The Labyrinth of Lunacy

Ψ

A Pandora Belfry Adventure
(Book Two)

Kristina Schram, Ph.D.

*Mischief*Maker*Media*

Published by Mischief Maker Media (USA)

First printing: October, 2013

Cover Design, Interior, and Technical Expertise: GorKee

ISBN: 978-1-939397-06-5

Visit Kristina Schram on the World Wide Web at:
www.KristinaSchram.com

Acknowledgements

I'd like to thank my loyal readers, Elizabeth Schram, Heather Duane, and Gordon Unzen. You point out the error of my ways and enjoy it. Thanks. But seriously, you really do make me a better writer and a better person, too. I bow to you.

Thank you, Dan, for sorting everything out for me—you know, all that technical gobbledygook. This world is a messy maze and you help me navigate it like a wise old seafarer. I think I'm mixing my metaphors here, but you know what I mean. You always do.

Thank you to the great and countless readers who buy my books. A special thanks to those who not only buy my books, but say good things about them. You keep me keepin' on.

~~~~~~~~~~

*Dedicated to all those folks I've met along the way
who taught me more than any book could.*

~~~~~~~~~~

Sometimes the job of a writer is to reveal the truth, and sometimes it's to create a more palatable truth. In writing about the residents of Nepenthe Manor, I have attempted to do both. While I hope to turn a light on the very real issues with which the mentally ill struggle every day, I also want to give these unique individuals a chance at a life I imagine few get to experience in the real world—one full of adventure, mystery, healing, and plain old fun.

1

Better be Sleeping

AFTER A THOROUGHLY rotten week, during which she'd learned she had a half-brother, discovered her supposedly dead father was still alive, and scored bruised ribs, Pandora Belfry was feeling a bit sorry for herself. On top of everything else, the caffeine from the five bottles of Coke she'd downed in a six-hour time span was starting to elucidate some extremely stupid decisions she'd made in the wake of those events.

The first extremely stupid decision was accepting Dougie Daft's invitation to his private school's dance just to get back at her mother. The second was to drink all that Coke. The third, and last, was deciding to head outside at two o'clock in the morning, in her nightgown, to determine what that strange light on the beach was.

If it weren't so late, she'd have invited the posse to join her on her quest. Unfortunately, while she was relatively free to come and go (making good use of the secret passages hidden in the manor's walls), the inmates' movements were much more restricted, especially at night, and especially since they didn't know about the secret passages.

Even so, she could have snuck them out, but then someone— probably Skippy—would likely wonder how she'd seen the light on the beach when her bedroom faced the opposite direction, looking out over the asylum's gravel driveway instead of the Atlantic Ocean.

The truth was that she'd spotted the light while in the attic looking for a cane, preferably of the lethal persuasion, with a dagger hidden within its seemingly innocent façade, to bring to the dance. But this explanation wouldn't help for two reasons. First, because she hadn't yet told them about the dance, and second, because then someone would want to know why she hadn't invited them to go to the attic with her in the first place. None of the posse liked being left out of any potential adventure. In this respect, Birdy was especially troublesome. She had a nose for sniffing out drama, followed by an irritating flair for topping it with some crisis of her own. By the time she was through with her calamity, any opportunity for doing something worthwhile (like finding a lethal cane) had long since passed.

Besides that, Sinclair, with his OCD, hated any change in routine. Charles had a heart condition and needed his sleep. Lucy, dear Lucy, would have a hard time not letting on that they'd left the mansion, and at night, no less. It was difficult enough for her to keep secrets, but this one would be a biggie, a challenge a fifteen-year-old with the mental age of a young child wouldn't be able to meet. The news would be out before Pandora's head hit her pillow.

Pandora reasoned to herself that she wasn't leaving the posse out of things; she was simply protecting them. Of course, she was also protecting her own interests. Nobody in their right mind gives away all their secrets. Having lived all her life at the Nepenthe Manor Insane Asylum, though, it was a wonder that she had any sort of right mind left at all. Not for the first time she considered running away and never coming back.

But first, the light…

With all the doors locked up tight for the night, Pandora decided to take the underground tunnel, which led outside. She supposed she could have used her illicit set of keys, which she kept in her sporran, to unlock one of the doors on the main level, but it was best not to rouse Frank's suspicions, or alert him to any strange activity. As Nepenthe Manor's only security guard, the hulk of a man wasn't the sharpest of tacks, but he possessed the uncannily keen senses of a wild animal and the stamina of a camel (he rarely took time off). No way was Pandora going to mess with that sort of power. She had enough troubles.

After pausing to listen for anyone passing by, Pandora pushed open the door, which resembled something straight out of a medieval castle, and stepped outside. The early May night air was cool on her skin as she forced her way through the overgrown shrubs growing around the heavy door. Dew had already settled on the grass, coating and chilling Pandora's bare feet. The black, star-dotted sky was clear now, the remnants of last week's nor'easter having passed on. Pandora typically liked stormy days—they suited her personality—but was grateful at this moment not to get poured on. Being sopping wet only looked good in Hollywood. Pandora, with her long, black hair, braids undone, and not exactly brushed out because it hurt her bruised ribs to do so, would look like a drowned rat nibbled on by sharks.

With this intriguing image in mind, Pandora headed for the fifteen-foot high wrought-iron fence that surrounded Nepenthe Manor's thirty acres.

Can a shark nibble on anything? she wondered. *Wouldn't it just devour the rat whole? And what's a rat doing swimming in the ocean? Abandoning a sinking ship?*

Questions like these occupied her caffeinated mind as she unlocked one of numerous gates spread around the estate. While this particular gate was used by the therapists, who lived in the cottages on the other side of the fence, and kept locked at all times, Pandora had the key and could get in and out whenever she wanted. Luckily her mother was as unaware that Pandora possessed the keys to many prohibited areas of Nepenthe Manor as she was of the existence of the other gates, most of which were hidden by trees and vines. Her ignorance suited Pandora just fine. If Vicki wanted to devote all her energy to saving the poor and downtrodden of the world instead of stopping her daughter from doing everything she could to avoid living a banal life, then so be it.

To Pandora's right, on the other side of the ivy-covered fence, eight cottages lined the crescent curve of the cliff. Light from a three-quarters moon made them glow in the dark like phosphorescent mushrooms. Pandora paused. All the cottages were dark, except for the one at the far end, which was occupied by Dr. Andrew Steele. He was the new Jungian therapist, who'd started work only this Monday, but had already made his delectable presence known *and* felt by many Nepenthe Manor residents.

What's he doing up this late at night? she wondered, her eyes focused on the rectangle of light. *Paperwork? Secret experiments? Socializing?*

Pandora made a sour face. Paperwork, while boring, she could accept. Secret experiments were even more acceptable, being infinitely more interesting. But socializing? The very idea of it made her sick. The god-like Dr. Steele should be above such goings-on. Besides, she thought of him as hers. So if someone was moving in on her territory, it behooved her to find out who and take the necessary measures to ensure the insolent creature never approached him again.

Torn on what to do—spy on Dr. Steele, or discover the source of the strange light on the beach—Pandora glanced back and forth between the two, her head like a tennis ball at a Wimbledon match. As her eyes landed on the cottage for the fifth time, the light winked out and the cottage plunged into darkness.

Pandora hesitated another moment, then leaned forward and peered down the long, straight driveway to the cottages, which ran parallel to the fence. No one was coming. She checked the first cottage, which stood only about twenty feet away, but it appeared as dark and soulless as its current inhabitant, Dr. Snyder. She slipped quickly through the gate and closed it softly behind her.

Before continuing down the path to the beach, she glanced once more at Dr. Steele's cottage. Crap. Whatever was going on in there now, it was going on in the dark. "It had better be sleeping," Pandora muttered, then wondered if Dr. Steele liked to lie on his back, like she did, or on his side or stomach. Probably on his back with his hands tucked under his head, elbows out. It made for a much better picture.

It occurred to her as she made her way down the rocky path that Dr. Steele could have been the source of the light on the beach. It would be just like him to wander at night, his incredible mind whirling with ideas, his romantic sensibilities astir. If he were anything like she thought he was, he, like her, would be unable to resist the allure of the sea at night.

But wait… There was that light on the beach again. Perhaps Dr. Steele had left the lights on in his cottage while out walking, to make it easier to find his way back. But if he was on the beach at this very moment, who had turned off the lights in his cottage? She didn't even want to think about *that*.

She stopped where she was, one foot balanced precariously on a rock, and squinted into the darkness. As bright as the moon was, it didn't aid in her identification of the light's source or who was moving it, merely blackening the holder into a dark silhouette. Her eyes quickly moved to study the light itself. *How terribly odd*, she thought to herself, in a voice reminiscent of an upper crust British matron. She blinked a few times to be sure of what she was seeing. Unlike a flashlight, the glow was more encompassing, as though the mysterious walker carried a lantern—the old-fashioned kind, judging by the light's flickering movement, and exactly like one she'd found in the secret room, which lay at the heart of Nepenthe Manor.

So who would be on the beach carrying a lantern, and at this time of night? Pandora's heart rate speeded up as though someone were running in her chest. Could it be? Rumors abounded that Nepenthe Manor was haunted. Pandora half-believed the stories, even though she herself was often the source of the strange sights and sounds the inmates and staff witnessed. There were times when she wasn't as stealthy as she meant to be.

Even knowing she was more than likely the 'spirit' of Nepenthe Manor, seeing the strange figure with the old lamp conjured up images of phantoms from days gone by. For all intents and purposes, the dark figure looked like a ghost as it moved steadily along the sandy beach.

Hoping to see a little better, Pandora leaned forward and the wobbly rock gave way beneath her foot. It bounced down the cliff side and ended with a sharp crack on a flat rock at the bottom. At the same time she jerked backward to keep from falling, instigating a burning pain that raged through her ribcage like a bad case of heartburn.

"Son of a sassafras!" she cursed more loudly than she'd meant to.

Her indignant voice carried down to the beach, the expanse of water amplifying the sound. Pandora froze. Surely the figure would have heard all that noise, even over the waves lunging against the shore. But whoever, or *whatever* it was, didn't react, merely kept up its slow, methodical plodding toward the jagged outcrop of rocks, which she called The Fangs, and which served as the northern boundary to Nepenthe Manor's beach. At high tide, the stretch of rocks made the beach impassable, and the tide was coming in fast. Soon the figure would reach the outcrop and be out of her reach.

Ignoring the pain in her ribs, Pandora scrambled down the remaining path, scratching the backs of her hands on the wild rosebushes that crowded the narrow stretch. She hit the beach running. The thought occurred to her that she made quite a sight herself, her black hair streaming behind her like a witch on a broom, her white nightgown billowing about her as she ran. She cackled. Hopefully someone was watching and getting the crap scared out of them right about now.

The hard packed sand gave little beneath her bare feet as she raced down the disappearing beach. It wasn't long before the pain in her ribs made her gasp for air. Her mind went dizzy and her temples throbbed from lack of oxygen. At this rate, she wasn't going to be able to catch up to the mystery figure before the tide cut her off. If only she had Shadow. But even if her horse were here and saddled up, Pandora wouldn't be able to ride her with her stupid ribs. She had to do something else, and quick.

"Hey!" she shouted as she ran. "You there!" The figure didn't pause or react in any way. No human would act like that, she determined. Thrilled, she pushed herself harder. "Fire!" she screamed. "Help me!" she tried again.

Nothing.

The figure had nearly reached The Fangs. And then…it disappeared.

"Wait!" Pandora cried. "Don't go!"

But the mysterious figure had vanished like a shadow in the night, leaving Pandora alone on the beach.

Curses at Poseidon

2

PANDORA URGED HER weary legs on, reaching the pile of stones at last. Not stopping to think, she scrambled up onto the wet, jagged rocks, searching for any sign of anyone or anything that resembled a human being or a light. Waves crashed against the rocks, spraying her face, and dark, wet spots dotted her gown like a moldy rash. The tide was growing hungry, and before long the outcrop would be underwater.

As she didn't fancy drowning—considering it the worst of all ways to die, well, that and being poisoned—Pandora jumped off the pile and raced away from a ravenous wave that licked at her heels like a dragon's tongue. Damn ocean. Couldn't it have waited another ten minutes?

Wet, tired, and thoroughly miffed, Pandora made her way back down the beach to the rocky path. Slipping and muttering curses at Poseidon—*may his trident forever be lodged in a vastly uncomfortable spot*—she finally made it to the top of the cliff and through the gate, locking it behind her. Shivering uncontrollably, she snapped off the flashlight to avoid being seen and started across the lawn, anxious now to get inside and warm up.

"Pandora Belfry, what in the name of Sam Hill are you doing out here?"

Pandora spun around. "D-D-Dr. S-S-Steele!" Her teeth chattered like a scolding squirrel, making it nearly impossible to speak. "I didn't see you th-th-there." She wrapped her arms around her quivering torso, belatedly remembering she was dressed only in her nightgown.

"You didn't answer my question." In the moonlight she could just make out the new doctor. The white t-shirt he wore practically glowed, though his dark pants and shoes made him look legless. With his back to the moon, she couldn't see his face, but she thought he sounded angry. His crossed arms and more pronounced Irish accent certainly made it seem that way.

"I-I-I thought I saw something."

"So you decided to come out in the middle of the night and go after it?" Yes, definitely angry. Something, she determined, that the good doctor had no right to be. He was merely a newly hired employee at

Nepenthe Manor, not her nanny. She felt her own ire spark up like a brush fire.

"Someone has to look after this place! You know the cretinous, and less than honorable, Mayor Daft would shut it down at the drop of a hat. I'm surprised he didn't try after our little incident in the foyer." She crossed her arms. "I think the real question here is what are *you* doing out and about at this time of night?" She'd learned at an early age that it was much better to go on the offensive than be on the defensive. "It's very late, you know."

"I was closing my window when I saw you." So unless he was possessed of magic powers, it hadn't been him out there on the beach. "You were running as though fleeing from demons."

"I wasn't fleeing, I was chasing someone…some *thing*." She had an idea. "Didn't you see it?"

There was a pause. "I didn't see anyone but you, Pandora."

A chill, like an icy-toed mouse, dashed up her spine. "But he was there! I *saw* him. And his light. He was holding a lantern. Surely you saw that?"

"I didn't see a figure, and I didn't see a light."

"Well, I saw them, and I don't make things up, Dr. Steele."

"I'm sure you *thought* you saw something…" he began.

Pandora rushed in to cut off the ending to this oft-repeated, and very patronizing sentence therapists at Nepenthe Manor loved to utter. "I *did* see something. Very clearly, as a matter of fact, and I'm shocked you didn't. Maybe you need glasses. You are getting to that age when everything starts to go."

He didn't speak for long enough that Pandora began to feel a tickle of apprehension. "No need to be insulting, Pandora," he said at last, breaking the tension. "I'm worried about you. I don't like the idea of you running about in the middle of the night chasing whatever it was that you were chasing. I doubt your mother would be too pleased, either."

"Surely you won't tell her?" Pandora begged.

"I won't tell her. But only if you promise to be more careful."

Pandora grinned. "I promise…" *not to call you Shirley anymore*, she added in her head. She never liked to be beholden to anything, even if it was in her best interests. *Especially* if it was in her best interests.

"Good." He sounded relieved, which was gratifying. "Now you'd better get to bed. It's Visitor's Day tomorrow. We must all be, as your mother puts it, 'on the top of our game.'"

Pandora groaned. "Don't remind me. I hate VD. It never fails to get the posse all riled up and there are always hurt feelings and fights."

"You really care about them, don't you?" Dr. Steele didn't sound surprised so much as impressed.

"Somebody's got to," Pandora rose to the implied compliment. "If I don't look after them, who will?"

"The staff?" he ventured. "Myself and your mother?"

Pandora snorted. "Not like I can." But before she could start feeling too satisfied with herself, she remembered how appalled she'd felt upon first meeting Dr. Steele when he'd assumed she was an inmate. Then she thought about all the secrets she kept from her friends. Not the best track record for someone who was supposedly looking out for them. "And maybe I'm not all that great at it, either," she mumbled.

"You can't save everyone," he said in a softer voice.

"Yeah, well, tell that to my mother. She thinks she can save the whole world." She bit her lip. No need to turn this into a confessional. "Listen, I've gotta go." Sometimes she wondered why she liked seeing Dr. Steele. He had a way of provoking self-examination that did not sit well with her general well-being.

"I'll see you tomorrow, Pandora."

"I suppose."

"I could use your help with introductions," he persisted.

"I might be busy." Which was true. Heading off disaster for the inmates on Visitor's Day wasn't easy. Birdy was the worst of the lot and did her best to crank up the theatrics. She was a lot like her mother, Mrs. Peacock, both of them being dramatic, narcissistic pains in the behind. The competition between those two for the 'worst crisis' started days before VD Saturday arrived, with much thought and angst put into preparation for the special day. Pandora was afraid that Birdy's latest diagnosis, a hysterical womb, would set off a recitation of symptoms that could last the entire day. Often called on to act as referee and/or judge, Pandora found the whole process exhausting.

Then there was Lucy's mother. Mrs. Landry had six other children, all younger than Lucy, and a husband whose greatest and most consistent job skill was getting fired. Mrs. Landry tried her best to visit, but she worked some Saturdays and when she didn't work she had all those kids to look after. Oftentimes she brought them with her—those days were the worst.

Charles's parents were dead and his Grandma Pippen, whom he'd stayed with for a couple years before coming to Nepenthe Manor, didn't leave the house, *ever.* Not coming would be one thing. Unfortunately, she possessed the irritating habit of writing letters filled with promises that this time could be it, "wouldn't that be wonderful, my little Pipken?" A gurgling *Urrrgh!* pretty much summed up how Pandora felt about Grandma Pippen and her worthless promises.

Skippy's mom would likely either be too high on heroin to attend or coming down off a bender. Mr. Stone was out, too. He'd deserted his wife and child when Skippy was six. Latest reports were that against all warnings he'd married the daughter of an African tribal chief (apparently the man courted disaster, or at least bad marriages). That being so, chances were he wouldn't be hopping on the next plane to make VD. Sadly, Skippy never gave up hope that his parents would finally get their act together and come fetch him home. Pandora hoped they wouldn't ever do that. They were more screwed up than their son. Unfortunately, each time they disappointed him, he plunged into a black depression that threatened to drag everyone nearby down with him. Every VD, Pandora had to work her butt off to avert this potential disaster. Despite her best efforts, she didn't always succeed.

Sinclair's parents were yet another piece of work, their odd, robot-like behavior a clear indicator of why obsessive-compulsive Sinclair was the way he was. Luckily, the Prims didn't usually come on VD, not liking to mingle with the dirty, sticky masses of Nepenthe Manor. While Sinclair held a similar opinion about the inmates, he didn't judge them for it, simply did his best to maneuver around their dirty stickiness. At any rate, the Prims rarely showed and when they did, they often set him back with their endless poking and picking at imagined defects, nearly always prompting a fit.

"I'll see what I can do," she finally said. Dr. Steele could be trouble—meddlesome as he was in her affairs—but the idea of missing out on time with him made Pandora's chest hurt.

"I'd appreciate it," he replied, his voice slightly amused.

"You owe me one."

"I don't think so since I'm keeping your gallivanting about after dark a secret. I'd say we're even Steven."

"More like odd Todd," she grumbled, feeling put out. She liked it when people owed her favors and Dr. Steele was annoyingly adept at avoiding getting under her finger.

He chuckled. "But I *will* be grateful."

"Gratitude, unless it can be cashed in, doesn't do me a heck of a lot of good. My Coke habit doesn't support itself, you know."

Dr. Steele made a choking noise. "Coke?"

"The most refreshing taste around?"

"Oh, you mean, cola."

"What you'd think I meant?" she asked innocently, though she knew exactly what he thought she'd meant because that's what she'd wanted him to think. "Oh, you thought I did drugs. I hope you don't think I'd waste this brilliant mind. What a tragedy that would be."

"Tragedy, indeed."

"Exactly. Well, it's been real, Wise Old Man, but I'm freezing my pa-tootie off so I'm outta here."

"Wise Old Man, hm? Are you sure Jung would agree with your as-sessment?"

"Like I said, you're getting old."

He laughed. "At least you think I'm wise."

"And what archetype would I fit?" she wondered, her skin growing itchy in anticipation of his answer. The Damsel in Distress, maybe?

"Oh, the Trickster, definitely." Hmmm… She rather liked that. "So how are you going to get back inside? Doesn't the security guard—"

"Frank…"

"Yes, Frank. Doesn't he lock the doors?"

She made an attempt to sound delightfully wicked as she laughed. "Of course he does. But I have my ways, Dr. Steele."

"Why am I not surprised?" he mused dryly.

"Because you're starting to understand the magic that is me," she half-joked. "Later, doc. Old people need their sleep."

"As do growing girls. Good night, then." Pandora turned to go. "Sleep tight," he called after her.

"Don't let the bed bugs bite," she called over her shoulder. And be-fore he could follow her and discover her secret entrance, she took off across the lawn, stifling the urge to whistle the tune to *Hogan's Heroes.* She flitted around the corner of the manor, then stopped and peered back. Dr. Steele was standing where she'd left him, his figure a dark silhouette. The image of her 'spirit' flashed through her mind. Could Dr. Steele be her ghost? If so, what had he been doing outside so late at night? Unlike her, he could do as he pleased, but then why deny be-ing on the beach? And why pretend not to have seen anything other than her? It didn't make sense.

She had to wonder, was their meeting tonight a case of synchronicity, or mere random chance? Jung would say it was a meaningful coinci-dence, and she wanted to agree. But if so, then what was the meaning behind their illicit encounter? That was always the question, wasn't it? Because really, what is the meaning behind anything? It's what every-one wanted to know.

As though he'd been waiting to see that she was safe, Dr. Steele at last turned to go, letting himself through the gate and locking it behind him. She hoped he wouldn't question how she'd gotten through a locked gate. If luck were on her side, he'd just think she rightfully owned a key, or that a careless staff member had left it unlocked. Either way, she'd have to be more careful from here on out.

Pandora counted to one hundred and then made her way to the secret door. As quietly as she could, she pushed aside the shrub's branches and slipped through the opening. Once inside, she hurried up to the third floor suite where she and her mother lived. Her feet were icy cold, her body shaking with fatigue and chill. She stifled two sneezes while in the secret passage, and three in the bathroom. But once in bed, she let four fly out in quick succession, clutching her ribs and cursing after each one.

Crossing her fingers, she sent up a wish to the powers that be not to let her get a cold. Bruised ribs and a cough would likely make her sloppy, which she couldn't afford. She had to be at her best tomorrow morning, keeping the posse distracted so they wouldn't suffer any emotional or psychological setbacks. She needed them to be strong. She needed them to help her with a plan that was forming in her mind.

Seeing the mysterious figure on the beach, then watching helplessly as it eluded her, had aroused a strange, but compelling question in Pandora's mind. What if the stranger had been her *father*? What if he *did* want to see her, but Vicki wouldn't let him? What if he was trying to reach his daughter, but couldn't? The idea was so bold as to be near genius.

Tomorrow—fate and posse be willing—the search for her father would begin!

3

Emphasis on the Nut

PANDORA AWOKE THE next morning feeling downright peppy. Ahead lay an adventure to undertake, and not even her runny nose, aching ribs, or painful lack of sleep could bring her down. She was the Trickster! She felt invincible!

Until she tried to get out of bed, that is. Peering over the edge of her bunk, she decided that doing her usual ninja-style jump to the floor probably wouldn't be the most intelligent move. Climbing down the ladder wasn't a much better alternative, but she had little choice. She had to get down somehow and falling on her head didn't seem like a good option.

The descent was agonizing, but after a hot shower, a bowl of Choco Bombs, a pain pill, and a bottle of Coke (her last), Pandora thought she might be able to face the day. She dressed in black jeans, pinned at the cuff, and donned a black Violent Femmes t-shirt. Yesterday during her Coke drinking spree, she'd scrawled 'Gone, Daddy, Gone' on the back with white paint.

After perfecting her Goth make-up, she gave her appearance in the mirror an enthusiastic thumbs-up, made a few kooky faces, then checked her watch. Half past nine. She smiled. Funny what a little motivation did to her sleeping patterns. Being a night owl, most days she typically slept in until eleven or twelve. But since Xavier, her new half-brother, had arrived on that fateful day a week ago, Pandora had been waking up early.

Full of purpose, she headed down to the arts and craft room, whistling the tune to *Gone, Daddy, Gone*. Every other Saturday from ten to two, the large room was transformed into a gathering place for family and inmates. On Friday night, extra chairs were carried in, all tables except one dragged to corners, and glue, paint, musical instruments, and inmate-friendly scissors all hidden away in the white cupboards that lined two of the walls. A rolled out rug the color of tangerines brightened the room, along with hundreds of paintings, most amateur, some very good, all slightly weird, taped on the other two walls. Pandora typically helped out with set-up, but last night her ribs had kept her on the sidelines nursing a Coke as J.T., the Rec Director, gave orders.

Although J.T. was irritatingly cheery and possessed more energy than a nuclear power plant, Pandora felt a grudging admiration for him. The vast majority of the inmates liked him, with the exception of Mrs. Johnson, one of Vicki's charity cases (she wasn't mentally ill, just evil, which Vicki mistakenly thought qualified the woman to stay). Mrs. Johnson didn't like J.T., but then she didn't much like anyone.

"*Pandora!*" J.T. greeted as she walked into the room. He wasn't much taller than her and a little on the doughy side, which was surprising considering how much energy he put into everything he did. Today he wore a neon yellow, long-sleeved shirt. Orange and green-striped suspenders held up navy blue, high-waisted, parachute pants he'd had the nerve to don. Red sneakers completed the colorful ensemble. No doubt his socks and underwear were equally bright. J.T. was a walking rainbow. "How are you this fine morning?" He scampered over to her with open arms and pulled her into a hug before she had a chance to run the other way. He squeezed her tight, then jerked back as she gasped in pain. "Oh, your ribs! Sorry, hon. Brain fart!" He held her at arm's length, his sparkling brown eyes full of sympathy, his feathered blond head cocked as he examined her. He tut-tutted. "You look awful, girl! You should go right back to bed this instant. You could get pneumonia!"

She wiggled uncomfortably. Sometimes J.T. was just so *intense*. With his slightly protruding teeth, he reminded her of a chipmunk whose diet consisted of acorns and coffee beans. "I'm fine," she insisted. He pursed his glossy lips (he never went anywhere without a Bonne Bell strawberry lip-smacker in his pocket). "Really!" She gently pulled out of his grasp. "I didn't sleep well last night, but I'll be okay."

"Goody!" He clapped his soft, clean hands—J.T. always kept himself immaculate, a bit of a challenge when working with paints, glue, glitter, and the mentally ill. "But I don't want you doing any heavy lifting, okay, my little ray o' sunshine?"

"Okay," she muttered.

"Turn that frown upside down, missy! Or you know what J.T. will do!" Knowing quite well what J.T. would do, Pandora worked very hard to dredge up a smile. Apparently it didn't pass muster. "Now you've done it!" He broke into song…and dance. "Life is good!" he sang, his tasseled loafers tapping away, his stubby fingers snapping. "Life is great! Let's show how much we appreciate…LIFE!" He threw his hands into the air, incorporated a little soft shoe, and ended with a ta-dah flourish.

The sound of clapping filled the room, echoing dimly in the open space. J.T. spun around and his round face lit up. "Dr. *Steele*! I just knew *you'd* come! Sometimes the counselors come. Sometimes they don't!"

"Mostly they don't," Pandora felt compelled to add.

He crossed the room and took hold of Dr. Steele's hand, pumping it up and down like a well handle. "This is so totally awesome!"

Dr. Steele gave J.T. a friendly smile. Pandora didn't know how he did it. Up late, rising early, and he still looked amazing, his blue eyes bright above his white Oxford shirt and red paisley tie. He wore khaki slacks and a navy blue blazer a shade tight in the shoulders. To his credit, he didn't look like he'd happily boot J.T. to the moon like a lot of the other counselors did. While the inmates loved J.T., the staff found him irritating. Pandora figured it was because he made them feel guilty. They were the ones who were supposed to make people feel better, but J.T. was much more skilled at it than they were. Pandora could understand their jealousy. How does one compete with sunshine and puppy dogs, rainbows and unicorns? That was J.T., in a nutshell.

Emphasis on the nut.

"I'm happy to be here, J.T.," Dr. Steele said, casually removing his hand from J.T's delighted grasp. "Is there anything I can do?"

"Is there anything you can *do*?" He rolled his eyes ecstatically. "Is there anything he can *do*, Pandora?" He peered at her expectantly.

"Ummm…"

"Of course there is, silly!" he cried, his head spinning back around. "Dr. Steele…I just *love* saying that name, don't you?" He glanced back at Pandora and gave a delicious shudder. "*Dr. Steele* must sit at the table and look important." He consulted his Mickey Mouse watch. "Oh, dear. Our special friends will be here any moment. Places, people!" He clapped his hands together as though marshalling together an army, even though it was just the three of them. With a brief nod of acknowledgment at Pandora, Dr. Steele headed for the table and sat down. J.T. took his customary position in the center of the room, applied a layer of strawberry lip-gloss, and spread his arms in a welcoming gesture. Pandora headed for a wall and leaned against it, arms crossed. She hated Visitor's Day.

Within moments, the first of the inmates, herded by the Hessian, a female psych assistant more closely related to Neanderthal than Homo sapiens, arrived and J.T. beamed at them. "Come in, friends! Come in!" The inmates filed into the room, basking in his ready smile and compliments.

"Love your new leg warmers, Lady Lucy!" he called. Giggling, Lucy twirled around him, kicking her stubby, rainbow leg-warmer covered legs into the air like a drunken ballerina. He high-fived Charles, who was looking particularly sassy in his red Superman cape and freshly brushed golden curls, and gave a nervous looking Sinclair the thumbs-up. Sinclair fingered the hem of his argyle sweater vest and gave J.T. a small nod in return. It had been a while since the Prim's last visit and Sinclair's pale, freckled complexion could only be described as under-cooked pancake. Pandora hoped he wouldn't puke.

"Marilyn Monroe…" J.T. started, then checked himself. "I mean, Birdy Peacock, you have topped yourself today!" She simpered and smoothed her stiff platinum bouffant with a plump hand. He turned to Skippy, who was trailing after her. "Skippy, that hat is too fabulous!" Skippy, wearing a black blazer too short in the sleeves and ratty red Chuck Taylor high-tops, grinned and doffed his gangster-style hat, which covered his mop of brown hair, which hid his oversized ears and pimply forehead.

Pandora sneaked a peek at Dr. Steele, curious to see how he was reacting to J.T.'s effusions. He was sitting, pushed away from the table, long legs crossed, leaning back against the metal folding chair and smil-ing. He seemed to be enjoying J.T.'s antics, or at least appreciating what J.T. did for the inmates, all of whom were chatting happily.

"Wienie butt!" Little Gustav cried as he entered the room. He was the resident Tourette's guy, hairless as a baby rat, and all-around enter-taining personage, to boot. "Pee-pee doodie head!"

"And hello to you, too, Gustav!" J.T. replied, not missing a beat. Lit-tle Gustav grinned and saluted J.T., who returned the salute with ap-propriate solemnity. The Hessian, perma-frown firmly in place, steered Little Gustav, twitching and blinking, toward a corner.

When Mrs. Johnson, in pink fuzzy slippers that had seen better days, shuffled into the room, J.T. hurried up to her and threw his arms around her flour sack of a body before she had a chance to retreat. "Eloise! So glad you could make it!"

She fought him off using the oatmeal-colored knitting bag she carried with her everywhere. He quickly backed away, but instead of looking offended, his eyes glinted mischievously. It was moments like these when J.T. showed this other side of himself that made him alluring to Pandora. He was no dummy, yet for some obscure, no doubt screwed-up reason of his own, he liked to pretend he was. Whatever those rea-sons were didn't matter, though. What mattered is that he made the inmates happy. Pandora just hoped he was truly as sincere as he always seemed to be. Having worked at the asylum for five years, he'd never once given her reason to doubt him. She certainly couldn't say that of anyone else.

"Insolent man!" Mrs. Johnson snapped as she passed by Pandora, hurrying to join her hypochondriac friend, Mrs. Bodkin. Neither of the two elderly women had anyone to visit them, but they came to VD anyway, both to sit in judgment and to eavesdrop. "Ought to be taken out and shot!"

"Don't make me hug you again, Frownykins!" he called after her. She hobbled faster. Togs arrived at that moment and readied himself to take a photo of J.T., who quickly posed as *The Thinker*. Unless someone in his family brought him film, however, Togs typically shot with an empty camera.

"Hey, Pandora Matadora!" Lucy greeted, giving Pandora a hug that would do a sumo wrestler proud. Luckily Pandora had braced herself for it and didn't pass out. She fondly squeezed one of Lucy's pom-pom pigtails.

"Hey, Lucy. Hey, guys," she greeted the rest of the posse flocking toward her.

Birdy joined her on the wall, leaning close to whisper loudly, "He's here." She nodded over at Dr. Steele, who was attempting to have a conversation with Professor Robertson. Talking to the professor was an exercise in patience. He never remembered your name or previous conversations. Absentminded and constantly mumbling to himself, he spent his days roaming the halls and grounds of Nepenthe Manor, magnifying glass and several baggies in hand, in search of new bug specimens. Further patience was required since he also delighted in talking about the insect world in excruciating detail.

Despite the lectures, Pandora rather liked him. She especially liked his room. Bugs plastered every wall as thoroughly as wallpaper, and even the ceiling and a few spots on the floor were used. Because sharps weren't allowed, the professor used glue or tape to keep those little buggers from getting away until they eventually expired. The effect was eerie, like a haunted madhouse. To be allowed into the room was an honor he didn't bestow on just anyone and most were grateful for that. Not Pandora. She loved visiting his room, even if she could only handle it in small doses. Even for her those tiny, staring eyes were a bit unnerving. After half an hour she swore she could hear the imprisoned creatures clicking, chirping, crawling as though still alive and their tiny voices would squeak, "Help me!"

"He's radalicious, isn't he?" Birdy continued, sending sweet-smelling waves of Juicy Fruit bubblegum up Pandora's nose. Birdy was never without a bottle of nail polish or a pack of gum on her person.

Skippy groaned, "Give it a rest, Birdy." He faced Pandora. "She's been going on and on about him since he arrived. Tell her he's a schmuck, Pandora." His eyes were desperate behind his round glasses.

Pandora shrugged, feeling trapped. She wanted to help Skippy out, but not at Dr. Steele's expense. "I'm sure he has a girlfriend," she said instead, quickly looking away, her hand darting up to twirl her braid round her index finger.

"What makes you say that?" Birdy demanded, staring at Pandora's averted face.

"I don't know…"

"You know something you're not telling." She chewed her gum ferociously.

Pandora dropped her braid. "Well, it's just that I find it hard to believe that a guy like him doesn't have *some*one."

"He better not," Birdy moaned. "And he better not be gay, either. That would be just my luck."

"Who's gay?" Lucy asked loudly. "I want to be gay, too!" She clapped her hands excitedly.

Pandora sighed. One of these days she was going to have to explain to Lucy what that word meant in modern times. But not today. She didn't have the kind of energy necessary to handle the barrage of questions such an explanation would evoke.

"No one's gay. Where'd you get the leg warmers?" she asked, hoping to distract the annoyingly inquisitive girl.

Tongue protruding slightly, Lucy stuck out a sturdy brown leg and studied the colorful, knitted wraps. "From Birdy."

"They're very nice."

"I hope my mama likes them. Do you think she'll come this time?" Her big dark eyes scanned the room. "She said she'd try. Maybe bring my dada and my brothers and sisters, too."

Pandora's throat tightened. "I don't know, Lucy. I hope so. But if she doesn't, then we'll go do something cool to make up for it."

"Like what?" Lucy stared up at her, waiting.

"Ummm…"

Birdy grabbed her sleeve and gave a vicious tug. "He's here."

Pandora looked around. "Lucy's father?"

"No, idiot! Xavier's here."

"Don't do that, Birdy!" Pandora scolded, glancing down at Lucy. "You got Lucy's hopes up."

But Lucy didn't look particularly crushed as she waved frantically at Xavier. He waved back with his good hand. A dark blue sling supported his left wrist, which was broken. She wasn't sure why they were so impressed. He looked like a bum in his faded Levis, with holes in both knees, and a ragged red t-shirt that would do better service as a dust rag. And his blond hair, spiky on top and longer in the back, needed a trim.

"What are you doing here?" Pandora barked at him as he joined them, feeling out of sorts and not quite up to his unexpected visit. Despite the connection they'd made yesterday, she didn't quite know how to act around her new half-brother and that made her nervous. She needed more caffeine, and stat. Too bad Vicki had finished the last of the coffee this morning. Pandora hated the taste, but at times of desperate need, one couldn't be fussy.

"Thought I'd see what was up." Lucy immediately abandoned Pandora and attached herself to Xavier's lean torso. He absently patted the top of her head as he nodded at the others. "How's it going?"

A chorus of "Hey, Xavier!" came back at him.

"It's Visitor's Day," Birdy explained, her voice breathless as she looked him up and down like a starving wolf. She had apparently forgiven him for not taking her side in yesterday's stuffed bra incident. "That's when our parents are *supposed* to come visit us."

"I know. Carl told me. That's why I came."

Pandora frowned. "You came to watch people get disappointed?"

He sucked thoughtfully on a lemon drop. "Nope. I came to see if our dad would show up."

Hysterical Babies

4

"WHAT?" PANDORA CHOKED out. Had Xavier gone mad? *"Here?"* Then she remembered what she'd thought about the mysterious figure on the beach last night. That it might be her father.

He shrugged. "Why not? Have you ever had any visitors you didn't recognize, who didn't really talk to anyone?"

Pandora stared at him for a moment. "I'd have to think about it. But why would he come in secret?"

"Because he's a spy? Or maybe because he's married?" Xavier tugged on his gold hoop earring. "I don't know. It could be anything."

Pandora wondered if she should tell him about the stranger on the beach and her theories about who he might be. "Maybe he's a member of the royal family," she offered, testing him.

He laughed. "I never pictured you as the princess type."

"Well, *you'd* fit right in," she snapped. "Being a royal pain in the ass."

Lucy giggled. "You said a bad word, Pandora!"

"Well, don't repeat it, all right?" Pandora grumbled, feeling worse by the second. She really needed some hair of the dog that bit her…a big bottle of Coke.

"Hey, here they come!" Skippy yelled, pointing at the doorway. Pandora was relieved to see a crowd of people surge into the room. The majority of visitors arrived during the first hour of Visitor's Day. After an hour and a half, the inmates who hadn't had visitors returned to their everyday activities, hopeful someone still might come. Usually they didn't.

"My family's not coming," Birdy grumbled. She crossed her plump arms and set her lips in full pout mode.

"What's happened this time?" Skippy asked.

"My mom says her womb is acting hysterical and she can't possibly leave the house."

"But I thought *your* womb was hysterical," Charles said, looking bewildered.

"It is," she replied indignantly. "But I made the mistake of telling my mom when she called last night and she *stole* my diagnosis!"

Xavier glanced at Pandora. "Is she serious with this?"

"Of course I'm serious!" Birdy cried, her freshly manicured hands flying into the air. "This is awful. Terrible. Devastating!"

"But you're fighting over who has a hysterical womb," he argued. "I say, let your mom have it and get on with your life."

"But it's mine!" Birdy clapped her hand to her chest, which was back to its normal size since she'd decided not to stuff her bra anymore. "I earned it!"

The corner of Xavier's mouth twitched upward. "*Earned* it?" The twitch turned into a grin.

She frowned. "You know what I mean. My doctor diagnosed it. It's mine. I have to live with it. It's terribly painful."

"Do you even know what a hysterical womb means?"

Birdy narrowed her green eyes at him. She might have given up the stuffed bra, but damned if she'd let go of her unnaturally colored contact lenses. "It means I have anxiety problems in my womanly parts."

Xavier snorted, then laughed outright. Pandora's fingers curled into fists, ready to go at him. "Are you making fun of Birdy's illness?" Only members of the posse were allowed the privilege of insulting other posse members.

"I'm making fun of her doctor," he replied. "He sounds like a real quack."

Being that her doctor was Dr. Snyder, the twisted Freudian, Pandora couldn't have agreed more, so she decided to keep her mouth shut.

"He's supposed to be one of the best," Birdy argued.

"By telling you that all your problems relate to your womb your doctor is basically saying you're sick because you're female," Xavier explained. "Doesn't that bring out the feminist in you at all?"

Birdy pursed her lips. "I don't do feminism. It's not attractive."

Xavier sighed. "But having a hysterical womb is?"

Lucy tugged on Pandora's sleeve. "What's a womb?"

Pandora groaned inwardly. "It's, um, the place where babies grow."

Lucy gasped, her tiny hand flying to her mouth. "Are Birdy's babies going to be hysterical?"

Pandora bit the inside of her lip. "Um…it's quite possible."

Lucy's brown eyes widened. "Then I don't think Birdy should have babies. Hysterical babies are bad news."

Xavier, unable to hold it in any longer, exploded into laughter. Lucy crossed her eyes, wagged her tongue, and cried, "Aggle, aggle!" Charles started giggling uncontrollably. It *was* pretty funny and Pandora found herself smiling, then laughing when Skippy clutched at his belly and cried, "Oh, my hysterical baby! It's having a fit! Somebody stop it before it wreaks havoc upon my womanly parts!" He pranced around and Xavier looked like he was going to heave, he was laughing so hard.

Despite herself, Birdy's eyes filled with mirth. She wanted to be mad. She wanted to maintain her righteous indignation. Her puckered mouth fought against the laughter, but when Skippy simulated a convulsive birth, replete with groans, she finally gave in, howling wildly.

After several minutes of raucous laughter, the posse finally settled down to a few snorts and breezy sighs. "You do realize everyone's looking at us," Birdy said happily, wiping away smeared mascara beneath her eyes.

"They're just jealous," Pandora declared. "They want their own hysterical baby."

"I've decided that a hysterical womb is not my problem," Birdy announced, her good humor restored. "Won't Mother be furious when she finds out?"

"That's the spirit." Xavier gave her an approving look and she primped with pride. "You can't believe everything adults tell you, right Pandora?"

"That's for sure," Pandora agreed. "One of my many tutors said I'd be dead before I turned fourteen and look at me now, alive and kicking. And my mother told me my father's dead, but he's alive and well." She paused. "Speaking of which, I suppose we should be looking for him."

Pandora's eyes, a vexingly peppy blue color, swept the room and what she didn't see made her fists clench. Not one of the posse's parents had made it today. That had to be a new record. An awful one, in some ways, but in the end, probably better for everyone. The day was young, but the chances of someone showing decreased with every passing second. People seemed to want to get the unpleasant task out of the way as soon as they could so they could enjoy the rest of their day knowing they had done their duty.

She had to distract the posse before they realized their families hadn't come. "Does anyone see any viable candidates?" she asked loudly.

"We'd have to look for males old enough to be your dad," Skippy surmised, "but not *too* old, if you know what I mean."

"What does he mean?" Lucy wanted to know.

"He means old men are too tired to be dads," Xavier answered, tweaking her pom-pom ponytail. Lucy nodded, satisfied. Pandora gave him a grateful glance, but he didn't notice. He was doing his own search of the room, his coffee-colored eyes unreadable.

"So who here is young enough?" Birdy asked, tapping her lower lip with a glossy pink fingernail, which matched her form-fitting dress. "Hey! J.T. is young enough—"

"It has to be a *stranger*!" Pandora practically shouted. "I mean, it has to be someone I don't know, right?" J.T. could not be her father. No way, no how.

Xavier shrugged. "I don't see why."

"If my parents were married," Pandora insisted, "then they'd still be living together."

"Ever heard of divorce?" Xavier asked, his tone clipped.

"Maybe they never got married," Birdy offered.

Trust the tramp to make that sort of comment. "I'm sure they got married. Can you imagine Vicki doing anything else?"

"Let's just look around, okay?" Xavier growled.

"What's your problem?" Pandora asked.

"Nothing," he muttered. "Just look."

"You might be a bastard, Pandora," Birdy persisted, speaking the word with particular relish.

"Pandora's a fish poop?" Lucy yelped.

"*Fish poop?*" Pandora stared down at Lucy.

"Yeah, Birdy said bass turd. And I know that a bass is a fish and turd is poop."

"Oh, Lucy." Pandora stifled a laugh. "I love your strange brain. But no, bastard only means my parents weren't married when I was conceived. When I was made, I mean."

"But I *can* call you a bastard," she fluttered her eyelashes innocently, "and I won't get in trouble?"

"You could," Pandora said quickly. "But I'd rather be called a love child…" *pause* "uh, better make that illegitimate or misbegotten."

"I'm sure your parents were married, Pandora," Charles said earnestly. "And still are."

Xavier looked ready to explode. "I really doubt *that*, Charles."

Charles gripped the sides of his red cape, looking hurt. "But they can't be divorced, Xavier. Divorce is really bad for kids!"

"Hey, I know," Birdy blurted out, either oblivious to the growing tension, or desirous of making it worse. Likely the latter. "Dr. Steele is the one!"

"Dr. Steele is the one *what?*"

The posse froze. Ten feet away and surrounded by a crowd of people all talking at once and Dr. Steele still had been able to hear Birdy. Pandora stored this little nugget of information away. Man of Steele, indeed. He stood and approached the group, his stride casual, though his blue eyes on Pandora were not casual at all.

"Hi, Dr. Steele," Birdy greeted him with a flirty giggle, curled eyelashes fluttering madly.

"Miss Peacock," he acknowledged Birdy with a slight bow. Her eyes widened at such a wondrous display of chivalry. "I'm the one what?" he repeated.

"You're the *one*," Pandora rushed to answer, "who's going to pay for the curtains." She did not need him hearing Birdy's scandalous, and totally false, theory.

Birdy giggled again. "Yeah, sure. *Curtains.*"

He glanced at Birdy with a raised eyebrow, then over at Pandora. "I'm going into Bedlam tomorrow to buy the material."

"I was just telling everyone that there's nothing to worry about," she answered quickly. "That you'll come through."

"Do you often worry about curtains?" he asked, his eyes light with a humorous gleam.

Sinclair was the only one who nodded. Everyone else snickered. "We like our privacy," Birdy replied saucily. "There's no telling what kind of *hysterical* weirdo could be lurking outside trying to catch us in our skivvies." The snickering turned to snorts of laughter.

"Well, we certainly can't have that," Dr. Steele said smoothly. "So what are you kids up to today?"

"I'm waiting for my mama," Lucy lisped. "And my sisters and my brothers and maybe my dada, if he can get off his patootie."

"My grandma wrote me a letter last week and said she'd try real hard to come today," Charles said earnestly when Dr. Steele looked at him. His words made it sound as though he really believed that this time she'd come, but his trembling lower lip said otherwise.

"One can only hope. How about you, Skippy?"

"My mom's probably sick," he mumbled and turned away. "She's *always* sick."

Birdy gave a heartrending sigh. "*My* mother won't be coming today, Dr. Steele. She says she has a hysterical womb."

"Does she now?" Dr. Steele did his best to look serious. "Well, thank goodness you don't suffer from the same."

"Thank goodness," Birdy heartily agreed, forgetting that only minutes ago she'd have bet her life she had a womb filled with hysteria. "My true diagnosis remains a mystery, but I believe you might be just the *man* to figure me out, Dr. Steele."

"Some mysteries are never meant to be solved, Birdy," he responded. "And sometimes that's a good thing. Imagine the world—imagine Birdy Peacock—with no secrets?"

Her green eyes looked positively thrilled. "I never thought of it that way."

He nodded. "You should." He faced Sinclair and Pandora felt increasingly jumpy. Why did he have to keep bringing up everyone's parents? She'd told him this was a bad day for the inmates, that their parents often didn't show. Why rub it in? "I imagine your parents had to work today?" Sinclair blinked twice for yes. "That's too bad. Maybe next time." Sinclair blinked once for no but Dr. Steele ignored his response, just kept talking. "It can be fun having visitors, but sometimes—"

Pandora quickly stepped forward. She had to stop him from making everything worse. "Thanks for dropping by, Dr. Steele. I imagine those people want to talk to you." She pointed behind him and he turned to see a crowd gathered around the chair he'd recently vacated. All were eyeing him avariciously, like starving jackals. Any time a new therapist started work at Nepenthe Manor, friends and family of the inmates pounced on the newbie. The hope for a cure never died.

"Oh!" He seemed surprised. "Looks like I'm wanted."

"Boy, are you ever!" Birdy said softly, but not so soft he couldn't hear. He didn't respond, though. At least not visibly.

"I will leave you to your day, then. Have a good one." He left them with a smile and was soon surrounded by anxious relatives desperate for hope.

"I hate Visitor's Day," Skippy groused. He pulled a pair of drumsticks out of his back pocket and began spinning them. "I hate my life, and I hate my mom."

"Your mom not coming has nothing to do with you," Pandora told him, not for the first time.

"Then what does it have to do with? Both her and my dad want nothing to do with me, so the problem must be with *me*, not them." He cracked the sticks against the wall over her head. "I'm so awful my mom does drugs and my dad ran away."

"That's not true!" Pandora cried. "Just because they're selfish and blind doesn't mean you're bad, too."

"Yes, it does," he said stubbornly, and his eyes welled up.

"My dad always picks my mom over me," Birdy complained. "She's totally got him wrapped around her finger. I'll never come first with him or her or, or…anyone!"

"My dad's a patootie!" Lucy cried. "He won't come. He won't ever come."

"My grandma always says she'll come, but she never does," Charles said in a voice barely above a whisper.

Sinclair tugged at his sweater vest and his rust-colored eyes darted about the room like twin hummingbirds. It was clear what he was feeling.

The posse was on the verge of a meltdown and Pandora suddenly felt perilously close to one herself. She was tired from her late night, her ribs hurt, and not one strange man had entered the room that fit her notion of an ideal father.

"Tell me about that labyrinth," Xavier asked suddenly.

Pandora started. What a strange question. "What do you want to know?" she asked warily.

"The most important thing…"

"And that would be…"

He grinned. "How to get into it."

5

Faster Than a Dung Beetle

PANDORA DUG HER short nails into her palm—it was the only way to keep her expression reasonably bland. "And what makes you think I'd have any idea how to go about that?"

He gave her a charming grin. "I can't imagine you guys would stay out of it. You're too adventurous."

She grimaced. "It's off-limits. Vicki's rule."

"And you always follow Vicki's rules?"

"Not me," Birdy interjected, her mother and father disappearing from her mind like magicians.

"Me, either," Skippy piped up. Pandora gazed at him in surprise. He was making an alarmingly quick recovery from his depression, and without her help.

"We can't just go outside," she told Xavier. "We could all get into trouble and we're already skating on thin ice as it is."

"All we have to do is ask for permission, Pandora," Birdy spoke up. "It's Saturday, after all. We get more freedom today." It was true. Weekends were typically more lax. The staff was often part-timers looking to make a few extra bucks. They had less invested in the job than the regulars. And on Visitor's Day Saturday, the staff was even more accommodating than usual. One might think they felt sorry for the inmates who didn't get any visitors. Maybe they did. Pandora thought it was probably only that they were lazy and used VD as an excuse to get out of work.

"You know Nurse Rackett is on duty?" Finding a good nurse to cover the weekends was next to impossible, so Nurse Rackett, a six-foot tall, solidly built Scandinavian ice queen with a no-nonsense attitude toward life and fashion, sometimes filled in on the weekends to help out. Some said she did it for the overtime pay. Others, who were more astute about these things, suggested her lack of a life outside the manor had something to do with her extreme work ethic. "She always says no if she thinks we're up to something no good and she always thinks we're up to no good."

"I'll talk to her," Xavier volunteered.

Pandora regarded him warily. "And why would she listen to you?"

He shrugged. "I'll think of something."

"Ha! You'll have to do better than that, Carlisle. The Rackett can sniff out b.s. faster than a dung beetle."

He gave her a confident smile. "And I can produce b.s. faster than a bull. Just you watch."

"I will."

"But don't let her see you."

"Me?" Pandora scowled. "Why not?"

"Because she doesn't like you."

She wanted to respond, opened her mouth to make the attempt, then snapped it shut. Crap. He had her there. "Fine. I'll watch from the stairwell."

"You do that."

"We're coming, too," Birdy cried.

"Sure," Xavier agreed cavalierly. "You can all come." Pandora smiled wickedly. Perfect. The more people who witnessed him falling flat on his behind, the better. Sure, she and Xavier had sort of made up, and yes, they shared a desire to find out who their father was, but that didn't mean she was going to let him take over. *She* was in charge of the posse. *She* was their leader.

"But what about my grandma?" Charles asked, his lips growing blue with worry.

"And what if my mama and dada come?" Lucy wondered. "How are they gonna find me?"

"I'm sure someone will come get you, okay?" Xavier patted her lightly on the head.

She nodded. "They'd better. Cause if dada comes and I miss him I'm going to have to burn something."

"I promise you won't miss them. Same for you, Charles." Charles nodded solemnly in response. "So let's get this party started, okay?" Xavier ushered the posse ahead of him.

When they were a good ten feet in front, Pandora hissed to his back, "You'd better know what you're doing."

"Do they ever come late?" he asked simply, his long stride almost arrogant in its confidence.

"Skippy's mom and Charles's grandma never come and no, I guess Lucy's mom always arrives right on time. Even with all those kids."

"Then I think it's better to get them outside and away from this depressing heap, don't you?"

"I suppose," she mumbled and let him get ahead of her. What he said made good sense, but she was angry. Angry that he'd come up with the idea and not her. Furious beyond belief that he was going to find out she didn't have access to everything at Nepenthe Manor. And royally perturbed that he had the gall to think he could convince Nurse Rackett of anything. The only thing that made Pandora feel better was the anticipation of watching him fail miserably.

Xavier made his way to the front of the pack and hustled up the stairs to the second floor, the posse close behind. Pandora tried to hurry, but her ribs, after all that running on the beach, decided they didn't like speed. She slowed down. At the top stair, Xavier turned around, and his eyes found hers, all the way at the bottom. He gave her a salute, then pushed open the door. Everyone fought to get into a good position in the narrow space to watch through the crack. The office, its upper half composed of unbreakable Plexiglas, was directly across from the door. Pandora struggled up the last few steps and shoved her way through the posse so that she could see.

Xavier lifted his hand and knocked. "One moment," a cool, crisp voice ordered. A few seconds later, the top half of the door swung inward to reveal Nurse Rackett in all her glory—uniform white as snow, her pale blond hair tightly wound into a bun, and unsmiling, icy blue eyes in the middle of a long, plain face. "Oh, Mr. Carlisle. I didn't expect it to be you." Her cold demeanor melted like an ice cube in a volcano. Pandora gaped at her, unable to believe what she was seeing.

"Good morning, Nurse Rackett." Xavier smiled brightly. "Beautiful day, isn't it?"

"I hadn't noticed," she declared dryly. "I've been doing paperwork since seven o'clock this morning."

He shook his head. "To think you have to be cooped up in here all day."

"I don't regret doing my duty, young man."

"You're a trooper, Nurse Rackett. Nepenthe Manor would be a wreck without you."

"I imagine it would be." False modesty was not one of Nurse Rackett's strong points.

"The Director means well, I suppose, but she doesn't have your keen mind. Your ability to organize."

"She certainly doesn't make my job any easier with all her strange ideas." Her tone softened. "Though I do believe allowing you to remain was one of her better ones. I agree with Dr. Steele that having you here will be an asset to Nepenthe Manor." Pandora bit down hard on her lip to keep from protesting. Dr. Steele couldn't possibly have spoken such drivel. "He seems to have taken a liking to you. I'm not quite sure why. You're a bit of a rogue, Xavier Carlisle, with that silly earring you wear. But I fancy myself a good judge of character and I find that I agree with Dr. Steele."

"I'm honored you've placed such faith in me," Xavier replied in a humble tone reminiscent of a butt kissing minion. Pandora bit her tongue to keep from losing her breakfast. "I hope that I don't let you down."

"I hope the same, Mr. Carlisle."

Xavier ducked his head for a moment, then swung it back up to look Nurse Rackett directly in the eye. "That's why I was wondering, Nurse Rackett—" He stopped himself and lowered his head again. "Oh, never mind. It's too much."

Nurse Rackett pursed her thin, pale lips. "What is it, Mr. Carlisle? No need to be shy with me. Shyness is a learned trait that often wastes a person's time and energy and should be discouraged whenever possible."

"Uh, yeah. You're right." He looked at her again. "Well, you see, I know you're busy, especially having to take on an extra shift so often, so I thought I might take some of the patients off your hands for a few hours—get them outside into the fresh air."

One pale eyebrow arched suspiciously. "Well, I don't know about that. They are a handful." She stared at him for what seemed like minutes. Xavier met her gaze unflinchingly. "But it isn't against the rules, and you do work here now. I suppose it couldn't do any harm. What do you have in mind?"

He shrugged. "I don't know. A little basketball…or maybe just a walk."

"A walk," she decided. "We don't want *certain* individuals to overdo."

"Definitely not."

"All right. You have my permission." Behind a stunned Pandora Lucy whispered a "*Woo-hoo.*" "Just be sure to get them back in time for lunch and dinner. Proper nutrition is essential to maintaining order."

"Absolutely. Thank you, Nurse Rackett. You're a credit to your profession."

She nodded briskly. "And you're a credit to…well, I suppose to all young people. Too bad they can't all be as polite and helpful as you." She leaned around him and stared directly at Pandora. Pandora jerked back, letting the door fall shut. Nurse Rackett had known she was there all along! She also knew perfectly well that Pandora wasn't supposed to be hanging around the inmates, yet had given Xavier, Pandora's half-*brother*, free rein. The nerve of the lady. How devious and manipulative. Pandora felt a grudging respect stir inside her. Letting

Xavier take charge of the inmates to teach Pandora a lesson was a bold move on Nurse Rackett's part. If only her behavior hadn't been so decidedly unfair Pandora might like the old witch a little better for it.

A moment later the door opened and the posse backed down the stairs to make way for Xavier. He waited for the door to close behind him. "We are good to go," he announced, looking immensely pleased with himself. He was wearing that look altogether too often lately. She would be *pleased* to wipe it off his face.

"Well, good luck, Xavier." She pushed her way through the excited posse and headed down the stairs. "I'll see you guys around."

"Wait!" he cried. "Aren't you coming?"

She stopped, but didn't turn around. "I'm feeling a bit under the weather at the moment." She clutched her waist and grimaced. "And Nurse Devine told me to take it easy. I probably shouldn't be gallivanting around."

"You gotta come, Pandora!" Lucy wailed, hopping down the steps. She grabbed Pandora's arm and hung on tight. "You're our leader."

"I agree," Xavier said, and she slowly turned around to face him, unable to hide a victorious smirk. "We need you, Pandora. *I* need you." He gazed at her earnestly.

"Well…"

"Great!" He clapped his hands together. "Let's do this." He whisked past her and the posse followed after him, leaving her alone on the stairs.

Damn him. He had outmaneuvered her again.

Pay the Price

6

IN A SHORT time they were clattering down the wide stone steps of Nepenthe Manor, past the carved griffins perched on either side, and out onto the front lawn. The air was warm for early May and its sweet smell put an extra skip in everyone's step. Spring was finally here.

Xavier led the posse around a copse of trees to a picnic table on the other side. Once everyone was seated, he looked at each of them, then over at the looming labyrinth. "So what do you guys know about the maze?" His eyes turned to rest on Pandora. "You must at least know where the door is."

"I have no idea where it is." She gave him a meaningful stare. "If I did, we'd have been inside ages ago."

"What if there's no way in?" Charles asked worriedly.

"There's always a way in," Birdy replied. She looked down at her dress. "Maybe I should go change. I don't want to get my dress dirty. My daddy gave it to me." Her lower lip jutted out. "Though why I bothered dressing up for him…"

"You dress up every day," Skippy pointed out.

"But I look especially nice today! Didn't you notice? How could you not have noticed?" Skippy drew back from her tirade. "I'm sure Xavier noticed, didn't you?" She fluttered her lashes at him.

"Ummm…" he replied, avoiding meeting her eyes. "Uhhh…"

"Maybe this is like *The Secret Garden*," Pandora intervened, before the conversation veered way off topic. She'd discovered the novel in the hidden room and devoured it in one day. Like all the books, the initials, *EN*, had been stamped on the inside cover. "You guys remember I read it to you? There's this girl, Mary Lennox, and her parents are in India, dead from the plague. So she's sent to live with her uncle in England. While she's there she finds a walled-in garden, but she can't find the door to get inside." Pandora sighed wistfully as she remembered the first time she'd read the story and how much she'd related to the contrary Mary. "I really love that book."

"So how'd she get in?" Xavier wanted to know.

"Well, it was a robin, actually, that showed her the door."

"But she already had the key to the door, *didn't* she?" Xavier persisted. Pandora glared at him. She would give good money to stick a fork in his hand right now.

"Yes, *she* did, because the robin showed her where it was."

"There's a robin right there!" Lucy shrieked, pointing at a black bird. "Cheeky little bugger!"

"That's a crow," Skippy informed her. "We need a robin."

"It doesn't have to be a robin," Birdy said disgustedly. "Any bird will do."

"Let's chase it!" Lucy cried and slid off the bench. Soon the entire posse was tearing after Lucy, who was chasing after a stupid bird. When they got within fifteen feet of the crow, it cawed loudly in disgust before flying up to land on top of one of the labyrinth's fifteen-foot high, spike covered walls. Everyone looked up, shading their eyes in the bright morning sun. "It's on top of the wall!"

"The bird, the key, or the door?" Skippy wanted to know.

"The key, stupid poopid!" Lucy retorted, sticking her tongue out at him.

Xavier looked around. "I just realized that nobody at the manor can see this part of the maze." They were standing between the north wall of the labyrinth and the copse. The trees curved outward just enough to block any view the staff might have of this stretch of the labyrinth.

Pandora already knew this because she'd spent hours searching amongst the wild tangle of ivy for the hidden door. "But that doesn't do us any good if the door's not on this side."

"Well, it's not going to be on the opposite side," he replied knowingly. "The wall's too close to the fence. But the entry could be on the wall parallel to the road." He pointed to his right.

"It's not," Pandora forced herself to say.

Skippy and Birdy looked at her. "How do you know that?" Birdy demanded.

"Because I've looked."

"Without *us*?"

Pandora put on her exasperated expression. "Unlike you guys, I have a lot of spare time on my hands. When you're in therapy or making macaroni picture frames, what do I have to do? I've got to keep myself busy."

"Makes me wonder what else you've been up to over the years," Birdy accused. "What other secrets you've hidden from us..."

Pandora glanced at Xavier, but he was staring up at the crow, who was cleaning under his wing with his humpy, black beak. "I don't know what you're talking about," she grumbled. "I can get out and about more than you guys, sure, but that doesn't mean I have a lot of freedom. You know the staff is always watching me, waiting for an opportunity to get me into trouble so they can go running to Rackett."

Birdy chewed on her lower lip. "True. But I still think you're holding out—"

"I'm not," Pandora declared. "In fact I have something I was going to tell you as soon as I had the chance."

Birdy crossed her plump arms. "And that would be…"

Pandora pulled in a deep breath, silently cursing Birdy and her suspicious nature. She had meant to keep this little tidbit to herself, at least until she'd done more investigating. Now she was going to have to share it whether she liked it or not.

"Last night I saw a stranger."

The rest of the posse drew closer; even Xavier stopped his examination of the wall to look at her. "What stranger?" he asked. "Where?"

"I couldn't sleep. Not after… Well…" she paused before continuing, "You see, I did something stupid." She hadn't wanted to share this part, either, but mainly because it made her look foolish. "After I said yes to Dougie Daft's invitation to the Spring Ball I drank almost a whole six-pack of Coke."

"You did *what?*" Xavier roared.

"I drank a six-pack of—"

"Not that part!" he cried. "The part about you going on a date with that bastard."

"Fish poop!" Lucy chuckled.

"Why you sly dog, you." Birdy eyed Pandora with new respect. "I knew you were keeping things from us, but I wouldn't have guessed it concerned a boy."

"No, no, no," cried Lucy, throwing her arms around Pandora. "Say it isn't so." Lucy only knew about Dougie through Pandora, and what Pandora had to say about the slimy, dog-kicking son of the equally slimy mayor of Bedlam wasn't good. Lucy had taken an immediate dislike to him, threatening to douse him in gasoline and light him on fire if he even so much as looked at Pandora.

For his part, Charles looked sick. Skippy didn't look much better, though he seemed more shocked than anything. "Why would you do that?" Charles wondered, shaking his golden head. "Why would you go to the dark side, Pandora?"

"I didn't go to the dark side, Charles," she snapped. "I was trying to get back at Vicki."

"You know, there are better ways to do that, ways where you wouldn't have to suffer so much," Skippy put in, his long fingers rubbing at the brim of his hat. "I mean, Dougie Daft? That's messed up."

"I can't believe you did something so stupid!" Xavier's good hand clenched into a fist that made his knuckles glow white. "That guy is a jerk. He's evil. I won't allow it."

Birdy frowned. "It's her life, Xavier. She can do what she wants."

"How would you stop it anyway?" Pandora wondered, feeling desperate enough to consider the option of having her older brother come to the rescue.

"I don't know," he growled. "But it'll be something bad."

"I'll stick him in an oven!" Lucy sobbed. "I'll boil him in a pot."

"Geez, Lucy." Pandora patted Lucy's head and the girl clung tighter. "No more fairy tales for you." She looked up at the rest of the posse, all of them waiting to hear what she had to say next. "Listen, guys, thanks for your concern, but I said I would go. It's the price I have to pay to make Vicki see the error of her ways. If she wants to lie to me, let me run around wild without so much as a reprimand to set me straight, well, then, she'll pay the price." She fought the urge to shake her fist at the sky, but only because she'd first have to pry her arm from Lucy's grasp, spoiling the whole effect.

"I think you're going to pay more than her, Pandora," Charles said sadly. His blue-tinged fingers tugged at the cape around his neck, as though it were choking him.

Pandora blinked. "I'll be okay," she said gruffly. "Don't you worry about me," she added with an enthusiasm she did not feel.

"You're crazy," Xavier said angrily. "Stupid *and* crazy."

"Not according to the people who matter," she replied testily, pulling away from Lucy. "You know, the doctors? The psychologists?"

He turned away. "*They* aren't the people that matter."

Pandora appealed to the posse. "Can't you see I had no choice? Vicki doesn't care that I hurt my ribs, and worse, she lied to me about my dad. She won't even tell me who he is. She's impossible."

"I still think there are better ways," Skippy mumbled.

She glared at him. "Like what?"

He shrugged, not looking at her. "I don't know. You could've staged a rally or done a sit-in or something."

Lucy tugged on her shirtsleeve. "Do the rally, Pandora."

"It's the eighties, Lucy, not the sixties."

"I want to know more about this stranger," Birdy demanded loudly.

Pandora stared blankly at her, then remembered. "Oh, yeah. The stranger." She'd almost gotten out of that one, but once again Birdy had to ruin things. "Well, as I was saying, I couldn't sleep from all that caffeine, so I was wandering around the manor when I saw a light outside on the beach. I knew Frank had already checked the kitchen so I was able to use the back door without being seen. I nearly knocked over a stack of boxes on my way out and—" She burst into a coughing fit, interrupting herself. She had to be careful not to use too much detail when lying. That sort of thing always tripped her up down the road. "Anyway, I headed for the beach and when I got to the cliff I saw someone carrying what looked like a lantern." She lowered her voice and whispered, "I think it was a ghost."

"Ghosts aren't real," Xavier grumbled and stepped away from the little group, distancing himself. He was obviously still angry about Dougie, though Pandora didn't know why he cared. He wasn't the one who had to go on a date with the overgrown wart.

"They are too real!" Lucy yelled at him. "There's Casper and the ghosts on Ghostbusters and our own ghost, too."

He turned to face her. "What ghost is that?"

"We don't know who it is," Birdy admitted. "But I've heard it was a girl my age who jumped off the cliffs and died a horrible death. Her ghost haunts the manor now."

Xavier glanced at Pandora. "How do you know she haunts the place? What proof do you have?"

"People have seen her and heard her, that's what proof we have," Birdy answered, determined to keep the spotlight focused firmly on her. "She's there one minute and gone the next."

"Have *you* seen her?" he asked with a challenging gleam in his eye.

"Hundreds of times!" Birdy declared, though this was the first Pandora had heard mention of it. She gave Birdy a funny look and Birdy glowered in response. "Well, I think it's a ghost I'm seeing." She nodded. "Yes, I'm sure it is."

Xavier snorted, showing what he thought of that. "It's probably just rats in the attic or you overdosing on your meds."

"What do you know about rats or my meds?" Birdy shouted, shaking a pink-lacquered finger at him. "You don't know the first thing about my suffering. My meds barely keep me functioning. Without them I would be nothing. I would be—"

"You'd be like any other person," Xavier finished for her.

She grimaced. "Dull and boring?"

"Normal."

She gave a hearty guffaw. "Whoever told you normal was good? Who made *you* the judge?"

"Can we talk about the stranger?" Skippy implored, glancing back and forth between Birdy and Xavier with a worried look on his face. He pulled out his drumsticks and began twirling them really fast.

"Fine," Xavier responded. He stared at Pandora. "So did you find out who it was?"

She shook her head. "When he reached the rocks, he disappeared." She snapped her fingers. "Just like that. Before, when I made a noise he didn't react. A human—well, a live one—would have at least turned around. Whoever it was didn't even flinch."

"That doesn't mean anything. He was by the ocean, right? It's hard to hear over the waves."

"True, but I was awfully close to him when I yelled."

"So what did you do after that?" Charles asked, watching her breathlessly. "Did you jump over the rocks, chase the guy down, and demand to know what's going on?" He flew around her, arms outstretched, cape flapping.

"I started to, then the figure disappeared. Exactly like a ghost."

Xavier gave a disgusted sigh. "Just because the guy disappeared doesn't mean he's a ghost."

"All right, then, Mr. Smarty Pants," Birdy began. "If the stranger wasn't a ghost, then who was he?"

He shrugged. "Someone taking a walk on the beach?"

"At two o'clock in the morning?" Pandora questioned.

"Two o'clock?" Birdy exclaimed, indignant. "You were up at two in the morning?"

"I told you, I couldn't sleep."

"Let's stick to the point," Xavier interrupted. "People take walks on the beach all the time, in all kinds of weather and at all times of the day or night. Still…it does seem rather late," he conceded. "Especially for this place."

"That's what I'm saying," Pandora insisted. "There was something about the whole thing that didn't seem right. So late at night, the way the guy just disappeared, the old-fashioned lantern he, or *she*, used for a light." She shook her head. "Very odd."

"We should set up a watch," Skippy suggested eagerly. "We'll take turns keeping an eye out for our elusive stranger."

Xavier nodded. "All right. I'll go along with that, if only to prove to you guys that it's something perfectly ordinary. Sinclair's room overlooks the ocean, right, Sinclair?" He looked around. "Where's Sinclair?"

"Over there," Lucy pointed. "Staring at the wall."

Pandora caught sight of him right away, his red hair and red and blue argyle sweater vest impossible to miss. He was staring at a spot about six feet up, centered exactly in the middle of the wall. "What's he looking at?"

Sinclair turned at that moment and saw them all staring at him. He faced the wall again and pointed up. The posse glanced at one another, then took off running to join him. When they reached his side, they looked up at the spot where he was pointing.

"Why are we all staring at a wall?" Birdy grumbled impatiently.

"That's it, Sinclair!" Xavier shouted suddenly and raced up to the wall. "Don't you see it?"

Pandora squinted, and ever so slowly a shadowy image formed in the ivy. It resembled the outline of a large door—a door that stood six feet off the ground. Sinclair had found the way into the labyrinth.

7

The Stink Eye

PANDORA GRINNED. "YOU really do see things others can't, don't you?" Sinclair ducked his head modestly as her finger traced the rectangular outline of the door in the wall. "Do you see it, Lucy? Charles?" They followed her finger, foreheads puckered. "Now you know why I call it the Labyrinth of Lunacy. Nobody sane puts a door up that high!"

"Labyrinth of Lunacy," Xavier laughed. "That's a good one!" Pandora preened a little.

"I see it now!" Charles yelped. "It's so high up, though. A person would have to have wings to get up there." He grabbed his cape. "Or one of these babies."

He was right that it would take wings, or a cape. What the entrance was doing six feet up was a mystery. Well, not such a big one. Placing a door that high made it almost impossible to find, because who in their right mind would be looking for a door six feet off the ground? No wonder she hadn't ever found it. But she was glad Sinclair had, and not Xavier. Sinclair needed a good dose of self-confidence, while Xavier could do with getting knocked down a peg, or twelve.

"The question is how do we reach it?" Xavier mused.

"We need a rope," Skippy replied, twirling his drumsticks. "Or we could form a human pyramid." He snapped his fingers. "I know! A hot air balloon could get us inside. We wouldn't even need the door. That would be so awesome." The drumsticks twirled faster.

"We could get a catapult to throw us all in," Xavier remarked dryly.

Skippy grinned. "I *like* it, Xavier. Or one of those cannons that shoots people."

"And what are we going to land on, dip wad?" Birdy demanded.

"You?" he suggested. She smacked him on the shoulder and he grinned as he rubbed at the spot. "Just a thought."

She glared at him. "Yeah, well, here's a suggestion, Einstein. Stop thinking."

"I think the door is our safest bet," Xavier said as he plunged his good hand into the ivy and began pulling on the vines. Thick from years of surviving New England winters, they shook and shimmied, but did not yield. After a minute, he pulled his hand back out. "We need something to cut through this crap." He examined the back of his hand, which was scratched and raw.

Pandora pulled out a pair of small shears from her sporran. She always carried them with her, along with countless other tools, and kept the blades sharp with a small whetstone she'd borrowed from the myriad heaps of treasure in the barn. One never knew when one would need to do some heavy-duty cutting.

"Would these do?"

Xavier eyed the shears. "You couldn't have mentioned those *before* I turned my hand into hamburger?" He grabbed a bunch of ivy. "I'll hold, you cut."

Pandora hurried forward, then stopped, experience from a lifetime of espionage kicking in. "We have to do it in a way that no one will notice."

Xavier nodded. "We could cut on three sides and let the rest hang like a curtain."

"Brilliant, Xavier!" Skippy cried. Pandora gave him the stink eye. "And fast thinking to you, too, Pandora."

She nodded, somewhat appeased. "The problem is that I won't be able to reach."

"We need a ladder," Xavier surmised.

"We can fetch one from the barn."

"All of us? Wouldn't that look suspicious?"

"No duh. Just you and I will go." She handed the shears to Skippy. "You're tall enough to reach the bottom of the door so cut along there. Charles and Lucy clean up any mess he makes and stash it in the woods. Sinclair and Birdy keep watch."

"Bo-ring!" Birdy complained. "I want to come with you two."

"It's really dirty in the barn," Pandora told her. "I think we have mice, too."

"Mice are cute."

"And bats."

"Oh." Birdy glanced down at her pristine pink dress. "Never mind."

Pandora managed to stifle a satisfied smile just in time. "Come on, Xavier. Before the kids get themselves into trouble," she added under her breath as they started to run.

Pandora led him on a narrow path through the copse. They didn't speak as they jogged through the bit of woods and across the driveway. When they arrived at the nearly century-old barn, she headed around back to a small door on the side of the building. This was the entrance Carl, the groundskeeper, used to get in and out of the barn whenever he needed tools. Three, much larger, doors, were only opened when Carl or Cracker Jack, an inmate who acted as gardener, needed anything too big to fit through the smaller door.

She waved Xavier inside then followed him. Before heading to the ladders, she took a brief moment to inhale the smell of dust, hay, and grease perfuming the dimly lit barn. She loved this barn. On stormy days it was like a cave, full of nooks and crannies for exploring or hiding out in. On sunny days, with shafts of sunlight slipping in through holes and cracks in the roof, it was more like a cathedral, the air filled with sparkling bits of dust swirling ever upward.

The main floor was dirt, and where the farm vehicles were kept. The u-shaped loft was accessed by a steep stairway built along the wall. Countless stacks of hay bales covered its rough-hewn planks, though the amount of hay had shrunk to about fifty bales after the long winter. The smell of hay reminded her of Shadow and she suddenly felt as though she'd lost her best friend. She promised herself to visit the stable before the day was done. She'd been terribly remiss these last couple days with the fire and her injury. Carl had promised to look after her horse, but still, Pandora missed her.

"Carl hangs the ladders here," she spoke into the hushed silence, indicating two steel bars jutting out from the wall opposite them. The bars supported six ladders ranging in length from two aluminum 10-footers to an ancient thirty-foot wood ladder that had once belonged to Bedlam High School. "We'll take the ladder closest to the wall because Carl will be less likely to miss it. And we'll have to be careful moving the wood ladder. It's very heavy."

Xavier, whose eyes had been taking in everything in the barn with intense interest, nodded. "I'll do it. You just stand back and let me work."

She waved at him. "Um, hello? Dumkopf? The medieval age just called and it wants its cretinous, arrogant stud back."

"Um, hello? They didn't have phones back then."

"Um, hello? No der."

"And it's cretinous with a long 'e' sound. If you're going to call me stupid, you should probably pronounce the word right."

Damn his eyes. "You're a real jerk, did you know that? How do you think I know those ladders are heavy? Because I've moved them by *myself*, idiot. That's how."

Xavier did not look impressed. "Whatever. You just keep a lookout so we don't get caught. The last thing I need is to get into trouble."

"The last thing you need is to get on my bad side, brother."

"Don't call me that." He walked over to the ladders and started inching the 30-foot ladder off the rack with his one good hand.

"Don't drop it on your foot," she warned, watching him with folded arms. He ignored her as he pulled hard on one end of the ladder. Pandora smiled with satisfaction as the end fell off and hit the dirt with a crack.

"Crap."

"Crap is right. That thing's practically an antique. If you break it, Carl will tan your hide. Now do you want my help or not, Captain Hook?"

He shrugged. "Either way."

She marched over and grabbed the side of the ladder still suspended in the air. With one smooth movement she pulled it off the rack. Two seconds too late, she remembered her bruised ribs. A sharp pain shot through her gut and she let go of the ladder. "Damnit to hell!" she cried as it crashed to the floor.

Xavier waved his finger at her. "No swears!"

"That rule only applies when you're inside Nepenthe Manor or around the posse," she grumbled. "And I had good reason to swear."

"Forgot about your ribs?" he mused.

She bit down on her lower lip. "Maybe."

"All right. Since you insist on playing the hero, we'll both work together."

"I've never had to rely on anyone for help, and I don't like it," she muttered.

"Me, either," he admitted. "But it looks like we don't have a choice."

"Fine."

Without another word, they lifted each ladder off the rack and set the 10-footer aside. Then they returned the remaining ladders in proper order. Sweating now, Pandora felt a desperate urge for a Coke. She'd have to make another trip to Simon's Supermarket soon, which meant she'd have to talk to Giganticus again since he'd probably be working at the store. She should probably find out his real name. People who were giants never seemed to appreciate being called one.

"You gonna make it?" Xavier asked, wiping his arm across his glistening forehead. The barn was cool, but the hard work, along with the pain of their injuries, had a way of making a person sweat.

She wrapped her arms around her torso to hide her discomfort. "I'm fine."

He leaned against a black tractor tire that came up to his chest. "Well, I need a break. Lemon drop?" He held out a powdery baggie full of them and she took one and popped it into her mouth. He helped himself, then looked around the barn as he shoved the bag back into his pocket. "This is a great place."

"Mr. Nepenthe built the place back in the 1880s and spared no expense. He was very rich."

"Sounds like my kind of guy." She tried to read the expression on his face, but a beam of sunlight whitewashed his features into obscurity. "Who do you think that stranger was?" he asked suddenly.

"What stranger?" She was still thinking about Mr. Nepenthe and what it might be like to have someone like him for a dad. "Oh, you mean the one on the beach." She shrugged. "I don't know."

"Do you really think it was a ghost?" She didn't need to see his face to know he was skeptical.

"Who knows? Whoever or whatever it was, he acted strangely."

"You say 'he' a lot. You must think it was a man."

"I guess. Or a big woman, like the Hessian."

He nodded thoughtfully. "She is a big woman. But if it's a guy, do you think it could be..." He stopped himself.

"...our dad?" she finished for him. "The thought crossed my mind."

He straightened up at the same time the beam disappeared, and his excited expression surprised her. "I'm going to find out."

"Not without me, you're not."

"Of course not," he agreed, but his eyes darted to the left. A sure sign of lying.

"Xavier, I mean it. I know that beach like the back of my hand. It's treacherous. You need me there, especially with your gimp hand."

"Sure. You're right, of course."

She eyed him suspiciously. He didn't look or sound like a person interested in her help. No, he looked and sounded like a guy who was going to do what he wanted to do...without her.

That wasn't acceptable. Nepenthe Manor was her territory, and damned if she was going to let some insolent brother of hers do what he wanted on her ground. If he insisted on going this alone, she'd have to come up with her own plan to teach him a lesson—one he wouldn't like at all.

A Fleshy Thud

8

"SHOULD WE GO?" Xavier indicated the ladder. "We probably shouldn't leave the posse alone too long, should we?"

Pandora's imagination kicked into overdrive. "We'd better hurry." She might want Xavier to get into trouble for failing to do his job, but not at the expense of her friends.

They each lifted one end and left the barn, moving as fast as they could with their awkward cargo. When they burst through the line of trees, they were stunned to see no one—not one single member of the posse. "Where are they?" Xavier cried. "I promised to look after them."

They raced to the labyrinth wall. When they reached it, they dropped the ladder and stared at the mass of vines. "Do you think they got in somehow?" Pandora asked, her stomach gurgling queasily.

"I don't know!" He paced back and forth. "Maybe Lucy climbed onto Skippy's shoulders."

"And did what? Climbed over the wall? She'd skewer herself on those spikes."

"I was only trying to make suggestions."

A light breeze picked up, rustling the ivy leaves. "Well, they aren't helping. This is awful. I knew I shouldn't have left them alone. Bad things happen when I'm not watching." The leaves rustled louder and louder, then a muffled giggle sounded to Pandora's left. She glanced at Xavier, who was staring at the spot where the giggle had come from.

He looked over at her with a relieved grin. "Well, I suppose we should go in there after them. But first I'll clear this spot." He reached into the dense foliage, grappled around for a bit, then pulled. A small arm came out, followed by a small body. Lucy. "Well, well, well. What do we have here? A wood nymph?"

She giggled and did a little dance. "Fooled you, fooled you! You thought we were gone!"

"We did," he acknowledged. "You got us good, Lucy Goosey."

"Not me." Pandora did not like being tricked. Gullibility was a weakness and at Nepenthe Manor, weaknesses were sniffed out and pounced on like lame rabbits. "I figured they were up to something no good. All right," she hollered. "Come on out."

Laughing, Skippy and Charles pushed their way out from under the thick ivy. "It's really cool in there!" Skippy exclaimed. "Like being in a jungle. You should give it a try, Xavier."

Xavier nodded. "I just might do that."

"Where are Birdy and Sinclair?" Pandora demanded peevishly. Skippy should have asked *her* to give it a try, not her baboony brother.

"They went around to the other side of the labyrinth. You know how they are about getting dirty."

Pandora looked to her right and saw Birdy and Sinclair coming toward them. Birdy was triumphant and even Sinclair looked rather pleased with himself. "You should've seen your faces when you thought we'd done a runner," Birdy crowed when they grew close.

Pandora scowled. "That's because I'm responsible for you guys. If something happened to you, *I'd* be the one in trouble."

"Not *you*, Pandora," Birdy snipped. "Xavier's the one who's in charge of us."

"Yeah, well, thanks for thinking of me," he drawled.

"It was just a joke," she giggled. "And a damned good one!" The posse gave a cheer and one corner of Sinclair's mouth slid up.

Pandora had a good mind to ban Birdy from the labyrinth and was about to suggest the idea when a yawn seized her. By the time it was finished, Xavier and Skippy were propping the ladder against the wall and the moment for revenge had passed. It was just as well, Pandora decided. She was too tired to wage battle against Birdy right now.

Skippy handed back her clippers. "I cut as high as I could. You might want to do the rest," he said hopefully as he eyed the ladder. Skippy wasn't too big on heights. "Unless your ribs hurt too much."

Pandora smiled. This was more like it. Really, life ran so much more smoothly when she was in charge. "I'm fine." She waved away his concern as she climbed. "You and Xavier hold the ladder and I'll finish the job."

But the job wasn't all that willing to be finished. Some of the vines were too thick for the small shears, but she made progress anyway. After about twenty minutes of cutting, she could see the outline of a solid wood door covered in moss. Encouraged, she had them move the ladder to the other side and cut for another twenty. "That's all I can do for now," she said as she wiped an arm across her forehead. "We'll need a saw for this last part."

"I'm hungry," Birdy complained. She'd spent the whole time sitting on the ground, alternating between giving everyone orders, which they ignored, complaining about how much her butt still hurt after falling on it during what Pandora now thought of as "The Foyer Fiasco," and picking grass to throw at Lucy. Charles had joined Skippy and Xavier to help "hold" the ladder while Skippy carted vines into the woods.

"All that work you're doing must have really worked up an appetite," Pandora replied dryly. She glanced at her watch. It was almost one. "I suppose we should go in for lunch. It's getting late." She backed down the rungs, probably looking like an old man. She'd been so focused on her job that she hadn't realized how much her ribs ached.

"We can come out after lunch and finish the job," Skippy suggested, rubbing his hands together to remove bits of ivy.

"I'll get the saw," Xavier volunteered. "I saw one in the barn."

"Don't take Carl's," Pandora warned him. "He calls it his 'Sweet Bitsy.'"

Xavier laughed. "Nice name."

"He names a lot of things. The orange tractor is Rufus and the lawn mower is The Cow."

"I thought you said he was a grumpy old man."

"He is. But that doesn't mean he doesn't have a good side. He just keeps it to himself."

Xavier looked suddenly thoughtful. "Hm. Well, maybe I can get him to open up a bit."

Pandora snorted. "Good luck. Carl is a tough nut to crack."

"I'm always up to a challenge." He grinned, and with Skippy's help, tucked the ladder behind the ivy.

"Whatever. I'll bring the saw. I have one in my room."

Xavier laughed. "Why am I not surprised?"

"Can we go now?" Birdy whined. "I'm starving!" She lazily pushed herself to her feet.

"Maybe my dada came for lunch!" Lucy cried, jumping up. On Visitor's Day, guests could stay and eat a free lunch at the cafeteria. Not many did. The ones who'd been around long enough knew better than to make that mistake. But Mrs. Landry, even though she knew better, also had a lot of mouths to feed, including her good for nothing husband. Whenever she visited, the whole family would stay for lunch and leave behind a gargantuan mess.

"And my grandma, too." Charles grew excited. "Maybe this is the day!"

Pandora stifled a sigh. "Maybe. But if they don't come, we'll be able to get back to work on getting into the labyrinth."

Lucy's lower lip jutted out. "I don't want to go in there. It's probably full of snakes and spiders."

"Then I'm definitely not going in!" Birdy screeched.

"There's no more chance of finding snakes and spiders in there than out here," Pandora told them, her tone more than a bit terse.

"I don't care," Birdy declared.

"I'll burn it down," Lucy promised. "That'll solve things."

"And miss out on its secrets?" Xavier said as he and Skippy brushed ivy leaves and bits of vine bark off each other's backs.

Lucy cocked her head. "Secrets?"

"Labyrinths are full of them," he told her in a low voice. "Our job is to ferret them out."

She grinned. "I like that. I'll be right behind you, Xavier."

"Me, too," Birdy gushed. Pandora could almost hear her adding, "Watching your butt the whole way."

She suppressed an urge to gag. "Let's just go before Old Corker closes the kitchen. You know how she likes to mess with us." Sometimes the cook would shut down before mealtime was over. When confronted with the error of her ways, she'd retort, "I opened early so you got your full hour. Not my fault you people can't read a clock!" Her logic made no sense, and hence, was irrefutable. Vicki refused to do anything about the old bat, only saying, as she always did when Pandora complained, "We have to keep her. No one else will take the job for so little pay." For her part, Pandora thought that was a load of crap, but had yet to come up with a good reason why Vicki would keep the old biddy on.

Xavier wouldn't let them leave the protection of the copse until he gave the all clear. "No sense raising suspicions," he explained. While he was absolutely right, Pandora wished she was the one who'd come up with the idea.

After Xavier gave the signal to move, Pandora walked slowly along, letting the others get ahead, and mulled over what her brother was planning to do about the stranger. He had no right encouraging the posse to keep a lookout. It was *her* stranger, after all. She'd spotted him first. To let anyone have first dibs at finding the man, or worse, be the one to prove it was their dad, wasn't sitting right with her. She wanted to be the first one to meet their father. Then maybe she'd have half a chance with the guy.

Plain and simple, she was going to have to sabotage Xavier's attempts. She had some serious thinking to do on how to go about it, but that would have to wait. Her mind was too fuzzy to be devious right now. Her early start and lack of sleep was starting to tell on her.

The posse disappeared inside and Pandora dragged her feet up the stairs after them. Xavier would probably be eating lunch with the posse. As he now had his lips fully planted on Nurse Rackett's behind, Vicki would let him do whatever he pleased.

Xavier works for Nepenthe Manor now, Pandora could hear her arguing when confronted on the unfairness of it all. *You don't.*

Once inside, she found the foyer empty. They'd gone on without her. She crossed the wide-open space, which still smelled of burnt velvet, and noticed a surprising amount of light pouring in. She preferred it dark. Squinting in the glare reflecting off the marble floor, she clumped unhappily across the foyer.

"Wait up, Pandora," a disembodied voice called out. She spun around, searching the numerous shadowy hallways that branched off the foyer. Her eyes lit on a tall figure stalking toward her from the narrow corridor she'd named Quack Central, which led to all of the therapists' offices. She crossed her arms and faced Dr. Steele, ready to duel.

"Don't you ever take time off?" she fired at him when he caught up to her.

He grinned. "Once a therapist, always a therapist."

"Once a masochist, always a masochist."

"Touché. So what are you up to, Trickster?"

"Why do you always assume I'm up to something?"

"My intuitive side tells me so."

"Well, you can tell your intuitive side that it can stick it. I'm off to get some lunch. All on the up and up and very innocent."

"I saw you and your friends coming across the lawn." She looked up at him, and he shrugged. "My office faces west."

"How'd you manage to get one of those?"

"Your mother gave it to me."

"Oh."

"Why?" He looked worried, and maybe a little suspicious.

"Well, it's just that all the therapists covet the offices with windows."

"You mean…" He stopped. "So that's why I've been getting dirty looks from the other therapists."

"Vicki doesn't always understand people as much as she thinks she does," Pandora explained.

"Hmmm…" was all he would commit to, though she sensed he agreed.

"Well, I'm outta here." She started to walk away. "See you around."

He hurried after her. "Why don't I join you for lunch? There's something I want to discuss with you."

Her stomach flipped. "I'm not supposed to fraternize with staff or inmates. You heard Vicki."

"Yet you do it anyway."

"Prove it, doc."

"Just eat lunch with me. I'm sure your mother won't care."

Pandora shrugged. "You're right. She probably won't." She looked up in time to catch a shadow crossing his face, and she felt a stir of satisfaction. Her pity arrow had hit a bulls-eye. "All right. But only because I'm too faint from hunger to argue."

Judging by the quiet that fell over the cafeteria as they entered what used to be the ballroom, one would think someone had pressed the mute button. Dr. Steele ignored the stares and whispers as he strolled toward the stainless steel lunch counter. Pandora, on the other hand, relished them.

"What's on the menu today, ladies?" he asked as he grabbed a tray. Two young college workers, brought in as extra help on Visitor's Day, giggled behind gloved fingers. Gladys, the lunch lady whose mother had served the Nepenthe family, glared at the witless idiots. They giggled again.

"Fried chicken, cornbread, and green beans, Dr. Steele," they replied in unison.

"Sounds delightful."

They served him with coquettish glances, barely noticing Pandora. They gave him twice as much chicken and cornbread as he was supposed to get while she only got a skinny chicken leg and her piece of cornbread looked like someone had taken a bite out of it. Somebody probably had. Somebody by the name of Agnes Corker. Pandora felt a little sick imagining that hefty ogre's greasy lips gnawing at food she was about to put in her own mouth.

But she immediately felt better when she saw Gladys reaching under the counter. Good old Gladys felt sorry for Pandora, and disliked the Corker, too, so she always tried to fix Pandora a little extra to make up for the pathetic fare they got at Nepenthe Manor.

The old woman said nothing as she placed a slice of French apple pie on Dr. Steele's tray, giving him a distorted wink. "That looks amazing, Gladys. Thank you."

Pandora slid her tray down the stainless steel counter and waited for her piece of pie. The toothless woman shrugged at her and it took a moment for Pandora to realize that Gladys had given Pandora's pie to Dr. Steele. Numb, she turned to go, and the sound of the two college girls' giggles followed her to the corner of the room. Three round tables, reserved for staff only, waited there. Pandora sat in an orange chair, her back to one of the two fireplaces, feeling both weird and special.

"Want to split the pie with me?" Dr. Steele asked as he unfolded a white paper napkin and placed it in his lap. Pandora copied his movements. Damned if she was going to let Vicki's neglect in teaching proper table etiquette make her look like a rube.

She shook her head. "I'm fine."

"Don't be a martyr," he scolded. "I know this was meant for you."

She glared at him. "Well, obviously you're Gladys's new favorite. Just like Xavier is the posse's new favorite." She bit down on her traitorous, quivering lip.

He sighed. "It's only because we're both new. Give it a few months and everything will go back to normal."

She desperately hoped so. All these changes were killing her. She picked up her pitiful excuse for a chicken leg. "So what did you want to talk about?"

He paused for a moment and looked her straight in the eye. "I wanted to talk to you about Douglas Daft."

The chicken leg dropped onto her plate with a fleshy thud.

9

No Way in Hades

"HOW DO YOU know about Dougie Daft?" Pandora demanded. "Did Vicki tell you?"

"Your mother is concerned about you," he answered calmly. He took a quick sip from his pink and white milk carton. "And apparently for good reason, don't you think?"

"So she asks a shrink to solve her problem for her?" Pandora couldn't believe what she was hearing.

"First of all, I'm not a shrink. We counseling psychologists reserve that term for the psychiatrists." He took in her unamused expression. "Note to self," he pretended to scribble on a notepad, "poor attempts at humor should not be used during difficult conversations with Miss Pandora Belfry."

"I'm leaving." She grabbed her tray and stood up.

His hand whipped out and encircled her wrist before she had a chance to take a step. "Sit down, Pandora."

Being that she had little choice in the matter—he was much stronger than her and she *was* curious—she sat back down and he let go of her wrist, though she wouldn't have minded if he hadn't. "Say what you're going to say," she pushed out through clenched teeth, "and then I'm leaving."

"Fine. I'll make it quick," he promised, but he did nothing of the sort. Instead, he took a bite of chicken, followed by a mouthful of cornbread. He nodded with approval. "This isn't half bad."

Shocked at his assessment of Corker's food, and then curious to test it, Pandora took a bite from her chicken leg and chewed thoughtfully. He was right. The chicken actually tasted like chicken instead of its usual paper bag flavor. Suddenly ravenous, she shoved half the tiny loaf-shaped piece of cornbread into her mouth, her mind blocking out the bite mark as best it could. It tasted relatively decent. Before she knew it, she had cleaned her plate and was looking for more. Dr. Steele pushed the pie toward her.

"Take it. You're still growing."

Pandora didn't touch it. "No thanks. Not when you're using your psychological tricks to loosen my tongue and make me talk when I don't want to."

He gave her a quick smile. "We can split it."

She considered this. "Fine." She grabbed her butter knife and split the pie down the middle. Scooping up half, she slid it onto her plate, then pushed the other half toward Dr. Steele.

They ate the still-warm delight in silence. When Dr. Steele finished his half, he set the white plate on his tray, then neatly crossed his silverware on top of it. "Can I ask you a question?"

Pandora sighed and swallowed her last bite. "You can ask it. Doesn't mean I'll answer."

"Fair enough. Why'd you do it?"

"Do what?"

"Why did you agree to go on a date with a boy who, from all accounts, is one bad egg?"

She laughed. "One bad *egg*? What is this? The Victorian era?"

He didn't react, his blue eyes calm and assessing. "Just answer the question, Pandora."

"I did it to get back at my mother. I thought you'd be able to figure that out yourself, having a Ph.D. and all." She wiped her mouth with her paper napkin. When she was sure she'd gotten every last crumb, she crumpled it up and threw it on top of her tray.

"I got that part," he replied patiently. "What I don't get is *why* you want to get back at her."

Pandora "tsked, tsked" at him, swiping one finger over the other. "For shame, Dr. Steele. You have not been paying attention. My mother thinks that she can lie to me and neglect me and there won't be any consequences for her misdeeds. She's wrong."

This seemed to bother him. "But aren't you the one who's going to pay the price?"

"We both will," Pandora replied with determination. "Vicki has never hidden the fact that she doesn't like Mayor Daft. One, because he's a certified idiot, and two, because he's always trying to shut us down. So if I go out on a date with his kid…well, you get the picture." She leaned back and crossed her arms.

"So you're attacking her pride." He said this without judgment, yet for some reason, Pandora felt judged.

"It's the only way I know how to get the job done," she answered angrily.

"Why don't you try to talk to her?" he asked, as though he'd never taken a relationship class in his life. "I can help mediate."

Pandora stared at him in horror. "Are you crazy? No offense, Dr. Steele, but that sounds like my worst nightmare. Stuck in a room with a shrink *and* my mother?" She clasped her hands together and fluttered her eyelashes. "Oh, can I? Please?" She unclasped her hands and shoved her tray away. "No way in Hades am I doing anything of the sort."

"All right, all right. How about you cancel the date with Douglas Daft and think of another way to get through to your mother."

Pandora looked Dr. Steele in the eye. "You don't seem to get it, doc. My mother never wanted me in the first place. She named me Pandora, for pity's sake! So talking to her and trying to work this out just isn't an option for me. Besides," she mumbled, "I've already tried that."

Dr. Steele tapped the orange tabletop with his index finger. "Then cancel the date for my sake. He's two years older than you, Pandora. I don't think he's safe for you right now."

"Have you ever met Dougie Daft?" she challenged.

He pulled back. "Me? Well, no, I haven't actually met the boy."

"So you've only heard things about him from my mother?"

"Yes, that's true." Dr. Steele frowned and Pandora knew she had him by the short hairs.

"And you consider her to be an objective, reliable source in this situation?"

"Well, um—"

She didn't give him a chance to finish, moving in for the kill like a rabid barracuda in the guise of an innocent goldfish. "You know, before this conversation I was thinking about ways to get out of the date myself. I don't think I'm ready for that sort of thing, plus I don't like dances. In my opinion, whoever invented them is a sadistic voyeur. But now that we've talked, I believe I'm going to honor my commitment." She scooted her chair back and stood up. "Thanks for clearing that up for me." She leaned forward to grab her tray and turned to leave.

His next words stopped her. "I won't let you go."

She peered sideways at him and laughed. "Try and stop me!"

"At least let me meet him first," he offered, his casual tone disarming.

She stared at him for a moment. Should she? But what would a meeting accomplish? Then again, what would it hurt? She wondered if Dougie would be able to fool Dr. Steele like he did other adults. It seemed an intriguing question. It might also tell her more about the doctor's character, whether or not he fell for Dougie's snake oil salesman charm. And anyway, she couldn't resist the temptation to plumb the depths of Dr. Andrew Steele. "All right," she agreed. "Tonight at 5:30. I'll invite him to have supper here at the cafeteria. Don't be late."

With that, she strode away, her back straight, her head held high as a princess. She passed the posse, all of whom were staring at her with wide eyes, having heard everything. Birdy's were more perturbed than shocked, of course, but that was just her natural jealousy shining through. "I'll see you guys outside at the *place* in half an hour," she told them, her tone brooking no argument. They nodded like robots, even Xavier.

After dropping off her tray, Pandora banged through the door, only to hear a roar of conversation spring up behind her as she left the cafeteria. She sighed and wished the inmates had a life of their own so they wouldn't feel the need to live vicariously through hers. Even so, she couldn't help grinning. It was nice leading a life deemed intriguing enough for others to want to emulate.

She headed up to her apartment. The Daft number was lying next to the telephone on the small table where she'd left it the day before. She quickly dialed the number, then listened to the wheel's hypnotic whir as it spun back to zero.

After a brief pause, the phone began to ring. "Daft residence," a cool voice answered before she could reconsider her plan. It was Bartles, the Daft family's snooty butler. That man was so cold he could use his pants pockets as coolers.

"I want to talk to Dougie," she said.

"Young Mr. Daft is busy."

"Tell him it's Pandora and be quick about it before I change my mind."

There was a short silence. "One moment, Miss Belfry."

Pandora counted to one hundred, then back down again. The sound of the phone being picked up stopped her at twenty-three. "Hello, Pandora," Dougie breathed into her ear. He always spoke in a low, creepy voice that reminded her of dirty secrets in dark alleyways. "To what do I owe this pleasure?"

"I'm inviting you to supper tonight…at the manor's cafeteria."

To give him credit, he didn't miss a beat. "Sounds delightful."

"Yeah, right. Anyway, be here at 5:30."

"I can't wait."

"Whatever. Okay, goodbye—"

"Wait…Pandora."

She gave an annoyed sigh. "What, Dougie?"

"How have you been?"

She stifled a groan. "Fine, good, whatever. What were you doing when I called?" she blurted out, then cursed her curiosity when he released a pleased sigh, a sound that reminded her of air escaping an evil balloon.

"I was preparing a specimen for dissection."

"And then having it for lunch afterward?" She snorted with mirth.

"That's funny, Pandora," he replied in a deadpan voice. "That's what I like about you. Such life."

"Yeah, well, I'm a regular spitfire. Look, I gotta go."

"Pandora?"

"What *now*?" Dang, why did she start this?

"I'm looking forward to our date."

"It's not a date." She should have hung up then, but she had to go and open her big mouth again. "Just so you know, the new doctor wants to meet you tonight. That's why I invited you."

"Oh, really?"

"Really."

"Is he checking up on me?"

"I suppose. I don't know. Anyway, don't be late. I hate it when people are late. It smacks of laziness and poor taste."

"If I were delayed for some reason, or couldn't come, I would need to call you."

"Fine." She rattled off their private number. "Only use it for an emergency."

"Whatever you say, Pandora."

A shudder ran up her back. The way he said her name, it was like he was licking each letter. Gag. "Bye." She slammed down the phone before she could do any more damage. Damnit all to hell! Why did she have to warn him about Dr. Steele? Well, she knew why. Because Dougie Daft had a way of making her want to bring him down a notch. He was just so damn confident about everything.

She grabbed her braid and twirled it around her finger. Something about all this was bothering her. Something to do with Dr. Steele, and something with the way Dougie had asked, "Is he checking up on me?"

Her brain worked at the problem like a nagging sliver in her flesh until at last she freed it. Dr. Steele wasn't just acting like a therapist; he was acting like her father.

The Electra Complex

10

HER *FATHER?* OH, please, no!

Though if this were true, it would explain so much—Vicki's flirtatious attitude toward Dr. Steele, her unwillingness to tell her daughter who her father was, Dr. Steele's constant concern. On the other hand, if the doc were her father, why wouldn't he tell her?

Unless he didn't know…

But if he *didn't* know, why would he be acting like her father? The question stymied her until she realized Dr. Steele might be acting like her father because he felt a blood connection—a bond that would likely arouse his protective instincts toward her.

The idea of Dr. Steele being her father was at once both intriguing and disturbing. Lord help her, she felt *urges* when she was around him, and had recently entertained vague fantasies about the two of them *being* together, stopping right about when he moved in to kiss her. Which, while frustrating at the time, was now a relief. According to Freud's theory on the Oedipus complex—where a boy falls in love with his mother—such feelings are a symptom of severe mental illness. Though strictly speaking, since she was a girl, she would manifest the Electra complex, which, while still messed up, was a much cooler sounding name.

Even so, Pandora rejected the possibility she was suffering from *any* complex, especially one that weird. Reasons being: One, she was quite mentally stable, thank you very much. Two, she hadn't known Dr. Steele might be her father before she developed urges for him. Three, she absolutely did not have penis envy, which was one of the freaky symptoms of the complex. And finally, she would never, *ever* compete with her mother over a man.

Talk about sick.

Still, even though she knew without a doubt that she didn't suffer from the Electra complex, the idea wouldn't die. She raced to her bedroom to escape her thoughts, but tethered by psychological strings, they followed her as she flew past her bunk bed and into her closet. In the darkness, persistent buggers that they were, they spoke to her in a patient, shrink-like voice. *You could've known unconsciously that Dr. Steele was your father, Pandora dear. And you're already competing with Vicki for him, aren't you?*

Feeling hot and prickly all over, Pandora dropped to her knees and began to dig through the pile of clothes covering the closet floor. *Where's that damn saw?* She typically kept it hanging on a hook on the wall behind the clothes rod, but she must have knocked it down the last time she'd entered the secret passage.

A few moments later, her fingers fastened around a long, smooth object. She pulled it out and examined it for a moment. It was a femur. With a frown, she shoved it back under a shirt and continued her search.

A painful prick on the tip of her pinkie finger told her she'd finally found the saw. Sticking her pinkie in her mouth, she proceeded to slowly and carefully push aside the dirty clothes with one hand. Beneath a black sock, a red painted handle emerged. It was the saw. Years ago, she'd confiscated it from the barn and cleaned it up. Since then, it had served her well.

Her pinkie had stopped bleeding by this time and she was able to slip the saw into a special pouch she'd made from an old pair of black jeans. She then looped the pouch through a belt that she cinched around her waist.

"I'm not Sylvia Plath," she told herself firmly as she left the closet. "I will not marry a man and make him my substitute father and then write a depressing poem about it."

She was about to pull open the door to her bedroom when a knock sounded on it. She jerked backward. "Who's that knocking at my chamber door?" she called, though she already had a good idea who it was. She just liked quoting Poe whenever possible.

"Your mother," came the dry response. "Who else would it be?" she had to add in that pedantic voice of hers.

"Maybe my *brother*?" Pandora answered as she opened the door to face her mother.

Vicki gave her daughter a keen, assessing look with eyes that were frighteningly intelligent. She held a Master's degree in business from an Ivy League school, but had chosen to use her expensive education to run Nepenthe Manor. Lately Pandora had begun to wonder if someone had the goods on Vicki and had blackmailed her into taking such a crappy job. Or maybe she was getting back at her snobby parents. The elderly Belfrys lived in an expensive Victorian in the nearby university town of Akmore and came from an old family, accompanied by a lot of money.

Her sharp eyes, the color of which reminded Pandora of green moss on brown bark, roamed around the room. Typically she would say something snarky about its messy state, but she didn't even seem to see the chaos today. "I wanted to talk to you."

"Don't you like to keep yourself available in case someone wants to talk to you?"

"This is more important, and besides, J.T. said he'd keep an eye on things."

Intrigued, and frankly, more than a little shocked by this atypical behavior, Pandora opened the door and gestured her mother inside. "So you're saying I'm more important than work? This is a banner day!" She grinned at her mother to show she wasn't being entirely flippant.

Vicki had the gall to look hurt as she entered the room. "Pandy, I'm always here for you. I've always looked out for your best interests. *Always*." She pressed a tight fist against her heart. "Perhaps I've spoiled you a bit—"

"Spoiled me?" Pandora echoed, dumbfounded. "I think you mean neglected."

Vicki shook her head, setting her brown curls dancing. "Oh, Pandy. One would think that living in an insane asylum would make you truly understand the meaning of that word you like to throw around so carelessly. I do *not* neglect you. But in letting you do what you want around here, I *do* spoil you. I admit that."

"Don't confuse your lack of parental supervision with spoiling me, Mommy Dearest. Spoiling someone is a decided action. Neglect is an absence of action."

Vicki waved this away and the light from the window made her blunt-tipped fingernails shine in an odd way. "Don't confuse the real issue with your psychobabble. I swear sometimes you're worse than the shrinks around here."

Pandora couldn't stop staring at Vicki's nails. "Are you wearing nail polish?" Her mother's wardrobe was typically so dull. Ever since Dr. Steele had arrived, however, she'd started to actually look feminine. Today she had donned a flowered skirt, navy blue heels, and a ruffled red blouse. Of course, it *was* VD, but still…ruffles?

Vicki blushed. "As a matter of fact, I am. Do you like it?"

Pandora really wanted to say no. Really, she did, if only to get back at Vicki for calling her spoiled. But saying no seemed counterproductive at this point and snottier than even *she* could rationalize in herself. "I'm sure Dr. Steele will like it," she said instead.

Vicki's blush spread like fire. "What does *he* have to do with it? I've only just realized I've spent so many years looking after this place that I've neglected myself. And you, young lady, have not missed many opportunities to point out my dowdiness. Now that I'm making an effort to look more presentable, you find fault with that, too." She sighed and ran a square hand through her tangled hair. "I can't win with you, Pandy."

"I just think your timing is interesting, that's all," she answered innocently, having learned that this was the best way to get at her mother.

Vicki blew a gush of air upward like a whale, the near gale force lifting her bangs an inch off her forehead. "I didn't come here to talk about me. I came to talk about you."

Pandora crossed her arms and waited. "Go on."

"I heard you were having Douglas Daft over for dinner tonight." Pandora stared at her, stunned. "To meet Dr. Steele," she added.

"You heard right." Damn Dr. Steele and his big mouth! How could he betray her like that? She was never going to trust him again. *Ever.*

"I'd like to join you."

"What? Why?"

"Because I'm your mother, that's why. Plus, I'd like to know why a sixteen-year-old boy feels the need to take a fourteen-year-old child to a dance."

"I'm not a child!"

"No, I suppose not," she replied, though she was nodding, as though negating her words. "But you're *my* child."

Hearing the motherly possessiveness in Vicki's tone, Pandora relented a little. "All right, you can come. But I already told Dr. Steele I'm not backing out of our date."

"Fine," Vicki agreed, almost too readily. "I won't try to convince you otherwise, but I'd still like to have dinner with you both."

Pandora sensed her mother was up to something but she hadn't quite sussed out what it was. "He's coming at 5:30."

"I'll meet you in the cafeteria." Vicki smiled, looking pleased. "See you then." Before Pandora could say any more, Vicki slipped out the door.

Pandora waited a few minutes for her mother to get ahead of her, then left the room. Her mind was spinning as she headed down the stairs to the main floor. She couldn't believe Dr. Steele had told Vicki about Dougie Daft coming for dinner. More accurately, she didn't *want* to believe he'd done something so heinous. The next time she saw him she'd be sure to let him know what a disaster he was as a therapist.

Confidentiality, indeed! He hadn't even waited ten minutes to tell Vicki everything about their conversation. What a toad!

Vexed to the point of wanting to scream, Pandora crossed the foyer quickly, her shoes squeaking across the marble floor. She needed to get inside that labyrinth—she needed to do something to take her mind off Dr. Steele and Dougie Daft and her mother. The three of them were really starting to get on her nerves.

Once she hit the lawn, she started running. As she rounded the copse, she spotted the posse standing just far enough from the labyrinth to avoid suspicion if seen. She pulled the saw out of its pouch and waved it at them. "Are we ready to enter the lair?"

Lucy ran toward her, her face streaked with tears. "The poopy head didn't come. And neither did Charles's grandma!"

Pandora patted the distraught girl on the back. "There, there, Lucy. I'm sorry they didn't visit, but maybe that's for the best. Adults screw things up. Haven't you learned that by now?"

Charles joined them, his shoulders hunched in misery. "But Grandma said—"

"Adults are always saying one thing and meaning another," Pandora interrupted, her voice fierce. "As soon as you understand that, Charles, you'll be free. They won't be able to hurt you anymore." She firmly turned Lucy around and herded her back toward the labyrinth. "Now come on, we have work to do."

"So you're saying we shouldn't trust anyone over thirty?" Xavier said with a smirk as she approached. Birdy was standing off by herself, busy smoothing out the wrinkles in her dress, and Skippy was watching her do it with an odd expression on his face.

"I'm not trusting anyone over *twenty*," Pandora asserted. "It seems like people become an adult and forget what it's like to be a kid. They start following every rule and walking around like they've got a stick up their butt. Frankly, I'm sick of it." She went to cross her arms, but stopped at the last second when she remembered the saw in her hand.

"Could your conversation with Dr. Steele have anything to do with this new attitude?" he wondered. His smile was light, but the expression in his eyes was inexplicably serious. *What did he care?* she wondered.

She fixed him with an equally serious gaze. "Well, if you have to know, yes, it does. Dr. Steele told me not to date Dougie Daft, but then, when I said I was still going to do it—that I'd made a *commitment*—he said he wanted to meet him."

"That doesn't sound too bad," Skippy remarked.

Sinclair didn't look too sure. He had a way of seeing the meaning behind the words and he shook his head, two sharp jerks, first to the left and then to the right. "Sinclair knows." Pandora pointed at him. "He sees what's coming." He frowned and looked down at his shoes—brown loafers that shined like polished walnuts.

"What's coming?" Birdy marched toward them, her heels sinking into the soft grassy ground with each step. Her approach brought with it a heavy, flowery odor that overwhelmed Pandora like a toxic cloud. The tramp must have sprayed on more perfume after lunch, enough to knock out an elephant.

"Dr. Steele," Pandora's hands shook with fury, "had to go and tell Vicki about Dougie coming to dinner and now she wants to join us!"

"He told on you?" Lucy lisped, her big eyes stunned. "What a big baby tattletale!" Her indignation was rather ironic being that she herself ratted people out on a regular basis.

"He most certainly did."

"Dr. Steele would never do such a thing!" Birdy declared. "He has integrity."

Pandora glared at her. "Then you tell me how Vicki found out about our conversation not ten minutes after I left him in the cafeteria."

"He did leave rather quickly," Skippy acknowledged.

"Maybe he had to go to the bathroom?" Birdy argued. "That food the Corker serves would give anyone the runs."

"It wasn't the runs," Skippy said. "We saw him outside Director Belfry's office on our way out, didn't we?"

Birdy scowled. "That doesn't mean anything. And whose side are you on?" Skippy shrugged and blushed, pressing his lips together.

Xavier looked thoughtful. "It doesn't look good for the doctor, though."

Pandora nodded, feeling vindicated. "So you agree with me, half-bro?"

"I've never trusted adults," he answered, dodging her question. "So it's nothing new to me."

"Do you got that?" She pointed at Lucy and Charles, who were playing stay-still tag, which is basically two people standing next to each other and exchanging wallops, yelling, "tag, you're it!" Their hands froze mid-air. "Xavier agrees. You can't ever trust adults. They only hurt people."

"I get it, Pandora," Lucy answered, her head lowered. "Adults are hurters."

"Charles?"

"Yes, Pandora," Charles sighed. "I understand."

"That includes Dr. Steele," she warned them. She made sure Birdy was looking at her when she said this. Her contemptuous gum snapping adequately expressed what she thought about that, so Pandora placed herself between the royal pain in the arse and Lucy and Charles. She needed to be sure they got what she was saying. She bent low and looked them both in the eye, her own orbs shifting back and forth between them a couple times for good measure.

"Dr. Steele is one of the bad guys, *right?*"

"Right, Pandora," they both echoed, their slumped shoulders mirroring each other.

But Pandora barely noticed their despondency. She was too busy being triumphant. In one fell swoop she'd gotten revenge on both Dr. Steele and Vicki. She'd won *this* battle! Now onto the next…

11

Storm the Castle

PANDORA BRANDISHED HER saw like a sword. "We're heading in!" Charles and Lucy, never able to stay down for long, chased after her, whooping and hollering.

"*Charge!*" Charles shouted with joyous ferocity, pretending he was holding his own sword. "Surrender or die!"

"We'll burn it to the ground!" Lucy cried, getting into the spirit of things. Pandora was glad she'd gotten her lighter back from the little pyro after the Foyer Fiasco. Knowing Lucy, she'd follow through on the threat.

When Pandora reached the wall where they'd begun clearing vines, she waited for the others to join her, with Birdy coming last. "I don't see what the hurry is," she grumbled, patting at her hair and smoothing her skirt. "All this gadding about is ruining my shoes."

"I want to at least get the door cleared before we have to go back to the manor," Pandora explained. "Then we can have all day tomorrow to explore the labyrinth."

"I'll hold the ladder," Xavier offered, his brown eyes gleaming. He wouldn't admit it, but she knew he was as excited as she was about getting inside. Unlike her, he hadn't been waiting for this moment for *years*. Even so, she was glad to see his face reflecting her own greedy anticipation. She'd long since discovered that just as misery loves company, so does mischief.

Kneeling down, Xavier and Skippy pulled out the ladder and set it against the wall. Ignoring her protesting ribs, Pandora climbed up the metal rungs and started sawing at the thick vines. This time, Sinclair, Lucy, and Charles took turns lugging the thick pieces of vine that Pandora sawed off into the woods. They only carried one piece at a time, and Sinclair held his out before him as though it were a smelly baby, but with the three of them working, they made good progress. Birdy did nothing, of course, spending her time complaining about the chill in the air, a stain on her new dress, and her mother's irritating habits, sprinkled in between with proclamations of Dr. Steele's innocence.

"I refuse to believe that man would ever betray anyone," she declared fervently, for about the thousandth time.

"Well, you better believe it, Toots," Pandora growled impatiently after the last declaration. "Once again, the adults of this world have let us down. I hope I never become one."

"You'd better not hope that," Xavier said as he let go of the ladder to grab the last of the vines from her.

"I mean, in spirit," Pandora clarified. "Being an adult doesn't necessarily mean someone who's turned eighteen, or who's done growing, or whatever. It's a state of mind."

"Adults are dumb, dumb poopy butts!" Lucy shouted as she and the boys returned from their trip to the woods. "I hate them all!"

"That's the spirit, Lucy!" Pandora cheered.

"Don't encourage her," Xavier scolded. "She's just a kid."

"And I hope she always stays one," she growled back. "Now mind your own business, Mr. Establishment. You don't know the posse like I do."

"Maybe not, but I know trouble when I see it."

"I'm *protecting* them from trouble," she hissed. "Just you watch."

He shrugged. "All right. But don't come running to me when it all goes wrong."

"Ha! Like I'd ever do that."

"You never know…"

"Oh, shut up, Negative Nellie." She cupped one hand to her mouth. "Get off that big butt of yours, Birdy, and get over here."

"Are we done?" Skippy looked up.

"Not only are we done, we're going in."

There was a change in the air as everyone gathered around the ladder. Even Birdy, still grumbling under her breath, was unable to hide the avid curiosity in her eyes.

"We just have to find a way to pry open the door—" Pandora stopped and reached up to push aside a few strands that made up the curtain they'd left behind to hide the door. "What's this?" She climbed one step higher to stand at the very top and grabbed hold of a thick vine to steady herself as she leaned closer. "Aha!"

"What is it, Pandora?" Charles asked, looking worried.

"Genius, that's what it is!"

"Would you mind elaborating?" Xavier asked, standing on his tiptoes to see better.

"Just don't let go of the ladder. I'm barely hanging on as it is."

"Fine. Now spill it."

"From what I can see, the door was made to be lowered like a draw-bridge. I can see the chains from here. We just have to find the bottom chains so we can open it from the outside."

"I don't see anything down here," Xavier called, his voice muffled by ivy. "It's probably just for show," he determined as he reemerged from the curtain.

"Then how do we get in? There's no way I'm going to be able to pry this open. At least, not without a crowbar."

"The chains are hidden," came a voice they were not accustomed to hearing. "The chains are hidden, the chains are hidden…" Sinclair softly repeated over and over.

"Hidden where?" Skippy wondered aloud. "There's nothing here but wall."

"This is stupid!" Birdy vented, examining her nails. "I have better things to do than search for non-existent chains."

"Like what?" Pandora snorted. "Look up new diagnoses? Pick your nose? Kiss up to Dr. Steele? Geez, Birdy, get over yourself. This stuff that's happening right now? This is life. Live it!"

"Easy for you to say," she drawled. "You're free. You don't have my history following you everywhere you go. You don't have my illness weighing down your every—"

"The Chains Are Hidden!" Sinclair shouted his last repetition with a fervor that startled everyone, even Birdy, who clamped her mouth shut and turned to stare at him. With uncharacteristic determination, he marched toward the wall, pushed aside the ivy, and disappeared beneath it.

Xavier started laughing. "That's it! The wall. They're hidden in the wall!"

"But where?" Pandora demanded, annoyed she wasn't in the thick of things down below so she could join in the search. Xavier and Skippy both let go of the ladder and ducked behind the ivy. "Hey!" she yelled. "Someone has to hold the ladder." She tightened her grip just as it shifted to the left when someone bumped against it. "Holy Schmidt, watch out!"

"Holy Schmidt! Sorry, Pandora." Lucy laughed. "I tripped."

"I'll save you!" Charles grabbed the ladder and steadied it under Pandora's feet.

She breathed a sigh of relief. "Thanks, Charles. Hang on tight. I'm coming down."

But at that moment the wall next to the ladder started to move. She jerked back, desperately clutching her vine. "The wall's coming down! Get out of the way, Lucy! Charles, *move!*"

"The wall's not coming down, you idiot," Birdy said calmly. "It's the drawbridge that's coming down."

Pandora looked at the wall and saw that Birdy was right. How annoying. But exciting, too. The boys had discovered the hidden chains. The time had come to storm the castle! She pulled back as a four-foot wide section of wall slowly fell away from the side of the labyrinth, the chains clunking, rattling, and screeching in protest every inch. They would need a good dose of WD-40, but luckily, still worked well enough to do the job. Pandora's heart beat excitedly. This was it—the moment of discovery!

The wide plank, its solid oak darkened with age, pushed the curtain of vines outward, slowly revealing the labyrinth within. But before Pandora could get a good look, Xavier cried, "It's too heavy. Get back!"

A groan shuddered through the air as Xavier fell backward. He hit the base of the ladder, knocking it out from Pandora at the same time the drawbridge slammed to the ground with a loud thud. She lunged for another vine and grabbed hold of it, her body slamming hard against the wall. Her ribs shrieked like mad ghosts, but she held on tight, her feet dangling in the air. If she fell now, she'd land on the ladder or Xavier, and damned if she was going to be blamed for breaking his *other* wrist.

"Pandora!" Lucy cried, jumping up and down. "Hang on!"

"I'm flying to your rescue!" Charles shouted, hopping and holding out his cape.

"I'm okay," she yelled down to him, though she really wasn't, not quite. Ivy tickled her nose and attempted to infiltrate her mouth. She wanted to sneeze and cough at the same time. "Just get that ladder!"

"You're gonna have to hang on," Xavier called up to her. "I'm tangled in the rungs and all this freakishly strong ivy, too."

"Well, hurry up. My ribs are killing me."

There was a scuffling noise down below. "Agh, don't pull so hard, Birdy!"

"Excuse me for living," she huffed. "I was just trying to help."

"You can't pull on his owie, Bird Brain," Lucy scolded. "Everyone knows that!"

"It's all I can reach, midget."

"Don't you call me a midget, Big Bird!"

Pandora's fingers grew numb and her breathing labored as she listened to them argue about the best way to handle the situation. "I'll lift you and the ladder, Xavier," Skippy offered. "I can do it. I've been working out."

"Um, probably not a good idea. I weigh more than you do, big guy. Why don't you grab me under the armpits and lift up. Lucy can untangle the vine that's wrapped around my leg and Birdy and Sinclair can *gently* pull on the ladder."

More scuffling noises rose up, then, "Agh! I said *gently*!"

"Wuss," Birdy grumbled. "I can only do so much, you know. That stupid ramp is in my way."

"I can't hold on much longer!" Pandora shouted over her shoulder, wishing she could see what was going on. They ignored her. "Hello? I'm slipping here!" No response, only a lot of grunting as they worked to free Xavier from the ladder and the lifelike vines.

Knowing she was going to drop like a brick if she didn't do something soon, Pandora started to swing her legs toward the labyrinth opening. On the first attempt, her toe touched the top of the drawbridge. On the second, her left hand slipped and she missed altogether. She rested a second. If she didn't get this next attempt right, she'd flatten Xavier.

Gritting her teeth, she made herself swing back and forth twice. On the second swing forward, she whipped her legs upward and with gritted teeth, let go of the vines. Her right foot hit first, followed by her left. Just when she thought she was going to make the landing, her left foot slipped on the mossy ramp and she pitched forward…right into the labyrinth.

Not a Normal Human Being

12

OH, THE PAIN.

Pandora spent several seconds staring up at the sky, waiting for the searing torture to go away. She was getting pretty darn sick of her rib injury; it was ruining a moment she'd been waiting for all her life. *Don't fight it*, she told herself sternly, and a memory of Giganticus placing his large, warm hand on her shoulder and speaking those very words sprouted in her mind. Instantly she felt better, as though he really had touched her. She shook her head and sat up.

"I'm in the labyrinth," she said wonderingly. "I'm *really* here."

"Pandora!" a distant voice called. She looked to her left, toward the wide stairway she'd rolled down when she'd fallen into the labyrinth. Charles appeared at the top of it, quickly joined by the others. "You're alive!"

"It'll take more than a fall down twenty stone steps to kill me," she groaned as she pushed herself to her feet. "But the pain was worth it. Will you look at this place?"

The posse clattered down the stairs to join her in an unusual courtyard with no apparent way out other than the way they'd come in. Ivy hung from every wall like mermaid's hair and encircled six figures nearly as tall as the labyrinth walls. Pandora hoped they were statues and not humans frozen in some sort of Narnian Ice Witch spell. Relief carvings of bats and skulls, gargoyles and other mythical monsters, protruded from bare spots on the walls, and hundreds more likely hid under the veil of ivy.

"It's the Garden of Eden!" Lucy lisped, her chubby little hands clasping together joyously.

"More like the Garden of Creepiness, if you ask me," Birdy replied, leaning over to break off a brittle twig. It snapped between her fingers, spooking a nearby bird. It was their crow, and he cawed at them in annoyance before flying away further into the labyrinth. Pandora wished she could follow after him.

"Where's the actual maze?" Xavier wondered as he looked around. "It has to be around here somewhere."

"On the other side of this wall, I suppose." Pandora flung her arm at the barrier. "The real question is, how do we get over there?"

"I imagine it's like how we got in here," he replied, "by triggering some sort of hidden mechanism."

"Speaking of which…what was the trick for the drawbridge?"

"It's made just like something you'd find in a medieval castle!" Skippy exclaimed. "There are two blocks about a foot off the ground, with a small groove on each side so you just stick your fingers in and slide them out. They aren't as thick as the regular blocks, and they hide the chains from sight. Once we grease everything up and move some more vines out of the way, everything should run smoothly."

"We should probably close the drawbridge in case someone comes along," Pandora said. "Vicki says it's not safe in here and has threatened to kill me if she ever hears that I got in. And being that I finally did it, I don't want my death to ruin the experience."

"I wonder why she didn't want you in here?" Xavier asked. "I mean, yeah, it's a mess, but otherwise everything looks to be in good shape."

"Maybe there are booby traps," Charles hoped.

"The only booby traps around here are on Birdy's chest," Pandora joked.

"Ha, ha. I, for one, am not getting locked up in this place. I vote we keep the door open. If it gets stuck, nobody will know where we are. We could be trapped in here for hours…days!"

Lucy clung to Pandora. "Trapped? I don't like that. I'm closet phobic, you know."

Pandora sighed. Leave it to Birdy to be sensible at the times when Pandora didn't want her to be. "You're not *claustro*phobic, Lucy, and we won't be trapped. Look." She pointed to the chains clearly visible on the wall. "We can open and close the drawbridge from this side."

"We'll be fine," Xavier spoke assertively. "Skippy and I will hide the ladder and we'll leave a small crack when we close the door so it won't get stuck. The curtain of vines should cover it enough so people won't see it's open."

"Not good enough," Birdy said, and Pandora wanted to smack her. Why, of all times, did she have to pick *now* to be dramatic? Wasn't this exciting enough for her?

"Come on, Birdy," Skippy pleaded. "It won't be the same without you."

"That's true," she mused. "But too bad." She crossed her arms and tapped the toe of her high-heeled shoe on the moss-covered stones that filled in the parts of the courtyard not covered by grass.

"Skippy's right," Xavier agreed, though he looked like he wished he didn't have to get involved. "We need you, Birdy."

"Oh, all right," she conceded, her lips curved in triumph. "I'll do it for *you*, Xavier."

Xavier shrugged at Skippy as though to say, *Sorry, dude, but it was the only way I could think of.* For his part, Skippy looked a little queasy.

"What about doing it for Skippy?" Pandora said quickly.

"Oh, him, too." Birdy fluttered her lashes at him and he inflated once more. "Can't have my man thinking I don't care, can I?"

"My *man*?" Pandora echoed.

"Oh," Birdy cooed triumphantly. "Didn't I tell you?"

"Tell me what?"

"Skippy and I are going out."

Going out? Pandora looked around. "Do all of you know about this?" Nobody met her eyes, so obviously the answer was yes. "Why didn't anyone tell me?"

"He asked me at lunch, when you were busy with Dr. Steele," Birdy answered for the others.

"Oh," Pandora replied, feeling better. The only reason she'd been left out of the loop was because Birdy was punishing her. And she'd probably made the rest of the posse promise not to say anything so she could announce it in her typical grand, dramatic fashion, as she was doing now.

"*And* I wanted to tell you myself, of course." Birdy always covered all her bases. "Didn't want you to have to hear it as gossip."

"Well, congratulations, you two," Pandora forced herself to say. "But I don't want to see any hysterical babies coming out of this, okay?"

"Eek!" Lucy shrieked. "Hysterical babies!"

"Very funny, Pandora," Birdy grumbled. Then she smiled. "No hard feelings, though, hm?"

Pandora eyed the gloating girl suspiciously. "Hard feelings about what?"

"Well, Skippy told me you liked him." Birdy's tone was deceptively sympathetic. "I didn't want to take him away from you, being that we're such good friends, but he insisted it was all right cause he doesn't feel that way about you."

Pandora glanced over at Skippy, whose eyes promptly darted over to look at one of the statues with such intense interest one would think it was Michelangelo's Pietà, or a naked woman. "He said that, did he?" Birdy nodded triumphantly and Skippy rolled his eyes like a nervous colt. Pandora bit her lip. "Well, he was right to pick you over me. You *are* twice the woman I am, and besides you two definitely deserve each other."

Birdy smiled sweetly. "I am, aren't I? And we most certainly do." She paused and frowned. It had just occurred to her that there might have been a double meaning behind Pandora's words.

"All right, let's get to work!" Pandora shouted before Birdy's little mind confirmed what her instincts were telling her. The last thing they needed was a hissy fit.

Not needing to be told twice, Skippy, relieved to escape the consequences of his little, white lie, dashed up the steps, followed by Xavier. Five minutes later, they were back inside the labyrinth, with Skippy pulling the drawbridge up and Xavier helping as best he could with one arm. The curtain of vines cooperated for the most part, though a few got caught between the wall and the bridge.

"We'll fix that when we leave," Xavier said as they descended the stairs. "But it should do for now."

"Great!" Pandora said heartily. "Now let's find out how to get on the other side of that wall and—"

"We should split up," Xavier interrupted, turning to face the others. "I want people to check every square inch of this wall for evidence of a door. The carvings might be triggers, so check them, too."

Pandora shot daggers of death at his back. "That's what I was going to say!"

He whirled around, looking innocent. "Sorry." His voice was unbearably smug, showing just how sorry he was *not*. "I guess you'll have to learn to talk faster."

"I wasn't expecting to be so rudely interrupted," she growled, taking a step toward him.

"Just trying to keep things running smoothly."

"Lucy and I will take this part over here!" Charles said in an anxious, high-pitched voice. "Okay, guys? We're a team and we have to each do our part, right?" He grabbed Lucy's hand and pulled her over toward one of the walls where she immediately stuck her finger up a gargoyle's nose.

Pandora sighed. Charles hated conflict of any kind. She wished Xavier would pick up on that. It looked like she was going to have to sit that boy down and explain to him how things ran around Nepenthe Manor. His constant "rocking the boat" attitude wasn't doing anyone any favors.

"Skippy, Xavier, and I will work on this part," Birdy announced, hooking each boy with an arm and whipping him toward the wall with a move that would have made a square dancer proud.

Pandora glanced around. That left her and Sinclair. But Sinclair, oblivious to the world around him, was already searching the wall on his own. She moved to join him. But as she neared his side, he backed away.

"Fine," she groused. "I know when I'm not wanted." Not surprisingly, he didn't respond.

She pushed her way through a clump of bushes toward the wall. On the way, she met up with a statue. Curiosity got the best of her and she yanked on the web of vines covering the tall figure. The thick branches were stubborn so she pulled out her shears and cut through several of them. As she worked, Sinclair kept stepping toward the wall, then retreating. After a few minutes she realized he hadn't been avoiding her, he'd been working something out. She knew better than to ask him what he was up to, however, so she continued cutting, occasional glimpses of pale stone tantalizing her.

Sweating like a Yeti in a fur coat, she finally finished cutting the worst of the vines. She tucked away her shears, then reached up and yanked down the leafy net covering the statue. With one fell swoop, the statue was revealed in all its glory. Pandora backed up and stared in wonder. The statue was a man and he was naked as the day he was born. And, holy crap, he was genitally correct. She couldn't stop staring at the muscled figure that looked any minute as though he might spring to life. The young man stood tall and straight on a five-foot platform, one fist pressed to his heart, the other hand stretching toward the skies as though reaching for God. He was beautiful.

"Enjoying the art?" Xavier asked. She spun around. He was right behind her and he was grinning.

"Yes, as a matter of fact, I am. I love stonework and this is an amazing piece of sculpture. Don't you think?" She was working very hard to sound nonchalant and sophisticated.

Xavier wasn't buying it. "Amazing piece, my patootie. You were staring right at his twigs and berries."

To her horror, her cheeks flamed hot. "I was *not!* I was wondering what he was reaching for. There must be some sort of symbolism in the gesture he's making, probably representing a connection between humankind and God, like in Michelangelo's *The Creation of Adam* in the Sistine Chapel."

"Yeah, right," Xavier snorted. "He's probably just reaching for a robe to hide his dainty bits."

Pandora glowered at him. "You wouldn't know a work of art from your ass, Xavier Carlisle."

He shrugged. "Probably not. But based on what you've been staring at, I doubt you would, either."

"Toad!"

"Hussy."

"Misogynist!"

"It's a soft 'g' and I happen to like women very much."

"Agh! Stop correcting me!"

"And let my sister sound like an uneducated miscreant? I don't think so."

"You arrogant son of a bi—" There was a movement to their left and Pandora bit down on the word racing across her palate. Sinclair pushed his way through the bushes, then, after a moment's hesitation, started to climb the statue. "Sinclair!" Pandora yelped. "What are you doing? Get down from there."

He didn't answer…of course.

"Leave him alone," Xavier said. "You treat him like a baby, you know."

She gaped at him. "I do not! Unlike some people, I respect Sinclair's illness and do what I can to make his life easier."

"My mom used to call that sort of 'help' mollycoddling and she said it never did anyone any good to be treated like they were a glass figurine. He's a human being, so treat him like one." Xavier's tone was bland, but his coffee eyes were shooting out passionate sparks.

"You just don't get it, Xavier," Pandora fired back indignantly. "Sinclair's not a normal human being. He's—"

"I've found the way in," Sinclair interrupted, his voice quiet, yet firm. He grabbed hold of the muscular stone arm pointing to the sky and pulled down hard. A rumbling noise rose from the statue's base and slowly the statue began to turn. Within seconds, Sinclair disappeared entirely from view, leaving Xavier and Pandora to stare incredulously at the statue's bare butt.

13

With a Cherry on Top

AND WHAT A butt it was, though it was not the sole reason Pandora was still staring. She'd never seen anything so awesome in her life. A moving statue, right here in her own backyard! Dang, she wished she'd found the way into the labyrinth years ago.

"Way to go, Sinclair!" Xavier shouted. "You're a genius." Sinclair popped his head around the side of the statue and his tightly pressed lips, which looked like they were trying very hard not to let loose his ritual repetition of words, lifted into a half-smile. "Guys, come on!" Xavier motioned for the others to join them. "Sinclair's found the way in." From various spots in the courtyard a bevy of cheers rose up.

Curious, and a little stunned by the fact that she had witnessed a statue move, Pandora hurried around to the other side to find a small opening in the seemingly solid base. She stepped back and peered up at the statue. The beautiful young man now faced the impenetrable wall, his well-muscled arm pointing toward it as though giving directions. *Incredible.*

"Sinclair?" she called through cupped hands. "Where'd you go?" She pushed the heavy stone door open a little wider. Ducking her head, she stepped inside the cobweb-filled space, large enough to fit five or six people if they didn't move too much and kept their knees bent. The light from outside spotlighted a set of stairs, and Sinclair was already halfway down them, peering up at her. He pointed to the wall on her left, next to the door. Hanging on a wrought-iron hook was an old-fashioned lantern, which reminded her of the one the stranger on the beach had been carrying. She pulled it down and wiped away a thick coating of dust. When the glass looked a little cleaner, she dug about in her sporran for her lighter.

"It's like magic!" Lucy cried excitedly, her voice drifting in through the opening. "Oh, Charles, isn't this the coolest thing, like, *ever*?"

"Like, totally!" he agreed heartily.

Pandora caught Sinclair's eye. "Just because you figured out the statue doesn't mean you can get all cocky now. So wait for us, all right?" He gave her a serious nod. Assured, she stepped back outside, crouched in front of the opening so no one could get past her, and handed the lantern to Lucy. "Hold this."

Lucy beamed as her tiny hands reached for the handle. "Pretty please, with a cherry on top, let me light it like a firebomb, Pretty Pandora!"

Pandora hesitated, remembering how Xavier accused her of treating the inmates like babies. "All right, fine, you can light it. Just keep the lantern still while I get it ready." Lucy did as she was told...to the best of her ability. She was so excited at the prospect of starting something on fire—even if it was *meant* to burn—she kept hopping up and down on her toes. Despite the challenge of working with a perpetually swinging object, Pandora managed to wrestle the glass from the wire arms holding it safely in place and set it on the ground away from Lucy's flying feet. Grasping the lantern once more, she turned the stiff wheel that raised the wick. After its blackened tip emerged, Pandora opened the cap to the fuel tank and sniffed at the opening.

"You'll fry your brain cells doing that," Xavier pointed out as he, Skippy, and a tottering Birdy rounded the base of the statue.

"Very funny. I'm checking the fuel."

"You couldn't just shake the lantern?"

"I know there's fuel in it, *dork*, I just wanted to be sure what type it was in case we use it all up and need to add more later." She screwed the cap back on.

"And it's..."

"Your garden variety kerosene and there's not much left. It won't last long." For obvious reasons, she didn't mention that the lantern in the secret room and this one were exactly the same, or that the stranger had one, too. Something odd was going on here, but she wasn't sure what.

"Good to know," he replied in a mocking tone of voice.

"It *is* good to know. Mixing fuels is dangerous."

One pale eyebrow shot up. It was annoying how he could make it do that on command. "You would know, wouldn't you?"

As a matter of fact, due to a few errors on her part resulting in the destruction of both eyebrows, she would, but she wasn't going to give him the satisfaction of being right by sharing such information.

She took the lamp from Lucy and set it on the ground. "Here." She handed the lighter to the feverishly excited girl as though presenting her with a Nobel Peace Prize. "You may do the honors."

Lucy chuckled like an old man as she swiped the lighter from Pandora. "Stand back, all of you!" Her tiny thumb rolled the lighter wheel three times in rapid succession, as though revving an engine. "And prepare to be amazed!" She lifted both arms into the air like a circus grandmaster.

"Just light the damn thing!" Birdy snapped.

"Birdy said *damn*!" Lucy cried, pointing her finger at the offending potty mouth. "Oops! Now I said it. Damn!" She started to titter, pressing her fingertips to her mouth.

"That's enough, Lucy," Xavier said gently, cutting off her descent into a gigglefest. "This is a sacred moment and we must treat it with utmost respect."

She stopped laughing and stared at him in awe. "Wow. You're right. I won't say damn anymore, okay?" He nodded his approval. "Here it goes!" With a solemnity befitting a queen, Lucy approached the lantern, spun the lighter's wheel, and lit the wick. The old fabric sputtered, hissed, then caught, quickly burgeoning into a healthy flame. "It's beautiful," she said as she stared at the fire.

Pandora slid the glass dome back into place and stood up. It was time to regain control of the situation. "All right, gang. Let's get moving before this thing goes out." Lantern firmly in her grasp, she ducked back through the opening. She was about to head down to join Sinclair when something above the arched doorway caught her eye—swirling script cut into the stone. "Hey, look!" she called to the others who were attempting to fit into the small space behind her. "It's a message." She lifted the lantern higher, took a step closer, and began to read aloud,

> "The Labyrinth of Lunacy is where you are.
> Here, normal is fallacy, a falling star.
> So if ye dare enter, this loony warns all…
> That finding the center takes more than one fall.
> When you hit a dead-end, for surely you will
> Don't go round the bend, just stand still.
> If you get stumped as the end grows near,
> Lean forward now and closer peer.
>
> See that you watch your step, my friend,
> The labyrinth is a queer old place.
> Its secrets might just be your end,
> So don't give up the chase!"

Tacked on at the end in less elegant script, as though written as an afterthought, were the words, "*And watch out for snakes.*"

"And I thought I was messed up." Birdy's expression was wry in the flickering light. "I don't think my nerves are up to this sort of drama."

"Your nerves have seen a lot worse in the mirror," Pandora muttered. Then more loudly, "I'm sure it's just a clue, Birdy, not a warning."

"I'll bet Charles was right and there are booby traps everywhere!" Skippy exclaimed.

Lucy giggled, her eyes bright. "Skippy said *booby*."

"We'll have to split up," he ignored Lucy, who had clapped her hand over her mouth. "Test every step, watch our every move. I volunteer to lead one of the groups. Who's with me?" He turned to face a mutinous Birdy.

"I'm staying here. You'll stay, too, won't you, Xavier?" she pleaded prettily.

"And miss the boobies?" he grinned. "Not on your life."

"Well, I think you're all idiots. I'm staying here alone. Outside, actually, where I can enjoy the view of Sir Bulgealot." She gave a dirty guffaw.

Skippy's long face stretched even longer. If Birdy were staying, then he would have to stay, too. Dating someone didn't come without a price. Pandora made a mental note not to date anyone any time soon. Skippy's shoulders dropped in disappointment as he accepted his fate, and Pandora knew it was time to intervene. She wondered, though, when the day would come that she could finally stop playing referee to these bozos.

"I'll stay with you, Birdy!" she said brightly. "We could talk about girl stuff. Like polishing our nails on a daily basis or how to rat our hair to attract men. Let the boys go on ahead without us. It'll be fun. Just you and me."

Birdy's eyes narrowed. She knew exactly what Pandora was up to and why. There was no way she was going to hang out with a girl when she could be vying for the attention of two young, virile men—one she'd already conquered, and one she was determined to—and she was quite aware Pandora knew that.

"Yeah, real fun, Belfry. But I don't think so. Can you move, please? It's getting cramped in here."

"Onward, soldiers!" Skippy commanded, brightening. Lucy and Charles repeated his call, filling the small space and stairway with their echoing cries.

Pandora stepped into the stairwell and tapped the narrow stone steps with the toe of her shoe. It seemed safe and she began her descent.

With each step that pulled them deeper below ground, the stairs grew increasingly moist and slippery. When she reached Sinclair, he pressed against the wall to let her pass. She went on ahead, her eyes darting back and forth searching for any signs of a booby trap, her breath growing louder in her ears with each step.

"Move faster, Pandora!" Birdy snapped. "My claustrophobia is kicking in."

"You're not claustrophobic, Birdy!" Pandora snapped back. "And I believe I've already had this discussion with Lucy."

"I could be claustrophobic," she insisted. "I've got everything else."

"Why couldn't you have a fear of talking?" Pandora mumbled.

"I *heard* that!"

"Oh, darn." Pandora was about to say more, but realized the steps had come to an end. She had survived. Heartened, she lifted the lantern, only to feel her stomach sink. "Oh, crud." Eight dark hallways split off from the stairwell like the arms of an octopus, or giant spider legs. "I can't believe it!" The posse crowded around her. "It's an *underground* maze."

"What do we do now?" Lucy moaned, clutching her hands together beneath her chin. "What if the ceiling caves in and we're buried alive! What if we have to eat each other like cannon balls do?"

Pandora sighed. Sometimes Lucy could be so morbid.

"We split up," Skippy suggested. "Each take a passage and see where it leads."

"And use what for light, Einstein?" Birdy snapped, her patience at an end.

"Maybe there's another clue written on the wall," Xavier suggested.

"Now that's using your head," Birdy purred.

Skippy frowned. "I thought of that, too, just didn't say it out loud. I was getting to it and—"

"Hold your light up, Pandora," Xavier interrupted. She grimaced. She hated being bossed around, especially by Xavier. He stepped toward one of the walls and began to inspect it closely. "Higher."

"It's as high as it's going to go."

"Then give it to Skippy."

She lifted the lantern higher. "No offense, Skippy, but you're too bouncy."

"None taken," he said, giving a few bounces before joining Xavier in his search. Soon everyone but Birdy was studying the walls as intensely as an archeologist in Tutankhamen's tomb.

"Anyone find anything?" Xavier asked after several minutes had passed.

Everyone shook their heads and Pandora rubbed at her temple. "There's nothing for it," she decided, "but to go down each passage."

Just as she said this, Sinclair did the unthinkable. He grabbed hold of her arm and pulled her over to the third passage. He let go and pointed, his expression more animated than she'd ever seen it— outside the times he was having a fit.

"How do you know it's this one?" He pointed to the stone blocks surrounding the opening. Instead of sitting horizontally like the rest, the blocks were set vertically. She looked at the rectangular stones, then at Sinclair. "*How* do you see these things?"

Xavier came up behind them. "I don't think I ever would've noticed these blocks were different. Good work, Sherlock." He gave Sinclair a salute, which Sinclair returned with a pleased smile. Pandora had never seen him look so confident and at ease. At first she felt happy for him, then her pleasure soured as a warning bell sounded in her mind. He was acting so different from his usual self.

She pushed away her misgivings. Sinclair was simply good at solving puzzles, that's all it was. He wasn't changing.

Nothing was changing.

So why did it feel as though everything was?

I'm a Real Man

14

"GOOD JOB, SINCLAIR!" the posse shouted, taking turns patting him on the back. Sinclair, returning to normal form, skittered away from the touching, or pounding, as was Lucy's case.

"Ladies first, Pandora." Xavier waved her forward like a general. She was tempted to shout her own orders, something akin to having the posse draw and quarter the arrogant bastard, but luckily for him her curiosity was stronger than her desire to crush him. She plunged into the dark, spider web-filled tunnel. After a few steps, it made a sharp left turn and had them heading back in the direction they'd come. Just as quickly, it made a right turn, followed by a series of turns back and forth. After the sixth one she lost track of how many times they turned.

She was starting to think they'd chosen the wrong passage and were going to get wrapped up in a massive spider web and eaten by a giant spider, when she spotted a pale light reaching toward them. At that same moment, two things happened. The floor sloped upward and the lantern's flame sputtered. She began to run. Seconds later she burst out of the tunnel and into the outside world. She blinked repeatedly, urging her eyes to adjust to the light. As though helping her in this effort, the sun slipped behind a wall of dark clouds and a shadow descended over the labyrinth.

Pandora blew out the lantern to save fuel for their return, then looked to her left and right with growing disbelief. "You've got to be kidding me." She was standing on the other side of the wall now, in a stone-paved corridor that spanned the length of a football field. On one side of the passage was the wall they'd just managed to get over, or under, as was the case. Running parallel to it, a new one, with about thirty doorways lining it, blocked their way. "Not again!"

"What'd you expect?" Xavier said from behind her. "It's a labyrinth."

"I *know* that! But it took us forever to get this far and now we have to pick from a million openings and we'll never get the right one!"

"Not to mention that it's getting late," he noted, peering up at the cloudy sky. "We won't be able to do it today. We'll have to come back tomorrow." He sounded disappointed, which made Pandora feel slightly better.

"Tomorrow?" Birdy echoed. "I thought we were done."

"I suppose we'll have to come back," Pandora reluctantly agreed. Privately she wondered if she would be able to return on her own after supper—if only to figure out which door was next. Her lips slid up into a smile, until she remembered who was coming for supper and the smile twisted into a scowl. Dougie. Damn his freaky eyes! Maybe if she hurried them through the meal there'd still be time to sneak out to the labyrinth. "We'll have to move fast," she told the others. "The lantern fuel is nearly gone."

"But I need light!" Birdy shrieked. "I've already found a spider crawling on my arm. It's dead now," she reassured them smugly.

"You can take my hand," Skippy offered.

She stared at it. "I suppose," she sighed when Xavier made no similar offer, even though her forceful stare was willing him to do so.

Pandora pulled out her lighter and re-lit the lamp. A lot of grumbling and sighs of disappointment accompanied the posse back through the tunnel. The lantern threatened to go out many times, but held on. As they reached the stairway, the flame flickered, then ceased to exist. Birdy cried out, but at this point her dramatics were pretty useless being that they could see where they were going now. Pandora waved everyone up the stairs, then followed after Sinclair, the last to head up.

When they reached the top, he looked up at the poem carved over the arched stairwell entry. His lips moved silently as he read the words to himself.

"Do you think you could memorize the whole thing and write it out for me?" Pandora asked. He nodded. "Don't forget the snakes part. I have a feeling everything has a meaning in this place." He nodded again. He obviously felt the same way.

She was about to hang the lantern on its hook, then remembered it was out of fuel. Although she planned to bring her flashlight next time, she still wanted to be sure the lantern was useable in case of an emergency. She ducked her head to leave the base and her eyes flashed toward the left side of the doorway. Another hook, identical to the first. She studied it for a moment. Two hooks should mean two lanterns, so what had happened to the other one?

After raising the statue's arm, returning the base to its normal position, they made their way out of the labyrinth, the posse chattering excitedly about their adventure. Pandora was glad to see that Lucy and Charles were in good spirits, seemingly having forgotten that their loved ones had once again failed them. Skippy and Xavier trimmed the ivy, then ensured the drawbridge was hidden beneath it, after which everyone headed back to the manor, talking and laughing and wondering what nasty concoction the Corker had brewed up for supper.

Pandora lagged behind, her mind full of nagging questions, foremost of which was, who had written that poem? It was so strange, it must have a hidden meaning, and she planned to find out what it was. She hoped Sinclair wrote it all down before supper. She didn't want him forgetting or misremembering parts, not that he was likely to. He had a mind like a steel trap, which was perhaps another reason why he had so many problems. Repression was one of Pandora's favorite defense mechanisms. She couldn't imagine how hard life would be being unable to forget what one didn't want to remember.

Then there was that missing lantern to consider. Was there a connection between it and the one the stranger had on the beach? A part of her thought there might be, but another part wasn't sure if she wanted there to be a link. People, she could handle. But real, live ghosts? They might be a bit trickier, and not so amenable to her kindly suggestions.

Her thoughts moved on to her impending dinner with Dougie. Would Dr. Steele like him? Would Vicki change her mind and agree to let them go to the dance? As Pandora climbed the front steps, she realized she was counting on her mother to put the kibosh on the whole scheme, which was probably why she didn't feel nearly as anxious as she should about it. Somewhere along the way she had decided that no way was Vicki going to let her 14-year-old daughter go on a date with a creepy guy whose father was even more of a creep.

Pandora laughed quietly to herself. Planning this dinner was a genius move. It was like her brain had a mind of its own, going about its business without tapping her conscious resources. When she died they should preserve her brain for science. Just in case, she had better write a letter to the Akmore University biology department and make the offer.

"Hey, Pandora!" Lucy cried as she entered the lobby, and she jumped, startled out of her thoughts. The entire posse gathered around her like a covey of spiders waiting for her to come inside before they pounced. "We're going to sit as close as we can to your table," she said.

"There's no need for that, you know."

"No, there's not," Xavier replied, a small smile on his lips.

Without meaning to, Pandora found herself smiling back. "See? Xavier *does* have some brains. Not much, but enough to know I can handle this myself."

"No," Xavier said firmly. "There's no need for them to sit close because I'm joining you for dinner."

She gaped at him. "Oh, no, you're not!"

He took a threatening step toward her. "Oh, yes, I am, Belfry. And if you try to stop me I'll tell Vicki about the labyrinth."

"You wouldn't!" she cried triumphantly, pointing at him. "Because if you do, you'll get in trouble. It's off-limits."

"But nobody told *me*." He batted his lashes innocently. "Besides, I wanted to be sure it was safe inside. She'll probably have me do maintenance when I tell her that the place could use some work."

Pandora let loose the growl building in her belly. "You beast! How could you?"

"It's for your own good, Pandora," Charles pleaded, his hands clasped together in front of him. "Someone has to watch over you with that villain around."

"I don't see what the big fuss is about," Birdy grumbled. "Pandora's a big girl. Let her fight her own battles." Xavier's only response was a bland glance in her direction. He'd obviously made up his mind. "Fine!" she huffed, her eyes shooting poison arrows at everyone in her line of sight. "I'm going to my room. You losers can do what you like." Pivoting about, she clacked across the marble floor like Attila the Hun heading off to battle…in heels.

"See you guys at dinner," Skippy called as he hurried after her. Lucy and Charles glanced at each other, then chased after Skippy. Sinclair followed at a more sedate pace, his expression furrowed as though deep in thought, likely he was repeating the rhyme to himself. She wanted to tell him to write it down before supper but she didn't want Xavier to know what she was plotting, so she kept her mouth shut.

As soon as Sinclair disappeared up the stairs, she turned on him. "Why do you have to come? If you're looking for entertainment, go watch TV."

He shrugged. "You can say what you like, but I'm coming. Now, why don't you go change?"

"Why would I want to do that? I'm not looking to impress anyone." She glanced down at her outfit. Little bits of vine, several leaves, and even a couple twigs clung to her person. She was also still holding the lantern. "Oh."

"We don't want Vicki asking too many questions, do we?" With a grin, he headed back outside to his room over the stables to change out of his own messy clothes.

Pandora pounded up the stairs to the third floor to change and clean up. She didn't want to look like she cared too much, so she picked out her typical ensemble of black jeans and a long-sleeved, black t-shirt graced by a picture of the Grim Reaper, his voluminous hood pulled back to reveal bloody, barbed wire encircling his skull. The words, "As ye reap, so shall ye sow" were on the front. For some reason, the simple switching of two little words really annoyed the crap out of a lot of people, especially cranky, old Mrs. Johnson, making the t-shirt worth the hard-earned fifteen bucks she'd paid for it. She spent the next ten minutes picking twigs and bits of moss out of her hair, then brushing and re-braiding it. Her glowering expression reflected precisely how thrilled she was to be having this meeting, but she knew it was a necessary evil. Xavier had better not ruin things, though. He had a bad habit of getting in her way.

Pulling her sporran over her head and positioning it over her left hip, she headed downstairs. As she crossed the foyer, she thought about waiting for Dougie to arrive, then thought better of it. Vicki's light was on in her office—she could show him the way to the cafeteria. Pandora moved a little faster. She'd told Dougie not to be late and he wouldn't be. He thought obeisance was the way to her heart, but he was wrong. The man she would love, *if* she ever decided to fall in love, would be feisty and strong, manly and smart. Like Dr. Steele.

Speaking of the handsome devil—and she did not use that word lightly after he betrayed her—he sat at one of the staff's round tables, hand wrapped around a coffee cup. The inmates watched him from a distance, their eyes glowing with worshipful fascination, as though he were the male version of Princess Diana or Madonna. They wouldn't stay away for long, though. The kinder therapists soon learned not to eat their lunch in the cafeteria. Like truffle pigs, the inmates could sniff out empathy from a mile away, and once a therapist was diagnosed as acceptable, he or she didn't stand a chance.

"You're already here," Pandora remarked inanely as she pulled out a chair across from him. She didn't trust herself sitting too close. She was angry and needed to convey her pique with full sincerity. Something about his presence messed with her head, crossing her wires so that she sent one message when she intended to send another. Maybe it was his 'I'm a real man' cologne. Or his intense blue eyes. Or his bulging muscles. Or his... "Don't you have paperwork to finish?"

"I figured I could take care of that later tonight."

"No big dates?" she couldn't resist asking.

"Just a little one."

Pandora bit her lip. "Oh, Nurse Joanna?"

He looked momentarily confused. "Who? Oh, yes! Nurse Burns. Um, no." He gave her a funny look. "I meant a date with my pillow. As you might recall I went to bed rather late last night." She did recall. "I imagine you're a bit tired, too."

She had to bite down on an overwhelming urge to yawn. Displaying her epiglottis did not fit with the mysterious and intriguing sexpot image she was trying to project. "Oh, I'm good."

He leaned back in his chair and crossed his arms. "So what did you do today?"

"Oh, not much. A little of this…a little of that."

"Did you get in?"

Pandora's heart seized and her mouth dropped open, spoiling the sexpot image. "Get in…*what?*"

A dark eyebrow lifted. "The labyrinth, of course."

She nearly choked. "How did you know?"

He grinned. "Haven't you figured it out yet?"

"Figured what out?"

"That I see everything."

"Everything?" she echoed breathily.

"*Everything.*"

15

Hit It Off

CRUD, CRUD, CRUD.

"You can close your mouth now."

She snapped her mouth shut, then opened it again just as quickly. "But *how* did you see? You were working inside and there are trees and I never saw *you...*" Her voice grew shriller with each word.

He laughed. "No need to look so stunned. And I wasn't spying. I went for a short walk after lunch and spotted you cutting vines. Do you think you should be doing that with your injury?"

Pandora glanced around her. "You can't tell Vicki I was there."

"Forbidden territory?" he guessed.

She nodded, feeling ill. "I mean it, Dr. Steele. You can't say *anything*. I know you've already told on me once—"

"Dr. Steele!" a voice called from behind them and they both turned. Vicki was marching toward them, smiling her Director smile. Trailing behind her was Dougie, looking slick as usual, and oddly deferent. Judging by Vicki's relaxed demeanor, his ruse of sweet, young man was already working. Damn, he moved quickly. "Good of you to join us."

Pandora leaped to her feet. "We should get our food now. The Corker sometimes closes down the cafeteria before she's supposed to."

Vicki gave a tinkly laugh. "Agnes is a character, isn't she?" She glanced conspiratorially at Pandora, as if they were both in on the joke.

Pandora scowled. "She's a character all right. An alcoholi—"

"But she's all we have," Vicki jumped in, "so we put up with her little eccentricities, don't we, Pandy?" The look in her eyes, one that only Pandora could see, translated to, "Don't mess with me on this, or I'll turn you into hamburger."

Pandora bit her lip and turned away, right into Dougie's arms. *Son of a biddy butt—*

"Hello, Pandora," Dougie greeted, his voice soft as curdled milk. A wave of revulsion swept over her and she jerked back.

"You're late," she snapped, even though he wasn't.

His pale lids slowly closed, stayed shut for a second, and opened once more, his empty blue eyes fastening on her like leeches. As usual, he looked immaculate, his pale blond hair slicked back with gel, and he wore his typical polo shirt, pale blue with a green alligator marking where his heart would have been if he had one, collar flipped up Count Dracula-style. Dark heather gray cords with cuffs were an exact fit, neither too baggy nor too tight, and his gray dress shoes shone in the fluorescent lighting of the cafeteria. Pandora found herself staring at him. When she realized what she was doing, she shook her head, feeling strangely dizzy as though waking from a long nap.

"Shall we get something to eat?" He held out his pale, nearly hairless arm for her to take.

She ignored the offer, charging on ahead. "Yeah, sure. Food's good."

Luckily the line was short and she didn't have to stand too long next to Dougie, who shifted along with her every move. If she stepped forward, he did too, as though attached to her with stretchy bands. He was creeping her out, yet at the same time, she found him oddly fascinating. He brought to mind the animal skull she'd once found out in the woods, the one she now had in her room. She cursed her natural morbid curiosity. It was something she was going to have to stifle, pronto, if she didn't want to end up doing something stupid.

Supper tonight was tater-tot casserole, green beans, and a roll, followed by butterscotch pudding for dessert. "Ladies." Dougie nodded at the two older women serving. "What's good tonight?" To Pandora's astonishment, Jackie and Linda, who'd been working at Nepenthe forever, and were as hardened as Pandora's roll, giggled and fluffed their hair through their hairnets.

"Ain't nothing ever good here," Jackie drawled. A two-pack a day smoker, she always talked as though she had a cigarette hanging out of her mouth, which she usually did if she could get away with it. "'Cept the service," she cackled.

Dougie did his slow blink. "I can see that. I'll take whatever you have to offer."

Linda fanned herself. "Lord, this one's a smoothie!"

"Can you just fill our trays?" Pandora demanded, exasperated. They were acting like trashy high school girls and Dougie was encouraging them in their childish, and frankly revolting, behavior. Had they not heard of the women's lib movement?

Jackie pointed a tater-tot encrusted serving spoon at Pandora, but was looking at Dougie as she spoke. "You sure you want to be hanging out with this one? She's a real pain in the ass."

"I like that in a woman," Dougie retorted, his voice soft, yet carrying. The two women roared and proceeded to dump a load of obnoxious food onto their trays. Pandora hurried away from the still laughing women to fill up a glass of milk at the milk station. When it was half-full, she hurried over to the staff table. The posse hadn't yet arrived so she had something to be grateful for. When she sat down, she heard Jackie and Linda still laughing and turned to give them a glare. But they weren't laughing at *her* anymore. Dr. Steele, standing in line to get his dinner, undoubtedly had said something witty, like "hello." Watching the two old biddies laugh, she felt a strange and violent urge to shove their faces into the tater-tot casserole. Instead, like a responsibly dull adult, she sat on her hands.

"What the hell was that?" she hissed at Dougie as he sat down. "You were flirting with women old enough to be your mother!"

"Don't tell that to my mother," he replied, inching his chair closer to hers. Everyone in town knew all about Mrs. Daft and her obsession with looking younger. A few years back she'd had some work done and now, with her pulled back eyes and an overstretched mouth, she looked like the Joker in Batman.

"Why do you do that?" she demanded, inching her chair away.

"Do what?"

"Act like you like people when you don't?"

He gave her his patented blank-faced stare. "What makes you think I don't like them, Pandora?"

"Don't put on that innocent act with me, Dougie Daft."

"But game playing is so fun,"—slow blink—"especially with you."

She raised a clenched fist. "You play games with me, boy, and I'll crack your head open."

His smile was grimly pleased. "Duly noted, *Pandy.*"

At that moment, the posse burst into the cafeteria, unwittingly saving Dougie from getting his head cracked open. Lucy spotted her and waved. When her eyes lit on Dougie, she stuck out her tongue and with her thumbs in her ears, waggled her fingers at him. He only blinked back at her like a reptile. Birdy didn't even so much as slow to look in their direction as she made a beeline toward Dr. Steele. Skippy followed after her, with Charles and Lucy tagging along. Sinclair paused as he entered the cafeteria, then turned and marched over to Pandora's table. She watched him as he approached, feeling that peculiar feeling again, as though things were changing. The Sinclair of old would never have broken the ritual he followed whenever he entered the cafeteria. Stop, count to ten, head directly to the line taking fifty steps, no more, no less, no stepping on cracks. Now, here he was, not only breaking form, but seemingly without distress.

Two feet from the table, he came to a stop and faced Pandora, his hand outstretched. In it was a folded piece of paper. He made a point of pretending Dougie didn't exist. She reached out and plucked the paper from his hand, quickly tucking it into her sporran. Then he pivoted on his heel and left the cafeteria. A second later, he re-entered, completed his ritual, and joined the others in line. Luckily, no one else arrived to get between him and the posse. He had sacrificed his comfort to do his duty, but he was the same old Sinclair, needing his routine to function. Pandora breathed a sigh of relief. Nothing was changing.

"A love letter from the imbecile?" Dougie breathed, leaning back in his chair as though it meant nothing to him. "How sweet."

She glared at him. "He's not an imbecile, you idiot. He's a savant. That means he's smarter than you any day of the week."

"*He's* the idiot," Dougie clarified. He held up his bony, Grim Reaper hands when Pandora made to protest. "Idiot savant, that is. Labels are so important, aren't they, Pandora? Especially in a place like this." He indicated the inmates and Little Gustav chose that moment to shout a few choice words.

"Dung nuts, wienie head!"

Pandora laughed. "Labels *are* important here, Dougie. Little Gustav was shouting that at you. And for your information, although intellectually gifted in one particular area, an idiot savant is mentally retarded. Sinclair is definitely not MR. In fact, I'll bet you he's a lot smarter than you."

Dougie's eyes narrowed, but before he could respond, Vicki and Dr. Steele pulled out their chairs to join them. "You certainly made a hit with Jackie and Linda, Douglas," Vicki noted as she sat down. She studied Dougie, who gave her a totally faux, self-deprecating smile.

"I think they simply enjoy meeting new people," he replied, his voice soft and sweet.

Vicki eyed him carefully. "I think they liked *you* in particular."

He shrugged. "I doubt it, Ms. Belfry. I'm not all that interesting." He speared a tater-tot. From where Pandora was sitting he looked like he wanted to keep spearing it over and over until it was mashed potatoes. He refrained.

"You're the mayor's son," she pointed out. "And the Dafts are a well-known family in Bedlam."

Dougie chewed thoughtfully on his tot. "My father likes everyone to think we're more important than we are." He spoke this so softly that Pandora barely heard him, but when she finally translated what he'd said, her eyes widened. Damn him! He knew exactly how to get on Vicki's good side. Quite aware of the animosity between his dad and

Pandora's mom, he was using it to his advantage. If it weren't also to Pandora's disadvantage, she'd applaud his audacity. In her head, anyway.

She glanced at Dr. Steele, who was studying Dougie like a detective about to grill a suspect. "So what's your take on Nepenthe Manor, Doug?" he asked, his face now devoid of any expression except innocent curiosity. Dougie looked up and met Dr. Steele's gaze. For a moment, his bland, blue eyes and Dr. Steele's own vivid ones locked in battle. Then Dougie smiled politely.

"I think that what Ms. Belfry is doing here is more important than what any politician could do. Politicians, like my father, promise change, but here at Nepenthe Manor, you actually follow through. You heal people. I can't help but be very impressed."

Pandora couldn't help being impressed, either. Here, at last, she was seeing why adults loved Dougie so much. He was as full of crap as a dung heap, but to give him credit, he was very good at shoveling that crap. Very good.

Vicki smiled. "Well, you're welcome here any time, Douglas, to learn more about what we do, if you'd like. You seem nothing like your father, you know. He never takes me up on my offers to visit."

Dougie slowly pulled a white paper napkin across his vampiric lips. "I take that as a compliment, Ms. Belfry. While I respect my father, I feel he too often forgets that his job is to serve others. I hope that in this respect I can make up for his deficits."

"Maybe you can work here as an intern," Pandora suggested brightly. "We have plenty of bedpans to dump and messes to clean up."

Xavier turned to look at her. She didn't know how he did it, but one half of his face—the half hidden from Dr. Steele and Vicki—looked downright evil, while the other half smiled sweetly, if rather sickly. "I regret to say that I have a weak stomach, but I'm happy to help in other ways."

Weak stomach, my ass, she wanted to shout, but she kept her mouth shut. Though only because she'd spotted her savior. Tray in hand, Xavier marched toward them, and he looked like a man on a mission. He would expose Dougie for the nasty nemesis that he was.

"Hello, everyone!" he called jovially. "What have I missed?"

Pandora grinned, she was so grateful to see him. "Dougie says he wants to help out here at Nepenthe Manor."

Xavier set his tray down, then sat across from Dougie. "Is that right?" Dougie nodded, unfazed. In fact, he seemed to relish the challenge that Xavier was about to throw at his feet. "Hmm… Well, I'm afraid we don't have any dogs or cats you can kick. We do have some horses, but I believe they kick back."

"Xavier!" Vicki exclaimed, her hazel eyes crackling like chestnuts in a fire. "Douglas is our guest. I expect you to treat him as such."

"It's all right, Ms. Belfry," Dougie soothed. "I'm afraid Mr. Carlisle and I got off on the wrong foot. When we first met, I was trying to help out an addled old dog, but when I went to pick him up, he snapped at me. I pushed him away with my foot so I wouldn't get bit, because of course then he would have to be put down. Xavier, in the dim light, thought I was kicking him. I understand his mistake and applaud his heroics. I only wish that I could've explained to him what I was doing before it all got out of hand. I did try…" His eyes filled with pity, he let his voice fade away.

Xavier stared at him, his expression a study in stunned disbelief. "You're kidding me, right?" He looked at Vicki. "You're buying his story?"

Her stern Director look took over. "He's trying to hold out the hand of friendship, Xavier. I suggest you take it."

Pandora glanced at Dr. Steele to see how he was taking this, but he was spooning butterscotch pudding into his mouth and seemed to have lost interest in the whole affair. Her fingers itched to scoop up a handful of pudding and fling it at him.

"But Director Belfry," Xavier cried. "He's an evil little cuss. If only you'd seen—"

"What I've seen," she interrupted, "is a polite young man who has earned the right to take my daughter to a dance."

"What?" Pandora yelped.

"What?" Xavier echoed.

"You heard me. Douglas Daft, you have my permission to take my daughter to the dance." She smiled at Pandora. "I think you two will hit it off wonderfully!"

16

PANDORA STIFLED THE urge to throw up the entire helping of butterscotch pudding she'd just shoveled into her mouth to keep herself from hurling it at Dr. Steele. What was Vicki thinking?

"I must admit, Douglas," Vicki continued, "that your father and I haven't always..." she paused, searching for the most politically correct way to communicate her belief that Mayor Daft was a supercilious, amoral joke for a human being. "Well, let's just say we haven't always seen eye to eye. But you're not your father, Douglas, and shouldn't be labeled by what he does. Working at a mental health institute, I should know better than to judge others by what I've heard, or by the people around them. I know what it's like to be judged by one's parents and feel awful that I've made the same mistake. The sins of your father, so to speak, should not be visited on his son."

Oh, crap, Pandora groaned inwardly. Not the sins of the father card! Vicki hated it when people thought she was like her parents, and now, thinking she had made the same mistake with Dougie, her guilt was blinding her to what Dougie was really like.

"Why thank you, Ms. Belfry. I'm honored to have earned your faith and trust." He turned his head, but not to look at Pandora. His dead eyes found Xavier and a spark of triumph briefly brought them to life before dying out.

Xavier shoved back his chair. "You know, I've seen some crazy things in my life, but this has got to take the cake. I'm sorry Director Belfry, but you're being taken for a fool." He stood up and pointed at Dougie. "He's bad news and if you let him take your daughter out on a date, you're basically writing her death sentence."

"Oh, Xavier," Vicki scowled. "There's no need to be so dramatic. You're as bad as Pandy."

He grabbed his tray. "Just you wait and see." Standing tall and majestic as a warrior, he gave Dougie one last glare, then stalked off to join the posse, who were, of course, absorbing everything like voracious amoebas. Pandora watched him go and a warm sensation tingled through her body. She hadn't realized he cared so much.

Vicki sighed. "Teenagers are so volatile!" She laughed, though it sounded forced.

Dougie leaned forward slightly. "I imagine jealousy can make a person say things they wouldn't normally say."

Vicki froze. "Jealousy?"

"Pandora is a beautiful young woman. It only makes sense that Xavier would find her attractive." The tip of his tongue flicked out like a snake.

"Pandora? Beautiful?" Vicki's voice shook. "Xavier find her attractive?"

"Xavier's my brother, Dougie," Pandora intervened. "My half-brother. We just found out."

Dougie peered at her closely. "You're *related* to him? I guess that makes it worse."

"Yes, well!" Vicki said brightly. "I'm quite sure we have nothing to worry about in that respect. Xavier is a nice boy."

"Oh, so you've known him since before he came to Bedlam…"

"Well, not exactly." Vicki frowned. "I knew his mother, though, and she was—" Here she stopped, flustered. "Well, she, I, um, she was a good friend," she finished lamely.

"I see," Dougie whispered, and said nothing more. But he didn't need to. The damage was done. He had planted the seed of doubt in Vicki's mind where it was already sprouting tendrils quick as Jack's beanstalk.

"Are you finished eating?" Pandora asked Dougie. He'd barely touched a morsel. "Good. I have homework to do and I'm sure you have more autopsies to perform."

He studied her for a moment and she had to fight off the desire to shudder that always came over her when he did that. "I could help you with your homework…" *up in your room*, his eyes added.

"Pandy could always use help in that department," Vicki said with a laugh that carried more than a hint of exasperation.

Pandora stared at her mother. Was she so desperate to keep Pandora and Xavier apart that she'd throw her daughter to the wolves, or the werewolf, in this case? "I can handle my homework myself. Besides, my ribs hurt and I didn't get much sleep last night."

Dr. Steele, who'd been inexcusably silent during most of the conversation, stifled a yawn. "I'm about done in, too. If you'll excuse me, I'm going to finish up some paperwork and hit the hay." He pushed back from the table and stood up. "It was nice to meet you, young man." He reached out to shake Dougie's hand. Dougie stared at the outstretched appendage as though each fingertip sported a head, then offered his own limp hand to be squeezed and jerked up and down in a strong shake. As soon as he could, he pulled his hand back.

"You, too, Dr. Steele. I'm glad we had this opportunity to get to know one another."

"Know one another? Why I imagine we've barely scratched the surface."

Dougie smiled. "I am what you see before you, Dr. Steele."

Dr. Steele's blue eyes flicked toward Pandora, then away. "If that's true, then the same can be said about me. Good night, everyone." He picked up his tray.

Vicki, who had been hurriedly finishing up her meal, pushed back her chair. "I'll walk you out, Andrew." She wiped her mouth with one quick dash, then threw the crumpled napkin onto her tray.

Before Pandora could say a word, they were gone from the table and she was left alone with Dougie. "Are you still here?" she growled, feeling sick to her stomach. The butterscotch pudding was fighting back.

His expression altered not one whit. "I want to see your room."

"And I want to fly to the moon. And since neither will be happening any time soon, let's call it a day."

"As long as there's a chance."

Pandora breathed out a long sigh that smelled of butterscotch. "My point, Dougie, is that there's not a snowball's chance in hell that you'll get in my room."

"I know you agreed to go to the dance with me to get back at your mother."

"I wasn't trying to be subtle about it."

"And yet I still want to go with you. I wonder why that is?"

"Because you like torturing people and having them under your slimy, little thumb."

"I imagine you're right, but it's more than that, Pandora."

She felt a prickling sensation in her armpits. "Well, whatever it is, I don't want to hear it. I've gotta go."

She stood and his hand snaked out and grabbed her arm, pulling her back down. Then he leaned close to her, his breath surprisingly hot on her cheek. "I like you, Pandora. Far more than anyone I've ever met. And I don't plan to let anyone get in the way of my having you."

"You'll never have me, Dougie Daft!" she declared defiantly, sounding an awful lot like Scarlett O'Hara. "I'll go to that stupid dance with you because I made a commitment and I honor my commitments. But when it's done, I want nothing to do with you."

Instead of looking angry, he looked pleased as he let go of her arm. "Did you know that your nostrils flare like a charging bull when you get mad? It's so pleasing to watch."

"Agghh!" she cried. "Don't say things like that."

She quickly stood, grabbed her tray, and headed for the dirty dish tub. They passed the posse and Dougie did something unexpected. He stopped.

"Hello," he greeted. No one said a word in reply. "I just wanted to introduce myself since we've never met. I'm Pandora's new boyfriend, Douglas Daft."

"You're not my boyfriend. I never said anything like that!"

"I only meant a boy who's your friend," he replied smoothly. "Anyway, you all seem like a nice group of people."

"You're so full of crap, Daft," Xavier spit out. Dougie blinked innocently, as though the words held no meaning to him.

"You're a mean-head!" Lucy cried. "Xavier said you kicked a dog."

"If I had kicked a dog, that officer would've arrested me, not Xavier. Xavier was doing what he thought was right, but he didn't realize I was only trying to help little Dobie." Xavier scowled.

"What about what Pandora saw?" Birdy demanded. "She said you booted a cat, too."

He gave Pandora a look that she supposed was meant to be fond. "We all know how Pandora likes to tell stories, don't we?" She did not! Though, truth be told, she hadn't actually *seen* Dougie kick the cat. Not that she'd ever admit that.

Birdy nodded. "She does. She's terrible."

"Hey!" Pandora protested, but neither of them was listening.

"You have beautiful hair, by the way, Miss…"

Birdy's eyes widened and her hand lifted to fluff her curls. "Peacock. Birdy Peacock. And you have great taste… In most things," she amended, looking pointedly at Pandora.

"I'm going," Pandora growled at Dougie.

"It was nice meeting all of you. When I come again, I'll bring some jawbreakers for you if you'd like." Lucy and Charles stared at each other in wonder. They loved jawbreakers, but couldn't have them at Nepenthe Manor. Vicki considered them a choking hazard. His eyes lit on Skippy's hat. "I also have a cowboy hat I never wear that you can have if you want. Girls seem to like cowboy hats." Skippy glanced at Birdy. Even though he said nothing, anyone could tell he was tempted by the offer.

"You're a lying scumbag, Daft," Xavier hissed. "And if it's the last thing I do, I'll show everyone the truth about you."

"I'm sorry if I upset you, Xavier. I only want to be friends with Pandora's friends. Maybe for her sake, you and I should let bygones be bygones."

"This has nothing to do with Pandora and you know it."

Pandora gaped at him. What happened to the protective older brother? "What are you talking about, Xavier? This has *everything* to do with me."

"There she goes again," Birdy drawled, "making it all about her. You can come back any time, Douglas. And bring that hat. I've always had a thing for cowboys."

"Bring those jawbreakers, too!" Lucy yelled, bouncing up and down excitedly.

Pandora stifled a groan. It was so easy to turn their heads, to buy their affection. First Xavier had done it and now Dougie. She was going to have to have a little talk with the posse. Skippy stood up at that moment and started pretending he was riding a horse. Lucy and Birdy clapped appreciatively.

Make that a *big* talk.

"I'm leaving now." She strode off and dumped her tray with a crash. Dougie did the same, trailing after her like a dog.

By the time they reached the foyer, she was incensed. "What were you doing in there? Don't you understand they're like children?"

"I understand perfectly," he replied as they headed toward the main door. "That's why I did what I did. I thought you of all people would understand manipulation."

"Me?" she gasped. "Understand manipulation? I don't know what you're talking about."

"There's no need to pretend around me, Pandora. You and I are more alike than you think."

"I'm nothing like you, Dougie." She stopped at the doorway and stood in front of him. She wanted him to see her face so he'd get how serious she was. "I don't even like you."

"And yet here I am." His soft voice penetrated to her core.

"Because I'm using you," she hissed. "That's the only reason."

"Which proves my original point. You *are* a manipulator. Just like me." He gave her his cool smile, then opened the door. Before she could say another word it shut in her face.

What had just happened? How had she so totally lost control? Her mother had given her permission to go to a dance with a monster. Dr.

Steele had done nothing to stop it, even though he was the one who'd wanted to meet Dougie in the first place. And her brother, whom she'd thought was protecting her, only wanted revenge.

If only she had magic beans of her own. Then she'd ride that bean plant high into the sky.

Where she'd find a giant...

...called Giganticus.

17

It's All Lies

PANDORA LAY IN her bunk, staring up at the mottled ceiling. A steady rain had started up during dinner and now tapped like beckoning fingers against the windowpanes, mocking her. The foul weather foiled any plans for heading out to the labyrinth tonight, and she wouldn't be able to set up a stakeout to watch the beach, either. It helped knowing that if the stranger was of the living, he'd more than likely stay home in this weather anyway. And Xavier, she felt reasonably assured, wouldn't be heading outdoors if he could help it. He was a bit of a wuss that way.

Before climbing into bed, she had refilled the lantern with kerosene, then taken a bath to soothe her sore muscles and aching ribs. The hot water made the tiny cuts all over her hands and arms sting like mosquito bites, and after climbing out, she rubbed Aloe Vera gel, squeezed from the plant in her room, on her scratches.

Physically, she felt better. Mentally, not so much. In fact, the urge to howl, like the screamer in the Edvard Munch print hanging on her wall, was almost overwhelming. If she thought she could get away with it, she'd let loose a frustrated screech that would shake the whole place down. Unfortunately, living in an insane asylum, they'd have her downing anti-psychotic cocktails before she could say, "I'm not crazy!" So she had to settle for yelling into her pillow and cursing the people in her life who insisted on making it miserable.

She was used to her mother failing her, but she had held high hopes for Dr. Steele. She'd even begun to accept the idea that he might be her father. At least then she'd have someone looking out for her best interests. But he'd failed her mightily. He'd barely spoken a word and had said nothing when Vicki gave Dougie her blessing. Even worse, he knew she'd gone into the labyrinth, which meant he now had something to hold over her head. Tonight he'd proven he was like every other adult. Useless.

But it wasn't just the adults bothering Pandora. Xavier hadn't exactly come off as a shining knight himself. Instead of looking out for his sister, he'd been more interested in seeking revenge against Dougie for getting him sent to Nepenthe Manor. Not only had he disappointed her with Dougie, he was hell-bent on finding their dad first so he could be the hero. Not cool.

Pandora sighed and turned over. After a moment of discomfort, she rolled onto her back again. Despite her efforts, the throbbing continued and Nurse Devine's pain pills beckoned with the allure of a Siren. The thought of taking a handful and forgetting everything sounded awfully good right now. It would be so nice not to feel anything anymore. Maybe not forever, but at least for tonight.

Unable to relax, Pandora climbed out of her bunk. Once on the floor, she paced back and forth along the pathways she'd made through the papers and clothes and shoes spread out all over the gray carpet. *Should I do it?* she wondered. *Why not?*

Because you won't be able to function at all tomorrow, her rational side pointed out.

I won't be able to function if I can't sleep, idiot, she answered back.

You take a handful and you might never wake up, you know. Her rational half was nicer than her darker, more wicked, half and kindly refrained from calling her an idiot.

Yeah, well, maybe I don't want to wake up.

Her rational mind worked through this before responding, *Then they win.*

Pandora stopped pacing. *Oh, no, they don't!*

That's the spirit! Now go take one pill, and one pill only. Then fetch Sinclair's note and look it over.

The note! She'd forgotten all about it. She hurried over to where her sporran hung on the bunk bed post. Her Scottish bag was one of the few things she stored in a certain spot, ready to go at a moment's notice. She'd long ago rationalized that she wasn't a total slob, just with things that didn't matter much—like homework and cafeteria trays.

Now to find her medication. Some digging produced it from under a pile of dirty clothes. She really needed to do some laundry, stat. She didn't own a lot of clothes in the first place and what she did have appeared to be in that pile. She swallowed the pill with the aid of a gulp of warm, stale water from a cup that had been sitting on her door cum desk for longer than Pandora cared to remember. With a forlorn expression, she gazed about her room and thought—not for the first time—that she was really going to have to clean this place up.

But later. More important things were calling.

Sinking to the floor and folding her legs Indian style, she opened Sinclair's perfectly folded piece of paper and ran her hand over it to flatten it out. He'd written the poem in tiny, careful script and she read it four or five times before setting the sheet down on the floor with a frown. Something was off. Sinclair had spelled 'see' wrong, which was very unlike him. He never made mistakes—his memory was infallible. Yet this time he'd made an error. Which meant he might have made more. What was going on with that boy?

Disappointed, she folded up the paper and tucked it back into her sporran. It was no use looking at it anymore. Following false leads could turn out to be more harmful than having no clues at all. The pill was kicking in now anyway, relaxing her enough to allow for the possibility of sleep. She climbed back into her bunk and collapsed with a groan on her bed. As she drifted into unconsciousness, one nagging thought accompanied her.

Who was the 'loony' in the poem?

Sunday morning arrived as dark and brooding as her mood. There was no wind to speak of, but a steady mist drizzled from the gray skies, soaking everything. No way would the nurse on duty allow the inmates to venture outdoors. Any change in weather was regarded as a threat to their welfare, which really meant a threat to the staff and their lack of desire to handle extra work.

The red line on the tiny temperature gauge nailed outside her window topped off at fifty-one degrees. Dang. Even if the staff agreed to allow the inmates out into the mist, they would balk at letting Charles get chilled. And if they couldn't include Charles, they might as well write his obituary now. He'd never forgive them for leaving him out and would subsequently die from a broken heart. No, they'd have to put off their search. But for how long?

Pandora dressed in a black turtleneck sweater, black miniskirt, and black tights. She glanced at her watch. Right now Vicki would be in the Chapel, a conservatory converted into a church for the inmates. She had long ago given up on asking Pandora to join her. The boring sermon, the stifling atmosphere, the 'thou shalt nots' all combined to give Pandora the hives. Talk about creating neuroses. According to the pastor who gave the sermons, Reverend Richus, if you so much as considered a bad thought, you were going to burn in hell. If that were true, Pandora was a lost cause. Bad thoughts composed most of her thinking. She didn't agree with Reverend Richus, anyway. She had her own beliefs about God, which pretty much contradicted everything that the pastor spouted, which was fine by her.

Unable to find anything palatable in the refrigerator or cupboards for breakfast, Pandora gave up and went to the phone. She dialed the number to the Chowder Shack and Bakery. Mrs. Hathaway answered on the first ring.

"Chowder Shack and Bakery, this is the proprietor, Mrs. Dolores J. Hathaway, speaking! How can I help you on this fine day?"

"Hey, Mrs. H. It's me, Pandora."

"Pandora, dear! I heard about your accident. You poor thing. How are you? You must be in terrible pain. I suppose it was only a matter of time something like this happened." She blew air down the line in a gusty sigh.

"Matter of time?"

"When that wild horse of yours fell on you and broke your ribs. He is quite the spirited little rascal, isn't he? I just can't believe your left lung was punctured. Does it hurt to breathe?"

Pandora pulled the receiver away from her ear and stared at it in disbelief. "Where'd you hear all that?" she continued after a few seconds of admiring the power of gossip.

"From Donna down at the dime store. I was filling my prescriptions for my sciatica, you see, and she told me everything. She heard it from Joe Wiedershin at Joe's Hardware, who heard it from his cousin's girlfriend, who—"

"Well, they've got it all wrong."

"All wrong? Heaven's to Betsy, what are you saying, dear? That it's all lies?" Mrs. Hathaway sounded delighted at this turn of events. "I can't wait to tell Donna." Donna Simmons owned the Five and Dime on Main Street and had dispensed prescriptions along with loads of unwanted advice for the past two decades. They were the best of friends, but nevertheless competed ruthlessly for the coveted title of town gossip.

"Not all of it is wrong. I *am* hurt, but my ribs are bruised, not broken, and my lungs are fine. I can't do your grease traps today, though, cause Dr. Gara said I'm not supposed to do anything too strenuous for the next couple weeks." No need to mention vine cutting and falling down stairs and exploring labyrinths.

"So your horse didn't have to be put down?"

Pandora suppressed a sigh. "Shadow had nothing to do with it, and *she's* fine. Maybe I'll stop by today and tell you everything. I can't ride yet, but I can walk."

"Oh, that would be delightful, dear. To see you, I mean. I want to be sure you're all right. I really was worried about you. I thought I might have to drag the mister away from Sally Jesse to come to your rescue. I know how your mother can be—"

"That's really nice of you, Mrs. H., but a rescue attempt isn't necessary. At least, not today." Mrs. Hathaway laughed loudly. "I'll see you in an hour or so and tell you everything, okay?"

"Oh, lovely. If you're sure you're up to it. I just baked a fresh batch of bread bowls and they— Eee! I forgot about the bread bowls! See you soon." A loud bang filled Pandora's ear, then a dial tone buzzed irately, as though she was the one who'd done the banging.

She hung up the phone and returned to her room. There she grabbed her raincoat and backpack and hurried downstairs to the stables. She wanted to visit Shadow before she left, which is why she'd said an hour instead of the thirty minutes it took to walk into Bedlam.

Pulling her hood over her head, she dashed outside into the cool, fresh air, and the mist coated her face as she scurried across the soaked grass to the horse stables. The main doors stood wide open and she burst through them into the dry, dusty world like a diva onto stage. Sensing her presence, Shadow gave a loud whinny from the far end of the stables, followed by several imperious hoof stomps. Pandora raced toward her horse, hand already digging around in her sporran where she kept sugar cubes for times like this.

She climbed up the locked gate and called, "Come on, girl. I've got some sugar for you!" Shadow tossed her head, showing her disdain for such a feeble attempt to win her favors after being abandoned for so long. "I'm sorry! I wanted to come earlier, but, well, I was hurt and then we got distracted by the labyrinth and you know how I hate seeing you when I can't ride you!"

Shadow snorted and stomped her foot, which in horse language, meant, "Nice try, but it ain't working. Now give me that sugar!"

Pandora held out her hand, palm flat, with the two sugar cubes resting on top. "Come on, Shadow. I really am sorry." She whispered this last part, staring at her pet with itchy fingers and a tingling sensation in her gut, all signs of a rider who hasn't ridden for way too long. This was another reason why she couldn't see Shadow—Pandora knew she'd be tempted to saddle her up and ride hard and fast until she rid herself of all her demons. But if she did that, she'd never recover. She was already in enough pain from yesterday's adventure. A hard ride might make her pass out, hit her head on a rock, and die a bloody death.

Shadow, never one to hold a grudge long enough to miss out on sugar, decided at that moment to forgive Pandora. Turning about, her soft, searching lips reached for the sugar and covered the cubes, tickling Pandora's skin. When she lifted her mouth, the sugar was gone, leaving only a spit bubble on Pandora's palm. Shadow whinnied and nuzzled Pandora's armpit. She was forgiven. For the next several minutes, she stroked Shadow's velvety black nose and reveled in being with her horse. After that, she brushed her and refreshed her water, talking to her all the while.

Too soon it was time to go. Not only did she have to see Mrs. Hathaway, she had to stop by Simon's Supermarket for more Coke. She didn't have any money, but thought she could exchange labor for goods. If Giganticus were there, he might let her do that, especially if she played the pity card. And she was desperate enough to do that.

She jumped down from the gate. "I'm off to Bedlam," she said. "Wish I could take you, too."

"You could take me," a voice came from behind her.

She spun around. "Or I could stick a fork in my eye."

Xavier sighed. "Do I have to threaten you again?"

"You're such a big tattletale, Xavier!"

"I prefer the term blackmailer. Nicer ring to it."

She brushed past him. "Fine. But if you so much as breathe a word of this to anyone, I'll have Shadow drag you around town in your birthday suit."

"Got it, Cap'n." He tipped an invisible hat, then threw his hand out with a flourish. "Lead the way."

She was tempted to lead him right off a cliff, but instead only muttered, "*Brothers!*" as they left the stables together.

Sir Galahad

18

THEY TROMPED THROUGH the dripping woods, neither of them speaking a word until they reached the hidden gate in the wrought-iron fence. "So this is how you do it," Xavier broke the silence. Both of them had long since pulled up their hoods, and Xavier stood hunched over against the rain that was coming down harder now. "I figured it was something like this."

"I'd climb a tree and jump if I had to," Pandora said as she locked the gate behind her. "Now let's get moving. Mrs. H. is waiting for us."

"Mrs. H.?"

"Mrs. Hathaway. She runs the Chowder Shack and Bakery. The plan is that she gives me food and I tell her about what happened to me. Then, come hell or high water, I'm going to get more Coke."

"I thought you seemed a bit irritable lately. Oh, wait. You're always irritable."

"Very funny," she snarled as she hurried along the muddy trail. The dirt path ran parallel to the main road and seemed a lot longer and harder going on foot.

"So what about me?" he asked.

"What about you?"

"Will Mrs. H. feed me?"

An idea occurred to Pandora. "She would if you cleaned her grease traps."

"Sounds delightful."

"I usually do it myself once a month, but I probably shouldn't with bruised ribs. If we worked together, we could get it done for her. She's a terrible gossip, but she's really nice to me so I like to help her out. Besides, her husband is a worthless bag of bones who sits on the couch all day watching TV while she works from dawn to dusk. She adores him, of course..." She shook her head in disgust. "Which makes me ask, why do women adore men who are jerks? I, for one, don't plan on having anything to do with any guy who doesn't treat me like the queen I was always meant to be."

Xavier picked up a thick branch, and after breaking off a few of its smaller branches, turned it into a walking stick. "Is that why you're going on a date with Dougie the Dork?"

"I would think you'd get it by now. I'm doing it to get back at Vicki."

"Thought she'd get you out of it, didn't you?"

"Yeah, well, I underestimated Dougie's dastardly powers of evil…and overestimated Vicki's resistance to bull."

"I tried to help you…"

"Help me?" She picked up a small rock and threw it at a tree. It ricocheted and nearly beaned her head. "You were only helping yourself."

"Not only. Why can't I do both?"

Pandora paused. In her experience, life was either/or, all or nothing, black and white. There were few gray areas. "I don't know," she grumbled, wanting to stay mad at him…at somebody. "I do know that Dr. Steele was useless. Why did he want to meet Dougie if he was just going to sit there and do nothing to stop the date?"

"Beats me. Maybe he didn't feel comfortable going against your mom."

"But if he were our—" Pandora bit her tongue hard. Damnit, she hadn't meant to bring that up.

"If he were our…what?" Pandora spotted the meadow that separated the wooded area from the town and hustled toward it. "Pandora!" Xavier persisted, catching up to her. When she wouldn't stop, he raced ahead of her and turned to face her, stopping her in the path. "What were you going to say?" She looked away from him, her traitorous cheeks darkening. "Oh, Pandora! You don't really think *he's* our dad, do you?"

She bit her lip angrily, meeting his eyes again. "Why not?"

He frowned. "Well, I don't think he's old enough for one thing. When I first met with him he told me he only recently got his Ph.D. so he's probably only twenty-seven or twenty-eight. He certainly doesn't look any older than that."

He had her there. While, biologically it would be possible for Dr. Steele to be their father, he would likely have been severely underage at the time. She didn't know whether to rejoice or mourn at the news. "Well, I just thought he could be a candidate."

Xavier turned around and they started walking again, following the path that cut through the meadow. "If it makes you feel any better, I'd take him as a dad."

Pandora grinned to herself. Funny, it did make her feel better. "So have you had any other ideas about who it might be?"

He shrugged, almost guiltily. "Actually, I've been thinking more about the labyrinth than our dad."

"Yeah, well," she said, feeling generous, "me, too. Sinclair copied out that poem in the statue."

"That's what he gave you in the cafeteria? I was wondering about that. Good thinking."

She basked in his praise for a moment before bursting his bubble. "It would've been, but Sinclair made a mistake in transposing the message so the translation isn't reliable."

"Sinclair? Make a mistake?"

"That's what I thought."

"You have it on you?" She opened her sporran and pulled out the paper. He laughed as he took it. "What else you got in there? A chainsaw? The kitchen sink?" He unfolded the paper and began to read. By the time he was finished, they had arrived at the outskirts of town.

"What do you think?"

"I see what you mean about the misspelling. Too bad." He handed the paper back and she tucked it into her sporran. "We're almost there, aren't we?" He inhaled deeply as they headed down the crowded back alleyway to the Chowder Shack. "I can already smell the donuts. I can see why you sneak into town whenever you can. That crap Corker serves isn't fit for prisoners."

"Exactly. So don't blow this, all right?" she warned. "While we're in town, we need to lay low and we need to tell Mrs. H. what she wants to hear."

"And she wants to hear…"

"Drama. I make up stories about what happens at Nepenthe Manor and in return she feeds me. It's a perfect system."

"So what are you going to tell her about your injury?"

Pandora tilted her head. "Actually, since it doesn't violate confidentiality, I think I'll just tell her the truth."

"Including that I'm your brother?"

"Of course. That bit alone will make her year."

"Are you sure you want everyone to know?"

"Everyone probably already knows. If they don't and I don't tell them the truth, they'll think we're dating."

"Oh." Xavier blanched. "Then tell away."

"Thought so." Pandora opened the back door to the shop, held it for Xavier, then stepped inside the warm, cozy interior that smelled of yeast and bread and sweet, glorious sugar. It was quiet, but not unusually so. Business at the bakery was nearly non-existent at ten o'clock on Sunday mornings. Bedlamites took the fate of their souls very seriously, attending one of ten churches in town. For a population of

2100, give or take, ten churches might seem like a bit much, but not for the citizens of Bedlam. They didn't especially like sharing their God.

"Mrs. H.?" Pandora called as she stepped in front of the glass display case.

"Back here!" came a fretful holler. "Oh, mercy!" A crash echoed from the kitchen and Pandora and Xavier dashed behind the bright orange counter. When they reached the kitchen, Mrs. Hathaway was leaning against the stainless steel sink, breathing heavily, her light brown eyes looking more crossed than usual. "Slipped out of my hands, blasted thing!" Luckily the grease trap had fallen back into place, keeping the grease contained within the fryer, except for a few drops splattered here and there.

"We'll do it, Mrs. H." Pandora strode over to the trap. The heavy smell of fried grease wafted toward her and she wrinkled her nose. When all was said and done, she was going to end up smelling like a French fry.

"Don't you lift another finger," Xavier added smoothly.

Mrs. Hathaway leaned toward Pandora, her flushed, round cheeks raised in a delighted smile. "It's that boy you were looking for!" she whispered loudly.

"Um, yeah. This is Xavier," Pandora said quickly. "He's my brother. Half-brother."

"Your *brother*? Oh, dear me."

"It's a pleasure to meet you, Mrs. Hathaway. Xavier Carlisle, at your service."

He grabbed Mrs. Hathaway's hand, and believe it or not, kissed the back of it. Pandora's palm mentally smacked her forehead. Talk about over the top. Who did he think he was—Sir Galahad?

Mrs. Hathaway, of course, ate it up. She loved that courtly crap. "Why, I didn't know... Pandora's your sister...? Oh, dear *me*!" Xavier released her hand, where it hovered in the air, uncertain what to do next.

"Why don't we clean up this mess and you go take care of your other work," Pandora offered. "When we're done, we'll tell you everything."

Mrs. Hathaway wiped her hands on her pink and yellow pinstriped apron, then straightened her beehive hair-do, which resembled the color of an actual beehive. "That would be lovely. I'll go make you a bite to eat." She beamed as she stared at Xavier. "And if I recall correctly, you loved my chowder."

Xavier ducked his head. "Best I've ever tasted."

She giggled girlishly as she scuttled out of the kitchen. Pandora sighed. "Laying it on a bit thick, don't you think?"

He grinned. "I thought she'd like it."

"I suppose. Just don't take it too far. She's not stupid."

He feigned offense, his hand clapping to his chest. "Did I ever suggest she was?"

"Just shut up and help me." They pulled off their raincoats and hung them, along with Pandora's backpack, on a coat hook near the back door. Half an hour later, they'd emptied out the gritty, dark brown grease, cleaned the grease traps, and put fresh oil in. When they were finished, they scrubbed up with lavender soap before heading out to the café.

"We're done," Pandora announced. Mrs. Hathaway, her ample hind end sticking out of the display case, was busily lining up Long Johns.

She pulled her head out. "Oh, lovely! Go sit down and I'll bring you two a bite to eat. You must be famished."

They headed for Pandora's favorite booth at the back of the shack and she reflected on how well she and Xavier had worked together. Neither had said much as they cleaned and scrubbed and lifted, and they'd gotten the job done despite their injuries. Maybe having Xavier along on this trip to Bedlam wouldn't be all bad.

As they slid over on the squeaky, red vinyl seats, the bell over the front door clanged like a fire engine. There was no way anyone could miss hearing it, which is exactly how Mrs. Hathaway, who claimed she couldn't hear out of her left ear, liked it.

Xavier, already forgetting Pandora's warning to lay low, leaned to the side to see who it was. His eyes lit up. "Hey!" Before she could stop him, he slid out of the booth and hurried toward the door. Overcome by curiosity, Pandora turned about to get a better look, then wished she hadn't. It was Giganticus, and he was greeting Xavier with a firm handshake.

Oh, brother.

The two boys approached the booth, Xavier talking a mile a minute, and Pandora promptly amended her hasty assessment that having her brother along might be a good thing.

19

Egg in a Nest

PANDORA PULLED BACK into the booth, wondering what to do. She didn't know how to handle Giganticus, with his perceptive gray eyes and infuriatingly calm manner. Something about him threw her and she didn't like being thrown. Should she treat him with haughty disdain? Complete indifference? Polite, but reserved dignity? Before she could decide on the best approach, he was at the table. He hung his dark gray trench coat on a hook and slid into the vinyl seat across from her, bringing the smell of fresh air and rain with him. He pulled a pair of headphones from his damp head and set them on the eggshell blue tabletop. A traitorous part of her wondered what he was listening to. Siouxsie and the Banshees? The Violent Femmes? The Cure?

Probably Air Supply.

"You've got to have lunch with us, Derek," Xavier ordered. Derek, was it? Not a bad name, she decided, though not as descriptive as Giganticus. He looked at her as though reading her thoughts and Pandora dropped her eyes to stare down at the table.

"I believe we haven't been properly introduced." He held out his hand. Lifting her eyes without actually moving her head, she could see the massive appendage hovering before her like a blimp, only this was a strong, tanned blimp. She reluctantly placed her hand in his, only to see it swallowed up like Jonah and the whale. "I'm Derek."

"Yeah, I heard that bit from the loudmouth." She nodded at Xavier. "I'm Pandora." She couldn't stop staring at their hands nestled together like an egg in a nest, his so big, hers so tiny. She didn't like how insignificant her hand seemed at that moment, especially since eggs are so easily crushed.

"I already know your name."

"You do?" She pulled her hand from his warm grasp, her head swinging up to meet his unwavering gaze. The forest green sweater he wore turned his gray eyes almost green and his short, dark hair, wet from the rain, seemed blacker than ever. "How? I've never seen you around town before last week. And I'm pretty sure I wouldn't have missed seeing you. You're a bit big for that."

"We've got a lot that needs tending to around the house and my ma, well," he shrugged, "she's on the sickly side."

Interesting. "Are you home schooled then?"

"My pa doesn't hold with that sort of thing. Thinks it's putting on airs. So I kind of school myself. Enough to keep the authorities away anyway." Hmmm… They had something in common.

"Authorities like Mrs. Nettle," she guessed. "School attendance officer from hell?"

For the first time since they'd met, he smiled. A slow smile, it revealed a roguish side that belied his serious features. "The same."

She laughed. "If the name fits…"

"Mrs. Belladonna fits even better."

As in deadly nightshade… She grinned. This Derek character was actually rather funny. Though he was distracting her from the business at hand. "This is all good information," she conceded, "but none of it explains how you know about *me*." She rather liked being known, but only for certain things—things that made her look good, like her stunning intellect or her outrageous fashion sense… Heck, she'd settle for people envying her knife and tomahawk throwing ability. It was such a practical skill, and downright scary, if it came down to it.

But if Giganticus had heard that her nickname around town was Bats (in-her) Belfry, he'd think she was crazy. Not that there was anything inherently wrong with being crazy, but some kinds of crazy are worse than others. Henrietta Bloomer, who was like a hundred years old, once stripped down to her lacy French skivvies and strutted around Nepenthe Manor like a peacock. Trouble was, she used to be a pastor's wife. At any rate, Pandora didn't want to be known for that sort of behavior. Besides, she didn't even own French underwear.

He leaned back in his seat and regarded her for several long moments. Pinned by his gaze, she found herself squirming and gave herself a harsh mental order to cease and desist! She was the one who made people squirm, not the other way around. "Is there anybody in this town who doesn't know about you?" he finally said.

She stared back at him, unsure if this was a compliment or not. "Sounds ominous," she answered, watching him carefully.

He nodded. "I like ominous."

"Derek!" Mrs. Hathaway cried, saving Pandora from having to come up with a snarky yet sophisticated reply to his peculiar response, especially being that she wasn't quite sure what he meant by it. Mrs. Hathaway waddled toward the table, a tray grasped firmly in her competent hands. "I heard you come in and brought you lunch." She set down the tray and slid turquoise plates bearing bread bowls filled with steaming chowder, and three sweaty Coke bottles, across the table like a pro.

Pandora leaned over and inhaled the fishy scent of chowder, her mouth instantly watering. Like an alcoholic who'd gone without a drink for too long, she grabbed her Coke bottle and took a swig. It burned her throat deliciously.

"You didn't need to do that, Mrs. Hathaway," he drawled, "though I do appreciate the thought."

"Oh, pish and tosh!" *Pish and tosh?* Pandora suppressed a grin. *Someone has been hitting the BBC lately.* "You've been a great help to me this past month. I'm so glad you started working at Simon's. You've certainly made my life easier, young man."

Pandora studied Derek, a growing uneasiness filling her gut as she listened to Mrs. Hathaway gush. "Just doing what I've been taught to do, Mrs. Hathaway."

"Which is more than I can say for most people, who've got far more than you, and fewer burdens, too."

Pandora found herself feeling a bit pouty, mainly because she wasn't the one on the receiving end of Mrs. Hathaway's raptures. It was pathetic and self-serving, but Mrs. Hathaway was Pandora's main, and probably only, source of praise, and she couldn't afford to lose her. She plunged her spoon into her chowder, making a grand show of devouring the first bite.

"This is your best chowder yet, Mrs. H.!" she gushed like those cheesy kids in TV commercials.

"Oh, go on, dear." Mrs. Hathaway beamed. "I don't think this chowder's different from any other day." She paused and laid a plump finger alongside her chin. "Come to think of it, I did add a bit more garlic this time." She frowned in thought, then shook her head. "Now you three get eating. I need to feed Woofy, and I'll be back in a few minutes to hear the whole story." She looked meaningfully at Pandora, then scurried off like a colorful mouse to tend to her bulldog.

After she left, Derek and Xavier dug into their chowder, tearing off pieces of their bread bowls to dip in the soup. Pandora surreptitiously watched Derek eat. It was like watching a giant vacuum cleaner swallowing up everything in its path…clean and thorough and almost magical. When he was done, he wiped his mouth with a yellow paper napkin. Then he folded his hands under his chin and planted his elbows on the table. "So what story is that, Pandora?"

She frowned. Derek Giganticus was a bit more forward—one might even say, nosy—than she'd realized. Time to put him firmly in his place. "You can just wait your turn and hear about it when Mrs. H. returns. Better yet, maybe you should get back to work now, don't you think?"

"Can't. I'm done for the day."

"Your dad probably wants you home, then."

"Pa doesn't expect me 'til four."

"Why do you always talk like you're on *Little House on the Prairie?*" she demanded, growing increasingly irritated.

"And what kind of talk is that?" he asked mildly.

"Country bumpkin talk," she said scornfully. "Like you're a dumb hick."

"Are you saying I'm *not* a dumb hick and so, shouldn't talk like one?"

"I'm saying—"

"Oh, shut up, Pandora!" Xavier exclaimed, pointing a chunk of bread at her. "Do you have to pick fights with everyone?"

She glared at him. "I'm not picking a fight. I just don't know why he needs to hear what I have to tell Mrs. H. And how do you two know each other anyway?"

"We met my first day here," Xavier replied. He took a swig of Coke, then burped. "Oh, man, that tasted much better going down." He pounded his chest with his fist and burped again.

"How? How did you meet, that is," she clarified, not wanting to know any more details about Xavier's chowder burp.

"I stopped in at Simon's Supermarket and showed him that picture of my dad. You know, the one you stole from me?"

She ignored that last bit and stared at Derek, who regarded her blandly. "You knew he was looking for his dad?" When she'd asked him about the photo last week, he hadn't mentioned that little fact.

"Nope."

"But—"

"I didn't tell him it was my dad, idiot," Xavier interrupted.

She looked at Derek. "But you said you hadn't seen that man before when I showed you the picture."

"I hadn't. Not in person. Didn't figure seeing a photograph of some-body counted."

Pandora suppressed an aggravated sigh. "You also asked if he might be *my* dad. Why would you say that?"

"I don't know. There was something there…"

Pandora's heart beat a little harder. "Like what?" she whispered.

He leaned closer. "I'm not sure. Just something in the way he looked."

"But what exactly—"

"I'm ready for my story!" Mrs. Hathaway called, sweeping toward them.

Pandora quickly shifted her expression from growing vexation to polite welcome as she scooted over to make room. "There's not much to tell, Mrs. H."

Mrs. Hathaway clasped her hands together. "But I'm sure that what there is to tell is going to be good…well, as far as getting hurt can be good. I mean, I don't think it's good that you got hurt. Oh, dear." She looked chagrined.

"I'll start at the beginning, okay?" Mrs. Hathaway smiled gratefully and Pandora proceeded to tell her and Derek everything, starting with her suspicions about Xavier's presence at Nepenthe Manor and ending with the revelation that she and Xavier shared a father. Xavier kept interrupting her to, as he put it, clarify things, when really he was just ruining a good storytelling. Derek listened to the entire saga without a word, his eyes fixed firmly on hers. Pandora wondered what he was thinking.

"And now Pandora is going on a date with Dougie Daft," Xavier couldn't help adding, his voice rough with disgust.

"A date with Daft?" Derek repeated, sitting up straight. "You don't want to do that."

"I don't have a choice," she growled, crossing her arms like a shield. She was getting awfully sick of hearing that old refrain.

"You always have a choice," he said firmly.

"And you're free to live your life the way you want?" she demanded. When he didn't answer, she added smugly, "I didn't think so. I'm stuck now, anyway, so I might as well make the best of it."

"Oh, Pandora!" Mrs. Hathaway bemoaned, her blue eyes worried. "You shouldn't get involved with the Dafts." She leaned closer and whispered, "Rumor has it that they worship the devil."

"Ha!" Xavier barked. "Dougie Daft *is* the devil."

"Speaking of the devil," Pandora ground out through gritted teeth, "we really should get going. Sometimes Vicki actually realizes I'm gone and sends someone looking for me." This was a rarity, like the eclipse of the sun, but a possibility all the same.

Mrs. Hathaway scooted out of the booth and proceeded to gather up their spoons, bottles, and napkins. "I can't believe this!" she exclaimed happily. "You have a brother, Pandora. You must feel so happy." She patted Pandora on the shoulder as Pandora slid out of the booth.

"Yeah, Pandora," Xavier gloated as he stood up. "You must feel *sooo* happy!"

"And you, too, young man," Mrs. Hathaway went on, missing his sarcasm. The little woman was sharp when it came to gossip and baking, but a bit slow on the uptake when it came to caustic humor. "Pandora is a lovely girl. I'm glad she has someone on her side at that *place*."

Xavier smiled down at her. "I'll do my best to take care of her."

Pandora's fingers curled into tight fists. As soon as he came into range, she'd pop him one. "Actually, Mrs. H., I'm the one looking after Xavier. He's not used to living in the midst of madness."

"Oh, dear me. I didn't think of that. You be careful!" she warned, wagging a plump finger at him.

"Oh, I will, Mrs. H. But I'll be fine." He looked directly at Pandora. "I sleep with one eye open at all times."

Derek pushed his way along the bench, grabbing his headphones and looping them around his neck before unfolding his long limbs to join them. He towered over the diminutive Mrs. Hathaway. "Thanks for the lunch. I'll be sure to make it up to you."

"Make it up to me?" She tittered. "Why, I still owe you for all that work you did out back."

He shook his head. "Just being neighborly, ma'am."

"Well, then, I'm being neighborly, too!" she said proudly, thrilled to have outsmarted him. "Your lunch is on me, and the next one, too, and that's that!" He smiled at her and nodded.

"We have to go now, Mrs. H." Pandora headed to the back of the bakery and grabbed their raincoats and her backpack. "I probably won't make it in tomorrow," she said as she returned. "The trails will likely be too muddy to walk."

"Then you must take some donuts now," she declared, hustling behind the display case and sliding open a glass door. Xavier glanced at Pandora and she gave an innocent shrug before handing him his coat.

"What's your poison, dears?" Pandora wanted to refuse, if only to strip Xavier of any idea that he could get in on the deal, but promptly changed her mind. Mrs. Hathaway had once told Pandora that being around young people made her feel young herself. Having three of them in the café at once was likely making her day. And feeding all three was probably the highlight of her life. It was rather sad, but who was Pandora to make a stink and ruin everything for the poor old thing?

Xavier asked for a Long John and Derek, after hesitating a moment, opted for a glazed applesauce donut, one of Pandora's personal favorites. Mrs. Hathaway handed the boys their donut on a piece of wax paper, then Pandora gave her order, picking out what the posse likely wanted. She felt staring eyes on her back as she took the two bags of donuts and one muffin for Sinclair and slid them into her pack.

"Thanks for lunch and the donuts, Mrs. H.," she said as she pulled on her backpack. "I'll see you next Monday. I should be able to ride then." Even if she wasn't supposed to, she was going to. Not being able to ride Shadow was making her feel like she'd swallowed a glass full of ants.

"That would be lovely, dear." She beamed. "And bring your brother!"

Fat chance. He'd be in school next week, and out of her hair at last.

After donning their coats, they said their goodbyes and headed out the door. Once outside, she and Xavier pulled up their hoods, but Derek remained bareheaded. Judging by the way he tilted his face into the heavy mist, he actually liked getting wet. Maybe he was a Selkie, part-seal, part human. Then again, maybe part-walrus was more accurate.

"Are you going home now?" he asked, turning a face pearled with beads of rainwater toward her. Xavier had wandered ahead and stood under the awning fronting Joe's Hardware, peering through the store window at a shiny red, ten-speed bike.

"I was hoping to get some Coke," Pandora admitted, though it cost her to do so. She hated asking for things. "But as I don't have any money, I guess it's home we go."

He stared at her without blinking for what was likely a record amount of time. "I'll tell you what. I'll buy you your Coke, and I'll give you a ride home. But on one condition."

She peered up at him, her eyes squinting with suspicion. "What's that?"

He took a step toward her. "That you don't go to that dance with Daft."

WHAT THE HELL? Why did everyone feel like Miss Pandora Belfry's business was their business and could tell her what to do, even when she never asked? Well, no more. She was tired of getting pushed around, told what to do, not being informed of important life issues, and generally being treated like she was six.

"I made a commitment, and I mean to honor it!" Dang. Now who was talking like Laura Ingalls?

"But why did you do it?" Derek wondered, looking truly baffled.

"To get back at my mom," she mumbled, and that's all she meant to say on the subject, but he stood there mute and unblinking, towering over her like a mutant force of nature, compelling her to say more. "She lied to me and now she won't tell me who my father is and I'm just sick of it all!" To her horror, her eyes watered up. She quickly looked away, finding a newly painted fire hydrant to focus on. "I don't want the Coke, and I can walk home."

"He's bad news, you know."

She sighed. She obviously wasn't getting out of this so easily. "So everyone keeps telling me." She paused. "And I know that for myself."

"You must hate your ma to do something like that."

"Not hate…just, oh, I don't know!" Her cold fingers curled into frustrated fists. "I guess I wish she'd notice me more." But only at certain times, she quickly amended, like when she wasn't getting into trouble. Which, unfortunately, probably occurred more often than not.

"I can't imagine anyone not noticing you, Pandora Belfry." Before she could respond, he went on, "And I'll get you that Coke and give you a ride home with no strings attached. All right?"

She frowned at him. "What made you change your mind?"

He looked away, over at Xavier, who was still staring covetously at the red bike. "Let's just say I understand how you feel."

She nodded knowingly, as though she got where he was coming from, but she didn't. Not at all. Further thinking was required. "I'll pay you back for the Coke."

"If you'd like."

"I would." She didn't like owing anybody anything. Owing someone meant they had a hold on you. Maybe that's why she was going ahead with this date with Dougie. She'd committed to it and if she didn't follow through, she had the feeling she'd owe him more than a dance, more like a pound of flesh, literally. Besides, the thought of owing Dougie anything made her want to ralph big time.

"You're cold," Derek noted. "Come on." He grabbed her arm and steered her to stand next to Xavier, out of the rain. "I'll be back in a bit." Just like that he was gone, lumbering away from them like the giant he was. Pandora watched him go, then turned to face the window.

"Isn't it awesome?" Xavier breathed. His forehead was pressed against the windowpane and his breath fogged the glass.

"I guess." She wasn't really looking at the bike but at her own soggy reflection. She squinted and instantly looked better. Delusion was such a great defense mechanism. "Looking to trade up?"

He turned his head, all the while keeping his forehead in contact with the window. "No. Never had one in the first place."

"You've never had a bike?"

"Have you?"

"No. But I've never wanted one. I have Shadow. She's enough for me."

"Well, you're lucky to have a mom who gave you a horse."

"She didn't *give* me a horse. Some jerk dumped her and I rescued her. The other horses would have been dog food, too, if I hadn't convinced Carl to rescue them, as well. I overheard this guy—Farmer Grewl—talking about turning them into glue. I told Carl and he went the next day and fetched them home."

"Still, Vicki lets you keep them."

"Whose side are you on, anyway? And she keeps the horses for the inmates, not for me."

"Boo, hoo," he replied, turning his head back to face the bike. "Poor little Pandora, so deprived and neglected by her mumsie."

"Screw you."

Xavier ignored this. "I wonder if they have it in midnight blue," he breathed against the glass, a round spot of fog appearing instantly.

Pandora gave a disgusted sigh and turned away from the window. Xavier didn't get it. The only person that seemed to understand about the horses was Carl and he— She paused. Wait a minute. Could Carl actually be her father? Sure he was a big grump, but when push came to shove, he looked after Pandora. He might be a Nazi about caring for the horses, but everyone knows how touchy horses can be, especially Shadow. One screw-up and the rider might end up paralyzed or dead as a dung patty. Carl's curmudgeonly ways could be seen as a form of taking care of his daughter, couldn't they?

She studied Xavier's profile. Right now he looked rather idiotic, drooling over a stupid bike. But there was something in the way he tilted his chin just so, and maybe the shape of his nose, too, that resembled Carl's profile. And what about herself? In the window's reflection, it was her black hair that stood out the most. The rest of her was too dark to really make a good comparison. What color hair did Carl have? Or what color did he use to have? Although his face looked relatively youthful, his hair had gone completely gray, the original color a mystery only he could solve. She knew he had blue eyes, though. Like her. And he liked horses. Like her. And he was a grouch. Like Xavier.

The sound of a horn behind her made her jump. She swung around to see a rusted orange pickup truck pull up to the curb. The door swung open. "Come on, Xavier," she pulled on his arm. "Derek's giving us a ride home."

Xavier reluctantly turned away from the bike, but when he saw the truck, he hurried over to it. "Dibs on the window," he called, pushing Pandora into the cab. There was no help for it; she would have to sit next to Derek. She pulled off her damp backpack and climbed inside. Xavier clambered in beside her and slammed the door shut. It didn't catch.

"Pull real hard," Derek directed. "She's ornery."

Xavier opened the door and slammed it shut again. This time it stayed that way. "Cool truck, man!" Xavier exclaimed, looking about the cab's worn interior. Despite its obvious age, it was clean and tidy. No litter on the floor, no empty cups on the seat. No dust, either, just the smell of oil, hot metal, and the old leather of the torn seats, patched by duct tape. Derek nodded an acknowledgment, then expertly shifted the truck into gear and pulled out onto Main Street.

"How long have you had your license, Derek?" Xavier asked around her. "I want to get mine soon, but with my mom dying, well, I haven't even taken driver's ed."

"I don't have a regular driver's license."

"Then what are you doing driving?" Pandora shrieked. "If I'm caught with you I might as well end it all cause Vicki'll kill me. First, for sneaking out, and second, for driving with someone who doesn't have a license."

"Oh, stuff it." Xavier elbowed her arm. "Like you follow all the rules, dissident."

"I prefer the term maverick, dorkwad." Personally, it didn't matter to Pandora one way or the other whether or not Derek had a license. She generally believed rules were for sissies who couldn't handle life without being told what to do. But rebellion that gained her nothing was something she simply could not support.

"You didn't let me finish," Derek said patiently. "I have a farmer's license."

"Ah." She'd heard about those. Kids who worked on farms could get them so they could drive the machinery. "So I'm not going to get busted?"

"I didn't say that." He waited a few seconds, his eyes amused. "At some point, I imagine you will. But probably not for riding with me."

"Just don't do anything stupid," she warned, fiddling with the zipper on her backpack.

"Like this?" he asked, and stepped on the gas. The truck leaped forward and Pandora jerked back against the seat, and then tilted hard to her left, right into Derek. Luckily they were at the edge of town, with no copper in sight. She tried to scoot back over to her right, but Xavier had taken the opportunity to spread out, his knee knocking against hers, effectively trapping her. *Drat.*

The trees sped by as they roared down the tar road. Derek shifted again, his massive trunk of an arm pushing against her. For some reason, she rather liked the sensation of his rough coat rubbing against her cheek. He also smelled nice. Like a meadow.

"Yeeha!" Xavier shouted, rolling down the window and sticking his head out. "Yeah!" After a few moments of getting pelted by rain, he returned his head to the safety of the cab, a goofy grin plastering his face. His blond, spiky hair glistened with water droplets. "You are so lucky, Derek!" Derek just smiled. His eyes dropped down to Pandora and lingered for a moment, the smile deepening before returning his attention to the road.

"Drop us off here," Pandora told him when they neared the trail. "There's a gate."

Derek nodded and after doing a u-turn, pulled off the road. Xavier opened the door and slid out. "Wait here a minute," Derek told her, getting out of the truck. She watched him head around to the back and lift a gray tarp. He pulled something red out from underneath it, then came over to her side. The door opened, and after grabbing her backpack, she scooted over to climb out. She found his arm blocking her way, then realized he was offering it to her. Feeling a little strange, she grabbed hold of it and used it to lower herself to the ground.

"Thanks," she mumbled.

"Here." He thrust the red object at her. It was a six-pack of Coke.

"Oh, wow. Thanks!" She unzipped her backpack. He reached down and pulled out the two bags of donuts, then slid the pack into the open mouth, replaced the bags, and zipped the pack shut. "I'll pay you back," she said again, pulling the pack onto her back. "Really, I will."

"All right."

"Fine."

"Scintillating conversation, folks." Xavier rubbed his hands together. "But I'm freezing my ass off. Let's go, Pandora. Thanks for the ride, Derek. Your truck is totally rad, and I'm totally jealous you can drive when you don't even have a license. You've got to go get the real thing so you can drive me to Akmore and we can hang with the college girls."

"Can't get it. I'm not sixteen yet."

Xavier and Pandora gaped at him, looking him up and down. "Holy crap, dude!" Xavier cried. "I coulda sworn you were at least eighteen! How old are you?"

"Just turned fourteen a couple months back."

"Wow," Xavier breathed, echoing Pandora's sentiment. She couldn't believe she and Giganticus were the same age. "Are you still growing?"

Derek shrugged. "My dad's six foot eight, so probably."

Suddenly Pandora laughed. "You really *are* a giant."

"Got a problem with giants?" His voice was calm, but his eyes were serious.

"As long as I don't hear, 'fe, fi, fo, fum, I smell the blood of an English mun,' coming out your mouth, I'll put up with you and your freakish size."

Derek studied her for a moment and she wondered if she'd gone too far. "Too bad," he replied. "That was my best pick-up line."

Xavier hooted and clapped Derek on the back. "That's a good one! 'Be ye live or be ye dead, lovely lady…'"

"I'll grind your bones to make my bread!" they all chimed in, then laughed. Morbid humor had a way of drawing people together, Pandora noted with a grin.

Smiling, Derek headed around to the driver's side, reattaching his headphones as he went. "I'll see you soon." He gave them a nod, his eyes settling on Pandora, then he started up his truck and drove off. She watched him go until the back of his head was only a speck. When he was gone, she turned to face Xavier. He was watching her, his eyes assessing.

"*What?*"

He smirked. "Oh, nothing."

Yeah, right. Nothing, my patootie. However, being that she had no desire to pursue a 'nothing' that, of course, meant *something*, she stalked off toward the woods.

It was time to return to her world, back to lying mothers and traitorous doctors, back to a place where life was fairly uncomplicated, yet perhaps just a tad more stifling than it had been this morning.

21

Breached by Intruders

XAVIER HEADED TO the stables to change clothes. Pandora asked him if he was coming inside afterwards, but he was vague in his response, never fully committing one way or the other. Her suspicions were immediately aroused.

When the front door to the manor flew open, Pandora wasn't surprised. The posse had been waiting for her. "Where were you?" Lucy cried, tap dancing down the stone steps in her pink, jelly sandals. The two pom-poms on each side of her head seemed extra frizzy today, creating a Minnie Mouse effect. "We've been looking for you for *hours*!" She grabbed Pandora's arm and pulled her up the steps. Waiting at the top were Sinclair and Charles.

"We went into town to get donuts," Pandora explained as they headed inside. "Do you think you could eat one?"

"I could eat twenty-six and have room for more!"

"Hey, Charles. Hey, Sinclair," she greeted. "Where are Skippy and Birdy?"

"Probably smooching somewhere." Lucy giggled and clapped a hand to her mouth. "Probably making hysterical babies," she said underneath it.

Charles rolled his eyes in disgust. "Do we have to talk about that?"

Lucy put her hands on her hips. "Yes, we do, Charles Boring Boy. You're such a dweeb!" She gave him a raspberry for good measure, spraying spit everywhere.

Charles sighed. Obviously Lucy was in a mood today. "I just don't see why they have to do that stuff in front of us." Sinclair nodded vigorously in agreement. "It's gross." Sinclair nodded even harder.

"It's not gross, it's love!" Lucy declared.

Charles mumbled something under his breath, but didn't pursue the argument. Lucy beamed, pleased she'd won. Or so she thought. Charles might be physically weak and he might be a very nice person, but there was a stubborn streak in that boy when it came to upholding his principles.

"Go to the TV room," Pandora directed. "You can eat your donuts there."

Being a Sunday afternoon, and rainy to boot, the room was crowded when they arrived. Pandora frowned. "Those ninnies took our seats again." She was referring to Mrs. Johnson and Mrs. Bodkin, neither of whom held any respect for the order of things. "Let's go somewhere else."

"Where?" Charles wondered. "There isn't anywhere else to go."

"Too bad you guys can't go outside," Pandora sighed. "We could go to the maze. It's dry inside the statue."

"Yeah!" Charles whooped and Pandora cursed her stupid brain. There was no way he'd be allowed outdoors on such a damp day. He pointed out the window. "It's stopped raining. I could go. I'll put on extra layers and my raincoat and rain boots. I won't get chilled. I promise!"

Lucy jumped up and down. "Let's do it! Let's do it! Let's go to the—"

"Shhh!" Pandora hissed. "Don't say that word."

Lucy slapped a hand over her mouth. "Sowwy," she apologized in a baby voice.

"Are you sure, Charles?" Pandora turned to him. "If you get sick, I'll never forgive myself."

He nodded solemnly. "If I don't take risks, Pandora, then I can neither call myself a man, nor a hero."

Pandora groaned, wondering which comic book he'd borrowed that line from. "Fine. But you know you're no good to me dead."

He puffed out his thin chest. "I'm no good to anyone, not even myself, sitting on the sidelines watching life pass me by."

Good gravy, how could she argue with that? "All right. Go get dressed. You, too, Lucy and Sinclair. I don't want you getting sick, either." With grins and nods all around, and Sinclair looking unnaturally peppy, the three ran to their rooms to change. "And be quiet about it!" she yelled after them.

Glancing down at her soaked shoes, Pandora decided to take this opportunity to get rid of her contraband Coke. Once in her room, she quickly yanked off her soggy socks and changed into a pair of old work boots. She found her flashlight and shoved it into her backpack. After pulling it back on, with half the donuts still inside, and grabbing the lantern, she headed for the apartment's small dining room. No one was there, which meant Vicki was likely in her office working, no surprise. Pandora would have to be careful sneaking the posse out to the labyrinth. The windows in Vicki's office looked directly out over the front lawn.

She turned to leave when she spotted a blinking light on the answering machine. Vicki had bought one last year, though Pandora wondered why she'd bothered with the useless contraption. They had their own private line, but no one, other than Grandfather and Grandmother Belfry, ever called them. And the last thing Vicki wanted to get was a message from her parents. So who the heck was she hoping to hear from?

Pandora stared down at the machine, wondering what she was supposed to do next. She saw a play button and figured it would be a good start. She pressed it and waited. There was a loud whirring noise, then a beep.

"Hello, Pandora. I wanted to thank you and your mother for a lovely evening last night. I also wanted to let you know that I saw you in town today with that boy. I'm not sure being around someone like him is a good idea. He seemed awfully old for you." There was a short pause, as though he were letting his words sink in for Vicki's sake. "So when can I see you again? I'll tell you what…I'll stop by." A click sounded, followed by a buzz, signaling he'd hung up.

Cursing roundly, Pandora hit the delete button three times. To be on the safe side, she pressed play again. When nothing came on, she felt satisfied she'd destroyed the evidence. Damn that Dougie! What was he playing at? To think he could stop by at any time. It was inconceivable! And who was he to threaten her like that, veiled as it was? She was an idiot for calling him in the first place, then giving him their private number. Anger really made people do terrible and stupid things. She vowed that the next time she got mad she'd think things through much longer before acting. Then maybe for once in her life she'd avert the crisis in the first place rather than have to put out the fires afterward.

Stewing over this latest predicament, Pandora hurried downstairs. As she crossed the foyer, Lucy, Charles, and Sinclair burst from the stairway.

"Ta-dah!" Lucy cried, flinging her arms wide. She was dressed in a rainbow raincoat and lime green rain boots. Charles and Sinclair's rain outfits, both overlarge and navy blue, were less colorful, but they appeared to be equally protected from the elements.

Pandora put her finger to her lips and nodded at Vicki's closed door. "Keep it down, Lucy. We don't want Herr Belfry catching us." Lucy drew a pretend zipper across her mouth. As quietly as she could, Pandora opened the main door and ushered the others outside. "Act casual," she warned as they crossed the lawn. "Look like we're just going for a walk."

For Lucy, acting casual meant hopping like a rabbit. Charles hunched his shoulders and took off after her, resembling a miniature caped avenger. Sinclair stayed behind with Pandora, walking at a sedate pace that, while necessary for subterfuge, was driving her crazy. She had to think of something to keep her from yelling at him to pick up the pace. Luckily, his copy of the poem came to mind.

"You made a mistake," she said, sounding like Nurse Rackett more than she would've liked. She softened her tone. "In the poem. You spelled 'see' wrong." Straight and rigid as always, he shook his head no. "I know," she went on, "I could hardly believe it myself. But there it is." She shrugged. "Don't worry about it. It just means you're fallible like the rest of us."

Sinclair stopped walking, his face a picture of exasperation. "What? Aren't you fond of being like us mere mortals?" This, of course, was the pot blatantly calling the kettle black. She didn't like to think of herself as a mere mortal, either, and anyone who made even the mere suggestion of such an idea would be shot down like a Soviet plane over D.C.

He shook his head, then proceeded to spell the word 'sea' in sign language. It took her a moment to translate—she always got 'a' and 'e' backwards. "No, Sinclair. S-e-e. You wrote it wrong. We can't use what you copied down because you might have gotten something else wrong."

He gave her a disgusted look that said, "What do you know?" and started walking again.

She sighed. It was hard being the leader, always having to give orders and point out errors. Did they think she liked doing these things? And besides, she did it for their sake, not her own. Maybe someday they'd see the light, but until then, she'd have to remain patient, yet persistent. Which reminded her…she needed to warn Charles and Lucy again about adults and their nefarious ways. Once was never enough with those two.

She couldn't see them around the outcropping of trees, but she could hear them yelling. Now what were they going on about? She glanced at Sinclair. He was staring straight ahead, his expression perplexed. "We'd better go see—" but he was already running. Her eyes widened. She didn't think she had ever seen that boy run. Ever.

She caught up with him as he rounded the tree line and what they saw up ahead spurred them both on. The drawbridge was down. Someone was in the labyrinth!

"Our fortress has been breached by intruders!" Charles cried out. Lucy was jumping up and down and waving her arms around like a stunted windmill. "Look!" He pointed at the lowered drawbridge, purple lips quivering. "This is terrible!"

Pandora passed him without breaking stride. "Damn and tarnation!" She shook her fist at the sky. "Let's get 'em, guys!" Letting loose a warrior whoop, she tore up the drawbridge, each step shaking the wide plank. The other three followed after her, uttering their own strange version of a battle cry, Sinclair's silent, of course.

The small group clattered down the stone steps, howling like deranged wolves. "The statue's been opened!" Pandora pointed at the now-exposed derriere of the god-like creature. She raced toward it and ducked inside the base, the others following after her. Such blatant disregard for track covering indicated a twisted mind arrogant enough to believe he or she wouldn't get caught. Or didn't care if they did. Whoever that person was was very dangerous, and must be caught and strung up by his heels as soon as physically possible.

Could it be Dougie? That didn't seem likely. He didn't strike her as the adventurous sort, plus she hadn't seen his car outside. Or maybe Ronny and Lonny, the twin gatekeepers, had spotted the posse the day before and decided to check things out. A disturbing thought hit her. Maybe the person had a right to be here. And the only people who had that right would be Carl or Vicki. Possibly even Dr. Steele. As far as she knew, he was the only one who was aware they'd gotten inside.

Freezing in her tracks, she held out her arm to stop the others from going down the stone steps. "Until we know who it is, we shouldn't give ourselves away." She didn't dare mention that the intruder could be Vicki herself. Despite her mother's savior persona, the inmates were intimidated by her. Though that might have an awful lot to do with Pandora's tendency to exaggerate Vicki's faults.

Charles saluted and whispered, "Aye, aye, Captain!" and Lucy made a zipping motion across her lips. Pandora sometimes wished the girl's mouth did come equipped with a zipper. Sinclair, the least of Pandora's worries, gave a serious nod. Before slipping down the steps, she re-hung the lantern on its hook and dug out her flashlight. As she pulled it out, she heard a sound. A giggle.

A very raunchy giggle.

Incensed, she stormed down the stairs. Just as she suspected, who-ever was down here had a light source of their own. When she reached the bottom, she turned and headed toward the flickering light. Seconds later she spotted two figures sitting on the floor, their torsos high-lighted in the glow of an old kerosene lantern.

"Ahem!" she called out. "What the Hades are *you* two doing here?"

Surrounded by Judases

22

STARTLED, BIRDY AND Skippy jerked back from each other. Before that moment they'd been noshing on each other like a potbelly pig at an all-you-can-eat buffet. Now they looked up at Pandora—Birdy triumphant, Skippy, mortified. He leaped to his feet, nearly tripping over his size twelve Chucks. Birdy remained seated on a gray wool blanket they must have brought along, calm as the Queen Majesty herself.

"Eww," Pandora made sure to say loudly. "Don't answer that."

Skippy tried to anyway. "We were, um, just, well—"

"We were making out," Birdy supplied, using her thumb to wipe each corner of her spit-moistened mouth.

"Yeah, I figured that out. Get up, will you? And you'd better come up with a better answer than that for Lucy, Charles, and Sinclair."

"Xavier isn't with you?" Birdy squawked. Pandora shook her head. She really wished the girl would give up on him already. He so obviously wasn't interested. "Then where is he?"

"How should I know? I'm not my brother's keeper."

Disgusted, Birdy pushed herself to her feet. Today she'd dressed more practically in tight blue jeans, pink sneakers, and a pink shaker knit sweater that peeked out from beneath a red raincoat. "You were with him earlier," she said it like an accusation.

"We went into town," Pandora informed her. "I promised Mrs. H. I'd help her clean the grease traps today, but I couldn't do it alone so Xavier came along to help." She was dancing with the truth here, but it was all for a good cause. "I got us donuts."

Birdy's expression mutated from disgust to delight. "Did you? You're my hero, Pandora," she purred, slinking up to take Pandora's arm. "Helping people, bringing us food. That's why you're our leader—always going the extra mile." Pandora could only roll her eyes. Birdy was so transparent, though she always thought she was being so devious.

"Can we come down now?" Lucy shouted.

"Yes!" Pandora cried desperately, pulling her arm from Birdy's grasp. "We can eat our donuts down here."

Seconds later the three burst into the small space. "Skippy? Birdy!" Lucy cried. "What are *you* guys doing here?"

"We thought we'd try to solve the next step in the labyrinth," Birdy lied smoothly. "We didn't get very far, though." Her smile was suggestive, but luckily the meaning behind it flew right over Lucy's head.

"Well, well, well," came a voice from behind them. "What do we have here?"

Pandora spun around to find Xavier facing them with crossed arms, looking superior. "You're here, too?" she gasped. "I can't believe this. I'm surrounded by Judases!"

"What are you talking about? I was going for a walk when I spotted the drawbridge down. I raised it back up, by the way. I thought we agreed not to leave it open," he added sternly, glaring at Pandora like a disappointed father.

"Tell that to these two." Pandora indicated Birdy and Skippy. "They came here *on their own* to do a little *exploring* and forgot to cover their tracks."

Birdy smiled seductively. "I guess we got so caught up in our exploring that we forgot."

Ignoring everything that was wrong with that statement, Pandora pointed at Xavier. "And do you think I'm going to buy your "I was just going for a walk" excuse? We just walked into town. Why would you need to do more?"

"I like to stay in shape."

"Oh, really? It doesn't show."

"It does under this jacket. Besides, I wasn't *just* going for a walk. I wanted to put WD-40 on the chains and make sure those vines are taken care of. What are *you* doing here?"

"If you must know, we were looking for a place to eat our pastries. The TV room was packed with snoops and tattletales." Not to mention thieves.

"You couldn't have tried the barn?" he accused, and she wanted most desperately to tell him what he could do with his arrogant attitude. It involved an ice pick and a shovel and it was messy.

"The barn is off-limits to the inmates," she informed him. Thankfully none of the posse felt the need to point out that they often ignored this rule when needing an alternative meeting place than the graveyard due to inclement weather. Seeing Xavier's skeptical expression, she gave a martyred sigh. It looked like she once again was going to have to take the high road. If she didn't, they'd waste the whole afternoon arguing about nothing. She'd seen it happen too many times with the posse. She pulled off her backpack and dug inside for the donuts. "Since we're all here, we might as well make the best of it." She quickly passed out the pastries, placing them in eager hands. Sinclair took the plastic baggie that held his cranberry muffin and slowly opened it. Pandora wondered why Mrs. H. never asked why she needed one muffin in a plastic bag, though the bakery owner was probably used to the weirdness that came out of Nepenthe Manor. She reluctantly retrieved a powdered donut—hers, by right—from the bag and handed it to Xavier. It was a big sacrifice, but necessary to keep things moving. He took it from her with an insolent grin and she had to restrain herself from shoving the white ring up his nose.

The posse ate their treat in companionable silence. When they were finished, they wiped their hands on their pants (actually Birdy wiped her hands on Skippy's pants) and thanked Pandora with satisfied, somewhat crumby, smiles. "You're welcome," she graciously replied, pulling her backpack on once more. She looked at everyone's expectant faces. "I guess since we're here, we should at least try to solve the next part of the labyrinth."

"I already solved it," Sinclair's rusty voice rumbled through the small space.

"What?" Pandora asked over the murmur of his repetitions. "How?" He finished the last one quickly, then motioned to her to follow him.

After a short time, they exited the tunnel, and Sinclair immediately headed toward a doorway. When he reached it, he stopped and peered upward. Pandora hurried to join him, with Lucy and Charles at her heels. Xavier headed in the opposite direction.

"What are you doing, Sinclair dee Dare?" Lucy asked. He didn't answer as he moved methodically to the next doorway. Pandora followed his intense gaze, which rested on the area above the opening. When her eyes settled on the source of his interest, she couldn't believe what she was seeing. Above the high-arched doorway stretched a series of stars and planets carved into the stone, each etching inlaid with brightly colored glass of varying colors. Tiny yellow stars hovered over multi-colored planets, big as grapes, all of which encircled a sun the size of a plum.

"Wow! This is totally awesome."

"We found treasure!" Lucy cried, clapping her hands. "We're rich, Charles. We're rich!" She grabbed his arm and jumped up and down like a kangaroo.

"It's only glass," Pandora told her as they followed Sinclair to the next door.

Lucy frowned. "No, it's not, fuddy-duddy Dora! It's precious jewels!"

"Don't be ridiculous, Lucy." She looked up to see a design exactly the same as the previous one. "If they were precious jewels, this place would be worth millions of dollars. Trust me. It's glass."

Lucy crossed her arms and pouted. "I was only pretending, you Bora!"

Pandora stifled a desire to take one of Lucy's pom-poms and stick it up her nose. "Fine, whatever." Lucy glared at her, her dark eyes threatening an imminent storm, and Pandora, with a mental sigh, amended her reply. "I mean, I wish they were real, too. I wouldn't mind being rich. I'd buy my own Coke machine with a lifetime contract for refills."

Lucy nodded her approval. "Now you're talking, Peter Pan-dora!" She rubbed her little hands together greedily. "You know what I'd do? I'd buy my own house and then I could see my dada *every* day." She giggled happily.

This time the sigh was quite vocal. "Lucy... What have I told you about adults?"

Lucy's lower lip jutted out, signaling an imminent meltdown. "You said they can't be trusted."

"Right. So maybe you could buy a house for you and your brothers and sisters. No adults allowed."

Lucy brightened. "I *love* it! Then I'd be queen of the house and I'd have fireplaces in every room."

"And Lucy?"

"Yeah, Pandora?"

"Just remember that adults aren't the only people we can't trust. Dougie Daft is even worse than the worst adult. You know he only told you he's bringing you and Charles jawbreakers to get on your good side."

"Well, it's working!" Lucy crowed, dancing about in a circle like a little fiend.

"Oh no, Lucy!" Charles gasped. "We can't give in to the dark side."

"It's just gobstoppers, Charles. It's not like I'm taking briberies."

They tagged along after Sinclair and argued about what constituted compromising your principles even though you might really, really want something tasty. After examining three more doors, Pandora stopped. "What are we doing, Sinclair?" He shook his head and continued on to the next door. Again, the design was exactly, boringly, the same as all the others. "This is a waste of time." But then, just as she was about to call for a change of plan, Sinclair stepped through the doorway in front of them.

"What are you doing?"

He stepped back through and gave her a look that spoke volumes, Volume One being: "Why do I always have to deal with such idiocy?" It was a look that Pandora herself liked giving to others. She didn't much like being its recipient. When she didn't respond, he pretended to open something up. She frowned at him. "You read it in a book?"

His shoulders dropped and he shook his head. He made the same gesture, then pointed at her sporran. She glanced down at it. "Oh. The poem. You read it in the poem. I think we talked about this, Sinclair. The poem you copied is probably wrong. We can't rely on it." Which reminded her that she'd walked right past it and forgot to check. She'd have to do it on the way out.

He gave her the look again. Shaking her head, she decided to humor him, but on their way out, she'd show him proof that he was wrong. Fetching the paper, she unfolded it. Sinclair pointed to the second line. *Here, normal is fallacy, a falling star.*

"So?"

He pointed at the galaxy scene, which looked exactly like all the other ones. She was about to tell him he either needed glasses or his medication tweaked when she saw it. A ball, trailing two silver streaks, raced toward one of the planets. She ran back to the previous doorway. No streaks or balls. Same as the next one down, and the one after that. She sprinted back to Sinclair.

"I can't believe it. You did it again." He made a circular motion, as though encouraging her to keep talking. When she didn't continue, not sure what he was looking for, his hand circled faster.

"He wants you to apologize," Charles explained.

"Apologize? Me? For what?"

"For doubting him."

She bit her lip. Damn these inmates and their sanctimonious ways. She looked at Sinclair, who was still making the motion. "Fine. I'm sorry. It's just that when you made that spelling mistake, I thought you'd screwed everything else up, too. I guess I was wrong."

He shook his head in disappointment, indicating what he thought of this sorry excuse for an apology. "S-e-a." He said each letter so loudly and with such emphasis that for a moment Pandora thought the veins on his forehead were going to pop. "S-e-a. S-e-a," he repeated over and over, louder than usual.

"All right! Have it your way." She looked down the empty corridor before them. "Guys, come on!" she shouted, signaling the others to hurry. "Sinclair has done it again." She reckoned she probably sounded a little sour, but she had every right to be peevish. With those smug looks Sinclair kept giving her, he might just as well be gyrating about in front of her yelling, "Eat that!"

Xavier was already heading in their direction, having given up on his search. Birdy, seeing that he was on the move, broke away from Skippy and hurried after him. Skippy, a little startled at her abrupt departure, followed after them.

Serves him right for dating a lunatic, Pandora thought crossly. She didn't feel the least bit sorry for him. He'd lied to Birdy about Pandora wanting to date him, and while she got why he'd done that—to make Birdy jealous enough to go out with him—that didn't make it right. She'd had to swallow her pride and go along with the lie, and in front of Birdy, of all people. Really, what did he expect from falling in love with that she-devil, anyway?

"What is it?" Xavier asked when he reached them.

"Yeah, what is it?" Birdy echoed a little breathlessly. Keeping up with Xavier wasn't easy. He had long legs, plus Pandora suspected he'd been using them to keep as far ahead of Birdy as possible.

"Sinclair cracked the code." She held up the paper. "I had him copy the poem in the statue. As you might recall, it says 'normal is fallacy, a falling star.' It doesn't make much sense on its own, but it's actually our first clue." She indicated the other doors up and down the corridor. "If you look carefully, you'll see that this is the only door with a meteor. Very clever." She might be annoyed with Sinclair for beating her to the punch and then rubbing it in, but she had to admire the way whoever had written the poem had presented the clue.

"What's a meteor got to do with a falling star?" Birdy asked. Her cheeks were flushed and she kept darting sideways glances at Xavier, who ignored her. It appeared as though her ploy to use Skippy to make Xavier jealous wasn't working.

"The term, falling star, is a fallacy," Skippy explained, stepping forward. The deft movement planted him firmly between Birdy and Xavier. "A falling star is a meteor, not a real star at all. A fallacy," he explained to a perplexed Lucy, "is a sort of mistake."

Birdy peered up at him, a faint hint of approval in her eyes. "How'd you know that?"

He shrugged. "I read it somewhere."

"Are you sure, Sinclair?" Xavier asked. Sinclair nodded confidently. "Well, that's good enough for me. I'm going in." With that, he walked through the doorway, and within moments, disappeared around the first corner. Sinclair and the others followed after him like five ducklings in a row.

Never one to cut off her nose to spite her face, Pandora took one last suspicious look at the shooting 'star,' then entered the labyrinth.

23

Let Her Id Run Wild

DETERMINED TO SOLVE the next clue, Pandora quietly scanned the poem as the posse walked ahead of her, eerily quiet in the close space of the passage that turned left and right and back again. *So if ye dare enter, this loony warns all…that finding the center takes more than one fall.*

Was that a clue or a warning? Should they watch out for hidden pits, which trapped victims in oubliettes, or giant swinging arms that would knock them off their feet? In this place, with all its spooky carvings, either seemed quite possible.

Which brought up the question: Who was the mastermind behind the labyrinth? She knew that Archibald Nepenthe had built Nepenthe Manor, but not why. Judging by how it had been built—with tunnels and hidden rooms and escape routes all over the place—the man must have been a bit on the paranoid side. Pandora liked all the secret places herself, because she was always surrounded by people and needed to get away from them sometimes. But this had been Archibald's home. What, or who, had he been hiding from? Why the need for such secrecy? And why build a labyrinth like this—so elaborate, so deviant?

Perhaps the answer lay in the increasing number of hideous stone faces jutting out from the walls, which rose up on either side, seemingly closing in on her. There were so many faces now that Pandora felt like she was wading through a crowd of jeering strangers, all watching greedily as she approached the hangman's noose. A part of her liked them; another part shuddered. This place, with its peculiar twists and turns, resembled the inner workings of a demented mind. It stood to reason that old Archie could very well have been crazy himself to create something like this. But had he written the poem, as well?

That was the six million dollar question.

She re-read the last part once more…*takes more than one fall*. If that wasn't a warning, then it had to be a clue. But what was it trying to tell her? She was pondering this when she slammed into Lucy.

"Ouch!" Lucy clutched the foot Pandora had stepped on.

"Sorry, Lucy. Wasn't watching where I was going."

Lucy grinned. "Almost torched you, there." Sometimes Lucy believed she could start something on fire just by sheer will.

"Thanks for holding back. So why'd everyone stop?" Then she saw why. The walls really had been closing in on her. Ahead, the posse stood huddled together, unable to go any further in the narrow passage. About five feet in front of them, the two walls came together, leaving a crack about four inches wide. There was no way they could get through to the other side, where it appeared the corridor continued onward. Pandora smiled, if a bit wickedly. Sinclair *had* been wrong. More importantly, *she'd* been right! But she wouldn't rub it in. She was more mature than that.

"Told you so, Sinclair!" she crowed.

Sinclair turned around. His agate-colored eyes looked so confused and disappointed that she felt a little crappy for acting so juvenile. Really, when did Sinclair ever get to be right? More specifically, her conscience berated her, when did Pandora Belfry ever *let* him be right? She groaned inwardly. Sometimes her superego was a real pain. Why couldn't she just obliterate it and let her id run wild? Being free to do and say whatever she wanted was a much more enjoyable way to live life.

"Okay, so maybe there's something we're missing," she corrected herself.

"Yeah, well, while you're figuring it out, I'm out of here!" Birdy cried, pushing her way through the posse and past Pandora. She was breathing hard, her cheeks flushed. "I don't like this one bit!" After several strides, she stopped and leaned against the wall in a tiny space between stone heads, her arms folded and lower lip trembling.

When Skippy made a move to join her, she shook her head at him like a bull about to charge. "Stay where you are." He froze. "I need space. Room to breathe!" She stared at Skippy as though he was one of the gargoyles come to life, and Pandora wondered if Birdy's words held a deeper meaning. She shook her head. No way. Deep, Birdy was not.

"Just hold on, everyone." She held up her hands for calm. "Don't leave, Birdy. We need to stick together. I have a feeling this place isn't safe." Birdy looked defiant, but didn't move, apparently deciding there might be some wisdom in what Pandora said.

Xavier, who'd been looking around, tilted his head at Pandora. "And what makes you say that?"

She shrugged. "Just a feeling. I mean, whoever built this place had a twisted mind, and twisted minds have been known to cause harm." She refrained from staring pointedly at Birdy.

"I think this place is cool," he said.

"Yeah, well, you say potato, I say pot*ah*to."

"We all see the world through our own lenses, you know."

"What's that supposed to mean?" she demanded, though she had a suspicion. One she didn't like.

"All I'm saying is that you're the type of person who sees a world full of traps and tricks, whereas I see it as one filled with opportunity and challenge."

"How clarifying, Pollyanna," she snapped, "but I think I know what I'm talking about." Dismissing Xavier with a wave of her hand, she turned her attention on Sinclair. "What do you think the next line means?" He had the whole poem memorized so he would know which line she was talking about. Even if his translation were wrong, as it undoubtedly was, it would make him feel better if she let him take over the reins, temporarily, that is.

Instead of answering he turned around and faced the nearly bisecting walls, his head swiveling back and forth and up and down as he searched for the answer. Meanwhile, Charles and Lucy started a game of tag, scurrying past Pandora and Birdy. "Don't go too far!" she yelled after them.

"What *is* the next line?" Xavier asked.

"Something about a fall, right?" Skippy said. He held out his hand. "Let me see it. I've been known to crack a code or two in my time."

She sighed. Was nothing sacred? *She* was the one who'd had the foresight to get Sinclair to copy down the poem. *She* was the one who'd kept it safe since then. So it stood to reason that *she* should be the only one who got to read it.

Even so, she handed the poem to Skippy, who skimmed it, his lips moving as he read the words. Xavier read it over his shoulder. "Sounds like the loony is telling us we're going to make mistakes, whether we like it or not," Xavier surmised. He threw his arm back at the walls. "Here's mistake number one." He didn't notice Sinclair flinch, though probably few people would notice Sinclair flinch, with only a slight lifting of the shoulders and a brief bob of the head to give him away.

"So we start over?" Skippy asked. "Try to figure out the correct door?"

"I guess," Pandora relented. She wanted to be right, and after seeing Sinclair's stunned expression, wanted him to be right, too. She wanted to have her cake and eat it, too. Dumb cake.

"If we have to start over," Birdy announced, "I'm going back to the manor. I don't have all day to be running about making a fool of myself."

"You live at Nepenthe Manor," Pandora pointed out. "You do have all day to be running around making a fool of yourself. Besides, what else are you going to do? Change the color of your fingernail polish? Brush your hair? Practice seductive poses in the mirror?"

"You wouldn't know a seductive pose if it bit you in the ass," Birdy growled. Xavier and Skippy broke into raucous guffaws.

"Thank the lord and hallelujah for that!" Pandora exclaimed over their laughter. Though inwardly she wondered why the two boys would be laughing so hard if there wasn't an element of truth in what Birdy said. Whatever. It wasn't that she couldn't be seductive; it was just that she didn't want to be. A world of difference.

A loud screech rang out. "What was that?" Skippy jerked toward the direction they'd come.

"That was Lucy. Come on!"

Pandora darted down the corridor past Birdy and around three corners before she found Lucy sprawled on the ground. Charles was bending over her, patting her awkwardly on the back. "She tripped," he told Pandora as she kneeled down beside him.

"Something jumped out of the wall and made me fall down!" she howled, which Pandora thought was an odd way to put it, though admittedly Lucy was always putting things oddly. She sat up and flew into Pandora's arms. "And I hurt my ass!"

"Lucy!" Pandora scolded, patting her on the back. "Don't use that word."

"But Birdy just used it like two seconds ago!" she sobbed.

Pandora glared up at the offender. "Yeah, well, Birdy is a potty mouth." Damnit all, if the staff heard Lucy swearing, it wouldn't be Lucy getting into trouble. First they'd blame the posse. But being that the posse had pretty much the solid gold excuse—*I'm crazy*—for any behavior they exhibited, blame would promptly pass on to Pandora. Oftentimes the staff skipped right over the others and went directly for her. "You have more class than that."

Lucy pulled back, sniffing. "I suppose I do go to class more than Birdy does." She frowned. "But I don't think that's so cool."

"Classy means that you have style and grace…like a princess."

Lucy wiped her nose on her sleeve. "You think I'm a princess?"

"Of the Land of Gullible," Birdy snipped, but luckily she was standing a few feet away and Lucy was blowing her nose loudly into her pink and white polka-dotted handkerchief.

She tucked the rag back into her pocket and used Pandora's shoulder to push herself up. Once she was on her feet, she grabbed Charles's elbow and pulled him up. "You're it!" she cried.

"Hold on." Pandora grabbed Lucy's plump arm before she could escape. "Why did you think something jumped out of the wall and made you fall?"

"Because she's delusional?" Birdy shouted, rolling her eyes. "Really, I don't know why I hang out with you people. I need some stability in my life, some normality. You guys are so far from normal, you'd need a rocket ship to get back."

"Feel free to leave," Pandora told her. Birdy was always threatening to quit the Secret Six, but she never did. She often made threats she didn't act on. It was the rare occasion that she did that had landed her in an insane asylum. "Go on, Lucy," Pandora encouraged the girl. "What happened?"

Lucy looked around, her eyes glowing from all the sudden attention. "Something just jumped out and I got scared and the earth tipped and I fell down on my ass...I mean, my butt!"

"Did you see it happen?" Pandora asked Charles.

He shook his head. "I had my eyes closed. We were playing blind man's bluff," he admitted sheepishly. "Cause there's nowhere to hide." *And because I can't run very fast*, he didn't add, but Pandora heard it all the same.

"Sounds fun," she said briskly. Sometimes Charles made her want to cry.

"Sounds stupid," Birdy muttered.

Pandora swung on her. "Why are you such a downer all the time, Birdy? Is it because you hate yourself? You should, you know. You're mean and vulgar and I'm sick of it." She'd gone too far, but she didn't care. Anger always felt better than submission.

"Hey, now—" Skippy began, but Birdy was already flying at Pandora, claws fully extended.

"You little bi—" But before she could finish her curse, the ground opened up and swallowed her whole, closing up once more with a gush of air like a belch.

24

STANDING BEHIND THE spot where Birdy had disappeared, Sinclair stared down at the ground, completely immobile. Finally— although really it was only two or three seconds—he looked up, his eyes wide, his mouth opening and closing like a fish out of water. He turned to look back the way he'd come, then swiveled around again. He did this three more times before settling at staring down once more at where Birdy had disappeared. Sinclair couldn't do anything an odd number of times.

It seemed the poem was a warning, after all, Pandora mused dazedly.

"What did you do?" Skippy cried, finally unfreezing. He and the others ran toward Sinclair, being careful not to step on the spot where Birdy had disappeared. Skippy sank to his knees and frantically pounded on the square stones. "Birdy!"

Sinclair's eyes widened even more. He shook his head and made twisting motions with both his hands. Then he pointed back down the corridor.

"You turned something?" Xavier guessed. Sinclair nodded. "Where? Show me!"

The two darted off down the corridor, back toward where the walls narrowed, and Pandora followed, shouting, "Stay where you are!" to the others. When they reached the spot, Sinclair strode directly up to the open crack and slid an arm through the space. He made a turning motion, then angled his body in the other direction before making another twisting motion. Behind them they heard a cry of surprise. Xavier looked at Sinclair, then hustled back down the corridor. Sinclair pulled his arm out and followed after him.

Pandora stayed behind. Pressing her nose to the narrow opening, she peered through and noticed something strange. Arranged in a circle, five leaves of assorted colors decorated each wall. Sticking out about an inch from the wall, the ten leaves appeared to be made of stone and were inlaid with bits of colored glass. The five colors, with its twin gracing the other wall, were pine green, pink, lilac purple, aqua blue, and orange. After that, the walls parted ways again, widening and returning to normal width about fifteen yards along.

Pandora slipped an arm through the crack. Straining a little, she managed to touch a purple leaf. To her surprise, it moved at her touch. She pushed down on one edge and the whole leaf turned. Using her fingertip, she spun the leaf completely around. Very cool. But nothing happened. She did the same to the purple leaf on the other wall. Again, nothing. Obviously Sinclair had discovered a trick she wasn't getting.

"Skippy, can you hear me?" Xavier's voice echoed down the corridor.

"The earth tilted and he fell in!" Lucy cried.

Pandora withdrew her arm and raced to join the others. "He's gone?" she asked when she saw Xavier on his knees pulling at the same area where Skippy had been only moments before. She dropped to the ground and put her face low to the damp stone. The smell of moss and wet dirt filled her nostrils. "Skippy? Birdy? Can you hear me?" Only the mocking caw of their crow answered from somewhere far off. "What the heck happened?" She looked up at Charles.

"After you guys left, I turned to help Lucy tie her shoe," he explained, panting slightly, his cheeks flushed and his eyes hectic, "and she screeched and pointed. When I turned around, Skippy had disappeared."

"I guess those two are gone for good," Lucy determined. "Bye-bye, Birdy!" She grinned wickedly. "I'll miss Skippy, though," she added as an afterthought. "He had such cool hats."

"Did something fly out of the wall again, Lucy?"

She frowned, the tip of her tongue sticking out as she thought. "Maybe…"

Pandora pushed herself to her feet and approached the wall. She leaned close to inspect the surface and immediately jerked back. "No way!"

"What is it?" Xavier quickly joined her.

"It's a leaf…like the other ones back there." She pointed. "But it's hard to see because it blends into the wall. All those weird faces don't help, either." She turned to Sinclair. "You have to do what you did before. I think it opens a trapdoor."

Sinclair nodded. "S-e-a," he said quietly, before running off to do what she'd asked.

After filing away his impertinent and tiresome insistence on repeating that misspelled word, she told the others to move back. "I don't want anyone standing on the trapdoor when it's triggered." They waited in silence, watching carefully for something to happen, but were still startled when the gray stone leaf, about four inches tall, popped out from the wall like a Jack-in-the-Box. Everyone jumped back, even though no one was in danger.

"Where's the trapdoor?" Lucy asked, inching forward.

Pandora frowned. "That should have opened it."

Xavier got down on his hands and knees and slowly crawled toward what they thought was the trapdoor, one hand patting at the earth. "Here it is," he announced. "I can see where the moss is torn."

Pandora joined him. "I see it, too. But why won't it give?"

"Get back," Xavier told her. "I want to try something."

After examining the spot a few more moments, he shifted around to the other side, put his good hand on the door, and pushed as hard as he could. There was a loud wrenching squeak and Xavier fell forward. Pandora lunged toward him and grabbed his belt to keep him from falling any farther. But the door had been triggered and Xavier's weight pulled her forward like a shark on the line. Her ribs burned and she started to pant.

"Just let go!" Xavier told her.

"No way!" she cried, but her words were mainly bravado. She either let him go or fall in with him. She was contemplating whether the posse could afford to lose her guiding presence when she felt hands encircle her waist and pull hard. She fell backward, and Xavier came with her. Luckily, this time he landed on his butt and not on her rib-cage. Nobody moved for several seconds as the sound of heavy breathing filled the air.

"Whoo, doggy!" Lucy cried, breaking the spell. "That was a close one! Good job, Sinclair!"

Pandora turned around to see Sinclair. He was looking down at himself sprawled on the ground, then lifted his hands to peer at them. Dirt and green moss covered his palms.

"Sinclair?" He didn't respond as he pushed himself to his feet and began to wipe off his pants. Following his example, she untangled herself and stood up. She held out her hand to Xavier, who was holding his broken wrist. "You okay?"

"I think so. Just jarred the wrist a bit."

She peered around him, into the dark slit that remained. "The trapdoor is still open."

"It must have gotten stuck."

"But when there's enough weight on it, it gives."

"Probably could use a good dose of WD-40."

"Yeah," she answered absently, turning to look at the protruding leaf. She thought about the other leaves she'd seen—how they had opened the trapdoor. Sinclair's initial actions had triggered the gray leaf, which had popped out and scared Lucy as she ran across the trapdoor. The door had given slightly under her weight, but not completely. Somehow Pandora herself had missed stepping on it when she'd gone to Lucy's aid, and Charles must have already been past it when Lucy had fallen. Xavier, Skippy, Birdy, and Sinclair had stayed on the other side of it, keeping clear of danger. Not having been used possibly for decades, the mechanism that made the door work had likely rusted, making the gears stick, even though the lever had been triggered. Birdy, however, had been heavy enough to overcome the years of rust. Once the door closed, the single leaf retracted, locking the door once more.

She kneeled down and examined the slightly depressed area. She pushed lightly on the spot and it went down. She pushed harder, then stuck her head into the dark space. "Skippy? Birdy? Can you hear me?" No answer. She pushed the door farther down and saw something metallic. From this angle, it looked like a slide. She leaned closer. It was a slide! She quickly started to lower herself into the hole.

Xavier grabbed her arm. "What are you doing?"

"I'm going down."

"No, you're not. We don't even know how to get back out."

"So we just leave them down there? They could be hurt!"

"I say we go for help."

"Oh, no, we don't! If we're caught in here—and that includes you, buddy—we won't ever see the light of day again."

"I won't get blamed—"

Pandora laughed. "You don't get it, do you? Whether you like it or not, you're one of us now." Realizing what she'd just said, Pandora could have bit off her own tongue.

Xavier grinned. "Really?"

"Really," she mumbled, though what she actually wanted to do was punch him in the nose. When she looked up to give him the full power of her disapproval, her anger fizzled. Anyone who looked as happy as Xavier did to be included in a bunch of crazy, or in her case, unconventional, misfits should be pitied, not scorned. She took a deep breath. "That means we have to figure this out ourselves. It's what we've always done."

"Am I part of the Secret Six, then?" He almost giggled, he was so thrilled.

She looked up at Sinclair, the one who would be most affected by this decision, given his fixation with even numbers. He gave one stiff nod, as though his chin was fighting against him.

"This means you have to follow our rules and learn our ways."

Xavier grinned again. "I can do that."

"Fine. You're in. Congratulations. You're an official member of our posse and of the Secret Six—Seven, that is." Lucy gave a cheer and Charles smiled happily. He loved it when everyone got along. "Keep in mind that I'm still the leader."

He gave her a salute. "Very good, Cap'n!"

"And I say we're going down."

"All right, but we have to think this through. You have your flashlight, right?"

She yanked off her backpack and pulled it out. "Right. So I'll go first, then I'll shine the light up the slide."

"Slide?" the other three echoed.

Pandora grinned. "You bet your booty!"

Lucy clapped her hands. "My booty loves slides. Slides rule! Me, first!"

Pandora laughed. "You can go second, Lucy. I'm going first to be sure it's safe. All right, guys," she motioned to Xavier and Charles, "hold the door open." The two boys flanked the trapdoor and pushed down. "Can you go last, Xavier?"

He glanced at his cast, then nodded. "No problem."

Pandora sat at the edge of the opening, resting her feet on the slide. Unable to see much, she flipped on the flashlight. Bright orange and dull patches of green reflected back at her and she realized that the slide was made of copper, which doesn't rust, but it does corrode, hence the green parts.

She readied herself to push off, but before she headed into the abyss, she had to know one thing. "Hey, Sinclair. What's the trick? How'd you know which leaves to turn?"

He bit his lip anxiously. "There's more than one fall," he croaked.

"I know that. It's what the poem says, but—" And then she got it. "It doesn't just mean 'fall' as in 'fall down.' It means the other kind, too. Autumn. You turned the orange leaves to open the trapdoor. More than one *fall*..." So simple, and yet so devious. Sinclair nodded, his eyes bright.

"You're a blasted genius!" Xavier declared, real admiration in his smile.

"You are, Sinclair," Pandora echoed. "You really are." She truly meant it this time. Even though she still wished she'd been the one to figure out the clue, she was proud of Sinclair. And being proud should make her feel happy for him, right? So why then did she feel like something precious was slipping through her fingers?

25

Such Terrible Thoughts

AS SOON AS the thought crossed her mind, Pandora shoved it out of her consciousness and into the deep, dark pit where such terrible thoughts resided. She had things to do, puzzles to solve, slides to ride. Anyway, she was being ridiculous. Sinclair wasn't changing. He couldn't.

"Catch you on the flip side," she called, then pushed off. As she plunged into the dark abyss, her light did little more than reflect off the stone walls while the slide dipped and curved. The sound of her pants whisking along, the heavy smell of damp, and the brisk, tangy odor of copper accompanied her as she sped along.

After thirty or forty heart pounding seconds, the slide began to level out and her momentum slowed. She was coming to a stop. Her flashlight caught two pale faces in its beam and two sets of relieved eyes stared back at her. They were alive!

"Are you all right?"

"It's about damn time!" Birdy pushed away from Skippy, who'd had his arms wrapped tightly around her. "Get us out of here."

"I take it that's a yes, and I don't know how yet. But I'll figure it out," she rushed to add as Birdy's bulging eyes threatened to pop out of their sockets.

"You'd better, Pandora. You got us into this mess, I expect you to get us out of it."

Pandora suppressed a sigh. If someone gave her a dollar every time she heard that phrase, she'd be richer than King Croesus. "You shouldn't worry so much," she told the frowning girl. "It'll give you wrinkles." Birdy's expression smoothed out faster than a fruit roll-up. "That's better." She turned around to face the slide, shouting, "Next contestant...come on down!"

Lucy appeared first, and after landing, bounced up and down and shouted, "Again, again!" Charles arrived next, wind-blown and thrilled. Sinclair took longer to show up and when he pushed himself off the slide he was mumbling something under his breath. Whether it was a curse or an accolade, Pandora couldn't tell.

"Maybe you shouldn't come down!" she shouted up to Xavier, deciding at the last second that maybe someone should stay above ground in case they couldn't get out.

"What?" Xavier shouted back, sounding awfully close. Seconds later, he skittered to a stop before her with a broad grin on his face. She'd obviously left it too late. "I *love* this place!" he shouted, and his voice echoed in the shadowy chamber.

"It's totally awesome, isn't it?" Birdy said, peppy as a cheerleader.

"I thought you said—" Skippy began.

"I could ride that slide all day!" Birdy ruthlessly cut him off, along with an elbow to the gut.

Skippy looked stricken. "But the whole time we were down here," he persisted, finally starting to get a little angry, "you complained about the labyrinth. I don't know why you're changing your story now."

Pandora stepped forward. "I know why." Despite Skippy's lie about her wanting to date him, she didn't like seeing Birdy treating him this way. It wasn't right. No, he wasn't the manliest of men. Yes, he had issues. And yes, Birdy had known him since they were kids. But he didn't deserve this. "I think we all know why."

"Mind your own business, Belfry," Birdy snarled.

"We all know you're using Skippy," Pandora went on relentlessly. "And it's got to stop. He's our friend. Yours, too. So treat him like one."

Skippy gave Pandora a grateful glance, but at the same time, he looked kind of sick. "Thanks, Pandora, but I don't mind—"

"Why would you?" Birdy snapped. "You have no backbone! When I ask you what you want to do, you ask, 'What do *you* want to do, Birdy?' When I ask what your favorite color is, you pick mine! Geez, Skippy. You have the personality of a water buffalo. Why can't you be more interesting? Like Xavier?"

Xavier held up his hands. "Hey, now. Whatever's going on here, leave me out of it."

Pandora laughed. "Ha! You're a part of us now, Xavier, and you're not going to escape the bloodletting so easily." She turned to Birdy and Skippy. "He's joined the Secret Seven."

"What?" Skippy responded, clearly stunned. His shoulders slumped dejectedly and Pandora noticed he was looking thinner than usual. "But don't we have to vote on that?"

"Sorry, Skippy," she replied, "but it was a last-second decision and a necessary one. We need him with us."

"What can he do that I can't?"

"Make a decision?" Birdy sniped.

"Oh, Birdy, why are you being so mean?" Lucy demanded. "Skippy loves you. I wish I had someone who loved me like that." She sighed wistfully, oblivious to Charles's simpering gaze. "I wish my dada loved me like that, with hugs and kisses and doing everything I want to do."

"Love like that suffocates," Birdy growled. "Is that what you want, dwarf? Not me," she went on, not waiting for an answer she had no desire to hear. "I'd rather be single for the rest of my life than stuck with a spineless wuss." Skippy gasped as though Birdy had cold-cocked him.

"Birdy!" Pandora cried. "Skippy isn't a spineless wuss."

Her cheeks were flushed. "I'm surprised he can even stand up he's so spineless."

"But I thought you were going to make babies," Lucy persisted, her voice sad. "I like babies."

"That's because you still are one," Birdy said, but she wasn't looking at Lucy anymore. She was looking at Skippy and the more wretched his expression grew, the fiercer hers became.

Charles, taking a deep breath from a trembling chest, said, "I think we need to get out of here."

"I agree," Xavier said, his voice loud and in command. "Being down here is enough to make anyone act a little weird. Let's get ourselves above ground and then *certain* people can work out their differences." Birdy looked as though she wanted to say something more, but thankfully she kept her mouth shut. "Pandora, can you lead the way with the flashlight?" Ordinarily her hackles would've risen at being ordered about and she'd have told Xavier off, but something warned her—a strange new sensation—that now was not the time to argue.

"No problem." She swung her flashlight around. "Looks like there's only one tunnel that leads out of here, near the slide."

The tunnel turned out to be short-lived, leading to a set of stairs rising sharply upward. Pandora quickly climbed the steep steps, anxious to get out. "We're almost there!" she cried. She reached up to touch a wooden door, just like the other trapdoor. At first it didn't give, but when she put her shoulder to it, it groaned and began to rise. Fresh air and bright light poured in. She shoved the door and it opened wide before falling to catch on the wall with a thud. She climbed the rest of the stairs and looked around, hoping to see the center of the maze and the end of their search. She didn't. "Damn!"

"What is it?" Xavier asked behind her.

"We're back where we started." She stared at the nearly touching walls a few feet behind her. Then she noticed something—the colored leaves. "No, wait. We're on the *other* side of the dead-end."

Birdy pushed past her. "Air. Sweet, blessed air!" The rest of the posse clambered up the steps, equally glad to be free, gasping and coughing as though they were miners who'd been trapped underground for days.

"Now what?" she wondered aloud as she watched the others lurch and stumble down the corridor.

"We look at the next clue?" Xavier replied. She swung around to find him still on the steps.

"I guess so." She wanted to get to the center already. She wanted answers.

"You know, you really should just enjoy the experience. Once this is over, it's over. We won't ever get to solve this labyrinth again."

She borrowed Dougie's reptile blink. "Enjoying the experience is not my style." She wasn't entirely sure this was true, and actually, it kind of made her sound stupid, but at this point, she didn't really care.

"It should be."

"Listen, we're supposed to be looking for our dad, not wasting our time trying to figure out some stupid maze. But now that we've started, I can't stop!"

"Maybe what we're doing is all a part of the process."

"What can a maze have to do with finding our dad?"

"Who knows?" Xavier shrugged. "Besides, I've been doing some of my own searching, so our time exploring the labyrinth hasn't been *totally* wasted." He gave her what was supposed to be a charming grin. She returned it with a grimace.

"What do you mean? Did you go down to the beach without me?"

"When would I do that? It's been raining the whole time and besides, I told you I wouldn't go alone." She didn't believe him, but then, she never believed people. That kind of weakness got a person screwed over. "No, I've been looking at all the possible candidates."

"Possible candidates? Where?"

"Here, *duh*. At Nepenthe Manor."

"Here?"

"We have to consider all the males who might fall within the correct age range to be our father. Basically, they have to be old enough for our moms to, um, consider for um, a prospective partner." His eyes flitted upward and his cheeks colored. "And then we have to add my age to that number."

"So anyone 36 or older, give or take?" Pandora answered, getting pulled in by his logic despite herself.

"I thought 35, so we're in the same ballpark."

Pandora cleared her throat. "I had considered Carl as an option, but not anybody else. Not even close."

"There's the security guard."

"Frank? Ugh. No way. Have you seen his offspring—Beetle? Being that neither of us look like warthogs, I think we can rule out Frank as our father."

Xavier laughed. "Still, we might've gotten lucky and ended up looking more like our mothers."

"So we can't rule Frank out?"

He shook his head. "Fraid not. There's J.T., too."

"No way. While I have no proof he's gay, I'd be totally shocked if he wasn't."

"Gay guys can still be dads, you know. Maybe he went through a period of denial."

She giggled. "Wouldn't that make him the *Queen* of Denial?"

"Funny." Xavier smiled. "But we still can't rule him out."

Pandora was almost afraid to ask, "Who else are you considering?"

"I've totally ruled out Dr. Steele." He watched her carefully as he said this. "I see you have, too," he went on, though she hadn't, not totally. "It's too bad. He'd have made a nice dad." She nodded without realizing she was doing it. "There's Dr. Malik and Dr. Snyder. That's all I know for staff."

"We don't exactly look Indian, do we? And Dr. Malik's only been here for about five years. Before that he lived in California, and as far as I know my mom has never traveled outside of New England."

"So that leaves Dr. Snyder."

"I'd rather have Hitler for a dad."

"Yeah, me, too. He's a bit on the uptight side."

"A bit? I mean, really, sometimes a cigar is just a cigar. But with him everything's a phallic symbol and everyone is a depraved sex maniac. That's why we call him the Snake."

Xavier laughed. "Good one. He tried to get me to admit that I struck out at Dougie Daft because I had an Oedipus complex. Can you believe that crap?"

"Ewww, no!" Pandora cried, conveniently forgetting that not so long ago she thought she might have developed her own complex for Dr. Steele. "But that sounds like Dr. Snyder. Sometimes I think the people who are supposed to be experts in this field are more screwed up than their patients."

"I agree." He nodded heartily.

"So that's it?"

"Well, there's one more candidate…" He paused and looked away.

"Who?" she asked suspiciously.

He screwed up his mouth. "Mayor Daft."

Boring and Clumsy and Stupid

26

"**HAVE YOU LOST** your mind?" Pandora shouted, then lowered her voice. The posse had headed down the corridor without them, but they were still close enough to hear, if they were listening. And they were *always* listening. "No way, no how."

"I don't like it, either. But he fits the age profile. And he's blond... like me."

Now that Pandora thought about it, there were a few similarities between Xavier and Dougie. Both were blond. Both were thin. Both were annoying. Even so, she wasn't going for it. "Do you really want to be related to someone like that? I'd just as soon not know."

"Me, too." He grimaced. "But I had to look at everyone who fit the profile."

"But Mayor Daft and my mom hate each other."

"But *why* do they hate each other?"

"Cause he's always trying to close this place down. He hates Nepenthe Manor. Says it's bad for business and bad for Bedlam."

"But don't you see?"

"What?"

"Maybe they were lovers and they had a fight and broke up. Then your mom found out she was pregnant and either never told him or did tell him and he washed his hands of you."

"Okay, first of all, don't ever use the word 'lover' in relation to my mother. Second, are you saying I've been dumped by a Daft?" *Oh, the gall of it.*

"I'm just saying he has to be considered."

"But what about your mom? How did he know her?"

"Your mom and my mom were friends, so it stands to reason that my mom and Mayor Daft could have met. According to my gran, some man ruined their friendship. She was more crude about it, but the point was that my mom and your mom were friends until some guy came between them. Mayor Daft sounds like that kind of person, don't you think?"

"I suppose," Pandora reluctantly acknowledged.

"And what kind of a mom names her kid Pandora?"

"Hey!"

His bony shoulders drew up and dropped again. "I'm only saying that she must have been pretty pissed at someone to do that to an innocent baby."

True. She was an innocent. "I guess what you're saying makes a weird sort of sense."

"It would solve your problem with the dance, you know."

She managed a strangled laugh. "Yeah, I guess it would."

"Nooo!" a shriek rang out. Looking at each other, Pandora and Xavier dashed up the last few steps and down the cobbled corridor to where the posse was gathered in front of a wall. Birdy was stomping her feet and yelling, "I want out of here!"

Pandora looked to the left, then to the right. Both walls had openings. "Did you try going through these?" It seemed like an obvious question, but she never assumed anything with this bunch.

"We did try," Charles informed her, looking pale and distraught. "They both lead to doors. We don't know which one to try and we don't want to make a mistake because Birdy's starting to lose it."

Sinclair was quiet but he was looking at the door on the left. "You think we should go that way?" Pandora asked him. He nodded. "And that will lead us to the center?" He shook his head, then stiffly mimed the pose of the statue in the labyrinth's courtyard. "You're saying it will take us back to the beginning of the maze?"

He gave one brief bob of his head. She studied the others. Charles looked wretched, worn out by all the excitement and drama, and Lucy's hair was starting to poof to the point of taking over her head. She knew Birdy was done and Skippy, well, after Birdy's rant, he looked like death warmed over. It was time to head back.

"All right. We'll go. If that's what everyone wants?" She had to make one last attempt.

"I think that's a good idea," Xavier said. "It's been a long day." For the first time she noticed he seemed a little peaky himself, cradling his broken wrist like a baby.

"All right. We'll head back. But remember... Not a word of this to anyone." She stared at Lucy meaningfully.

Lucy pretended to pull the zipper across her mouth, twisted the lock, and threw away the invisible key. Then she ruined it by laughing. "I'm not a tattletale, Pantaloon!"

"Not on purpose, you're not."

Lucy frowned. "You're as bad as mean old Birdy!"

"Loose lips sink ships," Pandora lectured.

"So do bombs!" Lucy cried. "Fire bombs!"

Before she could get a full head of steam going Charles grabbed her arm and steered her toward the opening on the left. "You can be first through the door," he offered with a flourish of his hand and Lucy beamed at him, anger forgotten. Pandora threw Charles a grateful look. She could always count on him.

"I hope there won't be monsters!" Lucy exclaimed, breaking free of Charles's grasp and running on ahead. When she reached the door, ten feet away, she cried, "Here goes nothing!" then pulled open the heavy door. It groaned and squeaked in protest and then gave way, nearly knocking Lucy to the ground. She steadied herself and pulled harder. "Bye!" She waved, then slipped through the crack. Charles grabbed the door before it could shut and hurried after her, followed by the rest of the posse.

As she waited her turn, Pandora realized she did want this door to lead out of here. She was feeling a bit tired herself, and she needed to think about a lot of things. Plus, tonight she planned to sneak down to the beach to do a little spirit patrol. But first, she needed a rest, a good meal in her belly, and a Coke to top it all off.

The last through, she heard the door clunk shut behind her, as final as the sound of an ax at a beheading. She turned around, suspicion tickling her insides, and spotted the source of her concern immediately. The door had no handle, no way of getting back through. Crud. She didn't dare tell the others, though. No sense getting people worked up.

After a couple minutes, they emerged from the narrow tunnel to find themselves back at the 30-door corridor, as she now thought of it. She looked back at the opening and made a note of it. It was a quick way out of the maze, but was not a way in. Very clever, she thought to herself, but also slightly worrying. How many more of these doors would just lead them back out again, only to have to start over?

It was a quiet group that stumbled along through the tunnel that led back to the statue. Rounding the last corner before the stairs, the beam of her flashlight caught the wool blanket that Birdy and Skippy had brought along to do their 'exploring.' Skippy bent his long frame in half and awkwardly gathered it up.

Something tugged at her mind. "Where did you get this lantern?" She pointed at it.

"At the beach. We were, um, exploring there."

"How'd you get down there?" she asked, surprised. She'd thought she was the only one who knew about the secret gates.

Normally he would've grinned, but he only looked woeful. "I can pick locks, remember?"

"Oh, yeah." He could. "So where'd you find it on the beach?"

"On a rock by The Fangs, turned on its side. Like it had been knocked over."

How odd. "Do you mind if I keep it? I want to fill it with kerosene."

He thrust it at her, the lantern suddenly distasteful to him. "Not at all. I'm sure we won't be needing it anymore."

"Thanks," she replied absently, wondering how the lantern, which was surely a twin to the one she'd found near the statue's doorway, had ended up on the beach. A shiver ran up her spine, quick as a snake. Could spirits carry lanterns? She'd read about ghosts being able to move things. They could also pass through walls...labyrinth walls. She bit her lip. This was all too bizarre to take in. She'd have to think more on it.

Xavier sprayed all the chains and any metal parts he could find with the WD-40 he'd brought along, then he and Skippy worked together to lift the drawbridge back up into place while Charles and Lucy stood watch. Birdy didn't stick around, storming off to the manor. She was in high dudgeon and Pandora hoped that for once she'd stay away from everyone while she sulked. Unfortunately, Birdy was a great believer in the saying, misery loves company. And when she was in misery, she wanted everyone else to be, too.

When everything was in place according to his majesty's standards, the motley crew headed back to the house. Only Lucy talked, chattering away about buying a house made of colored glass, filled to the top with gobstoppers and pop rocks.

"I'll see you guys tomorrow afternoon," Pandora announced as they entered the foyer. She did her best to sound tuckered out, as though the only plans she had that night involved her pillow and lots of sleep. She didn't have to act too much.

"Aren't you going to eat with us?" Lucy pleaded. "I want you to eat with us."

"I'm too tired, Lucy Goosey. I'm going to get something to eat, take a hot bath, and go straight to bed. Besides, you know how Vicki hates it when I hang out with the posse."

"Party pooper!" She stuck her tongue out and stomped her foot. "Chicken!" She started clucking and flapping her arms like a mad hen.

"Sorry, Lucy, but my ribs really hurt."

Lucy scowled. "That's not fair. I'm mad and I told you so, just like Dr. Hannah says I'm supposed to do. But you go and make me feel bad about it."

Pandora laughed. "I wasn't trying to, Lucy! I'm just not feeling up to company right now." Which was absolutely true. She needed space and quiet to think and plan.

"But we have therapy and classes and stuff tomorrow so we won't see each other all day!" Lucy liked it best when they were all together. Charles, too. He peered at her with big, wishing eyes.

"Fine," she sighed. "I'll eat with you guys. Then I'm going to bed."

"I'll join you," Xavier offered. "This will be my first official dinner as a posse member. Come on, Skippy. We'll make it a party."

Skippy tried to smile, but the effort failed miserably. "I'm not hungry," he croaked. Pandora regarded him worriedly. It was only a matter of time before the darkness claimed him and he'd descend into a deep depression.

"Sure you are," Xavier asserted. "You'll see as soon as you get into the cafeteria."

Skippy didn't look at all convinced, but he nodded. "All right."

"Good. Let's go."

"Just a minute," Pandora said. "Let me get rid of this." She held up the lantern. "I'll be right back." She raced up to her room and dumped her backpack and the lantern. When she returned, they headed into the cafeteria and got their trays of food. Supper was a mess of limp fish and chips, bitter tartar sauce, and flaccid green beans—in other words, back to normal. Sitting at their typical table, no one said much as they ate. Most everyone was hungry, but eating what Old Corker had brewed up was a challenge. The smell alone was enough to take out a skunk. Apparently yesterday's reasonably palatable meal had been an anomaly.

"I love her so much," Skippy declared in the middle of smashing his fish with his fork and mixing it and the tartar sauce into a quagmire of grossness. "So much."

"You're just having a lover's quarrel," Xavier replied matter-of-factly as he spooned the mess into his mouth. Despite his colorful descriptions of how bad the food was, the boy didn't seem all that put off by it. Pandora only ate because she knew she had to keep up her strength. Xavier, on the other hand, actually seemed to enjoy the meal. He was the first one done.

"It's over," Skippy said morosely. "I know it."

"Well, there are plenty of fish in the sea," Xavier replied heartily as he wiped his mouth.

"There's only one fish I want."

"It's certainly not the fish on your plate," Xavier joked. Skippy's only response was to sigh deeply. "Oh, come on, man! Cheer up. Birdy's playing games with you. All girls do."

"I don't!" Pandora protested, wondering if lightning could strike through a roof and a couple of floors.

"Ha!" Xavier snorted. "You're the biggest game player I know."

"I am not! I keep all my cards on the table. No secrets." Somewhere, someone's bullshit meter was dinging up a storm.

His eyebrows shot up. "Are you sure you want to keep going with this, Belfry?"

Damn him. "Okay, okay!" She held up her hands in mock surrender. This wasn't about her, after all. "Skippy, Xavier's right. Birdy's just messing with you. You know how she is."

One long finger slid beneath the frame of his glasses and tiredly rubbed his eye. "She thinks I'm a loser. A *wimp*."

"Then show her you're not. Show her you're made of sterner stuff."

"How?" he pleaded, leaning forward. "I'm not some big hotshot stud like Xavier. I'm not smart like Sinclair. I'm not nice like Charles. I'm boring and clumsy and stupid, and I hate myself." He stood abruptly. "I'm going to my room."

Before anyone could say anything to stop him, he was gone.

27

Crying His Fool Eyes Out

"WHERE'S SKIPPY GOING?" Lucy demanded, and Pandora had
to amend her earlier thought. The posse wasn't *always* listening. Especially when they were making sculptures with their fish and chips,
while discussing the joys of living in a house made entirely out of gobstoppers and pop rocks.

"He's not feeling well."

"I'd better go after him," Charles said, and Pandora breathed a sigh
of relief. The posse didn't like leaving Skippy alone when he was like
this, and since Charles was his roommate, there would be someone
watching him. Charles scooped the rest of his fish into his mouth,
chewed, and swallowed. "But first I'll escort you to your room, Lucy."

"Are we watching TV later?"

"Depends on what Skippy's doing," he replied with a shrug.

She sighed. "The poor son-of-a-bitch is probably crying his fool eyes
out."

"Lucy!" Charles exclaimed, his blue eyes shocked. "You shouldn't say
that word."

"Which one?" she asked, but the sparkle in her eyes told everyone
she knew perfectly well which one.

"Where'd you hear it, Lucy?" Pandora demanded.

"On the television," she replied slowly, testing out the lie to see if
anyone would fall for it.

"I don't think so, missy."

"Oh, I don't know!" she groaned dramatically. "Maybe from someone." She threw out her arms, indicating it could be anyone in the cafeteria.

"Which someone?" Xavier leaned forward, determined to get in on
the action.

Lucy struggled to stand up, getting her heel caught on the bench seat
before finally finding her feet. "Get off my back, you Nazis! I'll torch
your heads."

"You're not in trouble, Lucy." Pandora made calming gestures. "We
just want to know. It's an interesting thing for someone to say."

Lucy studied each of them for a moment, weighing her options, then
pointed over Pandora's shoulder. "He said it."

Pandora pivoted around in her seat. "Cracker Jack?" She found that hard to believe. The Vietnam vet was always a happy-go-lucky sort of fellow (except when he was experiencing flashbacks of the war), who tended the gardens with amazing success. He could never be found without his tinted sunglasses, reminiscent of John Lennon, which rode the hump of his thin nose. His long, dirty blond hair was woven together with bits of colorful material into one thick, messy braid. He dressed like a hippie and he lived the life of one. He'd have done better in the sixties, but he was stuck in the eighties, along with the rest of them. Pandora could relate. She preferred the roaring twenties herself.

"No, silly! The brown man with the wheels. You know…Jewelry."

Pandora's eyes shifted to rest on a short man with a potbelly holding court in his wheelchair. "Oh, you mean, Jun Li. Who was he talking about?"

Lucy shrugged. "Fart if I know." She giggled. "Did you see what I did? I said fart instead of hell so I wouldn't swear."

"Very clever, Lucy," Pandora sighed. "All right, why don't you and Charles head out? We don't want to leave Skippy alone for too long."

"I wonder who Jewelry was talking about," Xavier said when they were gone.

"It's *Jun Li*. And in this joint, it could have been anyone."

"Yeah, I suppose."

"Why?" She studied his pensive expression. "What are you thinking?"

"Remember what you said about Vicki not letting our dad see us? About how maybe he wanted to come, but didn't have a way to get to us?"

"Oh, yeah," she replied faintly. "And you think Jun Li knows something about this?"

Xavier studied the animated Asian. "I think that if anyone were to know something, it would be him."

Jun Li did seem to be friends with everyone. "So what are you going to do?"

"I'm going to ask him about what he said."

"Oh." Pandora was much better at using subversive tactics for gathering information, like sneaking down secret passages or hiding behind the massive curtains in the foyer, which had been burnt in the fire and were a great loss. She was always picking up tidbits by remaining unseen and unheard. Xavier's way—the direct approach—sounded much more dangerous, and much less efficient than she liked. "Well, good luck. I'm going to bed."

"You don't want to find out?"

She stifled a pretend yawn. "I'm too tired. You can tell me tomorrow."

"I start work tomorrow morning."

"Work? I thought you were going to school!"

He grinned happily. "Vicki is looking into letting me do homeschooling, like you."

"Crap."

He laughed. "I knew you'd be thrilled. So anyway, Carl's showing me how to plow the field. I can't do much with one arm, but it's a start. I won't see you until after lunch, though."

She weighed this. "Fine, I'll come with you. But if any of the staff come after me for harassing the inmates, I'm blaming you."

He grinned. "Got it."

They left their table, dumped their trays, and headed toward Cracker Jack and Jun Li. Surrounded by inmates, Jun was talking animatedly, his small hands in constant motion as though trying to make up for the immobility of his legs. Jun told all sorts of stories about what had happened to his legs, from stepping on a landmine to getting shot in the back to a poisonous spider bite on the butt. The impish expression on his round, brown face showed how much he loved telling whoppers. And the inmates loved falling for them. Jun was about the same age as the thirty-something Cracker Jack, but he looked and acted more like a teenager than an adult. The two men, although polar opposites, were best friends and could often be found together...except when Cracker Jack was working in the garden. Jun Li claimed work made him break out into hives, even if he was only watching someone else do it.

They approached the table and Jun looked up at them. "Greetings, jerk-offs!" He laughed jovially, his hands clutching his potbelly. "Just kidding. You're cool. Heard you were siblings. How's that going? Any fights yet?" He winked at them.

"It's going quite well," Xavier replied, holding out his hand. "I'm Xavier Carlisle." Jun grasped Xavier's good hand, giving him a gang-like handshake involving several different maneuvers. Xavier somehow managed to keep up with him. Cracker Jack settled for a plain old handshake, gripping Xavier's hand firmly, but not quite meeting his eyes. "How goes the planting?" Xavier asked him.

"Slow," Cracker Jack acknowledged ruefully, staring off to his left. "That nor'easter put me off a few days."

"I told him to plant in the rain!" Jun said loudly. "That's the only way to do it, but he won't. Stubborn son-of-a-bitch, ain't he?"

"I don't like the rain," Cracker Jack said softly.

Pandora knew why, but only after seeing him get caught in a storm one day. It rained a lot in Vietnam—quick, sudden downpours that covered the approach of Viet Cong attackers. "Oh, Jun," she jumped in. "You know Cracker Jack's got big feet. You get him in that muddy garden and there'll be holes all over the place."

Jun hooted. "She's right about that!" Cracker Jack gave a soft smile. "So what can I do you for? Unless this is a social chat?"

"We had a question for you, Jun."

He crossed his stubby arms and leaned back. "Of course you do. Everyone's got questions for Jun Li." He stared at them. "Well?"

"Um…" Xavier hesitated.

"Oh, got it. Private question." He clapped his hands. "Scram, you losers! We'll pick up where I left off later." The inmates protested good-naturedly, then finally shuffled off to dump their trays.

When they were gone, Xavier continued, "One of our friends over-heard you say something about a guy crying his eyes out."

Jun Li looked blank. "Run that by me again?"

"She said, 'The poor son-of-a-bitch is probably crying his fool eyes out,'" Pandora clarified.

"Oh, yeah! Yep, that was me. And you want to know who I was talk-ing about?" He laughed, a stuttering hyena-like bark. Then his mouth clamped shut like a puppet and he leaned forward, suddenly all busi-ness. "You'll have to tell my why first."

Pandora took a deep breath. "Because we're looking for our dad and it seemed like a good clue to follow up, you know?"

"Ahhh," he sighed. Pandora didn't miss the sideways glance Jun threw at Cracker Jack. "Well, we weren't talking about your dad. But we *were* talking about your mom." His slanted eyes narrowed to smug slits.

"My mom?"

"Yeah, and about that poor bastard, the new doctor. I said he'd be crying his eyes out when he found out the Director's in love with me." His thumbs pointed at his concave chest. "The lady's got it bad for me. No offense, Pan."

"None taken." Pandora's breath rattled painfully in her chest. "But why did you think he liked her?"

"Saw 'em eating together, didn't we?" Cracker Jack nodded, his typi-cally open face pinched as though the words hurt his ears. "And they're always talking in her office."

"Oh, that," Pandora breathed a sigh of relief. "She does that with all the new staff. I don't think you have anything to worry about there."

"Oh, I'm not worried about me," Jun said grandly. "Just about the doctor. No woman can resist this." He indicated his chubby torso with a flamboyant sweeping gesture.

"I'm sure he'll manage somehow," she replied dryly.

"Too bad your mother's so busy with her career," he went on, looking back and forth between Pandora and Cracker Jack like an avid tennis fan. "She needs a man in her life. A real man."

"Like you?" Pandora suggested.

"Yes, ma'am." He winked. "As long as she's not the jealous type, she'll be perfect for Jun Li, Lady's Man extraordinaire." He grinned, showing two chipped front teeth. "She's a pretty woman, though, ain't she, Cracker?" Cracker Jack nodded, his blue eyes distant. "So I might have to make an exception for her." He cackled. "Well, it's been real, for sure, but I got a date with a lucky lady tonight. She just doesn't know it yet. Later, losers!" His little, fat fingers gripped the tires of his wheelchair and he popped a wheelie before rolling off.

Cracker Jack stood and gathered up their trays. "See you around, Pandora. Xavier." He nodded at them. "I hope you find what you're looking for."

Xavier sighed as they watched Cracker Jack leave the cafeteria. "Well, I guess that was a dead-end."

"I guess so," Pandora replied. But if that were so, why couldn't she stop seeing the look on Cracker Jack's face whenever her mother came up?

Maybe because it was the look of a man madly in love.

28

THEY PARTED AT the main door. Xavier headed off to the stable, stretching his neck to the left and right as he muttered about needing to get some sleep. "Living directly above those demon beasts you like so much isn't exactly restful," he told her through a yawn.

Pandora watched him go, wondering if he was putting on an act, then closed the door, yawning herself. She desperately needed a Coke and a few minutes of shuteye, otherwise she'd never make it out to the beach tonight.

Dragging her feet, she started across the foyer for the staircase. She'd reached the first step when Dr. Steele called her name. She stopped, but didn't turn around before rearranging her features to convey the message, "I'm completely indifferent to you and cannot be affected by anything you say or do."

"Yes, Dr. Steele?" she inquired in her most mature voice. "What can I do for you?"

His expression was wry. "You can drop the act, for one."

His acuity nearly made her do something in a manner unbefitting a person of maturity, but she managed to keep her emotions under control. "What act is that, pray tell?" The moment the phrase, "pray tell" was out of her mouth, she winced, knowing she'd gone too far. Why was it that whenever she went into mature adult mode, she sounded like a character out of Jane Eyre?

"Pray tell?" He smiled. "How Shakespearean of you. I've done something to upset you, haven't I?" He paused, shaking his head. "No, wait. Don't bother saying no. I'm pretty sure I did. I remember now that you said something before our dinner with Douglas Daft yesterday. Something about me having told on you."

Pandora gripped the burnished wood railing, her knuckles whitening like popcorn. What was it with this man and his relentless plain speaking? She didn't know how to handle it. "Could you be more specific?"

He crossed his arms. She wondered vaguely if doing so made his muscles bulge beneath his tweed jacket. "I'm pretty sure that's about as specific as a person can get. Now stop buying time and answer my question."

"Are you like this as a therapist?" she asked, genuinely curious.

"Generally, yes, though I'm not as pushy. But since you're not a client of mine, I can act however I please. Now answer the question."

She backed up a step. "I don't have to do anything you say, you know."

"You do if you want me to stay quiet about all your shenanigans."

She gasped, pretending indignation as she clapped a hand to her chest. "Are you blackmailing me, Dr. Steele?"

He looked away for a second, then back at her, his head tilting to the right. "I guess I am. Now spill it, Belfry, because I need to ask you about something else and I don't have all day."

She had to admit she was intrigued by the 'something else.' Unfortunately, she was still mad at him, and worse, she was afraid he'd reveal that he *had* told on her, then go on to give all sorts of excuses for why. *I did it for your own good, Pandora.* Or, *I must have the trust of the Director, which means keeping no secrets from her.* And etc's of bullshit, after that.

She laughed lightly. "Simple miscommunication, Dr. Steele. You heard me wrong, and I also didn't finish my sentence. I said that you had *told me* to stay out of trouble and then I was going to add that here I was getting into it again."

His eyebrows rose by subtle tics as she spoke, mirrored by a narrowing of his blue eyes. "There are only two reasons I 'tell' on people, Pandora. One, if they are a threat to themselves. Two, if they are a threat to others."

"Oh," she replied, not really believing him, but desperately wanting to. "Well, it's a good thing I didn't think you'd told on me." The lie left a slimy taste in Pandora's mouth, something very unusual for her. She was used to manipulating the truth. Lying was a necessity here at Nepenthe Manor, a way to survive. Yet if she truly believed that, why did she feel like she wanted to gag? "So what else did you want to ask me?" she choked out.

"Was Saturday's Visitor's Day a typical one?"

"What do you mean?"

"Do your friends' families usually visit, just not yesterday?"

What an odd question. She wondered how much she should divulge. "Yesterday was typical. Some families are good and come every week, but many rarely visit, and a few don't come at all."

He nodded, looking thoughtful. "And what do you think of that?"

"I think it's a load of crap," she spewed, suddenly angry. "But Vicki says we can't force people to come. If it were up to me, though, I'd get a whip and—" She cut herself off, stopping her arm from completing the act. No need to jump headlong into the "threat to others" category and get trussed up in the Crazy Cocoon.

"And?" he asked politely.

"And nothing," she mumbled. "And stop trying to trick me into saying things that will get me into trouble!"

"I wasn't trying to trick you. I simply asked a question. The answer you give is solely dependent on you." He took in her glare. "I have another question, and just to be clear, it's not a trick." His smile met with a deepening of The Glare, a look she had borrowed from Grandmother Belfry and which she was working on perfecting. "Do you have any other ways to encourage family members to come visit?"

"Are you kidding me? They're all lazy, self-absorbed liars. Short of lighting a fire under them, I can't do anything to get them to come. I can only tell the inmates not to trust anyone who's an adult and that way they won't get hurt."

"Hmm…" he replied in a "tell me about your childhood" tone of voice.

"Is that all you can say?" His complacency irked her to no end.

"Actually, I have a lot to say on the subject, but not right now. You look tired. I *am* tired. And I need some time to think on this situation. If you have any ideas that don't involve bodily harm or defeatist advice, let me know."

"Sure." The word was not spoken with enthusiasm. *Defeatist advice*, indeed.

He regarded her steadily, and she met his gaze with equal force. "We're on the same side, Pandora. We both want to help your friends. So maybe we could get along for that reason?"

"I thought we did get along," she protested, suddenly forgetting that she was mad at him and he was not to be trusted.

"Not if you can't trust me and I can't trust you." She stared at him, wondering exactly how much he knew about what was going on, about the world of Nepenthe Manor, about her deepest thoughts and fears. "Goodnight, Pandora."

"Goodnight," she whispered to his retreating back. Unable to take her eyes off his perfect form, she watched—ready to bolt if he turned around—until he disappeared down the hall leading to the therapists' offices. When he was gone, she ran up to her apartment on the third floor. Inside her bedroom, she stood in front of the mirror and hugged herself, feeling weird and jittery. Her image reflected a girl on the verge of womanhood, face pale, dark circles under her eyes, shoulders bowed from the weight of the world. She tried striking a seductive pose, but only succeeded in looking constipated. She gave up the attempt. She needed to focus. To think.

Had Dr. Steele really told on her? She wasn't sure. Maybe he thought of it as a case of her being a threat to herself. But she wasn't going to kill herself, just go on a date with Dougie. A less intrepid person probably would want to off themselves at the prospect, but not her. As much as she wanted certain people to pay for neglecting her, hurting her, crossing her, Pandora had no intention of taking the long walk any time soon. Knowing this didn't make her life any easier, though. She still had to figure out what to do about Dr. Steele, her missing father, the labyrinth's tantalizing clues, which taunted her at every turn, and the stranger on the beach. *Don't forget Giganticus*, a little voice whispered in her head. *He needs some thinking on, too.*

One thing at a time, she told herself. *The best way to piece together a skeleton is bone by bone.* And that's what she would do…take things bone by bone, starting with a Coke and what lay ahead of her tonight.

Heading to her closet to fetch a bottle, she glanced at her watch. It was only a little after seven. She used the opener hanging on a string inside her closet to pop off the bottle top, and a hiss escaped followed by a whiff of fruity white smoke that made her think of ghosts.

It came to her that tonight, if only to maintain her own sanity, she had to prove that the beach walker was either very much alive or a spirit. But how could she do that? Bring a camera? While a good idea, it wasn't workable, being that she didn't have a camera and Vicki had forbidden her using the Polaroid anymore after one too many photos of a bloodied doll gripped between Shadow's teeth. Proclamations of 'homework assignment!' did nothing to sway her mother. Besides it would be too dark out for photographs.

Coke in hand, she walked over to one of the arched windows overlooking the front lawn and peered out the droplet-covered glass. In the dim light of the encroaching night, she could make out a series of mud puddles dotting the driveway like giant footprints. As she studied them, a slow smile turned up the corners of her mouth. Footprints. She would look for footprints on the beach. It was as simple as that.

Bone by bone.

Pandora figured she had only to wait another hour before it was safe to head out, which was enough time for a quick nap. She set her alarm and quickly fell into a fitful doze. When she awoke, groggy and needing to pee, the room was dark. For a brief moment she thought she'd slept too long, but a peek at her alarm clock perched on a shelf next to her bed, told her it was only 8:13. Perfect. Still a little disoriented, she slid out of bed and padded over to her closet to find her black trench coat and Doc Martens, which were still damp, but usable. After pulling them on, she slipped her sporran over her head and grabbed her flashlight out of her backpack. She spotted the lantern and studied it for a moment. It really did look exactly like the one from the labyrinth that she'd just filled. It had to have come from the same place. But then, how did it get to the beach? Perhaps tonight she'd find out!

After making a pit stop and checking to see that Vicki was in her office bent over her desk as usual catching up on the week's paperwork, Pandora headed for the secret passage.

The night air when she left the building felt balmy on her cheeks. A warm front was moving in, bringing with it swirling currents of moist, heated air. Pandora stood for a moment, breathing in the freshness of brine and salt, and looking around. She wouldn't put it past Dr. Steele to be lurking about, waiting to bust her for…well, for what? She had a right to be outside and she didn't have school in the morning, and after all, it wasn't even that late. Vicki couldn't care less that Pandora was heading to the beach at this hour. In fact, she'd probably encourage it. Anything to get her child out of her hair.

Emboldened by this reminder of her right to do as she pleased, Pandora marched toward the gate. Unlocking it, she swung it open with vigor. Rusted a bit after all the rain, it gave a loud squeal resembling that of a tormented cat.

At the same time Pandora cursed the tattling gate, her eyes caught sight of a large shadow on the beach, heading toward The Fangs. At the sound, the figure started to run.

29

Tender Bits

FOR A BRIEF moment Pandora could only stand and stare at the running figure. Only it wasn't racing toward the outcrop anymore, it was running in her direction. What the Hades was going on? Several possible courses of action tore through her mind as she watched whoever it was bound toward her. Run away? Scream for help? Throw rocks? Go on the attack *while* throwing rocks?

There was only one option, of course. She'd never run from any challenge, and screaming was for wussies. That left the good, old-fashioned berserker attack. Flashlight in one hand and a rock in the other, Pandora raced down the path to the beach.

As soon as her feet hit the sand, she turned on the speed, moving to meet her enemy as quickly as he raced to meet her. Whoever it was, it was likely not a she. Too tall, for one. Too fast, for another. And judging by the sound of his footsteps thudding on the sand, not a ghost, either.

Ten feet from the stranger, she hollered, "I've got you now, you insolent cur!" and threw the rock as hard as she could. It flew over his head, just missing knocking him out.

The figure, much to Pandora's gratification, skidded to a halt. "Ah, crap, Pandora!"

"Xavier?" She stalked toward him. "What the hell are you doing down here? You said you were going to bed, you lying sack of sh—"

"Oh, cut the crap," he said. She couldn't make out his face very well, but she could see he was breathing hard, his shoulders rising and falling. "I couldn't sleep. What's your excuse?"

"I, um, well…" Dang. It was so easy to talk her way out of things with the inmates, the staff, and/or her mother. But with the coming of Dr. Steele and her new half-brother and their low tolerance for bull, Pandora found herself at a loss for words more often than she liked. "I needed proof," she finally managed to get out.

"Proof of what? That you're an idiot? This is terrible weather. You shouldn't be out in it."

"This is great weather and you know it."

To her surprise, he laughed. "Yeah, it is kinda cool." He looked about him, and she could almost see his pleased expression in the dark.

"I've always wanted to live by the ocean. You know, right on it. Me and my mom would go to the beach once or twice a year, but it wasn't the same, you know?"

She did know. "I suppose," she acknowledged. "But it's dangerous out here for people who don't know their way around."

"You said that before."

"I know I did. And it wasn't *just* to keep you from looking for our dad on your own. There really are some spots you have to watch out for." This was somewhat true. You did have to watch out for them if you were swimming or if the tide was coming in fast. Neither of these events happened to be going on at the moment, but Xavier didn't need to know that.

"Like what?" Okay, apparently he *did* need to know.

"Um, like mudslides after heavy rains."

"It hasn't been raining all that much."

"There are certain rocks and, um, areas you have to avoid when the tide's coming in."

"Well, point them out to me."

"I can't right now. I have a job to do."

"Oh, right. Your proof gathering. What was that about again?"

"I was going to look for footprints, you turd. But your running on the beach ruined that idea."

"Ah, good idea. Ghosts don't leave footprints."

"Exactly," she grumbled, slightly mollified. "So how did you get down here anyway?"

"Skippy's not the only one who can pick locks."

"You came through the big gate? I hope you closed it after you."

"What do you take me for?"

She decided to take the high road and not give the obvious answer. "It's very important not to leave any trail."

"I didn't leave one, trust me." A moment of silence passed. "So now what?"

She stuck her flashlight under her chin and flicked it on so that he could catch the full effect of her death glare. "It's your turn to come up with bright ideas since you *ruined* mine."

"I guess we could hide out and watch for the intruder."

It was a decent idea, but unfortunately it involved hanging out with her brother. The same brother who had lied and told her he wouldn't come down to the beach alone. Perhaps now was the time to teach him a lesson about fibbing to the wrong person. "I guess we could do that. As long as you don't mind the crabs. Oh, and be sure to watch out for jellyfish washed up on the shore."

"Huh?"

"The crabs are no biggie. Just don't let them crawl up your pant leg. They tend to go straight for the tender bits, if you know what I mean."

"Tender bits." Xavier sounded a bit sick.

Pandora swung the flashlight to shine on the sand and the flat expanse glistened in the light. "The jellyfish are worse. You get stung by one of those and I'll have to pee on the wound."

"Pee on it?" His voice was hoarse, almost washed away by the waves.

"Well, if we can't find any vinegar," she said, deciding to throw in some solid facts to sound more convincing. Xavier was a bit of a doubting Thomas, she had learned. "The lion's mane jellyfish lives in this part of New England. Usually they stay farther out, but sometimes they die and get washed up onto the beach. But, even though they might be dead, their stingers still work just fine." She left out that this sort of thing didn't usually happen until late summer and fall, if it happened at all. Information like that should only be provided on a need-to-know basis and right now Xavier didn't need to know.

"I'm wearing boots, though," he said, sounding more confident. "And pants. I can tuck them in. I'll be fine."

"Good. Just don't trip," she replied casually. "If you get stung in the face and you're allergic, it's curtains for you. Anaphylactic shock is nothing to sneeze at."

"Oh, yeah?" Xavier was starting to get suspicious. "Then why aren't you worried?"

"Because I've already been stung right on the nose," she pointed, "and I survived. Though for an entire week, I looked like I'd grown a pig's snout." All this was true. "It hurt a lot." Also, true. Not just physically. The staff had gone after her like hyenas at a wounded gazelle, calling her, among other things, pigheaded, wild boar, and Miss Piggy. She almost hadn't survived, but pouring an entire bottle of liquid laxative into the staff's giant coffee maker had pulled her through.

"A whole week?"

"The face is a particularly sensitive area, but it's not the only one. There's your tender—"

Xavier held up his hands. "I get the picture."

She aimed her flashlight at her face again. "That's why I carry this with me. You should get one. They come in handy at times like this."

"We'll use yours, then," he said.

She shrugged. "Suit yourself. The problem is, you want the light to shine directly in your path. It's the best way to pick up the reflection off the jellyfish parts."

Xavier rubbed a hand over his face, looking suddenly tired. "Just do your best."

"Oh, you bet. I really don't want to have to pee on you. I have a nervous bladder."

"I seriously doubt that. In fact, I don't think anything about you could be nervous. You could probably pee in front of a crowd."

She laughed. "I once did, during a Visitor's Day picnic on the lawn. I was only five at the time, and I was trying to pee like a boy. It's so much more convenient. You boys have it good, you know? Though I don't think I'd like such a delicate instrument hanging out there, swinging in the wind like that. Not very safe."

"Can we just go?"

"Aye, aye, Cap'n!" She tossed him a salute and set off down the beach toward The Fangs. "There are places on the rocks where we can hide, but that's also where we might find crabs. So when we get there, be sure to tuck your pants in."

He didn't answer, but he did follow after her. She moved quickly along the beach, not in the least worried about encountering a jellyfish. The only reason she got stung last time was because she hadn't known what the gelatinous blob was and after touching it several times she decided, on a stupid whim, to stick her face in it. One of its tentacles had flipped up onto the body and that's just where her nose happened to hit. She'd learned a valuable lesson that day. If you're going to stick your face into something, you damn well better know what it is.

It wasn't long before they reached the outcrop. "Be careful here," she warned. "The rocks are slippery." After some curses on Xavier's part, with a few choice ones she hadn't heard before sprinkled in, they reached a boulder about his height, with a crevice to slip behind if necessary. She'd used this particular spot many times to spy on the staff, and had learned a lot about life on those afternoons. More than she'd wanted to on some occasions. Still, it was all grist for the mill. "Better to be informed than ignorant," was her motto.

Recalling one of those days—when a college p.a. had been making out with a nurse like he was vying for octopus of the year—ignited a river of heat in her body. She wondered what it would be like if that had been her and Dr. Steele instead, and then remembered he might be her dad, and all those lovely feelings evaporated like a bucket of water on a campfire.

"So who is it again that we're pretty sure isn't our dad?" she demanded as they sat down on a rock. Cold and damp seeped through her pants and she shivered as she clicked off the flashlight.

"Dr. Steele, for sure," he said and she relaxed a little. "And Dr. Malik. That's it. That leaves," he ticked off his fingers, "Frank, J.T., Mayor Daft, and Dr. Snyder."

"You forgot someone," she said, not wanting to bring him up, but feeling she had to. "Cracker Jack."

"Cracker Jack? Are you serious? No way is *he* our dad."

"Why? Because he's crazy?"

Xavier shifted uncomfortably on his rock. "That's not it at all."

"Then what is it?"

He paused. "Okay, maybe that is it. I mean, he's got some real problems, doesn't he? Yesterday after we got back from Bedlam I saw him working in the field and when I shouted hi to him, he dove to the ground and covered his head." He sighed. "How's he going to be a dad doing stuff like that?"

"Don't you really mean, if he's my dad, am I going to get what he has?"

Xavier didn't answer for several seconds. Pandora counted twelve waves crashing against the shore before he finally said, "I guess I mean both."

"He's got post-traumatic stress disorder, you idiot. PTSD. Shell shock. It's not a genetic defect so he can't pass it on to you. It's like getting a weak heart from rheumatic fever. He got his sickness from seeing too much war and death and killing, so it's not his fault!" By the time she was finished speaking she was breathing hard and her hands were in fists. She felt an overwhelming urge to smack Xavier upside the head. How could people be so ignorant? She saw it time and time again in people who should know better. Not just with the inmates' families, but from the very people who were supposed to be helping the mentally ill get better.

"Yeah, but most people fight in wars and don't get PT...whatever," he persisted. "So doesn't that mean there's something wrong? A sort of weakness?"

Pandora's knuckles cracked. "Don't you think it's more normal to be horrified watching your friends' body parts get blown off? To see blood everywhere? To never feel safe? In war, nothing is stable. Nothing is normal or good or right."

He breathed out through his nose. "Well, when you put it that way..."

"I put it that way because it makes sense. It's not normal to simply accept people you care about getting creamed. It's not normal to face hell and not be affected. If people reacted to evil by shrugging their shoulders, the world would be full of Dougie Dafts."

Xavier shuddered. "All right, I get it. But he still couldn't be a real dad to us, could he?" he pursued, though he sounded wistful.

Pandora wasn't sure what to say. Cracker Jack was a super guy, but he was a bit immature. He looked up to Jun Li, for Pete's sake, and who in their right mind would look up to that skeaze? And, she hated to admit it, but she sort of agreed with Xavier. She wanted her dad to be someone to lean on, someone who would listen to her and call her his little princess. She wanted a Norman Rockwell dad…strong, yet caring. Wise, yet accepting. Their current list of dad candidates contained men she couldn't imagine ever sharing anything personal with, much less a hug.

"Not like we'd want him to be," she finally answered, her voice quivering a little.

"No," he said sadly. "Which is too bad because I like Cracker Jack."

"Yeah. Me, too." They didn't speak after that.

After a half hour of listening to the ocean creep closer, Xavier stretched and yawned. "I'm cold, and I'm tired. Time to go to bed." He stood up. "Coming?"

"Yeah, I guess so." She was cold, too, and her eyelids kept slipping downward. After scanning the beach one last time, she clicked on the flashlight and stood up. Together they hiked up the stony path to the main gate, Xavier slipping and sliding on the wet rock. Pandora unlocked the gate, ushered him through, and followed after him. "I have to lock the other one." She gestured in the direction of the fence as she slipped the black padlock back through the hole.

"Don't stay up too late. I want to hit the labyrinth after lunch and we need to be focused to solve that next clue."

"I can take care of myself," she grumbled.

"Ha. I've seen evidence of how well you take care of yourself."

"Oh, bugger off."

"Buggering off," he called laughingly as he loped off toward the stables. "Goodnight, sister dear!"

When his form disappeared into the shadows, she turned and locked the gate, then headed for the other one. When she reached it, she grabbed hold of a bar and pulled the gate toward her, but just before it clanged shut, an odd feeling came over her. She looked out at the beach and something strange near the outcrop of rocks caught her eye. A light, bobbing in and out of sight.

A lantern.

Pandora paused for only a moment before taking off through the gate, after the light. The figure was quick, covering the beach with long, rapid strides. It couldn't be Xavier. He'd just left her and there was no way, without a light and with his clumsy feet, that he could have made it down to the beach that quickly.

She probably wouldn't catch the intruder, but she could do what she'd plan to do in the first place—see his footprints. Regrettably, the tide was coming in fast now. Where before it rolled inward with a casual ease, barely noticeable as it engulfed the sandy beach, now it moved with purpose, eager to fill in all spaces and crevices within reach. One narrow strip of beach remained and that's where Pandora headed, her feet flying over the rocks. She hit the sand running. The dark shadow pushed relentlessly onward, unaware of her pursuit. Knowing it was a risk, she flicked on her flashlight and scanned the sand, moving the beam from right to left.

No footprints, not even a whisper of an imprint, showed themselves. Swearing under her breath, she flicked off the beam and focused on the figure, which was halfway to The Fangs. If she sprinted at top speed, she might catch him. The water licked at her shoes as she dashed down the beach, her breath coming in ragged gasps. Still, she kept running, desperate now to catch her quarry.

It wasn't until her prey had reached the outcrop that she realized why she hadn't found any footprints in the sand. The crazy git was walking in the water! It was the swirling, tugging kind that made you stumble and fall, then the insatiable current would drag you out to sea, claiming you forever. And yet the stranger's gait had remained smooth and steady, as though he were floating. Even now, he rose out of the sea and up onto the pile of rocks, seemingly effortlessly. What human could do that?

She pushed herself harder, though her mind was growing dizzy with pain. *You can do it*, she told herself, watching her feet. *Push it, push it!* Just when she thought she couldn't go any further, the pile of jagged rocks was at her feet. She looked up, but couldn't see the stranger or the light anywhere. A rush of water soaked her shoes and she quickly scrambled up onto a slippery boulder. She'd catch him on the other side. There was nowhere to go over there. Not with the tide this high.

Her foot slipped and she cracked her knee on a rock. "Holy Mother of Mary!" she cried into the wind, but she valiantly kept going, ignoring the pain. This was her last chance. She had to catch him. She clambered down to the other side, but now she was trapped. The water was too high and it was too dangerous to go any farther. She looked around, her eyes darting here and there in the darkness. Not seeing anything, she flicked on her flashlight and its beam cut through the inky black like sunlight through a cloud.

Nothing.

Only the sound of surf and the whistling of the wind and... Wait, what was that?

Someone was singing.

Death Cheated

30

PANDORA CROUCHED DOWN like a gargoyle and strained to catch the words. Despite the crashing surf, she could just make them out.

Succumbing to a cold, dark wave
I fought to rise again
I begged to God; my life to save
I cannot leave my Gwen.

The voice was lovely, a tenor not unlike the Irish folk singers Professor Robertson listened to in his room as he counted specimens, and it was filled with such melancholy Pandora could feel the emotion winging its way toward her through the night air like a million moths. "Dr. Steele?" she cried through cupped hands. He was the only person she knew who would be out here *and* singing an Irish tune. "Is that you?"

The singing abruptly cut off. She leaned forward, hearing only the sucking sound of the waves. Whoever was singing did not want to be found. But whoever it was was also in danger. Soon they would be trapped between the overhang of rocks and the deadly water below. Pandora waited, hoping to hear some sort of answer. She called again, "Dr. Steele! *Andrew!* You can't stay there—you'll die!"

At last she saw movement. A shadow pushed away from behind a rock pile and despite the crashing waves, entered the dark, swirling water. It strode through the ripping, tugging liquid as though it weren't there. What human would take such a risk? What human had that sort of strength? The singing began again.

I cannot leave my Gwen, you see
She's everything to me.
Don't make me go, I'll give my soul.
Death's shadow, hear my plea.

Pandora wanted more than anything to follow after the figure, nearly did, in fact, when a shout from behind stopped her cold. "Pandora Belfry, not another step!"

She spun around, teetered, and nearly fell backward, her arms pinwheeling like twin windmills. Just as she was about to fall into the sea, she threw herself forward, cracking her knees on the rocks.

"Dr. Steele?" she called into the darkness. She looked over her shoulder and saw nothing. Her stranger was gone. She turned back to face the figure climbing up The Fangs toward her. "How'd you get over here?"

He soon reached her side and grabbed her arm. Despite the cold and her raincoat, she could feel the heat of his fingers. "Are you daft, girl?" He pushed her down onto a rock. "What are you doing out here in the dark? Does your mother know you're here?"

She knew then that he was not the one who'd been singing. Her heart pulsed in her chest and throughout her body and everything suddenly seemed lighter, as though the world was bathed in a strange light. "Not certifiably," she answered his first question shakily. "And I...I was looking for the stranger," she admitted. "The one I saw the other night."

He sighed and sat down beside her, his hand still gripping her arm. "And I'll bet a pretty penny your mother doesn't know you're down here."

"I imagine she thinks I'm tucked safely in bed reading *Pippi Longstocking*."

He repressed a snort. "Why do you do these things, Pandora?"

"What things?" He groaned in response. "Oh, all right!" she relented. "I've already told you why. I'm looking out for Nepenthe Manor. I'm protecting it. What I'd like to know," she added, taking on a tone of righteous indignation, "is why you always seem to catch me doing these things?"

This time he laughed. "Maybe because now I know you don't listen to reason. I feel protective of those who aren't able to look out for themselves."

She bristled. "I can watch out for myself just fine, Dr. Steele. Been doing it for years."

"But what if this 'stranger' of yours attacked you? What then?"

"If he did, I'd use this on his head." She flicked on her flashlight and held it up for him to see.

He looked at it and sighed, the sound blending in with the rushing of the tide. "I admire your bravery, Pandora, but there comes a point when bravery turns into stupidity."

"But life isn't worth living if you aren't willing to take a few risks to—" She stopped herself. She'd been about to admit she was searching for her father and she wasn't ready for Dr. Steele to know about that. Not yet. Maybe not ever.

"To what?" he pursued. "Come now, Pandora. I can't let this go this time. You're going to get hurt and if I knew about your activities and didn't say something, well, then it'd be like I had hurt you myself."

She wanted to remind him that he'd already told on her to Vicki, but she decided now was not the time to get into that argument. She might need to use that bit of information against him at a later date. Besides, she wasn't ready to get into a confrontation with him. "I want to know if this person on the beach is real or a, well, a ghost." She waited for him to laugh.

"You're chasing a ghost?"

"I don't know. He's not like any human I know. I couldn't find any footprints. He walks through water like it's not there. I even heard him singing. Did you hear him?"

"I didn't hear anything. Just the waves and the wind." Pandora caught the taint of doubt flitting in and out amongst his words. He didn't believe she'd seen or heard anyone, which didn't surprise her. It was a common trait amongst those in the loony business to doubt anything they could not confirm with their own senses.

"You *do* think I'm daft."

He let go of her arm. "I don't think that. I just think that living here, with people who have serious issues, has inspired in you a very active imagination."

"Very nice turn of phrase, doc, but that's a load of crap and you know it."

"I don't think you're daft, Pandora," he tried again. "But I also believe that growing up in a mental health institute hasn't exactly been healthy for you. I don't think it's healthy for anyone, actually. That's why I've made it my goal to encourage patients to seek out a better life."

"Are you saying the inmates shouldn't be here?" This was going from bad to worse.

"Not all of them."

"Even though others put them here?"

"It isn't healthy to blame others for your problems. Patients must take personal ownership of their illness, or they'll never get better."

"Are you saying it's their fault they're sick? That they did this to themselves?" She could not believe what she was hearing.

"Yes and no," he replied calmly. "The mentally ill cannot get better if they keep those that have harmed them alive and well in their minds.

They didn't get this way on their own, but now they have to rely on themselves to beat their illness."

"*Beat* their illness?"

"Yes of course. How else will they be able to leave Nepenthe Manor, live on their own? They have just as much right as you do to a normal life."

"A normal life?" She snorted disdainfully. "I don't think anyone lives a normal life, Dr. Steele. Do you?" She shifted the flashlight to highlight his face.

For once he looked disconcerted, as though her words had found a way past his professional suit of armor. "I suppose no one does. But we must aim for equilibrium, don't you think? We *must* keep trying or…" His words, which had grown softer with each syllable, petered out. She glanced up at him. His eyes were focused on something far away.

"What's worse?" she wondered aloud. "Giving up, or giving false hope?"

"Giving up," he said fiercely, then rose with the suddenness of a startled bird. "I'm heading back. I'd appreciate it if you came with me."

She stood, feeling like a chastised child, and followed after him. Neither spoke another word as they climbed up to the gate. When they reached it, Dr. Steele ushered her through, then closed it behind him and locked it with his key.

"Goodnight, Pandora."

"Are you going to tell my mom?" she asked, realizing she actually hoped he would. That strange, stupid urge of wanting Vicki to know what her daughter was doing while her mother wasn't looking surged through her.

"No," he said wearily. "Just promise me you won't do this again. The beach at night is a dangerous place."

"He was singing," she said quietly, wanting to distract him from promises she couldn't keep, wanting his opinion, too.

"What?"

"He was singing a song. It sounded Irish. I thought it was you, but you were behind me."

"Irish, hm? Do you remember the words?" He was testing her, making her give him details.

"He was singing about a woman named Gwen. He was drowning, and he didn't want to die because then he'd never see her again. He begged death not to take him."

An eternity passed before Dr. Steele responded. This far up on the cliffs the ocean waves were muffled, but she could hear them all the same. She could also hear Dr. Steele's breathing. He sounded like he'd just run a mile. A hard mile.

"It's called *Gwen's Last Love*," he said finally. "It's a very old Irish song."

"You know it?"

"Yes, in fact, I sing it myself. I sing it when I walk on this beach every evening. That's why I happened to see you. When you turned on your light."

She stared at him. He was standing just outside the ring of light her flashlight threw and she couldn't see his face very well. "What happens to him? The drowning man?"

"He doesn't die."

"Oh," she breathed. "That's a relief."

"But Gwen does."

"What? Why?"

"Death takes her instead."

Her heart pounded in her head. "But the man said he couldn't leave his Gwen. That's why he wanted to live. Death cheated him!"

"Death is wily, Pandora. The man did not leave his Gwen. She left him."

"Oh, crap. That's still a cheat." Her fists clenched at the unfairness.

"I agree with you," he said. "Now go inside and get some sleep."

"Okay, I will," she replied softly.

He left her then and for a long time she stared at the empty space where he'd stood and wondered about what he'd said about death. And then she wondered who'd taken his song from him and made it his own? At last she turned to go, whistling the eerie tune to herself as she went inside to get some sleep.

31

Laughing Ghosts

AFTER WAKING FROM a dream of chasing laughing ghosts up and down the empty halls of Nepenthe Manor, Pandora lay in bed and decided that Dr. Steele was totally and utterly full of horse doodie. Giving false hope was not better than giving up. She'd seen enough cases, even her own, to know false hope was as insidious as snake poison, creeping through one's veins unseen until it's too late. By the time you realized you'd been foolish enough to believe life was going to get better, you were already screwed.

Encouraging the inmates to believe they could survive in the outside world was just plain codswallop. Simply put, they couldn't do it. Within days of being released, Lucy would burn someone's house down. Skippy would attempt suicide, and Birdy would threaten to murder the first person who pissed her off, and then try to make good on her threat. Charles was apt to jump in front of a bus to save a dog, fully believing he could stop the massive hunk of speeding steel with the palm of his hand. As far as Sinclair was concerned, the chaos of the outside world was sure to finish him off. He'd get caught in a fit that wouldn't end, and eventually it would kill him.

Or would it? Pandora realized suddenly that she wasn't so sure about that anymore. This past week Sinclair had been acting very strangely, putting up with all sorts of unusual events, and despite everything, even thriving. Maybe, just maybe, he was stronger than she thought he was.

It was all so confusing, but she was sure about one thing. Dr. Steele wasn't her stranger on the beach. But was her stranger a ghost and visible only to her, or was it just that Dr. Steele hadn't been able to see him, or the lantern, for some reason or another, like hysterical blindness? She didn't know, nor was she any closer to answering the question: If not Dr. Steele, then who?

Feeling out of sorts, Pandora crawled down from her bunk and shuffled over to one of the windows. She leaned her forehead against the cool glass and sighed heavily. It was pouring. Again. She almost couldn't believe it. The rain was coming down so hard she could barely see across the lawn. She wouldn't be able to explore the labyrinth, head into town, or even exercise Shadow in the paddock. It was going to be a long day.

It turned out to be a long week. Day after day the rain continued, initially inspiring jokes about building an Ark and sprouting gills, jokes that grew more half-hearted with each passing hour. The endless rain and the strangely warm air outdoors made everything inside feel damp and heavy. The dense moisture weighted everything down—Pandora's eyelids, her lungs, even her limbs. Several times she checked to see if fungus was growing between her fingers.

Each day, the posse grew increasingly out of sorts, with Birdy acting as the spark to the tinder. She didn't go quite as far as to completely avoid the inmates; she'd stay in the same room, but she wouldn't sit with them or talk to anyone, which was even worse. On Tuesday afternoon, and the third straight day of rain, when Lucy tried for the tenth time to get Birdy to talk, she snarled at her to "go to hell and take your stupid friendship bracelet with you."

Lucy, of course, started up one of her own funks after that, which meant harassing the other inmates. Her first target was poor Charles, who was trying to work on his comic strip. She only stopped making fun of his "baby butt" drawings when he started crying and his lips turned purple. After that came Sinclair. He was performing his counting ritual in the TV room and she kept throwing cushions at his head and throwing him off count, and he had a fit. As the p.a.s took him away on a stretcher, Pandora thought she could detect relief in his frantically rolling eyes. This was more like the old Sinclair, though it did nothing to soothe Pandora's worries.

For his part, Skippy shuffled around the room like a zombie, circles darkening the hollows beneath his glazed eyes, his shoelaces untied and his t-shirt on backwards. Pandora tried talking to him, but he wasn't up to listening. He'd nod every few seconds, but his eyes were far away. He didn't even want to set up a special watch out Sinclair's window to see if they could spot the stranger, or attend the weekly Midnight Meeting in the attic, so Pandora was forced to cancel it. The rule was, if someone couldn't come, then it didn't happen.

She wasn't happy to be proven right about the posse, but she *was* right. They couldn't handle the stressors of everyday life. And now she was starting to wonder about her own ability to cope. With each passing hour, she felt herself growing more and more desperate. No one wanted to do anything, and everyone was grumpy, even the doctors and nurses. The whole manor felt like it was under siege, bombarded by endless issues, from excessive bedwetting to irrational outbursts to

Jun Li pouring glue into the arts and craft paint bottles. All of this doubled the staff's workload and when the staff was overworked, they, with the exception of Nurse Joanna and J.T., became downright belligerent. Even Dr. Steele wasn't his usual self. Several times a day, Nurse Rackett hunted him down to seek his opinion on one thing or another, and while he was polite and patient with her, his shoulders would drop and he'd tiredly rub his face after she turned to leave.

Through necessity (a belligerent staff was not her friend) and boredom, Pandora took up watch from various hiding places throughout the manor. But by Wednesday, the charm of spying had worn off. The breakdown in order wasn't enough to keep her mind off all the mysteries swirling around in her head, nor did it keep her from thinking about Dougie and the looming dance. She had to *do* something.

But there was nothing to do. She'd already refilled the lantern and even checked to see if the one in the secret room was still there—it was. Not even the forbidden library-cum-therapists' lounge offered any solace. She simply couldn't settle to reading any of the books, most of which she'd already read anyway. Xavier was lucky. Except for meals, he generally stayed away from the manor, likely helping Carl or unpacking. When she woke yesterday morning she found a note from Vicki telling her she was going to accompany Xavier back home to pack his stuff and to be sure his grandmother knew where he was. Pandora envied Xavier's freedom to escape at will, with something useful to do, to boot. She also envied him his room away from the never-ending chaos in the manor.

To prove how despairing she was, she actually dug in for the next two days and completed her entire homework list for the rest of the school year, except her experiment on pheromones (which was more of a long-term assignment). By the time she was finished it was late Thursday night. She should've been ecstatic, but she only felt numb as she hauled the pile of papers and assignments down to Vicki's office.

Vicki wasn't there, which was strange, and the door wasn't locked, which was stranger. Pandora had been hoping to get a little praise for all her hard work, so where was the woman? After scouting around to be sure mommy dearest wasn't in her secretary, Bennington's office, either, she plopped down in Vicki's squeaky chair and dropped the load of homework onto her desk. Damn the woman. When Pandora actually wanted to see her, she was impossible to find.

Too tired to seek her out, she decided to head up to bed and get some sleep. Her fingers were cramped from writing and her eyes blurry from reading instructions written by Nazis intent on brainwashing her.

She was crossing the foyer when she heard voices drifting toward her from Quack Central. Quick as a deer, she scampered behind a large urn near the curved staircase and squatted low.

"We're not doing enough to prepare these people to re-enter society," Dr. Steele argued passionately, his voice carrying like an echo down the hallway.

"Oh, Andrew," Vicki sighed, solving the mystery of where she'd been—with Dr. Steele. Pandora's stomach churned. "I thought we discussed this. The patients here will never be able to function normally. They're very sick and need my, *our* protection to keep them safe."

"So you're determined to sentence them to a life of institutional living?" He sounded angry. Pandora leaned closer. They were passing through the foyer now, heading for the main door.

Vicki stopped suddenly and spun around to face Dr. Steele, her flowered skirt flaring. Her finger pointed accusingly at his chest. "Let me tell you something, doctor. I've been running this place for almost fifteen years now and I've learned a thing or two about life. And what I've learned is that it's not all it's cracked up to be. The people living here are special. I won't have them suffer. And out in the real world they *will* suffer. I can guarantee you that because that's exactly what they were doing when I found them."

He ran a tired hand over his face. "Life *is* suffering, Director Belfry. It's also about joy and freedom and taking risks. When do the residents of Nepenthe Manor ever get to experience any of these basic rights that you and I enjoy every day?"

"So you're saying they're miserable here?" Vicki challenged.

He shook his head, then held out his hands as though making a plea to her. "Don't you see what's happening to them? They're so protected here that the slightest thing, like a few rainy days, sets them off. We need to strengthen them, teach them healthy ways to cope with the difficulties of life so they know how to handle it when something challenging happens. And then, when they're ready, we need to set them free."

"Free?" Vicki's voice was harsh. "I'm afraid, Dr. Steele, that you have no idea what you're talking about. You've been working here for what, two weeks? And suddenly you're an expert on life at Nepenthe Manor? Freedom will kill them."

He bowed his head a moment, then looked directly into Vicki's eyes. "I think I have a fresh perspective, that's all. As a newcomer I'm going to see things you no longer see. And what I see is a group of young people who are rotting inside these walls. I see a 14-year-old girl who thinks just like you do and sees herself as appointed protector of this place. She doesn't see a future for herself outside the manor. Is that what you want for your patients? For your own daughter?"

Pandora's heart thudded in her chest. What was he doing? What was he trying to say?

"Don't you dare tell me what's best for my daughter. And the next time I want your opinion on how to run Nepenthe Manor, I'll ask you. Until then, I expect you to do your work according to my rules and standards. If you're unable to comply, say so now." Pandora wondered if her mother had any idea how much she resembled her own mother at that moment. Vicki was not a fan of Grandmother Belfry, who, with her icy blue eyes and white blond hair, was very possibly a reincarnation of some Nordic war goddess.

"I don't have any plans of leaving," he replied, his voice equally cool. Pandora let loose a huge sigh of relief. She couldn't bear the idea of him abandoning her. Despite his ratting her out, he was the one ray of light in this place. If he ended up going because her mother couldn't handle a little freethinking, Pandora would run away and never come back. She'd wanted to leave for as long as she could remember, anyway. Hadn't she?

Vicki nodded brusquely. "Good. I hope we can set aside our differences and do what's best for the residents living here. We can't let our emotions get in the way of making good decisions. I'll see you tomorrow." With one last nod, she pivoted on her heel and marched toward her office like a general who'd just given the order to attack. Dr. Steele watched her go, flinching slightly as the heavy office door slammed hard. Then, slowly, as though in pain, he crossed to the main door, opened it, and disappeared outside. The door clicked shut behind him.

Pandora fell back against the wall, stunned. Had she really just witnessed Vicki and Dr. Steele fighting? She pulled in a deep breath and smiled. She had. And Dr. Steele was worried about her, too. He cared about her. More than Vicki did anyway.

Too bad he didn't get it about Nepenthe Manor. Pandora hated to admit it, but Vicki knew what she was talking about. The inmates were special and they needed protection. They wouldn't get that in the outside world.

Of course, if she believed what Dr. Steele was saying, neither would they experience freedom or the joy of independence, the wonder of making their own decisions, having families of their own. They wouldn't get hurt, true. But they also wouldn't be truly living, would they?

And if staying here meant missing out on life, Pandora herself was stuck in the same boat as the inmates—a boat that sailed safely onward, yet never going anywhere. Never landing. Never sinking. But safe, always safe.

A Bit Hypocritical

32

PANDORA WOKE TO a strange phenomenon. Sunshine. It filled her room with near blinding light and her entire being with hope. The rain had gone. It was going to be a beautiful day. She yawned and stretched as she padded over to the window and her eyes, as they had for most mornings of her life, fastened on the labyrinth.

Today's the day I'm going to crack it, she told herself. And she believed she would. She could feel the answers waiting for her like children in a game of hide and seek. Today she would crack the code, figure out the secret, find the center. *And then what?* Would any of it help her find her father? Get her out of her date with Dougie tomorrow night? Learn the identity of the stranger on the beach? Keep things from changing?

Likely not.

But that wasn't going to stop her from trying. Whistling cheerfully, she headed off to the bathroom. It was almost eleven already so she hurried through her lukewarm shower, drying off haphazardly when she was done. She braided her wet hair, got dressed, then scarfed down a bowl of Cheerios.

The phone rang as she was rinsing out her dishes in the sink. She turned off the water and stared at the ringing instrument in annoyance. She hated telephones. They never imparted good news. Not for her, anyway. She set the bowl to dry in the dish rack, then picked up the phone with dripping fingers.

"Addam's residence," she growled in her best Lurch imitation.

"Hello, Pandora," Dougie whispered.

She fumbled the phone and nearly dropped it before clapping it to her ear. "What is it, Dougie? I have a busy morning ahead of me."

"I stopped by the other day. You were nowhere to be found."

Oh, crap. She'd forgotten all about his threat to visit. "I imagine I was somewhere."

"I told you I was coming."

"I thought that was an open-ended thing. Like you might stop by some afternoon. Didn't think you meant that day."

"I did." He paused. "But that's not why I'm calling. I was wondering if you bought your dress for the dance yet."

"Dress?" The thought of what she was going to wear had never once occurred to her.

"Yes. Typically that's what the female wears to a dance. I'll be wearing a white tuxedo."

"Isn't wearing white a bit hypocritical for someone like you?"

There was silence. "The cummerbund is Devil's Red."

"That's more like it."

"I thought it was a nice touch."

"I don't own a proper dress," she said, hope surging through her, "and I can't afford to buy one."

"I thought you'd say that," he replied, almost gleefully. "So I picked one out for you. When can I bring it over for you to try on?"

From his tone, Pandora guessed he was picturing himself watching her through the whole 'trying on' process. "How about never?"

"You really are funny, Pandora. One of the many reasons why I like you. My parents were quite surprised at my choice of a date, however. Especially father. I think he suffered a minor stroke when I mentioned that I was bringing you. Mother, of course, hasn't talked to me since I told her. It's been delightfully quiet for the last couple of days."

Pandora stifled a laugh. Dougie might be a poisonous toad, but she had to admit, sometimes he was quite amusing. "Your dad nearly popped a vein, huh?"

"He says you're crazy, you know. It's what everyone in town says. They tell me that if I take Bats Belfry to the dance you'll probably turn on me and stab me in the heart."

Wow, the townsfolk were more astute than she'd given them credit. Still, she felt an urge to prove them wrong. "All right. I suppose since the dance is tomorrow," she paused to catch her suddenly absent breath, "you'd better have Bartles bring it over this afternoon. Tell him to leave it in the foyer. I'll find it."

"The dress cost five hundred dollars, so there is no chance it will be left unattended anywhere in that building, and I'll bring it to you myself."

"Five hundred bucks? Are you kidding me? That could buy a lot of food."

"Yes, I imagine it could buy bags and bags of tater tots."

"Right. So I think you should return it and donate the money to the manor."

"It's long and black."

"You bought me a black dress?" Despite herself, she was intrigued.

"You'll like it. I certainly do." She shuddered, glad he couldn't see her face. "And it's not returnable."

"Oh, fine. I'll meet you at the door at 5:30." She could always sell it to Diana's Dress Emporium afterward.

"Five," he amended.

She was tempted to argue, just because he sounded so sure of himself. Lucky for him she had a lot to get done before then and couldn't afford to waste any more time. "All right. Five."

"I'm looking forward to it."

"Great," she mumbled. "See you then."

"Yes you will." He hung up.

She did the same, but with more emphasis, the phone's bell ringing lightly as she slammed the receiver into its cradle. "Damn his creepy eyes." She peered at her watch. Crap. Most of the morning was gone. She'd hoped to have a solid two hours to scout out the labyrinth before Xavier was free from his morning chores. After all this rain, he'd be chomping at the bit to get in. The posse had their classes and therapy so they wouldn't be free until three. She looked around the kitchen. Maybe if she brought along a lunch she could get two hours without interruption.

There was little to choose from, but in the end she managed to whip together a pb & j sandwich using the end pieces of a loaf of bread. She stuffed potato chips into a baggie and grabbed a Granny Smith apple, the same color as the spring leaves outside, from the crisper drawer. After fetching her sporran, a backpack, a bottle of Coke, and whipping up a note for Charles, she was ready to go.

Even though everyone was otherwise occupied at this time, she made sure to check all hallways and the foyer before entering them, and practiced extra caution when she delivered the note to the posse's secret spot behind the potted fern in the foyer. Charles was the only one who checked it daily, so she'd made the note out to him, telling the posse to come to the maze at three o'clock. By the time they showed up, the labyrinth's secret would be exposed!

Ordinarily, she might feel a little guilty about leaving the posse out, but it wasn't like they enjoyed working out the clues, so she wasn't taking anything away from them. They would like seeing the center of the labyrinth, however, she was sure of that. Besides, she had to do it this way. Figuring out the secret wouldn't solve her problems, but she needed to feel successful at *something*, even if it was solving a dumb old maze.

She made it outside and across the lawn without anyone seeing her. The scent of plum tree blossoms followed her as she ran and she began to feel a lifting of her spirits. Spring, with its warm breezes, vivid blue skies, and explosion of life all around, was here at last. How could anyone stay down for long at such a time?

Well, Skippy could. If Dr. Steele really understood Skippy he would know that a boy like him would never survive in the real world. If Skippy couldn't handle his problems at Nepenthe Manor, where great efforts were made to reduce one's chances of ever being exposed to reality, he wouldn't be able to handle it out in the real world where no such buffers existed. Of course, if he were taught better ways to cope like Dr. Steele had said, he wouldn't need to be so protected. *She* wouldn't have to protect him. It was a strange and troubling thought.

She'd almost made it to the labyrinth when a voice boomed out from the trees, startling her. "Just what do you think you're doing?" She froze, then slowly turned around to see Xavier emerge from the copse. "I've been keeping an eye out for you," he said. He was wearing jeans with holes in the knees and a dirt-streaked Red Sox t-shirt. His good hand grasped a muddy spade.

"I was only looking," she protested. *For the center of the labyrinth.*

"For the center of the labyrinth," he finished for her. He already knew her too well. Which really sucked.

"Yeah, so? There's no law against looking, is there?"

"No, but wouldn't it be nice to share the discovery with your beloved brother and friends?"

"I imagine it would be thrilling. But frankly, I don't care anymore. I need to find the answer," she gestured wildly at the labyrinth, "before I lose my mind!"

"Well, you're going to have to wait. I wasn't spying on you, actually—Carl wants you to walk the horses in the paddock. He figures your ribs can handle that by now. No riding, though."

She groaned. "Can't you do it?"

"Can't." He lifted the shovel. "I'm transplanting apple trees. And I hate horses."

A howl of frustration burned in Pandora's chest. If she didn't do what Carl said, he'd take away her horse privileges. "Can't you say you didn't see me?"

Xavier smiled. It wasn't a nice one. "Too late. I was working with Carl when I spotted you. Of course I had to tell him what I was staring at."

She regarded him suspiciously. "So how are you digging with one hand?"

"Very carefully." He grinned. "Now come along, squirt. We've work to do."

Feeling very much like kicking something, or *someone*, Pandora followed after him, grumbling and cursing his future progeny. She begrudgingly waved to Carl, who was spitting out tobacco juice while watching her stumbling progress to the stables with hawkish intensity.

Two hours later, she finally finished walking, feeding, and brushing down all the horses. Shadow, of course, had been troublesome. The frantic horse needed a real ride, but with all this rain, not even Carl had been able to get her out for a good gallop. Like a spoiled toddler, she nipped at Pandora's hands, stomped her hoof, and did everything she could to be a pain in the butt. Pandora had to spend extra time with her, making her do tricks and jumps, anything to wear her out a little. In the end, she gave up and pushed her back in her stall and locked the gate.

After wolfing down her sandwich and chips, Pandora finally made it back to the labyrinth by a quarter after one, which gave her almost two hours to do what needed to be done before the posse showed. Hopefully Xavier and Carl would remain working out in the apple orchard for a good while longer.

She lowered the drawbridge, scrambled inside, and raised it once more. Determined, she quickly made her way to the spot where they'd left off—the corridor that ended with a door to the left, which led back out, and a door to the right, which was a mystery. What did the mystery door hide behind it? She scampered down the passage to find out.

The doorknob, when she turned it, protested like old bones. Remembering Xavier's words about savoring the experience, she hesitated a moment and realized she felt like an archeologist about to enter the pyramids for the first time. Her heart beat excitedly and butterflies inside her stomach fluttered madly. She obviously wasn't the first person to pass through this door, but it likely had been a long time since anyone had. She could feel her fellow explorers standing beside her with bated breath, listening as she did to the strange noise on the other side of the door—a sort of thunk, thunk, thunk, and a continual splashing sound, like water running into a tub. Perhaps it was a good thing to savor the moment once in a while, as Xavier had suggested, because this particular experience, which was vastly exciting, would never happen again.

Filled with the thrill of anticipation, she pushed on the door, and at first, it resisted her push, before giving in with a jerk. Unprepared, she fell forward and landed on her knees. A pain in her left knee flared up like an angry bird. She'd bruised it good on the rocks last night, turning her kneecap a wondrous purple.

Gritting her teeth, she pushed herself to her feet and looked around. Not far from where she stood was a round, dark pool, which reflected the sun like an old mirror. Next to it stood a tall, narrow stone building, dotted with round, dusty windows and capped by a cone-shaped roof. Attached to the building, a wheel, pale green with lichen and algae, and rising nearly as high as the wall, spun around and around—thunk, thunk, thunk—water falling from its paddles to the pool below. A ten-foot long sluice above the wheel provided the water, but where the water came from was a mystery.

Pandora ran over to the pool, thrilled with her discovery. After a few minutes of exploration she determined that the system was self-perpetuating via a strange contraption operated by cogs and chains inside the building. For something that had been built such a long time ago the mechanism appeared to be quite complex. But why was the water wheel here in the labyrinth? And how did it keep running after all these years?

A large, flat stone, moist and dark and sitting parallel to the wheel, served as a sort of platform. Pandora stepped onto it and stuck her hand into the water. The sun was hot here and the cold water felt good on her skin. She slid her other hand into the stream, then splashed a few handfuls onto her face. Dripping, but refreshed, she looked around, wondering where to go next. This spot was certainly cool, but she sensed it wasn't the center.

She wasn't surprised when she realized she couldn't see any way out. Whoever had built the labyrinth was quite fond of such antics. She left the stone and wandered around the enclosed area, searching high and low for any sign of a door. When she couldn't find any, she explored the ground. Unlike in the passages, this area was covered in moss and dirt, with not a stone to be seen. No trapdoors here.

Reluctantly she headed back to the door, pulling off her jacket and tying it around her waist as she walked. This spot was a red herring—a trick to throw her off the trail. It looked like she was going to have to backtrack all the way to the trapdoor and start over. *Typical labyrinth tricks*, she thought to herself. Irritated, but determined to keep trying, she faced the door and reached for the handle…

…a handle that didn't exist.

33

Grist to the Mill

SHE SHOULD'VE KNOWN. The other door, the one that led back to the 30-door corridor, was exactly the same…no handle. No way back. She had no choice now. She had to keep moving forward. But how? There seemed to be no way out. Not one that she could find anyway. There had to be a secret, but what was it?

Shading her eyes, she glanced up at the sky. She had to get herself out of this predicament, and soon. She wasn't a claustrophobic, but she could become one if she stayed trapped in here much longer. She spun around, her eyes searching for answers. Something nagged at her mind. A clue. There must be a clue. But where?

She found a stone and sat down, forcing herself to breathe deeply and evenly. When she'd calmed down, she opened her sporran for a stick of gum. Chewing sometimes helped her think. She rooted around, searching for a pack of Bubble Yum, and pulled out a piece of paper instead. It was the poem. She smacked herself on the forehead. Why hadn't she thought of it earlier? Now that it was in her mind she could even remember a bit of it. Something about a dead-end and a bend. She quickly scanned the next line in the rhyme:

When you hit a dead-end, for surely you will, don't go round the bend, put grist to the mill.

Put grist to the mill. She glanced up at the wheel. She'd definitely met a dead-end so she'd gotten that part right. But, put grist to the mill? What did that mean? She didn't have any grist. A lot of moss and bits of grass, certainly, but they would only fill the pool with shredded moss and grass. And besides, didn't the saying go, grist *for* the mill? Was this another Sinclair screw-up?

Oh, crud. In her hurry she hadn't stopped to check the poem and fix the mistakes. She'd had the perfect opportunity and she'd blown it. "I hate this place!" A loud whooshing sound startled her and she looked up to see a crow flapping his wings at her. "Go away, fiend!" He didn't go away. Instead he glided down to land on a rung of the water wheel and glared at her with beady eyes, his posture arrogant as he rode the plank like a Ferris wheel.

"Envy me, earthbound creature," he seemed to be saying. "Because, truly, I'm so much cooler than you."

"I'd fly if I could," she grumbled. When the crow reached the wheel's summit, he pushed off with a squawk and flew over the wall out of sight. "Show-off."

She propped her chin on her hand and watched the wheel circle around and around. It reminded her of the old spinning wheel in her Grandmother Belfry's perfect showcase of a living room. She didn't actually use the ancient contraption, but Vicki knew how to work it. She'd once taught Pandora how to turn a puff of wool into yarn. At the time Grandmother Belfry was out in the garden or she would've stopped such nonsense. Her precious antiques were for looking at, never for touching. Maybe that's why they didn't often visit the Grand ol' Belfrys.

Unable to figure out what could be the grist and what could be the mill, Pandora stood up and wandered over to the back part of the wheel. She let the rungs slap against her hand and the resulting sound was almost metallic. Metallic? She leaned closer to get a better look and water sprayed her face. She wiped her eyes, then reached out and rubbed away a bit of the pale green coating. What she saw underneath answered one of her questions—how the wheel was still intact after all these years. It was made from metal—aluminum, she guessed, being that it hadn't rusted.

With a flat palm, she pushed down on a paddle and it pushed back as it lifted upward. She pushed harder, wondering if putting fist to the mill counted. Likely not, but it would make her feel better. Grabbing hold of one of the metal rungs, she relaxed and let it rise, taking all her weight. Soon the wheel would have to stop. She was far too heavy to lift.

But it didn't stop. In the blink of an eye, her feet left the ground and she was rising up into the air. "Hey!" Her fingers on the wet metal started to slip. Already about four feet off the ground, her feet kicked about, looking for something to catch her weight. Her fingers slipped again and she nearly fell. Using the last of her strength, she renewed her grip and let her feet search for leverage. A searching toe found another rung and Pandora cautiously slid her feet onto the plank and let it take her weight. It held. She was safe.

That is, until she realized that the wheel was near its apex, whereafter it must go down again, taking her with it. At the very least, she'd end up in the pool. At the worst, she'd slip and fall and break her neck. Panicking, her glanced around, fearing imminent death. There was no way out of this.

But then, as she rose higher into the air, she noticed something. The tall building had a flat platform at the back, tucked in beneath the conical roof. She had a chance to get off the wheel, but only if she could get her timing right and jump from wheel to platform in one try.

She scooted closer to the building, counted to three, and then jumped. Her stomach leaped into her throat as she soared through the air, and for a moment she thought she wasn't going to make it. But then her feet hit metal and she landed far more easily than she would've thought possible. She looked back and saw that the platform sat slightly lower than the top of the wheel, so a person really only had to jump down. It was a leap even Lucy could make, especially if someone helped her.

Following the platform around a corner, Pandora spotted where to go next. Hidden from observers on the ground, the platform slanted up, leading toward the wall. Pandora hurried up the ramp, grateful for the iron bars on each side, which kept one from falling fifteen to a horrendous death, or, at the very least, to a very painful sprained ankle.

She soon realized that she'd be able to see the entire labyrinth from up on the wall, and when she reached the top, she turned around with a happy grin. At last she was going to find the way to the center! But her expectations were soon dashed. For while she could see most of the grounds of the estate from this position, and even parts of the first half of the labyrinth, she couldn't see the rest because of another, higher wall blocking her view. She couldn't help thinking it had been built solely for the purpose of spoiling any chance she might have at solving the puzzle simply by looking down. Her stomach gurgled with frustration. More trickery!

Her only choice now, it seemed, was to enter what looked like a covered, stone bridge. Feeling like a pot about to boil over, she entered the dark tunnel and began to make her way through it. Cool and quiet, it was a place that conjured up images of secret meetings, where the passing of confidential information occurred on a regular basis. Pandora pulled out her flashlight and clicked it on. She shined it along the arched ceiling and down at the dead leaves lining the cobbled walk, but its beam found nothing more interesting than spider webs and their many-legged inhabitants. As she walked she ran her hand along the rough stone surface. Halfway along the passage her fingers hit a blip. She stopped and backed up. Shining her light at the wall, she saw that someone had carved something into the stone.

Six letters. *PRJCVB*. Pandora stared at them for several moments, then reached up and traced each one with her fingertip. Someone had spent some time carving these. She wondered what they stood for and thought it might be a code. She'd once come across a code in a spy book where each letter stood for the 'opposite' letter in the alphabet. That is, A = Z, B = Y. She tried it and came up with: KIQXEY. Kiqxey? That didn't make any sense. She mentally rearranged the letters into two words. Key and Qix. Key and kicks, maybe? Perhaps she was supposed to kick a key. Right.

To make matters worse, her beam found two more letters, set apart from the other six—*EN*. She was going to have to start over! She sighed. Forget that. The letters probably meant nothing and time was a-ticking.

She glanced at her watch. Holy crap, it was after three already! *Why* did she leave that note for Charles and the others, telling them to join her? Why did she always feel like she had to watch out for them? She glanced back and forth between the way she'd come and the light at the end of the tunnel. What should she do? They would be arriving at the labyrinth at any moment; Xavier might already be here. She could return to the wheel and wait for them, or she could forge on ahead. Either way she was going to look guilty.

Damned if I do. Damned if I don't. She lifted her shoulders in a shrug. She might as well be damned for a sinner as a saint. Hunching her shoulders determinedly, she continued on down the tunnel. The posse was on its own. And so was she.

When she reached the end of the bridge she realized suddenly that she wasn't alone. She stopped walking and listened. A voice off in the distance, soft and murmuring, drifted toward her. Stone steps led downward and her feet flew over them. Was the posse already in the labyrinth? It was quite possible, especially if Xavier had gone to fetch them. So if they were here already, the question now was, how far had they gotten? Sinclair had memorized the poem and he was quick. He'd figure out the last clue faster than she had. She didn't have much time.

But when she saw what awaited her at the bottom of the steps, she couldn't help herself. She had to stop. Before her a white stone forest stretched on and on like the tombstones at Arlington National Cemetery. What must be at least a hundred trees, their tops level with the surrounding walls, grew from the stone floor. Pandora took a tentative step forward to touch one. The bark was smooth, the branches strong. She took another step, then another. Soon she was walking through the eerie white forest. In the middle of it, she found the stumpy remains of a giant stone tree, cut down nearly to its roots. She skirted around it and continued forward. Several steps farther on, she spotted a curved wall, and within that wall was a doorway. Things were looking up. She glanced back one last time before stepping through the opening...and into hell.

Corridor after corridor sprouted like spider legs from an eight-foot long, oval stone. Along each corridor open doorways beckoned to her, beguiling as sirens. She sprinted down the closest corridor. It curved to the right, then to the left, then back again. And then it stopped. Pandora's fists banged against the dead-end wall, then she kicked it with all her might, stubbing her big toe. She cursed loudly and hopped around clutching her foot. Stupid labyrinth! Once again, the fiendish mind that had created this infuriating hellhole had outwitted her, and she didn't like it one bit.

Luckily, this time she remembered the poem right away. Not feeling particularly hopeful, she fished it out and studied it with increasing frustration. *If you get stumped as the end grows near, lean forward now and closer peer.* Well, she was definitely stumped so she went ahead and did what it told her. She leaned closer to the paper and peered at it with all her might, hoping to pick out some sort of message hidden between the lines. *End. Grows. Lean. Peer.* Each word could be a potential clue, but in and of itself, was pretty senseless. She rearranged the words and snickered as she read aloud, "The lean peer's end grows." Did it mean she had to look for a skinny, noble guy with a big butt? No problem. There should be lots of those hiding in a forest of trees.

Having no other ideas, Pandora pushed herself to her feet and stumbled back into the stone forest. The leafless trees looked more foreboding now. She weaved in and out amongst them, searching for big-butted peers. After several minutes of aimless wandering, she plopped down on the huge tree stump and tried to think. But it was getting late, the sun was casting sinister shadows through the lifeless branches, and the ideas just wouldn't come. Damn it all, the posse was on its way and she was stumped while sitting on a stump and...

"Oh, you've got to be kidding me!" She slid off her seat and peered closely at the stone stump. At first all she saw was a dizzying spiral of rings, then she leaned closer and the answer appeared to her like a boat's prow splitting the fog. She laughed out loud. For the last several minutes, while she had moped and despaired, she'd been sitting on the answer all along. The rings in the tree stump represented the corridors in the labyrinth.

Unable to decipher anything, she pulled a magnifying glass out of her sporran. Tiny pictures slowly sharpened and came into focus. She made out the 30-door corridor and the trapdoor, the water wheel and bridge, and now the stone forest with its storytelling stump, all right before her.

She traced the path from the stone forest to the center of the maze. When her finger arrived at the middle, she found the space blank. No tiny pictures. No symbols. Nothing. Perhaps nothing was there. Then again, maybe amazing wonders and treasure filled the space from wall to wall. Finger tapping, she counted the number of passages to reach the center of the labyrinth, all the while thinking of the owl asking how many licks did it take to reach the center of a tootsie pop?

Realizing the path was more complicated than she'd thought, she pulled a pen out of her sporran and wrote: *At door 9, turn right. At 1, turn left. 13, right.* And so on…

When she was finished jotting down the key, she hustled back to the opening on the other side of the forest. She was about to re-enter the maze when she heard voices again. The posse was coming! But wait…it wasn't a group of voices she was hearing, merely one, and it was singing.

The spirit was in the maze.

34

BUT WHERE WAS it, and what was it doing in *here?* Pandora knew the answer to the first question before she'd even finished asking the second. He was at the center of the maze, of course. Waiting for her.

The spirit's voice could still be heard as she sprinted down the corridor, sheet of paper in hand, searching for the first turn. She rounded a corner and ended up passing under the covered bridge. Overhead, the sound of echoing voices filled her ears, this time a whole slew of them. The posse had almost caught up to her. She stopped to listen.

"I'm not taking another step," Birdy whined. "I really don't know why you had to drag me along, Xavier. I was perfectly happy doing my nails."

"I didn't drag you along," Xavier replied testily. "I simply asked if anyone wanted to come with me to the labyrinth."

"You were looking directly at me when you asked. I know you, Xavier Carlisle! You couldn't stand not having me along."

"Can we just go?" he snapped.

"But I'm famished," she replied. "Whatever that crap was for lunch today just didn't cut it."

"I can fetch you something to eat," Skippy volunteered. "I'll be back before you know it."

"Oh, right. And how are you going to carry anything without a spine?"

"Will you shut up about the boy's spine?" Xavier shouted, sounding on the verge of losing it. "Just because he wants to please you doesn't make him spineless." There was silence. "Now we have to hurry," he went on in a calmer voice. "Come on, Sinclair. Lead the way."

"This is so stupid!" Birdy complained again, but hearing the click of her heels on the stone bridge, Pandora knew she wasn't about to get left behind. Complaining was her way of making sure she wasn't forgotten.

Before Pandora started up again, she pulled out a piece of chalk to mark the way. At the ninth passage on the right, she drew an X next to the arched opening and turned. She took the first left, then the thirteenth right, marking each turn as she went. For the next several minutes, she followed the pattern she'd written down, until at last she reached the final corridor. She paused to catch her breath and look around. There were no openings on either side of this corridor, just one at the end, like a proverbial light at the end of the tunnel, leading to heaven.

Or to slaughter. She'd read *The Shining*. She'd seen the movie, too (by sneaking into the matinee at the century-old theater in Bedlam), so she knew what could happen in a maze when a crazy person is involved.

An image of Jack Nicholson's manic grin firmly planted in her mind, Pandora set off once more. After about forty steps, the path began to curve around and around. Pandora warily followed the spiral until there it was…the center of the labyrinth. She'd made it!

She soon forgot about her fear of ax-wielding maniacs as she spun around and around, trying to take everything in. From all appearances, she was standing in the courtyard of a miniature castle, though a terribly overgrown and neglected one. The crenellated stone walls looked like gappy teeth, and four towers, wrapped in thorny rose stems, sat at each of the corners. Off to her right, a miniature Stonehenge tempted one to go sit amongst the upright stones and think ancient thoughts.

A rectangular pool, darkened by black leaves and muck, dominated the middle of the courtyard. A carved mermaid, frolicking in its center, would likely spit streams of water into the air when the fountain worked. Donut-shaped stones, smooth and inviting, begged to be crawled through and sat in.

Near one tower a giant chess set awaited players. Near another, a long, stone table and chairs invited hungry guests for a summer day picnic. A large tree, big enough for climbing and sitting in, supported a swing, tilting drunkenly to one side due to a broken rope. It looked like a medieval playground set in the Secret Garden.

There was so much to see and do that she didn't know where to begin. But what did that matter? She'd solved the last two clues, and all on her own. She should feel great! Yet she didn't; she only felt deflated. Nothing had changed. Her other questions remained unanswered, and she didn't see the spirit anywhere.

Numb and confused, she could only stare at the wonders before her, taking in very little as the thought, *Now what?* flitted through her mind like a chant. Here she was, in this amazing and beautiful place, and she didn't even want to explore it. What was wrong with her?

"Pan, Pan, Pan! Dora, Dora, Dora!" Lucy's voice echoed all around her, and Pandora spun around in time to see Lucy charge into the courtyard. "I'm first! I'm first!" She did a victory dance. "Oh, yeah, that's right. I'm awesome!"

"Lucy!" Pandora waved her hand. "I've been waiting for you guys."

Charles followed after Lucy, his face lighting up when he saw Pandora. "I got your note," he said breathlessly. "But you didn't wait for us!"

"I tried to…" she began, her mind working overtime to produce a plausible lie. "But I didn't try very hard," she finished lamely.

"You wanted to solve it yourself," Xavier announced smugly as he and Birdy stalked toward her like the archangel, Gabriel, bent on seeking justice. Skippy trailed mournfully along behind them.

"I told you she always wants the spotlight," Birdy accused, fiddling with a red scarf wrapped stylishly around her neck. "It's like she's addicted to it."

"Look who's talking," Pandora grumbled. "You can't even have a relationship without turning it into a soap opera. And why are you here anyway? I thought you'd had enough of us."

"I've had enough of *you*." She pointed a red fingernail at Pandora.

"That's an impossibility."

"Very funny."

"So you're back to liking Skippy now?"

Birdy's smile was pleased as punch. "Xavier asked me to come."

"That's not what I heard. Really, Birdy! How could you treat Skippy this way? He's fragile!"

"That's the problem, you idiot," Birdy snapped. "I need a real man, not a pansy." In a lower voice she added, "It's bad enough having a dad who can't stand up for himself."

Pandora didn't process the last part, focusing only on Birdy's insult. "Skippy's not a pansy. He has an illness. It's not his fault he's so weak."

"Please don't, Pandora," Skippy pleaded. He looked awful, like a shriveled up pea. "She's right, you know. I *am* a pansy."

"You shouldn't defend her, Skippy."

Like a weary knight heading into a battle he knows will be his last, he drew up his bowed shoulders. "I'll defend her with my dying breath."

Everyone was silent until Lucy clasped her hands together and sighed, "That's so romantic, Skip-to-my-Lou!"

"Romantic, my a——" Pandora began.

"So this is it?" Xavier interrupted, pushing past her. His shoulder connected with hers, making her swallow the S's, and they slithered back down her throat. "This is the center of the labyrinth?"

"There aren't any more clues," she replied slowly, as she tried to change gears. "So this has to be it." Sinclair shook his head vigorously at her and pointed to his eyes. "Well, I haven't looked around, if that's what you're getting at, Sinclair. I was waiting for you guys to catch up."

"You were, were you?" Xavier challenged.

"Hard to believe as it is, I was waiting for you. Why else would I mark the path? Besides, it just wasn't the same on my own." Mulling this over, she realized it was true. Now that the posse was here with her she did feel a bit more like exploring. She wondered what that said about her. Was she becoming co-dependent?

Heaven forbid.

Lucy clapped her hands. "It's like a fairy tale in here! And I shall be the damsel in distress. Oh, save me, Charles! Save me!" She giggled as Charles turned bright red.

"Where should we start?" Pandora asked, trying to ignore Lucy's cries, meant to sound like a damsel in distress, but which came across more like a dying pig.

Sinclair pointed at his eyes again, this time more vehemently. It if he wasn't careful, he'd poke them out. "Okay, I get it. We're going to look around. Keep your knickers on, will you?"

"See!" Sinclair shouted. "See!"

"That's what we're about to do, ninny. We're going to 'see' what's here. I am speaking English, aren't I?" she appealed to the posse.

"You appear to be," Charles answered as Sinclair repeated "see" over and over, his expression mulish.

"Hey, look what I found," Xavier called to the others. He stood by a small well, holding a magnifying glass. "I wonder whose it is?"

Pandora hurried over and peered at the object. The thick glass and black handle were dusty and grimy, as though the magnifying glass had been sitting idle for years. "Whoever it was left it a long time ago," she deduced.

"Maybe it's the ghost's!" Lucy shouted.

"What would a ghost want with a magnifying glass?" Birdy argued. "They can already *see-through* everything." She laughed. "Hey, that was a good one." Lucy giggled, though Pandora was pretty sure she didn't get it.

Sinclair tugged on Pandora's shirt. "See!"

"Is that what you're talking about? The magnifying glass?" He shook his head, then pointed at her sporran. She frowned. "You want me to look at the rhyme again? The part about *seeing*?"

He gave her such a disgusted look that she took a step backward in surprise. When he didn't answer, she shrugged and did as he asked, holding the paper in front of her. "Sea that you watch your step, my friend," she intoned like a grand orator, "the labyrinth is a queer old place. Its secrets might just be your end, but don't give up the chase!" She folded the paper and stuffed it back in her sporran. "Yes, I *see* that you misspelled see. I believe that was your only mistake, though, so I won't hold it against you."

"See, you ninny!" he shouted, his hands gripped into fists. "S-e-a!"

"Did you just call me a ninny?" she demanded, shocked.

"He called you a ninny," Xavier stepped between them, "because you're acting like one. He's trying to tell us there's another clue and you're too stupid to get it."

She glared at him. "So what is it then? We're at the center. I figured out the labyrinth."

"Looks like you didn't figure it *all* out." He grinned.

"I did—" But she didn't get to finish her thought because she heard something. The soft sound of singing was coming from all around her, as though echoing through a cave.

I cannot leave my Gwen, you see
She's everything to me.

"Did you hear that?" she gasped. "The singing?"

Everyone looked at her funny. "What singing?" Lucy asked. "I don't hear nothing."

"Just listen," Pandora urged. Heads cocked and lips pursed, they reluctantly obeyed.

Don't make me go, I'll give my soul.
Death's shadow, hear my plea.

Everyone's eyes widened. "Who is that?" Xavier demanded.

"It's the ghost!" Lucy answered, eyes wide with feigned terror.

"It's the stranger," Pandora rushed to explain. "The one on the beach. He was singing that song. After you left that night, I heard him and ran after him, but he disappeared."

"Sea!" Sinclair insisted one last time and finally Pandora understood what he'd been trying to tell her. She felt a twinge of embarrassment at her obtusity. Luckily it was only a twinge.

"The poem is talking about the sea, the ocean. You didn't spell it wrong, Sinclair."

He actually smiled as he chanted, "Sea, sea, sea."

"But what's it trying to tell us?"

"To look for something to do with the ocean," Skippy patiently explained. "Like shells and tridents and all that."

"Its secrets might just be your end, but don't give up the chase," Birdy quoted in Shakespearean fashion, arm extended, voice deep and carrying. "That's the ending, right?" she said in a more normal voice. "So we should probably just be happy we found the center and call it good."

"No way." Pandora crossed her arms. "I'm not leaving until we figure it all out."

"Fine," Birdy sneered. "We'll be sure to tell them where your tired old bones are when you don't show up after a few months. As for me, I'm out of here."

"And how are you getting out? You can't go back through the door at the water wheel. There isn't a handle."

Birdy's eyes fixed on Pandora. "You're lying."

"I'm not. I couldn't figure out the poem and thought I had to start over so I tried to go back out that way. But there was no handle on the door."

"She's right," Xavier said. "I noticed that, too."

"So what do we do?" Birdy cried. "I don't like enclosed spaces. Everyone knows that. I feel like I can't breathe!" She started staggering about, gasping for air.

"Oh, put a cork in it, Birdy," Pandora snapped.

"If I had a cork, I'd shove it up your behind!" she shouted back, her hand clutching her chest as she wheezed.

"That I'd like to see!" Lucy snickered.

"I'm going to pass out!" Birdy screeched to the heavens.

"Oh, for pity's sake," Xavier groaned. He grabbed Birdy's arm and dragged her toward him. "There's a fresh breeze right here. That should help."

She sucked it in, her wheezing slowly fading. When she could breathe normally again, she rounded on Pandora. "You are so hardhearted, Pandora Belfry. I could've died!"

"Well, you didn't, so can we look for the sea clues now?" Birdy's only answer was to shoot Pandora with eye darts. "Good. I'm glad you're on board."

Charles stepped forward. "While you and Birdy were arguing, I scouted out the place with my x-ray vision, but I didn't see anything related to the ocean other than the mermaid fountain." He pointed at it. "I also didn't see a way out of here other than the way we came in."

Birdy backed away from the group. "There's no way I'm getting anywhere near that nasty old pool. I'll go over a wall if I have to!" She spun around to run, but after ten or so steps, she skidded to a halt, her hands flying into the air. She ran in the other direction, only to stop again. "Agh! They're everywhere!" She stood frozen, her chest pitching up and down in hysterical bursts. The posse stared at her, then, as though released from a spell, raced toward her.

"What is it, my love?" Skippy shouted as he neared her.

Wordlessly, she pointed at the ground. It was covered in snakes.

35

She's Gone

IN FACT, IT seemed like there were snakes everywhere. Apparently Pandora had lied to Birdy and Lucy when she'd said there wasn't any more chance of finding snakes inside the labyrinth than outside of it. "Kill them!" Birdy shouted, her voice shrill. "Stomp on them. Smear them into the ground!"

Xavier bent down on one knee to get a closer look. "They aren't real, Birdy. See?" He pointed to one. It was about a foot long and laid out in an s-shape. He tried to pick it up but the gray and rusty brown reptile didn't budge. "They're made from some sort of metal," he went on as he stroked the snake's back. "They look real, though, don't they?"

"They're all heading that way," Lucy pointed toward one of the towers.

"Watch out for snakes," Pandora breathed, suddenly remembering. "The rhyme told us to watch out for snakes! I thought it was a warning, but it was a clue. We need to follow them." She weaved her way through the mass exodus of snakes, heading resolutely toward the tower. The closer she got, the stronger the breeze, carrying a hint of ocean, grew. A couple steps from the arched doorway of the tower, a voice beckoned like an entreaty from the grave.

> *Death's shadow heard my plea that night*
> *He did not take my life.*
> *Instead he took my Gwen, my light.*
> *She'd never be my wife.*
>
> *She's gone, she's gone, my lovely Gwen*
> *She's gone forevermore*
> *Yet still I search the world for her*
> *My Gwen, I do adore.*

Drawn like a butterfly to a flower, Pandora followed the voice. Her stranger was singing to her, luring her onward.

My Gwen, I do adore.

"Pandora!" Xavier called as she stepped into the tower. It was cool and dark inside, a relief from the hot sun. "Be careful!"

She smiled when she saw the gray stone stairs leading downward and didn't hesitate to follow them. The scent of brine grew stronger with every step, as did the breeze. Nothing could stop her now. She was going to find the stranger. She was going to confront him and find out once and for all if he was real, or a spirit. She had to know.

Pulling her flashlight from her sporran, she ignored the posse's calls to wait up, and hurried down the stairs. She couldn't let him get away. She heard only the frantic sound of her own breathing as she raced through the tunnel that, for once, didn't turn or end or do anything but run straight ahead. The long corridor was mercifully cool, but relentlessly dark. The singing had stopped and Pandora wondered if her prey knew he was being pursued.

"I can't run anymore," Birdy wheezed from far behind. "I have a blister."

"We're almost there!" Pandora shouted back. "I can see a light up ahead."

Another few steps and she spotted the stranger, a black silhouette nearly filling the opening at the end of the tunnel. Behind him peeked blue sky and endless ocean. The sea. S-e-a. Damn that Sinclair, he'd been right all along! She was definitely going to have to eat crow this time. But only after she fried that sucker up, added a little salt and maybe a few sprigs of parsley.

She took off running. The stranger was right where she wanted him to be, and he wasn't moving. She had him now. Finally, she was going to get the answer to one of her questions.

When she heard a rumbling noise from far off, she thought at first it was thunder. Then a loud boom rang out and Birdy screeched. Pandora skidded to a stop and spun around. "Birdy! Where are you?" A huge rock dropped at her feet, followed by a shower of stones. She could see no one and nothing in the dust storm that kicked up around her. She ducked her head low, preparing to run through the falling debris toward her friends, when a hand grabbed her arm and yanked her backward. Before she could react, she was swept off her feet and carried toward the light. She struggled to get away, but the stranger was much stronger than she was. "We have to save my friends!"

The stranger didn't answer, only sped up. Behind them, a moan grew like the bellows of an angry witch. Pandora looked back to see a torrent of mud and stone raining down. The whole tunnel was collapsing. Rocks pelted her arms and dust attempted to infiltrate all her orifices. The stranger stumbled and the roar overtook them. With one last lunge, he plunged through the opening and fell to his knees just outside the passage. She rolled out of his arms and onto a flat stone. There she sat, stunned, as she watched the opening disappear.

When it was completely filled in with rubble, she shielded her eyes and looked up. Slowly the stranger's features came into focus. A fine coat of gray dust coated his dark hair and shoulders, and his ever-present headphones encircled his neck. Derek. He was smiling down at her, looking rather pleased with himself. "*You're* the stranger on the beach?"

"Who else would it be?"

"But, but—" She gaped at him. "How'd you know about this tunnel into the labyrinth? And how can you walk through water that could pull an elephant down? And why didn't you answer me when I called to you? And that song you were singing—"

He held up his hand. "All that can wait. First we need to help your friends."

She stared with disbelief at the filled-in tunnel and felt like she was going to be sick. "They're dead," she bleated. "It's my fault. I wanted to follow you. I wanted to see who you were…"

"It's not anyone's fault, Pandora. All that rain must have weakened the tunnel. I heard their voices before I grabbed you. There's still a chance they're alive, but we'll have to go in the other way to find out."

"The other way?" She glanced around the rocky beach and realized she was on the other side of The Fangs.

"It's hidden by boulders," he explained. "I moved a few to hide the openings."

"You did?" Well, that explained why she hadn't found the tunnels herself.

"Come on," he urged, pushing himself to his feet. He reached down to help her up. "Every second counts." He began to climb up the cliff side, and Pandora scrambled after him. His legs were long and his steps steady and Pandora had to move fast to keep up. Halfway up the cliff, he stopped before a large stone and put his shoulder to it. The boulder rolled away as though made out of Styrofoam, revealing a jagged opening. "I don't often use this one," he said over his shoulder. "I hope the tunnel's still okay."

"I have my flashlight." She handed it to him and he smiled at her, his gray eyes warm.

"Thanks."

She bit her lip. "No problem."

"Keep your ears open. If another cave-in happens, we need to be ready to run." He flipped on the light and led the way into the dark tunnel. Cobwebs hanging from the ceiling, and ocean detritus littering the floor, made the going painfully slow. But so far, there was no sign of a cave-in.

"Do you think they'll be all right?" she asked worriedly. "Maybe the cave-in missed them." She remembered Birdy's scream and shivered. "Or maybe not."

"I don't know. But there may still be hope if we get to them in time."

"Not if they got crushed under tons of dirt and rocks, their lungs pierced by sharp stones, their eyes bulging from pain and oxygen deprivation."

"Well, yes, if that happened, then probably not."

"I didn't know you could sing," she panted, anxious to keep her mind off the gruesome scenario she'd just conjured up. Sometimes she thought her macabre imagination ought to be taken out and shot.

"There are a lot of things you don't know about me."

True. What did she know about this giant of a boy other than that he liked to listen to music and could sing like a saint. "So I guess I better ask you some questions. Like, where'd you learn that song?"

"My mother used to sing it to me."

Used to? He made it sound like she was dead, when he'd only mentioned her a few days ago. Surely she hadn't bit the big one between then and now? Should she ask him? And tell him Dr. Steele sang that song, too? Maybe another time, she quickly decided. "You must live close by, to know this area so well."

"I do."

She frowned. "I thought I knew all the neighbors. There are the Clooneys to our south and then there's crazy old Choken who haunts the Humphrey's place to our north."

"Crazy old Choken is my father," he replied, his voice cool.

She nearly gagged on her surprise. "Your *father*?" Dang, that explained so much, and yet, left so much more unanswered.

"And he's not crazy."

"Oh."

"He just doesn't like people."

She could understand that. "I didn't know…"

"I do my best to keep it that way."

"I'm sorry. I shouldn't have called him crazy. I didn't mean it as an insult. It's just what people call him."

"Like people call you Bats?"

She swallowed hard. "Right."

"We're almost there." He shone the flashlight ahead to reveal a set of stone stairs. They raced up them, only to be blocked by a web of thorny vines at the opening. The roses had taken over. After some hackings and whackings, they pushed their way through, into the fresh air.

Pandora looked around, relieved they'd made it. They were back in the castle courtyard. "It's another tower."

"Just so you know," he said as he strode toward the tower where the posse was trapped and possibly dead, "the other two towers lead to locked doors, which I've yet to try out."

Once inside the other tower, they pelted down the stairs, their sense of urgency growing with each step. "Lucy! Charles!" Pandora shouted as she ran. "Are you all right?"

No one answered. She ran faster.

"Is there anyone who can hear me?" Derek shouted, his usually soft tone like a foghorn in the tunnel. The sound rumbled pleasantly in her chest.

"Help!" a tiny voice cried. "We're trapped!"

They ran as hard as they could until stopped by a pile of rubble that rose from floor to ceiling like a massive cairn. "Is anyone hurt?" Pandora yelled frantically through the pile of rocks and debris. "Speak to me!"

"Skippy's hurt!" Charles shouted back, his voice shaky. "His leg is stuck under a huge rock."

"Get us out of here, Pandora!" Birdy's voice boomed out from behind the rocks. Obviously her lungs remained unpunctured to summon up that sort of wind. "It's really dark and Skippy's dying!"

Pandora felt all the blood leave her head. "Don't you dare die on me, Skippy Stone! We're coming!" Derek propped up the flashlight to light the area, and together they started throwing rocks out of the way. Derek worked like a machine, the John Henry of rock movers, but every time they made progress, more rocks would slither down and fill the space. Minutes ticked by with not a sound coming from the other side. Pandora wondered if they were still alive, their air supply slowly depleting. She imagined the last of their oxygen being sucked into lungs that resembled shriveled balloons.

Just as she was about to shriek in frustration, Derek pulled loose a large stone and a crack appeared in the pile. After another ten minutes of shoveling and lifting, only one stubborn rock blocked their way. Fingers bloody and stinging fiercely, Pandora jerked and pulled at it, but it wouldn't budge.

"Move out of the way, please." Derek stepped forward and put his shoulder to the boulder. With all his might, he pushed. When it didn't move, he pushed again, and then again. The rock shifted slightly, but didn't give. Letting loose a tremendous roar, he pulled back, then crashed against the stone. At last it gave way and fell to the side, revealing a space large enough to climb through.

Pandora grabbed the flashlight and turned to shine it through the opening. "Come on, guys!" Soon Lucy and Charles were scrambling out of the well of darkness, followed by Sinclair. Lucy headed straight for Pandora and hugged her waist, threatening to cut off her air supply. Meanwhile Sinclair dusted himself off and Charles straightened his cape. They were okay. They were okay!

Charles pointed back the way they came, his lips quivering. "There's a rock crushing Skippy's leg. We can't get it off him! Xavier's arm is bad so he can't do it and I tried and I tried, but I couldn't do it, either." He hung his head.

Derek, who'd been standing off to one side, leaned down close to Charles. "I imagine you loosened it just enough. Now it's my turn to take care of the rest."

Charles's eyes widened as he looked up to take in all of Derek. "You're a giant!" he breathed reverently. "I've always wanted to be a giant, then I could've saved Skippy all by myself."

Derek smiled down at him. "There are many ways to be a giant, my friend." Then with a nod, he crawled through the opening. Pandora hurried after him, flashlight in hand. Inside the small area, they found Skippy lying on the floor, a large rock pinning his leg from the knee down. His face was pale, but he looked surprisingly chipper, likely because his head was resting on Birdy's chest while she held his hand tightly. She hadn't left him. Pandora had to give the girl credit for that. Big credit.

Xavier stood and grabbed Derek's hand. "You're a sight for sore eyes, man. I've been trying to lift this dang rock for ages, but I can't get it to budge."

"I'll need to get in there." Derek gestured toward Birdy.

She peered up at him. "I'm not going anywhere."

"Then I can't move the rock."

She frowned. "Okay, fine. But you be careful. If he dies, I'm coming after you."

"Upon my honor, I'll do my best," he told her solemnly.

"Well, all right then." She stood up, not even bothering to wipe the dust off her clothes. "I'll be right here, honeybun," she cooed. "Don't you die on me. I need my hero right by my side."

Derek kneeled down and wrapped the rock in a massive embrace. In the distance, a rumbling sounded.

"What's that?" Xavier called as dust and small stones showered down on his head.

Birdy looked around frantically. "I think the tunnel's collapsing again!"

An Ominous Roar

36

"HURRY!" SHE SHOUTED at Derek. "Help him!"

"Get out of here, you two," Xavier ordered, pushing Pandora with his good hand. "You'll only slow us down."

"I'm not leaving Skippy!" Birdy hollered.

Pandora grabbed her plump arm. "Come on, Birdy. Xavier's right. Besides, we have to get the others out of here." She thrust the flashlight at Xavier.

He grabbed it and pointed it at the opening. "I'll light your way for as far as I can."

Birdy fought Pandora, twisting her arm left and right. "I'm not leaving my man!"

"Go, Birdy!" Skippy shouted hoarsely. "I'll be with you soon."

"Darling dearest!" she cried, reaching for him.

The rumbling grew louder and rocks fell around them. Birdy screamed and Pandora took advantage of her distraction to yank her through to the other side. When Birdy realized what had happened, she lunged backward at the opening. Pandora threw herself in front of the girl, grabbing both her arms and holding tight. "Listen to me, Birdy, and listen good. Skippy will want you to live, because without you…" she paused to pull in enough air to dispense the next load of crap, "…he's nothing. Now come on!"

Hearing the thundering noise, and recognizing the logic behind Pandora's rationale, Birdy nodded. "You're right." She started trotting down the dim corridor without a backward glance, chanting in a low voice, "He better be all right. He better be all right."

Pandora grabbed Charles and Lucy's hands and they followed Sinclair down the hall, moving as fast as they could with so little light. Charles's wheezing worried her, but there wasn't time to stop. When she saw a bright light in the distance, she pushed the two on ahead of her. "Run!" she screamed, then turned around and plunged back into the darkness. Draping an arm over her head, she ducked and dodged around the rubble as rocks fell all about her. The ground shook beneath her feet and she nearly wiped out twice. She kept expecting to see the beam from the flashlight, but nothing appeared even though she knew she was close to the opening. She made herself slow down, letting her feet shuffle across the stone floor, and at last she spotted a light, dim and hazy in the dusty air.

"Are you all right, guys?" she shouted, wondering what was taking so long. The rest of the corridor could collapse at any moment. "Answer me right now, or I'm going to give you a hiding you won't soon forget!"

"Don't get your knickers in a bunch," Xavier shouted back. "We only just got the rock off Skippy's leg."

Her frantically beating heart slowed. "Why didn't you answer me, you idiot?"

"I just did. Now get out of the way."

Ignoring the order, she peeked through only to come face to face with Derek. A smile lit up his face, followed quickly by a frown. "You should be gone."

"And leave you ninnies to manage on your own?"

"I told you she was bossy," Xavier had the nerve to say.

"I'm not bossy, I'm a leader. There's a difference."

"That's like saying Hitler wasn't evil, he was just sensitive," Xavier retorted.

"Ha, ha. And I suppose you're docile as a lamb. I don't think so—"

"Stand back, Pandora," Derek interrupted. "We need to get through."

"Fine. But this isn't over, Xavier!" she yelled as she crawled out of the way.

Skippy's shaggy head appeared through the hole, followed by the rest of his long torso. She grabbed his arm and helped him through. "Are you okay?" She did her best to look him over in the dim light.

He pushed himself to his feet. "Bruised, but otherwise intact. Where's Birdy?"

"She's helping the others get out," she answered, telling a slight variation of the truth since Birdy *had* been praying for him. Sort of. Come to think of it, she'd sounded more like she'd been threatening God than praying to him. "Go join her, will you? Make sure everyone is okay."

For the first time in days he smiled. "Yes, my liege." He gave her a salute, then hobbled off down the corridor, his hand trailing along the wall to guide him. She'd never been more glad to see the back of him.

A rumbling sounded in the distance. "You better hurry, guys."

Xavier wiggled out through the opening. "I'm going as fast as I can," he managed to snip as he struggled to push himself forward with his one good hand.

"Yeah, well, move faster. I don't think this tunnel is through with us yet."

With one last kick he was out and Pandora shoved him aside. Derek pushed the flashlight through the opening. Pandora grabbed it and handed it to Xavier. "Hold this."

He took it and shined it on Derek's emerging head. "I think the rocks shifted," he warned him. "I nearly didn't get my shoulders through."

Oh, crud. If stickpin Xavier had trouble getting through, there was no way Derek was going to fit. "You've got to move faster," Pandora urged. "It's starting again." He wiggled and pushed, his shoulders butting up against large stones on either side. "Turn sideways," she instructed. "You'll fit better that way."

He did as he was told and began to make some progress. Soon his shoulders had cleared the opening, followed by his torso. She tugged and jerked on his arm, trying to help him along, but it was like moving a tree. Still, he was making progress when a loud crack, followed by an ominous roar, sounded behind him. Derek gasped and tried to move forward but after several more attempts, he was unable to get anywhere.

"My foot," he grimaced. "It's stuck."

"This whole place is ready to go at any minute," Xavier announced.

"No shit, Sherlock!" Pandora snapped. She took a deep breath. "All right, I'm going in."

"What?" Derek and Xavier both exclaimed in horror.

She pointed to a narrow gap between Derek's legs and the large rock. "I can fit through there. It's the only way to free his foot."

"No way." Derek's tone, steeled with an edge, brooked no argument.

She found she rather liked how manly he sounded, not that it changed her mind, or anything stupid like that. "Too late." She dove forward, and before he could grab her, she was halfway through the narrow space. With one more wiggle she found herself on the other side of the pile. It was dark and dusty and she coughed, setting off the pain in her ribs. She clutched them until the fit passed.

"Damnit, Pandora!" Xavier swore. The light shone through into the darkness. "Get out of there!"

"Do as he says," Derek commanded.

"No can do." Her fingers found his legs. "Now hold that light still, Xavier."

The beam found Derek's legs, then traveled down. The light caught not one, but two large stones trapping Derek's boot. One was lying on his foot. The other wedged it in tight. "You can't move those, pip-squeak," Xavier said. "I'm going to have to do it."

"You and what army?" she said through gritted teeth. "Or should I say what *arm*? I'm doing it, so shut up and let me work." She shoved hard on the first rock. It moved, but not far enough, catching against the other one as it rolled. The sound of gurgling pain reached her. "Sorry, Derek. I'll get it this time." She braced herself against the stone and pushed with all her remaining strength, and then some. "Aaaggghhh!" she roared. "Move, you son of a—" She stopped and listened. Thunder, low and menacing, echoed around her. The sound was moving, she realized. Fast. She ducked low and threw herself forward. The pain traveled up her arm and into her head as her shoulder smacked against her unyielding foe. She fought against the rock as it fought against her. "Move, you turd!"

A surge of adrenaline poured through her and suddenly the stone shifted. Her left hand shot out and caught the other rock, keeping it from landing on Derek's foot. "Go!" His foot slid forward as he pulled himself toward the opening. Within seconds he was out of what could have been his tomb.

The roar was so loud now that she couldn't hear anything. Xavier reached out for her. She threw herself forward, clasping his hand. He jerked hard and she slid toward him. Rocks pelted her back as she inched through the opening, and clouds of dust kicked up, blinding her. She was halfway through when Xavier's hand lost its grip, as though he'd been jerked backward.

"Xavier!" she cried, and pushed herself forward, seeing nothing. From out of the darkness, another, larger hand appeared.

"Grab hold," Derek mouthed at her. She grasped his hand like a life buoy and he pulled her through as easily as thread through a needle. Xavier was standing nearby, looking dazed, the flashlight spotlighting the blood streaking down his face. Derek pulled her to her feet, grabbed Xavier's elbow, and they were off running.

Pandora didn't dare turn around to look. She knew what she'd see—stones and dirt filling the air behind them. Her feet flew like wings as Derek dragged her along with him. Xavier stumbled, nearly falling. A rock hit her shoulder and she tripped. Derek's tight grip kept her from hitting the ground, dragging her along until she regained her feet.

"The light!" she gasped, peering ahead. "We're nearly there!"

At that moment, Xavier went down hard, and he didn't get back up. "Take him!" she screamed at Derek. After hesitating for a second, he let go of her and lifted Xavier's limp body into his arms. She chased after them as Derek loped along toward the stairway. Soon he reached the steps and clambered up them, Xavier's knees scraping against the wall. At the top, Derek lunged through the opening and disappeared.

Pandora started up the stairs after them, but halfway up, a rock smashed against her ankle. She fell onto the steps, gasping with pain. Despite what she'd promised herself, she turned around and what she saw was horrifying. A giant snake of rocks and dirt roared toward her. Her whole body went rigid as the thing reached out to engulf her. She closed her eyes and waited for the end.

37

The Elusive Eight

JUST AS THE cave-in's hellish mouth opened to take her, a massive hand encircled her arm and yanked her to her feet. She was half-dragged up the remaining steps and then flung forward like a Frisbee. She landed hard and Derek landed even harder right next to her. It took several seconds to catch her breath and several more for the rumblings below ground to subside. She rolled over and sat up with a groan.

Derek lay on his back beside her, unmoving. Still as a corpse, his face, even his eyelids, were coated in dust. Blood oozed down one cheek, forming a grayish red river. He looked horrid. No, he looked worse than horrid. He looked dead. She grabbed his muscled arm with both hands and shook it. "Wake up!" He didn't respond. "You wake up, Derek, or I'm going to beat the crap out of you!"

She leaned forward, close to his face. Was it her imagination, or had an eyelid flickered? Suddenly his hands shot up and grabbed her arms. Before she could utter a sound, he pulled her to him. They were so close she could feel his warm breath on her cheek, see the black flecks in his gray eyes, smell the intoxicating musk rising from his sweat-slicked skin. As they stared into each other's eyes, her head grew light as a helium balloon and she thought that if he let her go, she'd drift away on the breeze.

"You're alive," he wheezed. He glanced down at her arms, then suddenly let go of them. She slid sideways off him to land on the ground and could only watch with a blank stare as he sat up. After a moment he shook his head, then focused on her. "You all right?"

"You're bleeding," she forced out. "Is your head okay?"

"Just a scrape." He looked her over. "You didn't answer my question."

"I'm talking to you, aren't I?" she snapped, feeling weird and tingly all over.

"You look like the devil's mare."

She laughed and relaxed a bit. "Yeah, well, you don't look much better."

"The others must have got out of the maze," he surmised as he rubbed at one eye.

She looked around. "I guess they must have. Is that what you told them to do?"

He nodded. "I wasn't sure how safe it would be in here."

"But how did they get out?"

"There's a door over there." He pointed to a spot covered in ivy. "It's got four snakes carved on it. Hard to see them unless you know they're there."

"So snakes mark all the exits? Is that the meaning behind the last clue?"

"Yep." He lifted up his arm to survey a bloody wound on his elbow. "They allow you to get out, but not back in."

"Hm. I like that." She peered down at one of her own wounds—a gash on her ankle. "How'd you find the labyrinth?"

"From the beach. I walk there a lot. About a year ago I found the opening and followed it. After that, I explored the maze whenever I could. I used the lanterns to light my way."

"So that was you! I thought one was missing. But then Skippy found one on the beach…"

He shrugged. "Yeah, well, one's missing again. I'll return it when I can."

"Sure. Whenever. But I still don't know how you walked through water like that. Or why, when I called to you, you didn't answer."

"There's a flat ledge underwater, very sturdy, and I've got long legs." He touched his headphones. "I was probably wearing these when you called."

"I almost caught you once. You were singing that song. Why didn't you talk to me then?"

"I saw Dr. Steele behind you and didn't want to get you into trouble."

"Me? You were the one trespassing!"

He smiled. "If a boy is found alone with a girl, that's a good thing for him. But if a girl is found alone with a boy, well, that's not so good for her."

"That's so old-fashioned." But true, she realized. "So how come I've never seen you on the beach before now?"

A slow smile spread across his face. "That's how I preferred it to be."

Preferred it. Past tense. "What made you change your mind?"

"I was bored."

That made her laugh. "Well, I certainly fixed that, didn't I?"

He looked up at her, his eyes smiling. "Yes, you did."

Blushing madly, she ducked her head, aghast at her girly reaction. Then she wondered if he would grab her again, maybe kiss her, so she raised her head to be ready. When he didn't do either, she cleared her throat nervously and before she could make a fool of herself, said, "We should go find the others."

He pushed himself to his feet and lowered his hand to help her up. She liked how it felt wrapped around hers. Not so big and overpowering anymore. "I reckon our little cave-in didn't go unnoticed."

"Oh, crap, you're probably right! We have to get out of here."

Still holding her hand, he led her toward the wall, his massive feet picking their way through the slithering snakes like a linebacker. More often than not, her own caught on them as she followed after him.

Letting go of her hand, which now felt oddly bereft, he swept aside a web of ivy, pushed on a barely discernible door in the wall, and ducked through, holding it open for her. Before stepping through, she spotted four snakes on the door, which could easily be mistaken for scratches if you didn't know better. Derek took the lead, and eventually they ended up back in the 30-door corridor, to the left of the tunnel that led back to the statue. When they entered the tunnel, she was glad to see that it was still intact.

Fortunately, Xavier had left the drawbridge open for them. Derek gestured her up and out and when they were on the other side, they both pulled the drawbridge up again. Once the vines were back in place, they ran around the copse of trees, heading for the manor. Right away Pandora spotted Carl and Vicki, along with the posse and several staff members, staring into a gaping hole in the driveway.

Their shoes crunched on the gravel as they approached and Vicki spun around. "Pandy!" She hurried toward her. "Where *were* you?" Pandora reluctantly shuffled forward to meet her mother, with Derek matching her every step. "You're covered in dust and you're bleeding and..." She shook her head. "Damnit, Pandy, I thought you were safely inside the house!"

"Well, um, we, um, well..." Dang. In terms of imaginative excuses, she was tapped. It had been a long day.

"And you, young man!" Vicki turned her furious gaze on Derek. "What in Heaven's name happened here?" She threw a wild gesture back at the hole.

"We ran into a little trouble, ma'am," Derek answered.

"The area where we were standing gave way and we fell in," Pandora said, finally figuring out what to say. It wasn't the best story, but darned if she was going to put Derek in a position of having to lie for her. "We managed to climb out just in the nick of time."

Derek remained perfectly still while Vicki glanced back and forth between the two, her brow furrowed with suspicion. "Is this true?" she finally demanded of Derek, no doubt knowing her daughter would lie. Pandora wasn't sure if she liked that so much. She didn't *always* lie…only when necessary. And growing up in an insane asylum often made it necessary.

"He saved my life," she quickly added, which was the truth.

"He did?" Vicki's fierce expression softened a bit.

"He certainly did. Can I go check out that giant hole?" Pandora really did want to see it—it looked awesome from here—but she also needed to be sure the posse was okay. Especially Xavier. Last time she'd seen him he'd been lying limp as a cooked noodle in Derek's arms. Before Vicki could answer, she said, "Thanks, luv," and scurried toward the hole. Rule number one when dealing with adults: Don't give them time to come up with reasons why you shouldn't do something.

"Ma'am," Derek nodded at Vicki, then followed after Pandora.

She pushed her way through the posse and peered down into the hole. All she could see were rocks and dirt and tufts of grass. The tunnel would never be used again.

"I can't believe we were down there!" Skippy whispered, his eyes dancing. Birdy clung to his arm, her fingers white with the effort. She only gave Derek the once-over *once* as he approached. Even stranger, she made no pointed remarks about what a big man he was and how little ol' Birdy, all sugar and helplessness, could use a giant like him to protect her. And so on and so forth. For the moment, she had eyes only for Skippy.

Excellent.

"You kids go on now." Carl shooed them away with the shovel he'd been leaning on. "And if I catch anyone anywhere near this hole, I'll hide and tan him—or *her*—" here he looked directly at Pandora, his blue eyes deadly serious beneath his John Deere cap— "and hang the skin on my wall." Knowing he would, they all shuffled a good twenty feet away from the cave-in. Satisfied they'd gotten the message, Carl and Vicki, along with the staff, except for a few who stayed behind to get in a quick ciggie break, headed back inside the manor.

"You okay?" she asked Xavier when they were gone.

He looked surprisingly clean, as did the others. "I'll live. Birdy used her scarf to wipe the worst of the blood and dust off us before your mom saw. Sinclair was surprisingly dust-free." Sinclair looked rather smug at this.

Pandora was impressed. "Good thinking, Birdy."

She shrugged. "I wasn't about to get in trouble because of a stupid cave-in. We hardly get to do anything around here as it is. Imagine if the shackles were tightened even further?"

"Imagine," Pandora agreed. "So what happened when you were trapped?"

Birdy used her free hand to fan herself. "Skippy was *amazing*. He risked his life to save us. He's a genuine hero." She gripped his arm tighter, tilting her face to gaze adoringly up at him. He blushed and peered down at his dusty sneakers, but he couldn't hide his grin.

"Wow, Skippy. What'd you do?"

He shrugged modestly. "I only pushed them out of the way. No biggie."

"He wasn't just a hero, he was a superhero, Pandora!" Charles exclaimed.

Lucy spread out her arms and pretended to fly. "Super Skippy to the rescue!"

"It *was* a biggie!" Birdy protested. "After pushing us to safety, a bunch of rocks landed on his back. You should see it, Pandora. He'll probably have lots of scars."

"Can't wait for the big reveal."

Xavier turned to Derek. "Speaking of saving people, thanks for carrying me out, old boy. That rock did a number on my poor head."

Derek didn't even blush, just nodded. "Any time."

"This is Derek, by the way," Pandora introduced him. "And I've found out that he's the stranger. He lives at the old Humphrey's place next door and his dad is *Mr.* Choken."

The posse, showing remarkable restraint upon hearing the name Choken (especially since, for some strange reason, they thought he was the local bogey man), called out cheery hellos. Lucy slipped her tiny hand in his and looked up at him. Pandora closed her eyes and sent a mental command to Lucy not to mention the skinned squirrels Pandora had once found by an outbuilding near Derek's house. "Are you really a giant?"

He bent down and looked her in the eye. "Yes."

She giggled. "Good. The posse needs a giant."

"Lucy!" Charles cried. "He doesn't know—"

"He does now," Pandora said drily. "All those in favor of including Derek as a member of our posse say, 'aye.'"

Seven 'ayes' rang out, followed by Sinclair's louder than usual echoes. His enthusiasm was understandable. The number was now back to an acceptably even eight.

"But we can't be the Secret Six or Seven now," Charles pointed out.

"We'll be the Elusive Eight," Skippy suggested. "I like being elusive." He twirled the ends of an imaginary mustache and his eyes sparkled. Pandora smiled. She liked seeing Skippy happy. She just hoped Birdy wouldn't let him down again. Birdy was very good at letting people down.

"All agreed?" Pandora asked. Everyone, including Derek, nodded. "The Elusive Eight, it is."

"And here's our first task as the new eight," Xavier commented, nodding down the drive. Everyone spun around. A red car raced toward them, throwing up a plume of dust behind it. After maneuvering around the gaping hole, it skidded to a stop only a few feet from where they stood. Dougie stepped out of the car, his every move neat and precise.

Derek grabbed her arm and pulled her backward. "What's *he* doing here?" She glanced up at him in surprise. He sounded like a wild animal.

"He's bringing my dress for the dance. I don't have one," she added lamely.

"Tell him to leave."

"I can't do that! I told him I was going, and I am. Do you want me to be beholden to him forever?" She sounded as though she'd just stepped out of the Victorian era, but it seemed the right way to put it with someone like Derek.

He shook his head, his mouth stretched in tight lines. "No. But I also don't want you near him. He's bad news." He squeezed her arm possessively.

"I know he is. But if I get this over with, he'll be out of my life forever."

"People like the Dafts are never out of your life. Once they get their hooks in you, you're caught like a fish." The image, so close to how she imagined it being with Dougie, sent a shiver up her spine.

"I'll be fine," she managed to get out before Dougie pushed his way past Lucy, who was wondering loudly where her jawbreakers were.

His pale eyes looked Pandora over, then moved to examine Derek. "Did I miss something?"

Pandora shook her head. "It's just a sink hole. From all the rain."

"Strange place for one," he commented.

"Did you bring the candy or not?" Lucy tugged at his arm.

He looked down at her. "As a matter of fact, I did."

"Good. But just so you know, this doesn't make us friends." She glanced meaningfully at Pandora.

"How about acquaintances?" he proposed.

She considered this. "I suppose I could do that."

Pandora gave a disgusted snort. "Stop trying to bribe them, Dougie. They aren't for sale."

Dougie peered at their expectant faces, then strode over to his car and pulled out two bags, a paper one and a black plastic garment bag, and a cowboy hat that looked brand new.

"He bought you a dress?" Xavier hissed at her. "Are you serious?"

"I don't have one," she defended herself.

"Take it and run, Pandora," Birdy advised. "It's a Gucci."

"I'm not impressed by labels, Birdy."

"Is that so?" Dougie handed the paper bag to Charles, who set it on the ground. Once opened, he and Lucy went through it like ravenous dogs, pulling out packets of pop rocks and jawbreakers and a large bag of pixie sticks. Dougie held out the hat to Skippy. "This is for you."

Skippy stared at the hat, then swallowed hard. "Thanks, but I better not."

Birdy let go of his arm and plucked the hat out of Dougie's hand. "Skippy has principles, but I don't. Anytime you have some Gucci lying around, think of me, all right, sugar?" She gave him a seductive smile, then slipped the hat onto Skippy's head.

Pandora grabbed the garment bag from Dougie's outstretched hand. "You might be able to buy *them*," she nodded at the others, "but not me."

His eyelids slowly blinked at her. "Oh, I think we all have a price, Pandora. I just have to figure out what yours is."

Xavier stepped forward. "I think you should leave now."

Derek moved to stand by Xavier's side. "I second that."

Dougie coolly surveyed them both. He was either very brave or very good at controlling his emotions. "I don't recall the lady asking me to leave. Besides, I'm here to see that the dress fits."

"You'll do no such thing, you pervert!" Xavier shouted. "Now get out of here, scumbag, before I make you regret being born."

Derek took another step forward and towered over Dougie. To Dougie's credit, he didn't step back, nor did he cower. "Well, if it isn't Derek Choken. How's your mother these days, Derek? Still crazy as ever?"

Derek pulled his fist back and Pandora lunged at it, barely managing to grab hold of the giant ball of death. "Don't, Derek! He's not worth it."

Derek slowly lowered his arm and Pandora let go. "Leave now, Daft, and I won't grind your face into the ground." His tone of voice was calm and smooth, deceptively so.

For the first time, Dougie looked a little ruffled. "Pandora?"

"You'd better go."

"I'll be back. Tomorrow at 6:00."

"Fine. I'll see you then."

Derek rumbled beside her, his own personal storm cloud. Dougie spun on his heel and walked back to his car, his posture that of a person seemingly unconcerned that his life had just been threatened.

Lucy looked up to watch him go, her mouth full of fizzing pop rocks. "Bye, Dougie Daft!" she gurgled. "Bring more pop rocks next time!" He nodded to her as he climbed into his car. The engine roared to life and he sped off down the drive.

"Now that," Birdy declared, "was amazingly romantic!"

"ROMANTIC?" PANDORA ECHOED disbelievingly. "More like repugnant." But Birdy had already turned away, dragging Skippy toward the manor as she fussed over his scratches and bruises. He took it all good naturedly, smiling widely. Skippy was not often fussed over and he intended to take full advantage of it.

"That girl is messed up," Xavier observed, watching them go. "But Dougie Daft is worse."

"When is Dougie coming back with more candy?" Lucy asked.

"Never," Xavier growled.

"He's not giving you candy because he likes you, Lucy," Pandora interjected, trying to get it through Lucy's mind that people were manipulative and not to be trusted. "He's only trying to trick you."

Lucy snatched up the paper bag and stuffed the candy back inside, her large eyes tearing up. "Come on, Charles. Nobody likes us, not even our family, so we're outta here." Charles joined her, his lower lip trembling. He didn't look back once as he scurried after Lucy.

Sinclair didn't follow after the others as he usually did, his rigid stance communicating that he wanted something. "What is it, Sinclair?" she asked impatiently when he wouldn't stop staring at her. She frowned. "Oh, I suppose you're looking for an apology. Okay, you deserve it. I'm sorry I doubted you. You were brilliant at solving the riddles. You really were," she added more softly. He stared at her for several seconds, then a slow smile spread across his freckled face. It was the most relaxed, real smile she'd ever seen him produce. "Really, Sinclair. If your parents had half a brain between them, they'd see exactly how amazing you are."

"She's right," Xavier chimed in. "You're like a scientist. When you get out of here, you'll do great things."

Pandora glared at her hopelessly insensitive brother. "Don't give him false hope!"

"Hope can't be false, Pandora," Derek said. "It's just hope."

Sinclair looked up at Derek, nodding slowly. "Hope," he whispered.

Pandora wanted to argue with Derek, but she couldn't bring herself to ruin the beatific smile on Sinclair's face. He looked so normal in that moment…like any young boy seeing his future before him and believing it to be full of promise.

"There's just one thing I don't get," she switched tracks before she could change her mind. "Maybe you figured it out, Sinclair. What were those letters on the wall in the covered bridge?"

"PR…JC…VB," Xavier recited, grouping the letters by twos. He grinned at her expression. "I saw them, too, but no one else did. We were moving too fast." He turned to Derek. "Pandora went on ahead because she couldn't stand the idea of not knowing everything there is to know about everything." To her relief, Derek only smiled at her fondly.

"Okay, hotshot!" she snapped ungraciously. "If you're so dang smart, what do they mean?"

"I didn't get that far, but you know, they seem like initials to me." He frowned. "Actually, JC could stand for Judy Carlisle. That's my mom," he explained to Derek. His eyes suddenly lit up. "And VB is for Vicki Belfry!"

Pandora felt herself grow suddenly lightheaded. Vicki had been in the labyrinth? "I don't know. Maybe. But then, who's PR?"

"You got me." He tugged at his sling. "Dangit, I keep finding rocks in here." He pulled it over his head and shook it. Several small rocks flew out. After a few more shakes, a magnifying glass dropped to the ground.

Sinclair reached down and picked up the dusty object. He looked at Xavier, then at Pandora. "PR is for Peter Robertson."

"Who's Peter Robertson?" Xavier asked.

"Professor Robertson," Sinclair clarified.

Hearing the professor's name stunned Pandora to the point that it barely registered that Sinclair wasn't repeating himself. "But how did Professor Robertson's magnifying glass and his initials end up in the labyrinth?"

"It's what kids used to do around here," Derek explained. "A long time ago."

"What did they do?"

"They tried to solve the maze."

"Are you saying our mothers…and Professor Robertson…were inside the labyrinth?"

She glanced at Xavier, who was smiling. "Don't you get it, Pandora? This professor knew our mothers. *Both* of them."

She took a step backward, her mind reeling. "What are you saying?"

"He's our father, Pandora!"

"No. I don't believe it."

"It's the only explanation." He grinned. "He must be pretty well known at the university, so he didn't want it getting out that he has two kids with two different women."

"No, *you* don't get it," Pandora ground out. "Professor Robertson lives at Nepenthe Manor."

Xavier looked confused. "*Lives?*"

"As in, permanently. As in, he's schizophrenic." Her voice grew higher with each word. "As in, our father's not some illustrious figure. He's insane." This was why Vicki didn't want Pandora going in the labyrinth…because it hid the answer to her terrible secret.

Xavier coughed, rubbed his forehead, stared up at the sky, and looked sick. "Our father is schizophrenic? But-but…" He sputtered to a halt.

"Are you sure?" Derek asked her.

"That Professor Robertson is our father? Not absolutely. But it makes a lot of sense. Why Vicki couldn't tell us about him. And why he, himself, didn't want us to know."

"He's not my father," Xavier declared. "It's just not possible."

Pandora faced him. "You're only saying that because Professor Robertson is crazy. You've already made it clear that you don't want a father who's out of his mind. You can't stand the fact that you could have it inside you, too. Just waiting, biding its time. You could be crazy, too, Xavier. So could I!" She started laughing, a little hysterically. "I guess that's why my mom never wanted me to leave the grounds. Because she knows I'm a ticking time bomb!"

"Enough!" Derek roared. Pandora's mouth snapped shut and her hysteria snuffed out. It was the first time she'd ever seen Giganticus get angry. He shoved his hands into his pockets and pulled in a deep breath. "You both heard what Daft said about my ma," he continued, his eyes focusing on Pandora. "Well, it's true. Her mind turned when I was born and it never turned back. My pa, he kept me hidden at home because he thought I'd go crazy, too, that the madness could come out at any time. It was only when we needed money that he let me go into town to work."

"Oh, Derek," Pandora said softly. "That's horrible."

"Dude," Xavier assured him. "You're the least crazy person I know."

"Crazy is as crazy does," Derek replied, looking uncertain.

"I suppose," Xavier mumbled. "So maybe I'm crazy, too, and I just don't know it yet. Maybe—"

"You're not crazy," Pandora interrupted him. "Either of you. And I should know cause I've seen a *lot* of crazy. Heck, compared to the rest of the world, the people in Nepenthe Manor aren't all that crazy, either." She looked straight at Sinclair. He needed to hear this, too. "As Derek said, crazy is as crazy does. If you don't *do* crazy, then maybe you aren't. At least for a while. And for most of us, that's the best we can hope for."

Sinclair tapped his foot on the ground as he thought this over. "Hope," he said quietly.

"Yes, hope," she conceded, hoping dearly that she wasn't setting him up for the biggest fall he'd ever take. Because if he fell after going so high, he might not get back up again. No one's ever picked themselves up after falling off a cliff.

"How do we know for sure?" Xavier asked, his voice shaky. "About Professor Robertson being our dad?"

"I guess we ask Vicki."

"I guess," Xavier replied, though if his darting eyes and trembling fingers were any sign, the thought of it made him want to hurl.

"I have to go," Derek announced suddenly, glancing over at the woods separating Nepenthe Manor from his home. "My pa worries when I'm gone too long. But I'll see you soon. Both of you." He gave Pandora a quick nod and headed toward the beach at a fast lope.

Pandora didn't say goodbye. She couldn't. It was pathetic of her, but she felt like he was abandoning her. *Fine*, she harrumphed inwardly, sounding more like grumpy old Mrs. Johnson than she liked. *I don't need Derek's support during this trying time. I can handle things on my own, just like I always do.* But her words didn't sound all that convincing, even to her own ears.

After Derek disappeared around the corner of the house, the three of them headed toward the manor, each lost in their own thoughts. Once inside, Sinclair left them with a small wave. His step was lighter, she noticed, almost confident. She sighed. He was in for a brutal downfall, but she couldn't do anything about it right now. She and Xavier had business to take care of.

Coming out of Vicki's office, Carl marched past them as though they weren't there. Pandora glanced over at Xavier, then pushed open the office door. Vicki was sitting at her desk, staring down at a stack of papers in front of her. She looked up when the door clicked shut. She sighed gustily. "If it's bad news, I don't want to hear it."

"What's wrong?" Pandora asked as she draped her dress bag over the back of a chair.

"That sink hole is going to cost us money we don't have."

"What are you going to do?"

"Same as always…fly by the seat of my pants and hope for the best." She pushed back her bangs, looking defeated. It was not a look that Vicki often, if ever, wore. It threw Pandora. Could this be the straw that broke Nepenthe Manor's back? Could Mayor Daft shut them down for this? "Is there something you two wanted?"

"Nope! Nothing!" Pandora babbled. "We'll come back another time." She turned to go.

"Stop right there." Pandora slowly turned around. Vicki looked back and forth between them like a predator eyeing its prey. Pandora did her best to look innocent, while Xavier did his best not to look at Vicki at all. But Vicki was patient. Years of working at Nepenthe Manor had taught her how to outlast even the most stubborn of opponents. At last, Xavier, unable to stand the suspense any longer, sneaked a peek at her. She pounced immediately.

"What's going on, Xavier? Is this about your feelings for Pandy?"

Pandora gazed up at the ceiling, hoping for divine intervention. It didn't come. What did come was Xavier's indignation.

"*What?*"

Pandora sighed. "At lunch the other day, Dougie implied that your interest in helping me was because you find me irresistibly desirable." Xavier visibly gagged. "Yeah, well, thanks for that. Did you catch that, Vicki? My half-brother does not find me attractive."

Vicki had the grace to look embarrassed. "Sorry. I've been jumping to a lot of conclusions lately, haven't I?" She hurried on before Pandora could agree. "So what was the reason you wanted to talk to me?" She turned her full attention on Xavier.

"Um, we were just wondering…" He stopped, his eyes wide and panicky. "Um…well, um…"

"It's really a bad time for this," Pandora rushed in. "We'll come back when you're not so busy."

"Stop stalling, Pandy."

"I'm not stalling. It's just that what we wanted to know is kind of hard to ask."

"The easiest way is to just cut to the chase."

"Easiest for who?" Pandora mumbled.

"Just ask the question, Pandy." Vicki's voice was tired and she was running out of patience.

"Okay, fine. Here goes… Is Professor Robertson our father?"

Vicki's eyes widened in disbelief and her mouth went slack. "How…? How…?" She didn't seem able to get the rest of the question out of her mouth.

"So he *is*?" For some reason, Pandora had expected Vicki to laugh and wave a hand at them dismissively. Maybe, like Xavier, she, too, didn't want a crazy man for a dad. "Professor Robertson really is our father? Are you sure?"

A shadow darkened Vicki's eyes. "I've never been more sure of anything in my life."

39

Heavens to Buttsy

"YOUR FATHER WASN'T always like he is now," Vicki went on quietly. "He was once so full of life, so full of potential."

"Did he marry my mom?" Xavier asked gruffly. "Cause if he didn't…"

"They married and were divorced a year and a half later. You were only eight months old when the divorce went through."

"But why did they get a divorce, and so quickly?" he asked, sounding lost.

Vicki bit her lip. "It's complicated. The three of us grew up together, right next door to each other, in fact. And we were inseparable, the best of friends. Even though Peter was four years older than us, we did everything together, mostly stupid stuff. When we got bored, we'd play a game called Spectacular where we'd dare each other to do outrageous things." Pandora stared at her mother. Vicki *spectacular*? *Outrageous*? She couldn't picture it at all. Xavier looked as though he was thinking the same thing about his own mother. "I know it doesn't seem like it now," Vicki responded to their doubtful looks. "But in our day we were quite the hellions."

Now Pandora knew Vicki was exaggerating. A true hellion, even a former one, would *never* use the word hellion to describe themselves.

"But that doesn't explain the divorce," Xavier prompted. "Why did they get divorced?"

Vicki sighed and ran her fingers through her hair, revealing a few strands of gray. Pandora couldn't recall seeing them before. "Your mother and Peter were very passionate people, Xavier. They fancied themselves in love, but they really weren't a good match for each other. They fought a lot, even before they got married. Judy thought having a baby would settle Peter down, but he kept up his antics, staying out all night, tearing around on his motorcycle. When your Grandma Carlisle got cancer, Judy left him to take care of her. He didn't like that, but Judy wouldn't budge. So they ended their marriage."

"Just like that?" he breathed.

"Just like that." She rubbed her face tiredly.

"So how did *I* happen?" Pandora asked.

Vicki looked down at her desk, her eyes searching desperately for a pen. Finding one, she seized it and began to tap on a yellow legal pad.

"After the divorce, Peter came to me looking for comfort. He was an old friend—I didn't think anything of it at the time. I certainly didn't think it would lead to anything. But Peter was good at getting me to do things I didn't always want to do. Six months later, I was married and pregnant with you."

"*Six* months?" Xavier sputtered. "Some friend you were!"

Vicki cringed. "I know. It was a dreadful thing to do, even though Judy had initiated the divorce. I think I was always a bit in love with Peter. He was so charming. So outgoing and full of spirit."

"Are you sure we're talking about the same person?" Pandora asked. "Professor Robertson is about as charming as a rock, about as lively as one, too…unless he's talking about his specimens."

Vicki turned away, but not before Pandora saw her eyes tear up. She bit her lip, regretting her choice of words. Vicki never cried. "He's changed, of course," she explained. "And he's not really a professor. Some patient gave him that nickname. You know how he is with that magnifying glass of his. Before he came here, well, he always carried one with him—he'd use it for starting fires. Cheaper than a lighter, he often joked, conveniently forgetting that the sun doesn't always shine."

"So what happened to him?" Xavier asked.

"Well, it didn't take long for him to start doing to me what he'd done to Judy—staying out late, drinking too much. He wasn't one for being tied down, our Peter. The day I went into labor, I called around trying to find him. Between contractions, I finally managed to track him down at Bedlamite, a bar in Bedlam. He was drinking with friends, celebrating someone's birthday, I believe. When I told him what was happening, he promised he'd be right along. He never came. Fifteen long hours later I gave birth to Pandy."

"He never showed up at all?" Pandora exclaimed.

"I thought he'd abandoned me," Vicki recalled, her eyes as she re-lived that day focused on a faded print of Van Gogh's *A Starry Night*. For once, the pen remained still in her limp fingers. "But he hadn't. He was lying in a ditch with a crushed skull. His bike hit a tree. He died on the operating table twice. And afterwards, he was in a coma for six months. But eventually he woke and he recovered. In a way."

"So he's not crazy?" Xavier said.

Vicki shook her head wearily. "Not that I know of. Just, just damaged."

"But why wouldn't you tell us about him?" Pandora questioned. "I know I said he doesn't have much charm, but I like Professor Robertson."

The pen started tapping again. "After Peter came out of his coma, he was much like he is today—out of touch, difficult to reach. But in the early days he still had some lucid moments. During one of them, he made me and Judy promise not to tell you children about him. He said he'd rather you imagined he was someone like the man he used to be than the man he is today. Peter had a lot of pride," Vicki said sadly. "Foolish pride."

"Does he have any lucid moments now?" Xavier asked softly.

"I'm afraid not. After he came out of the coma, he started having seizures. The last one damaged his brain too badly and left him unable to recognize anyone or remember his life before. Medication keeps the seizures under control now, so he's able to live a sort of life."

"He seems happy enough," Pandora offered.

Vicki stared at her, and that damnable fiend, false hope, brightened her eyes. "Do you think so, Pandy? Really?"

"I do," Pandora choked out, though she didn't know if Professor Robertson was happy or not. It was hard to tell with him. He did seem to enjoy his specimens and the donuts she brought him. That was something.

Vicki fell back in her chair, dazed, and the pen slipped from her fingers. "I've always hoped and prayed he was at peace. But I couldn't be sure. I didn't know if I was only seeing what I wanted to see and ignoring the awful truth or—"

"I want to meet him," Xavier spoke up, his voice breaking twice as he pushed the words out. "It's my right," he added sternly.

Vicki's happiness curdled, her fingers turning white as they gripped the arms of her chair. "I'm not sure that would be a good idea, Xavier. He's so fragile, you see. I have to keep him safe. He's mine to keep safe."

Pandora realized something at that moment, something important. Her mother was still in love with Professor Robertson. A lump formed in her throat. She swallowed, but it refused to move along. "Are you…are you still married to him?"

Vicki lifted her chin. "Of course I am."

"But you changed your name back to Belfry."

"I never changed it in the first place. All my degrees are in my maiden name…and there was Judy, Xavier's mother. It just didn't feel right."

"You still could get a divorce," Pandora pushed. "No one would blame you."

"I'd never leave him, Pandy! Not after what happened. Not *ever*."

Xavier flinched, and Pandora looked over at him. His expression was confused, hurt. "I wouldn't do anything to harm him," he said in a gentler voice. "I just want to see him. He's my dad, Director Belfry. I need to see him. Know him, if only a little bit."

Vicki's grip relaxed slightly and she nodded as she made her decision. "All right, Xavier. I'll arrange it. But not today. I don't think I can take much more today."

"That's fine," he agreed. "Maybe next week."

"Next week would be good," Vicki replied vaguely, then revived herself. "We'll sit down and talk all this through. I promise." In an instant, she transformed herself back into the Director. She scooted her chair closer to her desk and picked up the phone. Her expression was all business, with no trace of sorrow remaining on her face. "Now if you two don't mind I have a few phone calls to make."

Pandora picked up her dress, grabbed Xavier's arm, and pulled him away. He stumbled after her, out into the foyer. "He likes donuts," she told him as she dragged him toward the cafeteria. Under the circumstances, she decided not to mention that he liked whiskey, too. As they passed the potted fern, she threw her dress behind it, not caring if it got wrinkled. They both needed food right now, and lots of it.

"Great. We can connect over pastries."

"I know it's not much, Xavier, but at least he's not crazy."

All the anger drained out of him and his shoulders slumped. "Yeah, I know."

"You should be happy," she pushed, peering up at him.

"You, too," he threw back at her.

She shrugged. "I guess."

"Aren't you mad?" They entered the cafeteria. She looked around for the posse and found them sitting at their regular table. Lucy spotted her and waved. She appeared to be over her snit. Pandora waved back.

"Mad about what?"

He glared at her. "Just answer the question."

"Okay, fine. I guess I'm more sad than mad." While strange, it was true. Usually when someone wronged her, she flew right past sadness and straight into outrage. But this time, she couldn't seem to muster the necessary zeal to be furious.

"Really?" They stopped at the serving counter. Two college students, wearing their atrocious hairnets like crowns, plopped piles of unrecognizable food onto their plates. "Cause right now I feel like I could kick in a door."

"Who are you mad at?" she wondered. "Professor Robertson, or our moms?"

"All of them! Him for being selfish and drinking too much and crashing his motorcycle. And my mom for not telling me about him. And your mom for being a bad friend."

"Now wait just a darn minute!" Pandora cried, her sadness taking a flying leap right out the window. "She wasn't being a bad friend. They were divorced. She didn't do anything wrong."

"Well, maybe Professor Robertson divorced my mom because your mom kept getting in the middle. I've seen it happen," he added darkly.

"Where? On *Days of Our Lives*?" She stalked toward the posse. "You heard Vicki. She didn't mean for it to happen, it just did."

"Yeah, well, like mother, like daughter."

She stopped mid-step and rounded on him. "What's that supposed to mean?"

"You want to know? Fine, I'll tell you. What kind of a person goes out on a date with a scumbag like Daft? A messed up one, that's what kind. Your mom knew the professor had problems, yet she went after him anyway. Insanity obviously runs in your family."

"And divorcing someone after only a year and a half is healthy?" Her voice echoed in a room that had gone quiet. "What kind of a person gives up that quickly? A messed up one, *that's* what kind."

He took a menacing step forward. "Take it back, Belfry."

"I won't!"

"My mother was a saint. She sacrificed her life for me. I won't have you talk about her that way!"

"My mother's not a saint, but she means well. So I won't have you talk about her that way, either!"

"Oh, just go to hell." Xavier swung around to face the whole cafeteria. "All of you can just go to hell!"

"Go to hell!" Little Gustav piped up. "Heavens to Buttsy, dingleberry, weenie head!"

"We are in hell, you idiot," Pandora growled as the cafeteria started buzzing like a disturbed beehive.

"Yeah, well, I'm leaving this hell!" he shouted. "As soon as I get my paycheck, I'm outta here!"

"Good. Leave! Just like your mom. Always running from your problems!"

"At least my mother was smart enough to get away from a raving lunatic!" he shot back. And with that, he smashed his tray down on the closest table and ran out of the cafeteria.

Pandora watched him go, her head pounding and her chest aching. When he was gone, she turned to face the roomful of inmates, all of whom were growing more and more agitated. "It's all right, guys," she called out, using her hands to calm them. "He didn't mean it. He just heard some bad news. Okay? Now go back to your meals or the Rackett will up your meds." That last bit did the trick. Nobody liked having their meds upped. Slowly the uproar died down and the attendants, who spent their mealtimes leaning against the walls and making sure nothing happened, relaxed.

"What was that about?" Birdy wanted to know when Pandora sat down. "Xavier sounded mighty pissed off with you."

"We just found out who our dad is," she replied in a dead voice.

The posse stopped eating and stared at her. "Well, go on!" Lucy urged. "Spill your guts!" After a moment, Pandora did, telling the group everything.

"No wonder Xavier's mad at the world," Skippy said when she was finished.

"Yeah, okay, I get it," Pandora snapped. "Life's been unfair to him. But that doesn't mean he gets to take his anger out on me. He can find another dog to kick."

"That's what my baby brothers and sisters do to me when they get mad," Lucy said. "But I don't mind. It's just what they do." Her brown eyes grew sad. "I sure wish I could see them. But I can't cause my mama won't bring them here anymore. She's bad, isn't she, Pandora?" Lucy looked up at her with wet, trusting eyes.

"Well, I wouldn't say bad—"

"But you said adults are bad," Lucy insisted, her lower lip trembling. "We can't trust them. They lie to us."

"Yeah," Charles put in. "You said that, Pandora."

"I didn't mean it like that," she hedged. "Not *all* adults are bad." The thing was, Lucy's mom always tried to visit Lucy as often as she could. It was Mr. Lazy-Ass Landry who was the problem.

"Which is it?" Birdy countered. "Are adults good or bad?"

Pandora felt trapped. "I don't know, all right? Maybe it isn't that simple. All I know is that Dr. Steele ratted me out. And if *he's* not to be trusted, who can we trust?"

"No one," Birdy replied morosely. She clutched Skippy's arm as though he were the only thing keeping her afloat on a stormy sea. "Just ourselves."

"Right," Pandora answered. But it didn't feel right. Not anymore.

Goodnight, Fair Maiden

40

AFTER SAYING GOODNIGHT to the posse, Pandora headed to the foyer to fetch her dress. They had spent the rest of the meal talking about Pandora's date with Dougie tomorrow night. By the time they were finished expounding all the horrific things he might do to her (from selling her on the black market to using her brain to create a monster), Pandora's stomach felt like a tiny dragon had taken up residence and was practicing its fire breathing while tap dancing with spiked shoes.

After a lot of tossing and turning in bed, she finally fell asleep only to dream of being trapped in the labyrinth with Professor Robertson when he was still only Peter—her image of him coming from Xavier's old photograph of a mysterious man wearing a fedora. She kept trying to talk to him, but he kept running away from her. Halfway through the dream, Dr. Steele showed up and wagged his finger at her like a disapproving Nurse Rackett. "I'm telling on you, Bats!" he sang. Then he disappeared as though he'd never been.

Xavier was in the dream, too, but only as an elusive figure that dogged her steps as persistently as her own shadow. He followed her wherever she went, but he wouldn't speak to her. At one point, she screamed at him to find his own body to follow. He didn't answer. The dream suddenly shifted and she was at the dance with Dougie. He looked even more like a vampire than usual, with his pale skin, red lips, and white tuxedo the color of a bloated corpse. Every time she tried to escape him, Derek, who was acting as bouncer, caught her and dragged her back.

"I told you not to go with him!" he declared triumphantly every time he returned her to Dougie's clutches.

At last she woke up, feeling like she'd just finished running a marathon through foul, nasty mud and freezing rain. Her watch when she peered at it through blurry eyes said a quarter to eleven. She groaned and turned over. She had no desire to talk to or see anyone today. It would be best to hide out. When the time came to go to the dance, she'd sneak out the kitchen door to wait for Dougie outside. The last thing she needed was another lecture, or worse, having to deal with Charles and Lucy's irritatingly adept ability to come up with disastrous endings for her date.

After a long shower that ended only because the water turned cold, she made herself a big lunch (Vicki must have had Bennington go grocery shopping yesterday) and methodically ate her way through it. After grabbing a handful of Fig Newtons from the Cookie Monster cookie jar on the counter, she headed back to her room and devoured them while downing a bottle of Coke and listening to the Sex Pistols.

Vexing thoughts kept surfacing and she briefly considered seeking out the posse and braving their gloomy forecasts, then thought better of it. Xavier might be with them and she didn't want to have anything to do with him right now. He'd likely rub it in about Dougie, anyway. She also didn't want to see Dr. Steele, the tattletale, or Vicki, her *married* mother. Sooner or later they were going to have to talk about what all this meant, but Pandora rather it was later. Much, much later.

She settled for reading *I Capture the Castle* for the fifth time. She felt a close connection to the heroine, Cassandra Mortmain, who had to put up with a lot, living in a decrepit castle with her nudist stepmother and well-known, but reclusive father. Pandora often fantasized about having tea with Cassandra and comparing notes. As strange as Cassandra's life was, Pandora was pretty sure she had the girl beat.

Seeing the time, she reluctantly put down her book and started getting ready for the dance. She spent a long time applying powder and black eyeliner, then brushing out her hair to achieve a Morticia Addams look—Wednesday's braids somehow just didn't cut it for a dance. It was getting late and she paused in her grooming to look about her. Crap. She didn't have shoes, not any that could be worn with a dress. Her anxiety grew as she unzipped the garment bag and pulled out a long, slinky black gown. She glanced at the tag. The size was a perfect match. Knowing exactly how well Dougie had guessed her dress size made her feel queasy.

Attempting to shake off her discomfort, she stripped down to her bland white bra and underwear, the only color Vicki would buy for her, then pulled the long-sleeved dress over her head. The gown, made of a silky material that was form-fitting without being clingy, slid down to land about an inch from the floor. It looked like it really did cost the fortune Dougie had said he paid for it. She examined herself in the mirror, stunned at what she saw before her. She looked like a wanton woman, a seductive siren, a desirable diva.

Holy crud.

She turned this way and that, relieved to find that her underwear line didn't show. She didn't own a slip and wasn't about to ask Vicki if she could borrow one. She'd probably want to loan her a bra, too. One of those lacy ones she kept hidden away at the back of her drawer. Pandora quickly turned her line of thought away from her mother and things relating to seduction. Learning that Vicki was married, and to Professor Robertson, changed things. Pandora felt like she didn't know her mother anymore, didn't even know how to think about the woman, and that made her feel all funny inside.

In the end, she had to settle for wearing her Doc Martens. She took comfort in their familiar presence as she headed downstairs to meet her doom. Halfway down the spiral staircase the sound of music and voices drifted up to greet her. Curious, she hurried down the rest of the stairs and across the foyer toward the cafeteria. The closer she got, the louder the noise grew.

She opened the cafeteria door a crack and nearly fell backwards. A miraculous transformation had taken place in the ballroom, returning it to its former glory. Paper streamers the color of the rainbow, strings of lights, and paper lanterns criss-crossed the space. The room was packed with people, dressed in their best, and a good majority of them were whirling back and forth across the floor, or packed together in one group, directed by J.T., and doing the Electric Slide while Togs took pictures. Even Jun Li and Cracker Jack were dancing. The rest sat in chairs, eating from paper plates and sipping from Styrofoam cups. What the heck was going on?

She scanned the scene looking for answers and found Lucy and Charles on the dance floor. Charles, sporting a matching bow tie and cape, bobbed up and down while Lucy bounced like a super ball, her every movement copied by a bunch of little kids surrounding her. They weren't just any kids, though, they were her brothers and sisters. Nearby, a dark-skinned man danced with Mrs. Landry, Lucy's mom, who was wearing a pretty pink dress that brought out the color in her pale skin. Pandora stared in disbelief. Could it be? Had Mr. Landry really come to Nepenthe Manor?

There was no sign of Charles's grandmother, but he looked radiant anyway as one of Lucy's little sisters grabbed onto his leg and rode it like a horse. At the sight, Pandora's eyes blinked rapidly. Lucy and Charles looked so full of joy, like they were part of one big happy family. It seemed a miracle.

In the center of the floor, Birdy and Skippy twirled around each other like ballroom dancers. Birdy wore her best finery—a tight polka-dot number with a flared skirt, and Skippy had donned, of all things, a black coat with tails. It was slightly too big on him, but still extremely dapper. They looked wonderful together. Mr. and Mrs. Peacock tried to keep up with the youngsters, especially the competitive Mrs. Peacock, with her glistening bosoms bouncing and cleavage roaring, but it was Birdy's moment and she worked it for all it was worth.

The spectacle got even more amazing. Sinclair's parents, the Prims, had come. They weren't dancing, but were sitting in two of the metal folding chairs lining the perimeter of the room. Several chairs down from them, Mrs. Johnson and Mrs. Bodkin sat in judgment of the dancers, looking very content. Mrs. Bodkin, her arm in a sling that bore a surprising resemblance to Xavier's, chattered and pointed while Mrs. Johnson knitted and nodded.

Sinclair sat straight as a board between his mother and father. Pandora's eyes fastened on his face, searching it for signs of an imminent breakdown, ready to run to his rescue. He'd come a long way these past few days, but the structure he'd built was fragile, like the little pig's straw house. One foul breath and he'd topple.

He didn't look fragile, though. His shiny, patent leather shoe tapped the floor as he sat between the rigid Prims. He didn't seem to care that no one was talking or interacting. For now it was enough that his parents had come. Pandora felt the lump in her throat, the one that had formed in Vicki's office and never quite gone away, grow a little bigger.

Too bad Xavier wasn't here to see this. He'd like knowing that the posse was doing well. The good vibes they were feeling tonight might be temporary—probably were—but still…joy was a rare commodity in Nepenthe Manor. Xavier could benefit from a little himself. Having lost his mom and then finding out his dad was a shell of a man who could never live outside an insane asylum had to be pretty depressing.

Pandora dug her fingernails into her palm. Damn. Now she was feeling sorry for him, and she knew this pesky feeling wouldn't go away until she did something about it. Heaving a martyred sigh, she turned away from the door. Dougie was just going to have to wait for her. She needed to fetch Xavier from the stables and make him go to the dance. If he said no, she'd tell him about the loads of delicious smelling food in there, just the incentive to get him to change his mind. If he was going to leave Nepenthe Manor, he might as well go out on a good note.

She entered the foyer right as the main door opened and the sound of voices filled the room. She shrank back into the shadows. Vicki entered first, firmly guiding Dougie Daft through the doorway and into the building. Behind them came Xavier and Dr. Steele and—she shook her head dizzily—*Derek*? What was he doing here? And how had he managed to make himself look so incredibly gorgeous?

"I know this is a change in plans, Douglas," Vicki announced apologetically, "but I've decided that Pandy is really too young to go to a high school dance. I'm sure you understand." She stopped halfway across the foyer and let go of Dougie's arm to smooth out her dress, a lovely lilac number. "But you're welcome to come to our dance. It's just a little something we put together for the residents and their families and friends. Please say you'll join us?" Was Vicki testing him? Had she finally seen past her guilt and through him?

Dougie, looking debonair in his white tuxedo and red sash, paused for a fraction of a second. "Are you saying the patients will be dancing with us?" His voice was soft; his expression was not. He didn't look at all pleased and Pandora gave a mental cheer.

"That's what she's saying," Dr. Steele spoke up, moving to stand close to him. "You could even dance with them if you'd like. I'm sure the Director would be okay with that."

Vicki nodded. "Absolutely. I trust you, Douglas. You have free reign with them."

Dougie started to cough, and Xavier came up behind him and clapped him on the back. "Getting a cold, Daft?"

Dougie straightened up. "I'm perfectly fine, and I would be honored to attend your dance, Ms. Belfry."

Pandora nearly whistled out loud. Dang, he had balls of steel! She couldn't stand the guy, but once again, she had to give him credit for doing something she'd never thought he'd do. She stepped forward, out of the shadows. "Hello, Dougie. I see you made it."

Xavier let loose a whistle. "Holy hell, Pandora! You scared the crap out of me. I thought you were the ghost of Nepenthe Manor."

She grinned and gave a little curtsy. "Thanks for the compliment, bro. You don't look so bad yourself." He was wearing a zoot suit of all things, complete with wing-tip shoes. He looked pretty darn good for a half-brother. She felt a strange sensation come over her and promptly realized what it was...she didn't want him to leave.

"Nice suit." She nodded at Derek. It was black like her dress and fit him surprisingly well.

He gave her his slow smile. "It suits me."

Everyone groaned at the bad pun, except Dougie. He only looked angry, his red lips pressed into two thin lines. He held out his arm to Pandora. "Shall we?" She sighed and went to take it. At the last second he grabbed her hand tightly in his. His skin was cold on her warm flesh and she shivered as he escorted her into the ballroom. As they walked through the doors, recently propped open to let in the cooler air, he leaned over and whispered in her ear, "You look ravishing. I could eat you up."

"Yeah, well, try to resist the urge. I'm pretty bitter."

"I like bitter." Before she could respond, he twirled her onto the floor. Soon they were dancing as gracefully as Fred Astaire and Ginger Rogers. He made her look good, she knew, because normally she wasn't the most graceful of girls, especially in her clunky Doc Martens. But right now the two of them could give Birdy and Skippy a run for their money.

Dougie wasn't going to be given much of a chance to do that, though. After the third dance, Xavier tapped him on the shoulder and Dougie reluctantly let her go.

"Is he behaving himself?" Xavier asked when Dougie went to stand near the drinks table, where he sipped fruit punch and watched their every move.

Pandora laughed. "With you and Derek giving him the evil eye, he'd better."

He spun her around with his one good arm. He wasn't a very good dancer, but he was a fun one. He smelled like Carl, she realized, who smelled like Old Spice and hay. It was rather a comforting smell. "I'm sorry about what I said yesterday. None of this is your fault."

"Thanks for pointing out the obvious, Einstein. So, um, when are you leaving?"

He looked away. "I changed my mind. That labyrinth isn't going to clean itself up."

"Ah. Well, good." She paused. "You know what's funny?"

"Your face?"

"Ha, ha, loser. I was just coming out to get you when you guys came in. Your life's been pretty sucky lately and I thought you could use a little distraction."

"Yours has been pretty sucky, too," he admitted, peering over her head.

"But I'm used to sucky. I grew up in an insane asylum, remember." She frowned. "You know, I think I just figured out why my mom works here. To be close to our dad. To watch over him, like she said."

Xavier nodded. "I never thought of that. She must really love him," he added thoughtfully.

Pandora didn't trust herself to respond. This lump in her throat was turning out to be a real pain. Her eyes roamed around the room, searching for her mother. She spotted the Hessian boogying with Beetle in her delightful caveman style, then caught sight of Vicki standing next to Professor Robertson. She was trying not to look like they were together, but the tilt of her shoulders, leaning toward him as though offering shelter from a storm, gave her away to anyone who knew her secret. What a sacrifice she'd made, all these years, for a man who would never be normal. "She really must," Pandora agreed in a tight voice, lump be damned.

"So do you think the dance is a success?" Xavier asked.

"Totally. The posse looks happier than I've seen them in a long time."

"Dr. Steele and your mom put it together. They both wanted to have a better way to get the families to come visit. Everyone helped decorate while you were hiding out in your room."

Pandora chose to ignore the part about her hiding out. "Well, this is definitely a success." And somehow her mother and Dr. Steele had come to a compromise, which meant nothing was going to change. He wasn't going to leave!

"I think so, too." The song ended at that moment and Derek swiftly stepped in to take Xavier's spot. Xavier grinned at him. "Glad you could come, dude."

"Glad to be here." He took Pandora in his arms and looked down at her. "Very glad."

A strange sensation washed over her. After a moment she realized what it was—shyness. No way. Absolutely not! She would not become one of those stupid heroines in romance novels, who lost their mind the moment a male entered the room, ending up giggling and blushing like idiots. "Um…well…um…" *Damn.*

"You look beautiful."

"Thank you," she whispered. "You're looking quite handsome yourself."

"It's my pa's suit. He got married in it." He pulled her tight against him and her heart beat hard.

"You really are going to be a giant."

He gave a slow chuckle as he spun her around. She felt like she was floating on air, then realized she *was* floating on air. He'd lifted her off the ground and was spinning her around and around like a fairy princess. Sweet Mary, she was giggling!

The rest of the night was magical. Between Xavier and Derek, Dougie had little chance to dance with Pandora again. He was wily, though, and managed to pull her into a dance while the boys were fetching drinks or food the parents and friends had brought potluck style. Dr. Steele's idea, Xavier told her earlier while sipping lemonade.

Near the end of the evening, the posse gathered together and chatted about the wonderful night. Birdy bragged about outdancing her mother, and then proceeded to go on and on about how little Skippy and her father were alike because Skippy wasn't spineless and actually used his brain for something other than doing what others told him to do. For his part, Skippy just stared at her like a spineless, brainless, lovesick puppy dog. Dougie had gone to use the bathroom, leaving her alone for the first time that night. Jun Li used his wheelchair to bully Cracker Jack into approaching Vicki. He didn't say anything to her, but when she saw him, she patted Professor Robertson's arm, then left him to dance with Cracker Jack. Pandora had never seen him looking so alive. She'd be happier for him, however, if it weren't for the specter of false hope raising its ugly head once again. The man had no chance with Vicki and when he found that out, he'd probably chop off his arm with a garden hoe.

While Xavier and Derek discussed cars, Lucy sidled over and took Pandora's hand, her big brown eyes welling up. "I really didn't mean to do it, Pancake."

It took a moment for her words to register. "Do what, Lucy?"

"Trust adults. I know you said I shouldn't."

"Oh, yeah. Well, I only said that because Dr. Steele told Vicki about Dougie coming by and I didn't want her to know that."

Lucy squeezed Pandora's hand like an old aunt. "Oh, Pandella! Haven't you learned by now?"

Pandora felt a tendril of suspicion sprout in her gut. "Learned what?"

"I was the one who told your mom about Dougie."

"You! But why did you do that?"

"I didn't mean to. After lunch, I wanted to ask her about my dada and somehow she got me to spill my guts. She's a good terror gator."

"Ahhh…" Pandora breathed a liberating sigh of relief. "I guess I should've known it was you." And Lucy had likely managed to spill the beans within ten seconds of approaching Vicki, with no effort on Vicki's part needed.

"Are you mad at poor little Lucy?" She blinked rapidly several times, all sweetness.

"No, I guess not. I'm relieved actually. I didn't want to believe that Dr. Steele had done—"

"Go on," a voice came from behind her. "You didn't want to believe that Dr. Steele had done, what?"

She swung around. "Dr. Steele! I didn't see you there."

"No, I imagine you didn't, being that you had your back to me." He held out his arm, crooked at the elbow. "Shall we dance, Miss Belfry?" He'd spent the entire evening dancing, but looked none the worse for wear. As it turned out there were more than a few ladies, young and old, who were quite eager to dance with the good-looking bachelor doctor. Nurse Rackett, dressed in a starched, white dress not all that different from her uniform, had elbowed her way into getting more than her fair share of turns. The gorgeous Nurse Burns only landed one dance, Pandora was pleased to note. J.T. even managed to include Dr. Steele in a group dance, making sure to stick close to his side despite all the chaos. Way to go, J.T.!

"I heard about the cave-in," he said as they danced what Pandora thought might be a waltz. Pandora had no clue how to waltz, but luckily Dr. Steele did, and guided her every step. He maintained a respectable, but boring, ruler-length away from her, though maybe they'd do the tango later. She shivered at the thought. "Lucy spilled the beans," he explained.

Pandora sighed. "Lucy is a bean spiller extraordinaire."

"So you got into the labyrinth, then? And you solved it?"

Pandora stared at him in shock. "How did you know that?"

"You know Lucy, once she gets started…"

"Oh, Lucy!" she moaned in her best Desi Arnaz voice. "It's like she's got diarrhea of the mouth."

Dr. Steele chose to ignore her bang on analogy. "I'd love to see it some time."

"You would? Um, sure! Okay. I could show you around. But it's sort of against the rules for me to be in there."

"It's sort of against the rules for you to do just about anything around here, isn't it?" She swallowed hard, unable to answer. He'd gotten it exactly right. She gave him a quick nod and he smiled kindly. "So mum's the word on my part. And anyway, I wouldn't want to add another burden to your mother's shoulders."

Pandora grinned. "You're a good guy, Dr. Steele."

"Yes, I am." He spun her around. "Your mother told me, reluctantly, mind you, that you and Xavier figured out who your father is. To be honest, I'm not sure whether to offer my condolences or congratulations."

"To be honest, I'm not sure which one, either," Pandora admitted. But she was glad he now knew Vicki was married…that there was no chance with her. She was also glad he didn't appear all that disappointed or upset at the idea.

"And did you ever find your ghost?" he asked casually, though his expression was more than curious. It seemed almost...hopeful.

She laughed. "I did. It was Derek walking on the beach."

"Oh." He sounded disappointed. "I imagine walking through water would be easy for someone like him."

"Yeah," she agreed, remembering the strange sight. "He's strong as a horse."

They twirled in silence for several seconds. "You did a good thing tonight, Pandora," he spoke up over the driving beat of a Madonna song. It was not the best tune for waltzing, but Pandora wasn't about to bring that up. She found she rather liked waltzing.

She peered up at him. "Me?"

"Yes, you. Who do you think made all this happen?"

"Duh. You and Vicki."

"We organized the dance, but it was your idea."

She thought back, vaguely remembering what she'd shouted so passionately, something about getting a whip. "Hm. I suppose I might have been the inspiration. But since I didn't do any of the work, I'll be okay giving you guys the credit for everything. This place looks reasonably respectable for once."

He smiled. "I'm glad you like it. And how was Mr. Daft tonight?"

"Bearable. I can't believe my mom put her foot down about having him take me to his dance. I didn't think she cared."

"Your mother wants to believe Mr. Daft has the best of intentions."

"That was her first mistake," Pandora grumbled.

"We all make mistakes, but if we do what we can to make amends, then we're halfway to redemption."

Pandora laughed. "That'd be great if it were true, but I don't think I'm the least bit redeemable, Dr. Steele."

"I think there are a lot of people here who'd disagree with that, including one young man who looks like he wants to dance with you...again."

"Not Dougie," she groaned.

"No. I meant Derek. I met him earlier. He seems like a nice young man. Douglas Daft, on the other hand... Well, let's just say I wouldn't mind sending him home."

"You wouldn't?"

His eyes twinkled. "And I'd enjoy doing it immensely."

"So you *do* care about me?" she blurted out, wishing the words back almost immediately.

His eyes grew serious. "Pandora Belfry, I care about you and your friends and Nepenthe Manor more than you could ever understand." With a brief bow, he stepped away. "Goodnight, fair maiden, and please, for my sake, stay inside tonight!"

41

Twists and Turns

BEFORE THE EVENING could conclude, this being Nepenthe Manor, something dramatic had to happen. It started when Vicki left the room for a moment to deal with a stuck elevator, something that happened on a regular basis.

Seizing his opportunity, Dougie pulled Pandora away from Derek and onto the dance floor. Before he could get far, Derek seized Pandora's arm, and there she stood stretched between the two of them like a wishbone.

"You've only danced with me four times tonight," Dougie said, his voice a threatening hiss. "I don't consider that adequate to settle our debt."

"I think Pandora has had enough dancing for tonight," Derek replied, his voice even and sure, his eyes flat and dangerous. "And a gentleman does not force a lady to do something she so obviously doesn't want to do."

Pandora yanked her arm out of Dougie's surprisingly strong grip. "How dare you threaten me! I said I'd go to a dance with you and here we are. Debt paid in full."

His blue eyes were icy. "I want another dance." His lips twitched lasciviously. "And a kiss."

"You creep!" She swung back her arm to smack him one, then remembered that Derek had referred to her as a lady and settled for giving him the death glare instead. It wasn't nearly as satisfying.

Dougie folded his arms. "I'm not leaving until I get my dance, and the kiss."

Derek let go of her arm and stepped forward. "You lay one hand on Pandora and I'll rip it off."

Dougie looked straight at Derek. "Are you sure you want to make an enemy of me, Choken?"

Derek took another step forward. "Don't make me say it again, Daft."

Xavier, who'd been loading up on more food, set down his plate and hurried toward them. "What's going on?"

She nodded at Dougie. "He says he won't leave without a dance and a kiss."

"Well, he can kiss my ass."

She stifled a laugh, then turned to Dougie, who was standing his ground despite Derek's looming. "Don't cause trouble. It upsets the inmates and when they get upset…" She shrugged. "Well, you know…"

"We'll escort you out," Xavier offered. "And we can be nice about it…or not."

Dougie looked at the two of them, then at Pandora. "This isn't over, Pandora. I told you I'd make you mine and I intend to. And when we meet again, I'll show you just how good we'll be together." He bowed low. "Until then." He straightened, gave her a nod, and pivoted on his heel to leave. Xavier and Derek trotted after him.

A minute later they returned with smiles on their lips. After reenacting the scene several times, *Girls Just Want to Have Fun* started playing and Lucy grabbed Xavier and pulled him onto the floor. After watching them for a bit, Derek took Pandora's hand and escorted her onto the dance floor, effectively making liars out of both of them. Apparently she had *not* had enough dancing for the evening.

After one last perfect dance to *Total Eclipse of the Heart*, Derek said he had to go. After promising Lucy he'd return as soon as he could to visit, he left Pandora with a kiss on the cheek and a warning to "watch out for snakes." Lying in bed later that night, she could still feel his warm lips on her skin and she couldn't help herself. She giggled.

Unable to sleep, she mulled over the past week in her mind. It had been a tumultuous run, full of shocks and surprises, up and downs. She wasn't sure how she, or the posse, had managed to survive. But they had.

But was she stronger for it, or better off? Rather than a deposed king or a Pulitzer prize-winning author, she had a head case for a father. Not once had it occurred to her that her father might be less than perfect, that he might have less to offer her than Vicki. Her image of him had become something of a refuge to her, a fantasy she could escape to when things at Nepenthe Manor were bad.

What an irony that she'd been living with her father all along, one whom her mother still loved dearly. It was going to be very hard to stay mad at a woman who'd sacrificed so much of her own happiness to keep them all together. But if she didn't have her anger with Vicki to keep her going, what did she have?

She hadn't yet told Derek about her father yet, either. She hadn't wanted to spoil the evening, plus she wasn't sure how to approach the topic. He might not be sympathetic to her troubles when his mother was supposedly in even worse shape. Then again, maybe he would be.

He had, after all, understood why she'd gone on a date with Dougie to get back at her mother. His cryptic words, *Let's just say I understand how you feel,* now made sense. His mother was crazy, after all, and likely not easy to get along with. So maybe she could trust him. Maybe.

It was all too much to deal with, and Pandora decided to think on it later, or not at all, as was her typical way of dealing with conflict. Instead she turned her thoughts toward something more appealing—her recent adventures in the labyrinth. Once again, she couldn't help wondering what kind of a person had built such an elaborate place? Mr. Nepenthe was its most likely architect, but had he written the poem, too? If he had, why would he refer to himself as a loony?

Suddenly the letters *EN*, the same ones carved into the wall of the covered bridge, appeared in her mind. Where had she seen them before? Then she remembered. They were the same letters as the ones inscribed in every book in the secret room. Pandora's heart started beating a little faster. Who was this mysterious *EN*? Was she related to Archibald Nepenthe? Both their last names ended in N, so it was possible.

A terrible and fascinating thought struck her. Could *EN* be the one who'd killed herself by jumping off the cliffs? Could she be the ghost of Nepenthe Manor? An overwhelming urge to find out gripped her. Unfortunately, she and Xavier were going to be busy for the next couple weeks, helping Carl fill in the sinkhole, planting the garden, and doing spring yard work, which took forever. But after that...well, it would be summer and she'd have all the time in the world.

She would, of course, include the posse in her search. She was glad Skippy and Birdy had made amends, but the peace wouldn't last long. Birdy was too dramatic for her own good. She'd find some way of screwing things up. Memories of the dance would help sustain Lucy and Charles for a little while, but what would happen when things went back to normal? And how long would Sinclair be able to hang onto the progress he'd made? She gave him a month, tops.

Because how could anyone get better, and *stay* better, while living in an insane world like Nepenthe Manor? Simply put, they couldn't.

That's why, as much as she wanted to, she could never leave this place. Dr. Steele seemed to think the inmates could leave Nepenthe Manor and survive, but she knew better. On their own, they'd sink faster than the Titanic. She'd seen it happen too many times. They needed her to keep them alive, to keep them reasonably sane.

But what if this time things have changed? a voice whispered in her mind, a voice that sounded very much like Dr. Steele.

What if she *were* to leave Nepenthe Manor someday? What if the inmates overcame their illnesses and thrived, going on to lead normal lives? The very idea of either event happening seemed as farfetched as little green men.

And yet…strangely thrilling, too.

Pandora punched her pillow, trying to get comfortable. She didn't want to think about any of this 'people leaving' stuff anymore. She'd rather think about Derek's warm lips on her cheek, his slow smile, his huge hands encircling her waist. How absurd that a month ago she'd entertained nary a thought about anything even remotely touching on romance and now such enticing thoughts wouldn't leave her alone.

She flipped over and imagined herself in the maze once again, running back and forth, solving riddles, climbing walls. Her life, she was starting to understand, resembled the Labyrinth of Lunacy, with its twists and turns and locked doors hiding secrets untold. Perhaps if she could solve the riddle of her own maze, life would become so much simpler for her. Unfortunately, all she seemed able to do lately was butt her head against the squishy walls of her labyrinthine brain.

Still, the idea of conquering the maze of her mind, with all its complexities and quirks, was intriguing. All she had to do was dig up its secrets, solve its mysteries, and *voila!* she would no longer be deranged. On the other hand, she thought sleepily, she rather liked her brain as it was. Better the devil you know, right?

Maybe I'll just stick to figuring out other mysteries, starting with the enigmatic EN, Pandora decided, her eyelids growing heavy. *And how I'm going to get to know my father as a person.* She liked the idea of being able to visit his little shop of horrors without fear of getting into trouble. *And I definitely have to figure out how to get Derek to kiss me again…on the lips this time.* She laughed wickedly until a wave of exhaustion swept over her. Within moments, she was breathing heavily, so heavily that she missed hearing the sound of singing passing beneath her window.

She's gone, she's gone, my lovely Gwen
She's gone forevermore
Yet still I search the world for her
My Gwen, I do adore.

About the Author

When author, Kristina Schram, was growing up she wanted to be a star. When that didn't turn out quite like she expected, she turned her mind to achieving other goals: Earning her Ph.D. in Counseling Psychology, working as an Artist-in-Residence at local schools, being a free-lance editor and reader, coaching parks & rec basketball, and publishing her first novel, a YA fantasy called The Chronicles of Anaedor: The Prophecies (Book One).

Knowing what it's like to struggle with self-doubt and lack of confidence, her biggest dream (in addition to owning a castle) is to stamp out low self-esteem for everyone, especially young people. "Feeling bad about yourself is the number one deterrent to achieving happiness," she says. "So for the sake of a better world, it's got to go." She lives in New Hampshire with her husband, three boys, her mother and various pets, and can also throw a tomahawk, if need be. For more information, visit her website: www.kristinaschram.com. She's also on Facebook and Twitter.

Other Books by Kristina Schram

Mayhem at Nepenthe Manor:
A Pandora Belfry Adventure (Book One)

Precocious and morbidly obsessed with death, Pandora Belfry has spent her entire life at Nepenthe Manor, a dark, Gothic mansion also known as the local loony bin. Recently turned fourteen and growing exasperated with her stifling life, Pandora wants two things more than anything else in the world—to make her escape from the asylum, and to get her mom to finally act like a real mom. Until these wishes are granted, she acts as self-imposed ringleader to a wayward posse of inmates. Known amongst themselves as the Secret Six, Pandora and her friends spend their time at Nepenthe Manor stirring up trouble—holding weekly Midnight Meetings to concoct schemes, sneaking into places like the Nepenthe family cemetery and the forbidden attic, and generally doing everything they can to avoid the curse of living a mundane life. But when a mysterious new inmate arrives at the manor, things change for Pandora, and not for the better. In retaliation for a trick she plays on him, the charming and handsome Xavier connives to take over the posse, threatens to divulge one of Pandora's biggest secrets, and refuses to tell her what he did to get himself locked up. This boy is obviously hiding something, and it's up to Pandora to use whatever nefarious means necessary to find out what it is, before he destroys the only world she's ever known.

The Chronicles of Anaedor: The Prophecies (Book One)

Strange things happen to fifteen-year-old Lavida Mors. Maybe that's why her father sends her to Portal Manor, a mysterious family estate she never knew existed. Lavida quickly discovers that not everything at Portal Manor is as it seems when she stumbles across a secret passage to a hidden world—Anaedor. Long ago, humans drove the Anaedorians, a civilization of magical and strange beings, into the dark world of huge caverns, frigid rivers, and bottomless pits deep within the earth. Malevolent forces, led by the evil Malvado, seek to control all of Anaedor, but an ancient prophecy tells of a hero who will save them from destruction. While trying to escape the dark realm, Lavida must battle overgrown leeches, survive a poisoned arrow, and outwit a giant, all while trying to convince the hopeful populace of Anaedor that she is not the savior they believe her to be.

The Chronicles of Anaedor: The Return to Anaedor (Book Two)

After escaping from Anaedor, fifteen-year-old Lavida Mors starts a training course with her guardian, Mrs. Keeper, in hopes of improving her magic skills before the dreaded Malvado returns. But while trying out a new spell, something awful happens, and she vows never to do magic again. When an unexpected discovery forces her to return to Anaedor, she is faced with her most terrifying challenges yet. Strife reigns in the hidden underground world as lootings and burnings break out, and numerous enemies conspire to capture Lavida, fight her, even kill her. Without magic, how can she possibly flee from dragons, escape the Goblins, outwit the ruthless Frio, and fight a duel with a young rebel intent on proving she's not the One? Time is running out. If Lavida doesn't learn to trust herself and her skills, a series of catastrophic events will ensure that she and her friends never make it out of Anaedor again.

The Chronicles of Anaedor: The Lost Ones (Book Three)

Sixteen-year-old Lavida Mors is in for a long, hot summer. With no way into Anaedor, the Lost Ones seeking refuge at Portal Manor are taking over the house, creating havoc and misery. Lavida is overwhelmed trying to keep up with her chores, learning magic, and fighting off the Pixies—tiny creatures who have made it their mission to harass Lavida at every turn. Meanwhile, unbeknownst to the residents of Portal Manor, the AAK is hard at work opening a Portal to the Upland. They are successful at last, and the twins, Loria and Darian, on the run from Malvado, and the AAK leader, Trey, manage to make it through the opening only to have it collapse behind them. With no way back into Anaedor, they are forced to take refuge at Portal Manor. As they try to settle into this strange new life, tensions between the humans and the Anaedorians grow, creating rifts between Lavida and her friends. To make matters worse, Frio, Amoral Hunter Leader, is hiding out in the Upland, and when he goes after Lavida, he starts in motion a series of events that could end up costing Lavida her life.

The Chronicles of Anaedor: The Uprising (Book Four)

In this final book of the Anaedor series, sixteen-year-old Lavida Mors is placed in grave danger when a group of young Anaedorians infiltrates the Upland. Their orders are to eliminate the evil one, whom they believe is Lavida, and then launch an Uprising to take over the Upland. Disguising themselves as humans, they befriend the unwitting Lavida and her friends, allowing them easy access to Portal Manor. Darian and Loria, Blendar twins and Lavida's friends, and Trey, ex-AAK rebel leader, have come to the Upland to warn Lavida about the intruders. But before they can, Darian learns something about Lavida's past that turns him against her. Surrounded by betrayal and danger, and faced with an astonishing revelation that makes her question everything about her existence, Lavida feels increasingly alone and afraid. If she cannot convince Darian and the others that she is not the evil being they think she is, she will lose everything to the Uprising.

The Wrath: A Paranormal Gothic Romance

When a cryptic letter arrives from Evalina Filmore's two aunts, she travels to England to find out what they want, figuring this will be the chance to experience the romantic adventure she has so often read about in her beloved gothic novels. When she arrives, she finds the eerie mansion, the strange atmosphere, and the adventure, as hoped. But there are troubles. On the train, she meets a man who, upon learning her name, walks away without a word of explanation. Not long after, she passes unharmed through a wood called the Wrath, even though, as she later learns, no one ever has. While in the Wrath, she meets a tantalizing and seductive stranger, one who just might be her gothic hero. But he has a secret. It seems everyone in the village does, including her aunts, and it's up to Evie to figure out what is going on before the Wrath lures her in and never lets her go.

The Battle to Become an Author: When Great Expectations Go Awry

Are you looking to find an agent and/or get published? Are you a published author frustrated with the whole process? Or have you simply heard the horror stories and are looking for a ray of light before plunging into the fray? In this short booklet, author Kristina Schram discusses how one's unrealistic expectations about becoming an author can contribute to feelings of negativity and isolation. Dr. Schram offers a real-world discussion of this growing issue, humorously incorporating her own experiences throughout. She also offers insights and ways to cope with the increasingly difficult battle to become a published author. Come prepared to challenge your own expectations, to laugh and to cry, and to battle against the forces conspiring to keep you from reaching your writing potential!

www.ingramcontent.com/pod-product-compliance
Lightning Source LLC
Chambersburg PA
CBHW020748250626
47155CB00003B/978